TEEN
RUT

10/05/23

Rutherford, Mara

A multitude of dreams

A MULTITUDE of DREAMS

A MULTITUDE of DREAMS

MARA RUTHERFORD

inkyard
PRESS

Recycling programs
for this product may
not exist in your area.

ISBN-13: 978-1-335-45796-7

A Multitude of Dreams

For questions and comments about the quality of this book, please contact us at CustomerService@Harlequin.com.

Inkyard Press
22 Adelaide St. West, 41st Floor
Toronto, Ontario M5H 4E3, Canada
www.InkyardPress.com

Printed in U.S.A.

For Will, because fair is fair.

I love you, small fry.

"O' happy posterity, who will not experience such abysmal woe and will look upon our testimony as a fable."
—Petrarch, 1348, regarding the Black Death

"There was much of the beautiful, much of the wanton, much of the bizarre, something of the terrible, and not a little of that which might have excited disgust. To and fro in the seven chambers there stalked, in fact, a multitude of dreams."
—Edgar Allan Poe, "The Masque of the Red Death"

CHAPTER 1

Eldridge Hall was a castle built on lies.

In the highest chamber of the tallest tower, where it was drafty on even the stillest day, Seraphina stood at the sole window's ledge. Even that window was a lie, for it had been hastily boarded up years ago, and a window that couldn't be seen through was just another wall. Any minute, the ebony clock in the great hall would send out three booming chimes, announcing the start of another elaborate dinner the kingdom couldn't afford.

The real time hardly mattered; the clock maker had died years ago of the mori roja, and if there was someone left outside the castle to repair it, the king would never risk the health of his beloved youngest daughter to find them. As she descended the steps to the dining hall, she hummed the tune to a children's nursery rhyme she'd heard in the early days of the plague, when it hadn't yet reached the city. The plague was called the mori roja in royal circles, but out there, beyond the castle walls, it had been called the Bloody Three.

Here was a fact: three was the unluckiest of all numbers.

It was the number of wretched older sisters Seraphina had; it was the number of times per day she had to visit the mad king in his chambers; it was the number of days it took a person to die of the mori roja.

And it was the time the ebony clock insisted on announcing every hour for years, as stubborn in its denial of reality as the king.

Squaring her shoulders and raising her royal chin, Seraphina entered the dining hall. Chairs scraped as lords and ladies rose to greet her. Beyond the exquisite cut crystal and bone china so fine you could nearly see through it, the king was already halfway out of his chair, ready to grace her with one of his kisses that were somehow too wet and too dry at the same time.

"Father," she said, dropping into the easy curtsy that hadn't come easily at all. "You're looking well this evening."

"Not as well as you, my dear. Doesn't she look lovely, Lord Greymont? Lord Greymont?" The king tottered in a circle, searching for his favorite young nobleman. "Ah, there you are. Doesn't my daughter look lovely tonight?"

"As fair as a rose," Lord Greymont said to Seraphina with a bow. "Please, allow me to accompany you to your chair."

She bit the inside of her cheek, already raw from her efforts not to groan every time she was forced to pretend. Lord Greymont was no better or worse than any of the other young men at Eldridge Hall, which was to say he was handsome, rich, and achingly dull.

"You always look lovely," he whispered, his breath on her bare shoulder as unwelcome as the skin on warm milk. "But I must say that pink gown suits your complexion." His eyes lingered at the delicate neckline a moment too long.

She arched a well-groomed brow. "And you look as dashing as ever. Though we're all a bit pale, wouldn't you say?"

"Years indoors will do that to a person, yes." He shooed a tabby cat off her chair. They were everywhere in the castle, having bred like rabbits for the past few years with no access to the outside, where predators would have kept their population in check. Seraphina sat and allowed Greymont to ease her chair into the table. He took the seat next to hers without asking. "Are you looking forward to your twentieth birthday party?"

"A lady doesn't like to be reminded of her age," she said, because it seemed like something a princess would say. In truth, she was seventeen and a half, and her favorite way to spend her birthday was with a picnic.

Lord Greymont had been paying her special attention lately, for reasons she had yet to deduce. "Forgive me, Your Highness. But if I may be so bold, you are even lovelier now than the day I met you."

She remembered the day well. She was barely fourteen, coarse and malnourished, starting at shadows as if they were specters. His compliment was hardly bold. But she pursed her lips and dropped her eyes in the appropriate display of femininity, which she had learned was a bizarre combination of modesty and coyness.

"Have you chosen a costume yet?" he asked.

"No, but I have no doubt my sisters are already scheming." She looked to the end of the table, where the young women sat. Sure enough, they were giggling behind their hands, their rouged cheeks almost garishly bright in the candlelight.

Lord Greymont cleared his throat and leaned closer. "I realize it's a bit premature, but may I request the first dance?"

"My birthday isn't for three weeks."

"True, but I have no doubt you will be booked solid within the fortnight. I can't risk losing out to our dear Lord Spottington."

Seraphina sighed. "Lord *Pottington* only asks because his father demands it. He's about as ambitious as a garden snail."

Lord Greymont grinned. "Don't underestimate him, Your Highness. Even the humble garden snail has aims, slow though he may be."

"If Lord Pottington is a snail, what does that make me? A leaf?"

His eyes drifted toward his peer, who was pantomiming something to her eldest sister. He was clumsy and awkward—and true, his complexion wasn't clear, even at twenty-five—but Seraphina knew better than to trust appearances. They were as much a lie as everything else here.

"You, Princess, are far from foliage."

"You did already compare me to a flower," she said.

He swirled his wine in its cut-crystal glass, and Seraphina noted absently that the gilded rim was chipped and flaking. "Is *fair as a rose* not the compliment I thought it was?"

"I can't say. I haven't seen a rose in ages."

"Then I shall make it my life's work to bring you one."

She almost snorted, before remembering that a princess would never snort. "Please don't waste your time on something as trivial as a rose."

"And what would you have me waste it on? It's not as if I'm doing anything of value here in the Hall."

Seraphina took a sip of her own wine, which was heavily watered down. They had to be running out by now. Heaven help the servant to whom it fell to deliver that news to the king. She lowered her voice so that Lord Greymont had to lean in closer. It wasn't his proximity she craved, but the pleasure of forcing others to bend to her will after so many years of doing it herself. Besides, he smelled nice, like perfumed soap, which was more than could be said of the boys she knew when she was younger.

"And what would you do if you weren't trapped in the castle?"

His eyes, which she noticed had green flecks in the brown, darted around. She wondered if he would ask her what she meant by *trapped*. No one was supposed to allude to the game they all played, particularly in the king's presence. But Lord Greymont's lips curled just a bit at the corners as he spoke. "I should like to travel the world. I think I might like sailing. I know I would, in fact."

She brightened unconsciously. "You've seen the ocean?"

"Indeed. More than once."

Not quite as dull as she'd thought, then. "You had access to a ship?"

He nodded. "Dance with me on your birthday, and I'll tell you all about it."

She'd learned long ago to couch her annoyance as teasing, though she couldn't quite keep the edge out of her voice. "You'd keep me waiting that long?"

Something in his eyes shifted, his smile suddenly wicked. He had knowledge she wanted now, and he would use it to draw her in. Not a lie, but more games. Fortunately, Seraphina was good at games, and she could be patient if the prize was something she wanted.

"It will be worth the wait," he purred. "I promise."

The wine must be stronger than she'd given it credit for, because Seraphina felt warm and a little giddy. What would the girls back home say if they could see her now, dressed in a beautiful pink gown with a handsome man at her side?

Seraphina pinched the inside of her wrist hard under the table, something she did whenever she found herself enjoying even a moment of her time at Eldridge. Happiness was complacency, and complacency was acceptance. She would never accept this life as her own, not as long as she drew breath.

Besides, what the girls back home thought of any of this didn't matter anymore. All the girls back home were dead.

After dinner Seraphina retired to the chambers she shared with her older sisters.

"A masquerade!" Rose, the youngest and most excitable of the three, squealed and fell dramatically onto one of the seven brocade fainting couches in their chambers—as if that was all ladies did: eat, sleep, swoon, repeat—upsetting a lounging longhaired ginger. "I can't decide what I should be!"

"We have weeks to decide," Seraphina said to her reflection in the vanity mirror. Behind her, Jocelyn, her lady-in-waiting and the only person at Eldridge Seraphina could tolerate, smiled.

"Lord Greymont will look handsome in a mask," she said, tugging on one of Seraphina's auburn curls. "Don't you think?"

She avoided Jocelyn's eyes as she reached for a silver brush, worth more than most men's lives, and handed it to her. It was maid's work, but Jocelyn said it relaxed her, and Seraphina couldn't deny it was soothing for her as well.

"Lord Greymont would look handsome in anything," Rose giggled.

"Or nothing." Nina, her eldest sister, flashed a wicked grin.

Seraphina rolled her eyes as her sisters and their ladies tittered and trilled like a small flock of sparrows. She wondered if there were any birds left outside the castle walls. Dalia, her best friend back when she'd had the luxury of choosing them, had loved songbirds. Goldfinches were a particular favorite. But when the king started hoarding the crops and livestock, people began to eat anything they could get their hands on. She hadn't heard a bird outside her window in ages.

"Thinking of your family?" Jocelyn whispered into Seraphina's ear.

She narrowed her downturned brown eyes, eyes so familiar that her "sisters" had gasped when they spotted her for the first time. She could still hear Giselle, her middle sister, whispering to the others in the entry of her family's home. *She's perfect. Well, she will be, once we clean away all the filth.*

Seraphina wouldn't cry. She would save her tears for later, when she went to her room in the tower. A room so cramped and dim that it allowed her to believe—for one bittersweet moment every morning—that she was home.

When they'd first brought her to the castle, she'd slept in her own royal chamber, more opulent and luxurious than anything she could have imagined. But a few months into her life here she'd discovered the empty tower and began sneaking up at night. The more she allowed herself to relish in the beautiful gowns and sumptuous meals, the more she let the flattery of men like Lord Greymont warm her cheeks—and worse, her belly—the easier it was to forget the people she had left behind to die of the mori roja. Not just her family, but her whole community. The whole world, for all she knew. For all anyone at the castle knew.

"I'm going to be a butterfly," Rose said. "A beautiful pink butterfly."

"There's no such thing as a pink butterfly." Nina plucked a candied cherry from one of the bowls of crystallized fruit that followed the princesses everywhere they went. Seraphina never touched it, no matter how tempting; she seemed to be the only one who remembered that the fruit was not neverending. None of this was.

They'd been sequestered in the castle for nearly four years, and she still didn't know where the fruit came from. No one was allowed out of the castle, and no one was allowed in. Jocelyn believed there was a secret tunnel the servants used, because though the king demanded his delicacies, he'd never told them how they were supposed to provide fresh food through what may as well be a siege. But Seraphina was rarely ever alone outside her tower—Giselle had made certain of that—and she had no idea where the tunnel could be.

"There might be pink butterflies," Rose insisted. "You've never even been outside of Goslind."

Nina plucked another cherry, mimicking Rose when her back was turned. "I'm going to be a siren."

"What does a siren costume consist of?" Jocelyn asked.

"Cleavage," Rose retorted before Nina could answer, and even Seraphina had to laugh. Rose wasn't usually quick or witty.

"Ha ha," Nina said, though she was admiring said cleavage

in the mirror. "I'm going to wear a long blue gown, with my hair down and flowing, and I'll leave my feet bare."

"Careful you don't wind up dancing with any of the Archer brothers," Jocelyn said. "They're as graceful as a herd of cattle."

"What will you be?" Rose asked Seraphina, perching on the arm of her chair. "A mermaid? A swan? Oh, what about a fairy? You'd look so lovely in a pair of wings."

"I imagine Giselle will choose for me." Giselle was in her own private room with her ladies-in-waiting. She avoided Seraphina whenever possible, forcing others to do the dirty work of keeping her in check.

"Come now, you must have some preference," Jocelyn pressed.

Seraphina raised an indifferent shoulder. Her entire life was one never-ending masquerade; she couldn't drum up enthusiasm for another. Jocelyn set the brush back down on the vanity and a shimmer caught Seraphina's eye. She plucked a golden strand of hair from the brush and held it up to Jocelyn.

"We'll need to dye it again this week," Jocelyn said. "I know you hate it."

"The henna irritates my scalp." Seraphina frowned, tilting her head to watch the light catch the trace of a scar on her jawline, rendered almost invisible by pearl powder.

"I'm sorry, darling. But what choice do we have?"

The question was rhetorical. They both knew they had no choices when it came to their lives at Eldridge. Jocelyn's entire family had died of the Bloody Three, including her infant sister. Her childhood nurse had written to Jocelyn several months after the castle gates were locked, warning her to stay away, not realizing Jocelyn couldn't leave even if she wanted to. But Jocelyn considered herself fortunate to be here, safe and sound from the mori roja, and she thought Seraphina should, too.

They were safe, perhaps, but nothing was sound. Life at Eldridge Hall was like a child's wooden block tower, only the blocks were lies, the king was the child, and one wrong move didn't just mean a few weepy minutes on a nursemaid's knee. It meant death.

"I think I'll go to bed," Seraphina said, rising from her vanity.

"Let me help you change out of your gown." Jocelyn wasn't a beauty like Rose, or a coquette like Nina, but she was kind and clever. She was the only one who knew what Seraphina was really thinking, even though Seraphina liked to believe she'd gotten quite good at playing princess by now.

"I can do it myself," she said gently. "Get some rest."

"At least take an extra blanket," Jocelyn insisted, kissing her on the cheek. "It's so drafty up there."

No one liked to think about Seraphina up in the tower. It distracted from the charade. Rose waved sleepily from the settee. "May you dream of Lord Greymont and a royal wedding."

"And a royal wedding *night*," Nina added.

"Good night, Princess Imogen," Jocelyn said as she closed the door behind Seraphina.

She climbed the stairs to her tower barefoot, relishing the way the cold stone bit into the soles of her pampered feet, a ritual that kept her from ever forgetting where she came from. After locking the thin wooden door behind her, she went to the windowsill and pressed her eye to a small crack in the wooden boards, relieved when she saw her: a girl clad in a white linen dress, her delicate features merely a smudge at this distance. She was the greatest reminder of home that Seraphina had. Every day Seraphina feared that she wouldn't come, but every night she did. Dalia, her best friend.

Seraphina waited for her to wave, just one raised hand before she disappeared into the forest as the clock began to chime once more. Dalia was the only true thing she had left, the last remaining vestige of a world she *would* return to, one day. Because she was not a princess, or the king's daughter, or even a lady.

Her name was Seraphina Blum. She was a Jew who had survived the plague because she was a pretty girl with sad eyes who happened to look like a dead princess.

And that was the most beautiful lie of all.

CHAPTER 2

Nico stabbed his shovel into the dirt, which thankfully wasn't yet frozen. Burying bodies was a miserable task under any circumstance; burying them in snow and ice was an altogether different breed of torture. He tossed a pile of dirt onto the rotting arm of a corpse, little more than a skeleton at this point, unlike its more freshly deceased neighbor.

His late father, a butcher who had turned the head of a nobleman's daughter—much to *her* father's chagrin—had reminded Nico often that he was made of softer stuff than his two older brothers. At least Nico had inherited Jeremiah's strong stomach. It came in handy for grave digging.

In all other ways Nico took after his mother, tall and lean with a perpetually furrowed brow. He'd always been Lucinda's favorite, a role he had cherished until she died of the mori roja in his arms. He hefted the shovel and drove it into the dirt harder than necessary, just to prove to himself that he wasn't as soft as he'd once been. His father and brothers would hardly recognize him now. Why, they'd be—

The shovel's head slammed into a rock, sending shock waves

through Nico's arm. He shook it out, scowling at the sky. Someone up there had a shit sense of humor.

"That's the last of them," Colin said, coming to stand next to Nico. Colin Chambers had been a chimney sweep before the plague, and now Nico, a gentleman—by birth if not manners—was working side by side with him. Death truly was the great equalizer.

Nico nodded. "Only three bodies this week. That's three less than last week."

Colin swiped his forearm over his brow, revealing branching red streaks on the light brown skin of his inner wrist that matched the marks on Nico's own. Built like a chimney, Colin was uniquely suited to life as a sweep, work he'd detested but which, in the end, had spared him witnessing the worst of the plague. Just before it hit, he'd been sent to the seaside for a few weeks by his employer, who had taken pity on him after listening to him cough all winter long. The plague hit while Colin was at the shore, and his employer's family had let him stay on there to look after the house while they sailed for even safer lands.

The plague had eventually spread throughout Goslind and beyond its borders to the surrounding kingdoms, but when it reached the shore, Colin found that, like Nico, he was one of the lucky few with blood immunity. He had come back eventually to check on his family, but they were all "dead or fled," as the saying went.

Nico's family never had the chance to flee. He'd been the one to care for them during their final three bloody days. His brothers may have been sturdy and strong like their father, but they'd died the same way his mother had: with blood spilling from their pores, their eyes, their ears, their noses, and every other orifice imaginable. He'd never know if his father had been immune. He'd died shortly before the plague hit.

"Most of these bodies have been out here for a good while, months and months. The plague is over," Colin said, then promptly knocked on Nico's head. "Touch wood."

"Ow." Nico rubbed at his brown hair, which had grown long enough to tie into a ponytail at the nape of his neck. The barber who'd once kept his hair fashionably styled was dead, along with his tailor, his cobbler, the butcher, the baker, and the bloody candlestick maker.

"We should get back to the house. It's nearly nightfall." Colin picked the empty wheelbarrow up by the handles and turned it around toward the stately stone manor on the hill. The place they now called home.

It was strange to be a servant after so many years of having them, but not a day went by that Nico didn't thank his lucky stars for his savior, Lord Crane. Nico had gone to his neighbors in the days immediately following the plague, hoping to be of some use with his medical knowledge, but they had all been too afraid to open their doors to anyone. And considering no one had ever come to him seeking aid or refuge, he had to assume a huge portion of the population had died.

For a while he had contemplated going to Esmoor, the capital city and the epicenter of the plague. Even if no one had need of him, perhaps he could learn more about the mori roja and how it spread. He wasn't brilliant enough to find a cure, but there was still a chance he could help *someone*. A chance that he wouldn't fail them the way he'd failed his mother.

Finally, after Nico had consumed everything edible at

home—and some things that were decidedly not—he had set out on his own to look for other survivors. Sadly, he had found nothing but corpses, sometimes still lying in the middle of the road where they had collapsed. There weren't even enough people left to bury them.

Lord Crane had found Nico in the forest, half-starved and delirious, nearly twenty miles from Crane Manor. Crane was also immune to the plague, and after most of his servants and the farmers on his lands had died, he started making trips out into the countryside.

So far he'd taken in more than a dozen survivors, all living and working together at Crane Manor. If he'd been braver, Nico liked to think he would have done the same. But even if he wasn't saving lives, he helped the rest of the household with his medical knowledge, and that gave him the sense of purpose he'd been lacking since his family died.

Nico wasn't paid money for his work, but he was given everything he needed to live a perfectly decent life. Someday maybe he'd go back to his ancestral home, if looters or animals hadn't taken over. But for now it was nice not to be alone. He'd always considered himself a solitary, independent sort, until he'd been truly alone for the first time. He quickly realized that the company he'd kept in his prior life wasn't nearly as witty or charming as he'd thought.

They knocked the mud off their boots and went to the servants' area downstairs, following the aroma of cooking meat.

"Hurry and wash up for supper," Mrs. Horner, the cook, said as she bustled around the kitchen. "The master has a guest tonight, and he wants a formal dinner at eight."

They all wore multiple hats in the manor; Nico served as

footman, valet, undertaker, and nurse, depending on what was needed that day. Tonight he'd be a server in the dining room.

"Who's the guest?" Colin asked, munching on a scraggly carrot plucked from the cutting board when Mrs. Horner's broad back was turned.

"A girl," said Abby, a young woman whom Colin himself had found over two years ago. She was short and plump with an angelic face, and Colin had fallen in love with her the moment he saw her. But Abby had aimed her sights higher, on the only other young aristocrat at the manor, Clifford Branson.

Not that any of it mattered. Lord Crane didn't tolerate tomfoolery amongst the staff. It was one of his requirements for living at the manor, one that had little effect on Nico. Romance was the furthest thing from his mind these days.

"An immaculate?" Colin asked.

Abby nodded. Immaculates and immunes were not the same. Immunes had been exposed to the plague and gone unaffected but for red marks that appeared along the veins of their inner wrists, whereas immaculates had somehow managed to escape exposure altogether. They were rare, especially now and especially in these parts, where the plague had hit hard. Sometimes they turned up—returning to look for survivors, or just now venturing out after locking themselves away for years in a manor. No one who caught the Bloody Three survived it, as far as Nico could tell. By his estimation, at least three quarters of the population of Goslind had been wiped out in the past three and a half years.

"She came upon the manor just as Lord Crane was heading out for a hunt," Abby explained. "She's headed home, she said. She was abroad when the plague hit, but she believes it's over. She doesn't know who survived."

Nico lowered his gaze in sympathy. He could imagine she must be very frightened, a young lady all on her own, not knowing what she'd encounter when she returned home. In the beginning Nico was certain that even without a cure, there were preventative measures they could take to slow the spread of the mori roja. Quarantines had saved villages from other plagues in the past. The Jews, for example, who were forced to remain in their walled quarters, often succumbed last. Of course, that led to their being accused of starting the plagues in the first place, so it was not the blessing it might have been. Between the Bloody Three or a pogrom, Nico thought it better to be betrayed by nature than slaughtered by your own neighbors.

But Nico still didn't know how the plague spread—whether it was airborne or passed through bodily fluids. Either way he had known it would eventually run out of hosts, as all plagues do. But a small part of him worried it could still be out there, biding its time, waiting for the population to recover enough for it to take root once again.

"She must be finding Goslind very much changed," Colin said. "She's fortunate to have come upon Lord Crane's lands."

Abby nodded. "She'll stay a few days and then be on her way. I'm to prepare the guest room."

"As if she'll need it," Branson said behind her. He had a nasty habit of appearing out of nowhere, with his oily black hair and leer of a smile. Abby tittered behind her hand, hiding the crooked tooth she was self-conscious of around Branson.

"Get to work, all of you," Mrs. Horner said, swatting Branson with a spoon. But even she was under his spell; she giggled like a schoolgirl when he untied her apron strings with one deft tug.

Colin and Nico rolled their eyes at each other as they went upstairs to wash and change for dinner. Nico had taken some of his brothers' clothes with him when he left home, and they were almost too small for him now, proof that he'd grown. Colin liked to tease that if *he* had "the body of a god and the soul of a poet," he'd have married Abby by now, titles be damned. But he said it mostly to make Nico blush, which wasn't difficult; Nico blushed whenever anyone complimented him, teased him, or looked at him too long.

They left the room together, Colin off to the kitchen and Nico to the dining room. He was making his way through the many corridors of Crane Manor when he nearly ran into someone he'd missed in the dimly lit hallway.

"Oof," Nico said, rather poetically.

"Who's there?" a small voice asked.

Nico looked down to find a petite young woman standing before him. This must be Crane's guest. "I beg your pardon, miss. Can I be of service?"

"That would be most welcome," she said, spinning in a circle. "This house is like a labyrinth."

"Please, allow me." It had been a while since Nico had been in the presence of a lady, and it took him a moment to shake off his new, more rustic persona. It didn't help that the lady in question was young and beautiful, and Nico was blushing like mad. He was suddenly grateful they didn't have enough tallow for candles to light all the halls of the manor.

"Are you a relation of Lord Crane?" the girl asked. She had wide-set brown eyes, giving her the look of a startled fawn.

"No, Miss..."

She smiled up at him. "Elisabeth Talbot."

"No, Miss Talbot. I am one of the many people Lord Crane has taken in after the plague. I came from Mayville."

She blinked at him with her doe eyes, clearly unfamiliar with the small hamlet.

"My mother's family was from Esmoor," he added. "Lucinda Templeton."

"Oh," she said, brightening. The Templetons were well known in Goslind. Several had served as kings' advisers, and Nico's uncle was a judge who had presided over the murder trial of a famous opera singer. "And what shall I call you?"

"You don't need to call me anything, Miss Talbot. I'm just a servant here."

Before they reached the end of the corridor, she stopped him with a delicate gloved hand on his arm. "The plague changed all of us, sir. But that doesn't mean we must completely abandon who we were beforehand."

He smiled and inclined his head. "Well said. My name is Nicodemus Mott."

"Well, then, Mr. Mott. Will you please escort me to dinner?" She crooked her elbow expectantly.

He bowed, a fancy trick for hiding the world's longest-sustained man-blush. "It would be my honor."

Crane Manor hadn't seen a guest in over six months, and something about Elisabeth's presence raised the spirits of the entire household. It wasn't just that she was charming and beautiful; it was knowing that there were survivors out there, immaculates who had made it through the plague without immunity. The world was changed, but not entirely. And with that came the hope that one day things could go back to how they had once been.

Nico helped Miss Talbot into her chair, noting that Crane had asked for the good china and silverware to be used tonight.

"Tell me, Mr. Mott," Elisabeth said, glancing up at him. In the candlelight, she was even more beautiful, her olive complexion glowing with health and vitality. "What would you be doing with your life if it hadn't been for the mori roja?"

Nico had been sixteen when the plague hit. As the youngest of three sons, he would have been lucky to inherit anything, but there had been no expectations placed on him, either. "I would have liked to study medicine," he said. His father had ridiculed the idea, but he could dream about those things now. There was no one left to tell him not to.

"Mott is one of the brightest young men I've ever met," Crane said, striding into the room. "He tends to all our injuries around the manor, human and animal alike. He would have made a fine physician."

"He *will*," Elisabeth said, smiling at Nico. "The world still needs physicians, surely."

Nico was about to say something brilliant, like "thank you," when Crane took his seat at the table, signaling that it was time for Nico to serve.

Nico's stomach hollowed in embarrassment, and he bowed before heading to the kitchen. He'd told himself for years that there was no place for romance in his life, and he was right.

He had nothing to offer someone like Miss Talbot. Not even a witty retort.

When he returned with the carrot soup, Nico was surprised to see Elisabeth and Crane sitting in awkward silence. Crane could be stern with the servants, but never without reason, and he was generally affable with guests. Perhaps he was rusty from not having entertained in so long.

Nico set the soup down and was turning to fade into the background like a proper servant when Elisabeth placed a hand on his forearm.

"Tell me more about your family," she said. "I'm curious how someone with noble blood came to work here at the manor."

Nico could feel Crane's eyes on him, and he licked his lips against the sudden dryness of his mouth.

Fortunately, he was saved by a heavy knock on the front door.

"Who the hell is *that*?" Crane asked, sounding profoundly unhappy about being interrupted.

"I'll go," Nico said, grateful for the excuse to leave the room. No one ever came to their door, and Nico had half a mind to grab one of the hunting rifles. But the pounding of a fist continued, and Nico found himself answering the door simply to spare Crane the noise.

A stranger stood on the threshold. He looked to be in his twenties, with sable hair to his shoulders and the fine clothing of a gentleman.

"Can I help you, sir?" Nico asked.

"I certainly hope so," the man replied. "I'm looking for my wife, you see. I lost her in the forest."

Nico suppressed a shiver as he glanced back into the manor. The stranger couldn't possibly mean Elisabeth.

"My name is Adrien Arnaud," the man said, drawing Nico's attention. "I live just a few miles from here. I don't suppose I could come in? It's awfully cold this evening."

"Do not invite that man inside, Mott."

He turned to see Crane standing behind him. He hadn't heard his master approach, but then, he hadn't been able to hear much over the pounding of blood in his ears.

"This gentleman says he's looking for his wife," Nico explained. Crane was several inches taller than Arnaud, but the stranger had the lean look of someone who spent plenty of time engaged in physical pursuits. Nico wouldn't want to face either of them in a fight.

"You're not welcome here," Crane said to the man. They stood nearly toe to toe, one on either side of the threshold.

"Come now. Surely we can be civil about this."

Crane was about to respond when they all heard a small cough behind them. Elisabeth stood watching, her hands folded daintily before her. "Dinner is getting cold."

There was no flicker of recognition in her eyes when she glanced at Arnaud. Not her husband, then. Who was this man, and why did Nico get the sense that he and Crane knew each other somehow?

"Leave now, before I have you driven off my land," Crane growled, slamming the door so hard it was a wonder he didn't break Arnaud's nose. Straightening his jacket, he turned to Elisabeth and took her arm.

"Nico," he called over his shoulder. "Watch from the window and be sure he leaves. Whatever you do, don't open the door for him again."

Nico nodded, unable to find his voice after witnessing the bizarre encounter.

But Lord Crane was already leading Elisabeth back to the dining room, speaking to her in a low, reassuring voice. "Come, my dear. Your hands are like ice. Nothing like a warm meal to get the blood pumping."

CHAPTER 3

It was Seraphina's midday visit with the king, who was in conversation with Lord Greymont. She sat to the side with her sisters and their ladies, embroidering a cushion. When she was a young girl in the confines of the Jewish quarter, she had daydreamed of being a lady. Not because she wanted a life of leisure, but because she wanted freedom.

Now she would give anything for her old life. Walling off the Jews was supposed to protect gentiles from their influence, but it also provided safety and community among the Jews. Then she and Dalia could go out into the woods and pick berries in the summer and mushrooms in the fall, or swim in the river when they were supposed to be doing the wash. She could still hear Dalia's giggle whenever she spoke of one of her many crushes.

"What are you thinking about, Princess Imogen?" Lord Greymont asked, coming to sit next to her. Jocelyn rose and absconded discreetly to a corner before Seraphina could catch her eye.

She flicked her gaze toward him for just a moment. "I'm

thinking about how wonderful this particular pillow will look amongst the dozens of nearly identical pillows in my room, Lord Greymont." Beside her, an old black cat she'd named Fig stretched languidly before slinking away.

Greymont leaned in, as if he wanted a closer look, but Seraphina thought his eyes were considerably farther north than the pillow. "Lovely," he declared before leaning back.

"Indeed," she drawled. "Shouldn't you be entertaining my father?"

"He looks like he's getting on just fine."

Seraphina turned and found that the king was, in fact, content. He was now playing a game of chess with Giselle, while Nina looked on in undisguised boredom. She was still bitter that she wasn't allowed to wear the siren costume she'd chosen for Seraphina's birthday masquerade. But a siren didn't complement the angel costume the king had decided on for Seraphina. She had been fitted for her white gown, feathered wings, and the golden circlet that would sit atop her freshly hennaed hair earlier this morning.

It was Giselle who decided that Nina, Rose, and their ladies-in-waiting should go as flowers, determined to take back some control after the king had chosen Seraphina's costume without consulting her. Nina may be the oldest, but Giselle was the craftiest, and she'd convinced their father of her plan before Nina had a chance to voice her opinion. Nina was to be an iris, Giselle a hyacinth, while Rose would go as her namesake blossom. *She* was happy, at least; she still got to wear pink.

"Now, then," continued Lord Greymont. "We know you're not that fond of embroidery, and the king is well in hand. What are you really thinking about?"

She wanted to tell him the truth. Not because she cared to confide in Lord Greymont, of all people, but because speaking Dalia's name out loud made her feel real. She had denied the existence of everyone she loved for nearly four years in what felt like the worst kind of betrayal. Seraphina hoped it was a relief to her parents that she'd been plucked from obscurity and sent to the castle—at least they would have died believing that their only child survived the plague—but she dishonored their memory by pretending they'd never lived.

The true princess had contracted the mori roja on a trip to a neighboring kingdom and died before she could return to Eldridge Hall. When Nina, Giselle, and Rose heard the news, they feared it would drive their already addled father straight into madness—as had the messenger who'd conveyed word of Imogen's death to the princesses first. Terrified of being trapped in a castle with their unpredictable and sometimes violent father after he'd ordered the walls closed to prevent the plague from reaching Eldridge Hall, they had done the only thing they could think of: create one of their father's beloved masquerades.

Seraphina remembered her last day outside the castle as if it were yesterday. She'd been scrounging around in the woods with Dalia, looking for anything edible, and her hands were covered in dark earth. They weren't supposed to leave the Jewish quarter, but as the plague struck towns closer and closer to Esmoor, the guards fled. At home it was all doom and gloom and panic, as everyone awaited the inevitable arrival of the plague. But out in the woods, it was like nothing had changed.

Dalia, so vibrant and joyful in Seraphina's memory, had

thrown a mushroom at her playfully, and it had left a smudge on Seraphina's cheek where it hit her. Her hair was in its usual loose braid over one shoulder, and she wore the shabbier of her two dresses. It was brown and plain, worlds removed from the gown she wore now, which was butter yellow and would have shown every stain, had she any reason to acquire one.

When a fine coach had traveled through the woods toward the city, they had followed it back. By the time they reached the Jewish quarter, people were already talking about how three noblewomen were passing around a portrait, asking if anyone knew the girl rendered in oils.

The women were offering a large reward for information. Seraphina's father found her in the crowd and immediately ordered her to the house, but people were staring and pointing at her. She hadn't understood why, having never seen the portrait herself. In good times her neighbors never would have turned on each other, but everyone was desperate now. Seraphina only had a moment to say goodbye to Dalia before she was ushered home.

Seraphina was horrified when the ladies and their attendants entered their house, and further mortified when one of them whispered to the other about the smudge on Seraphina's cheek, which she had quickly wiped away with her sleeve. That only made them giggle more.

Giselle, clearly the ringleader even then, whispered to her sisters that with a little hair dye and a bath, she would be perfect. Couldn't they look past the girl's *heritage* for a moment? Rose seemed afraid to touch anything and hardly said a word.

Finally, they came to some decision. "She'll do," Giselle said, though Seraphina still had no idea what for. Giselle handed a large purse to Seraphina's father, who shook his head and refused to take the money. The fear didn't set in until her mother started to cry. The two large guards had to stoop to enter through their front door. One took a hold of her arm without a word. That was when her mother began to wail and her father fell to his knees, pleading with them not to take her.

"Just think of it as one less mouth to feed," Giselle had said, gathering up her skirts and hurrying out the door. The guards dragged Seraphina with them.

"Careful," Giselle called over her shoulder. "Don't bruise her. Father wouldn't like that."

Seraphina had never forgotten those words. It made her relish hurting herself all the more. Now she pressed a thumb to a fresh bruise on her wrist and smiled at Lord Greymont.

"I'm thinking about the ocean. I'm wondering if you've really seen it, or if you were just trying to secure the first dance at my birthday."

"I would never lie to you."

She set her embroidery down and caught a maid's eye, who hurried away to fetch tea. "All right, then. Let's play a game. It's called 'fact or fiction.' I will tell you something about myself, and you guess if it's true or false."

When his brow furrowed, he looked younger than his twenty-two years, more like the boys Seraphina had known. She had kissed two or three in her day, and though they had not been as handsome, they had seemed infinitely more real than Lord Greymont or any of the other nobles here.

"But I just told you I would never lie to you," he protested.

"It's part of the game. And now I get to see what you look like when you tell the truth, and when you don't."

He grinned, his brown-flecked-with-green eyes gleaming.

His skin, which Seraphina remembered had been a burnished bronze when she was first brought here, was a lighter shade of brown now, reminding Seraphina of Dalia's olive complexion. Imogen had been just as pale as she was now from the start, albeit with more freckles. "Very well."

She smiled her most charming smile. "My favorite fruit is a clementine."

He bit his lip for a moment, considering. "Fiction."

"How do you know?"

"Because you always choose the strawberry tart for dessert. And you eat every other part of the tart first, the crust and the cream, before you savor the strawberries. You eat them like you might never have one again."

Seraphina felt a blush creeping all the way up her neck and into her cheeks. It wasn't her fault Princess Imogen had eaten her strawberry tarts like a lusty squirrel. "My, aren't we observant."

"It's hard to look away from," he said, his voice pitched low.

She could have kissed the maid who set the tea down in front of them at that very moment, sparing her from having to respond.

Lord Greymont cleared his throat and sat back. "My turn," he said, glancing up at the maid as she handed him his tea. "Thank you, miss."

The maid startled, sloshing the tea into the saucer, but he pretended not to notice. "I sailed on a ship when I was eleven," he said to Seraphina. "From here to the Isle of Wye and back."

"Wye? What on earth for?"

"My father imported wine before the… Before. Every year he'd go to Wye and check on his vineyard. He let me go with him, just the one time." He sipped his tea, and when he set it down, he was grinning. "You believed every word of that, didn't you?"

She blinked and realized she'd been staring. "I…well, yes. I suppose I did."

"That's because it was the truth."

If the rumors were true, the plague had spread over the entire continent. The only places that would have been safe were islands, assuming no one brought it over on a ship. "Did your family go to Wye when the—"

"It's your turn, Princess."

Seraphina wanted to throttle him for cutting her off mid-sentence, until she noticed that the king was no longer playing chess. He had come to stand behind them and was watching from above, frowning beneath his beard. A stormy look had come into his usually placid blue eyes, and she realized what she'd been about to say.

She set her teacup down and rose, smoothing her gown to wipe the moisture from her palms. "Tell me, Father, who won the game?"

Nina, who was standing next to him, smiled. "Why, Father, of course. How can a princess be expected to compete with a master strategist?"

There were some lies even Seraphina was happy to indulge. The king was rotten at chess. "Oh, well done, Father," she said, kissing him on the cheek. The princesses had spent weeks teaching her how to mimic their dead sister, from the way she kissed their father to calm his notorious temper, to the way she ate strawberry tarts. In truth, she didn't care for strawberries. Clementines really were her favorite, though she hadn't eaten one in years.

Placated, the darkness receded from the king's eyes as he held his arm out to his eldest daughter. "Nina can escort me today. Go back to your fun with Lord Greymont, my dear. I will see you at dinner."

After he'd gone, Seraphina took her seat again, releasing her breath slowly. She would have thought pretending to be someone else would get easier as time went on, but she only grew wearier with the passing years. To simply be herself was a luxury she'd taken for granted.

It took her a moment to realize that almost everyone had left the room. Rose and Giselle remained, playing a game of cards in a far corner. Jocelyn was observing Seraphina surreptitiously from another corner. Seraphina could never be left alone with a man, but Jocelyn knew how to be invisible.

She wasn't sure if Lord Greymont had been saving her from the king earlier or saving himself. It was forbidden to mention the plague inside the castle; anyone who attempted to escape was punished, though the attempts were short-lived after the first three servants were hanged. Everyone had to pretend that the plague had never come to Goslind at all. It was the only way to maintain the illusion, and to Seraphina's eyes, it was a role they were all happy to play. But if she was acting, maybe others were, too. It was impossible to know.

Or perhaps not impossible, after all.

"We can continue this game another time," he said, sensing the shift in her mood.

She had no idea if the king would ever willingly open the castle gates, but she couldn't go on like this forever. She had considered attempting an escape years ago, but she kept coming back to the words her father had whispered to her as she embraced him for the last time, the same thing the rabbi had told them when the kosher food in the Jewish quarter ran out and some people refused to eat: *You shall guard your life.*

If Lord Greymont's family had a vineyard on an island, then perhaps they had a ship. And if Seraphina had access to a ship, she could get far, far away from King Stuart and his court.

"Just one more round," she said, squaring her shoulders with a smile. The king hated it when she frowned.

Greymont lowered his eyes in deference. "I am at your disposal."

The tea had gone cold, so she picked up a biscuit and nibbled daintily at the edge. It was unsweetened, as she'd expected. The sugar supply was finally running out, and if the dry goods were dwindling, it didn't bode well for their fresh food. "I am turning twenty years old in two weeks."

"Fact, of course."

Not even a second of hesitation. She met his gaze and held it, for far longer than was proper. "Are you sure that is your answer, Lord Greymont?"

He started to reply, then narrowed his eyes and leaned back against the sofa. "Why do I get the sense you're playing a different game than I am, Your Highness?"

There was something about his gaze that made Seraphina's pulse quicken. Convincing the king she was Imogen was almost shockingly simple—he had no reason to believe she wasn't his daughter, and he was half-mad to begin with. But she sometimes wondered how no one else at court noticed that she was a stand-in. Yes, Imogen had been the shiest of the princesses, and as fourth in line to inherit, she hadn't attracted the same attention as Nina and Giselle, or even Rose. But still, Seraphina was an *entirely different person*, for heaven's sake.

"If you must call me anything, call me Princess Imogen. Please. *Your Highness* always sounds so fussy and formal."

He placed his hand on the sofa between them, so close one of his fingers brushed the fabric of her skirt. "Well, then, Princess Imogen." His lips curled in a small smile. "If your birthday isn't in two weeks, perhaps I can give you your gift sooner."

Her gaze drifted from his to the finger touching her velvet gown. Seraphina had never given any thought to finding a romantic attachment in Eldridge. Diverting though a dalliance may have been, allowing anyone to get too close to her was dangerous. She was bound to slip up and reveal her true identity eventually.

But this lord wasn't quite as dim as the others, and she knew enough of men to know he desired her. An ally at Eldridge Hall could be just what she needed; someone who would help her when the tower of lies came crumbling down around them. The plague *would* end, if it hadn't already, and there would be worse consequences when the stores ran out than bland biscuits.

She let her hand brush his, just for a moment, as she gathered her skirt and stood. "You win," she said as Rose and Jocelyn came rustling over.

He stood and cocked his head to the side. "Did I?"

"You were correct both times. Strawberries are my favorite fruit, and I am turning twenty in two weeks."

"At the masquerade!" Rose smiled prettily, but Jocelyn's eyes darted between Lord Greymont and Seraphina.

"I believe the game is still in play, Princess Imogen," he said with an exaggerated bow. And then, in a whisper that tickled her shoulder as he passed by, "I still owe you a lie."

CHAPTER 4

Lord Crane entertained Miss Talbot for several days. A wicked storm had swept through right after her arrival, and the master would never send a lady out in such conditions. Though when Nico found himself alone with her one afternoon in the study, she seemed eager to be on her way.

Nico was dusting a bookshelf, pretending that Elisabeth's sighs and mutterings weren't a distraction, when she came to hover next to his ladder.

"How can you stand it here?" she muttered, pulling a book off the shelf beneath him.

"I beg your pardon, Miss Talbot?"

She flipped absently through the pages, waving away the dust motes that floated out. If she had asked, Nico would have told her that the book in her hands was two centuries old, and that it included some rather lovely prose. "Lord Crane seems to control everyone and everything here. I told him I wanted to leave this morning and he forbade it. He said he'd tie me up if I even tried."

She was nineteen, the same age as Nico, but there was a

childish, petulant tone in her voice. "I'm sure he only wants to keep you safe. The forest will be a swamp by now, and if your horse goes lame, you'll be stranded out there." He stepped down from the ladder as she tried to stuff the book back into the wrong place on the shelf. "Here," he said, taking it from her and placing it reverently in its proper slot.

"I made it this far on my own, didn't I?" She plopped down on a sofa and folded her arms across her chest. "Eldridge Hall is only five more days from here, if I can make good time. And Locket would never let me come to harm."

Nico barely heard Elisabeth's comment about her gray mare, who, though docile and sweet, was still just a horse. His attention had snagged on something else. "Your family is at the castle?"

Elisabeth sighed and played with the golden fringe on a velvet pillow. "My brother was, the last I heard. But it's been years with no word."

Nico set down his duster and took a seat on the sofa across from Elisabeth. "I hate to be the one to tell you this, but all the rumors say the mad king locked the nobility up inside with him. They didn't have nearly enough food to last this long."

Worry flickered over her brow, but she set her chin at a stubborn angle. "If that's true, I'll continue to our home and see if anyone is left. Mother and Father sent me away as soon as they got word of the plague. They were supposed to come along after me, but it's possible they decided to stay and wait it out. Maybe they're all together now."

Nico wondered if she realized how deluded she sounded, but he decided not to press her. If there was any hope that some of his family members were still alive, he'd do the same thing. "I'm sure another day to wait for the weather to clear won't hurt," he said. "And another night in a warm bed can't hurt, either."

She glanced up at him, her eyes even wider than normal. "What's that supposed to mean?"

"I—er, nothing, Miss Talbot. Only that if you'll be sleeping in the woods on your way to Eldridge Hall, then staying at the manor one more night will give you some much-needed rest. Won't it?" The more he spoke the harder he blushed, but he wasn't alone. Elisabeth's cheeks were the same shade of mauve as her gown. Perhaps Branson was onto something when he insinuated that Elisabeth wouldn't need her own room.

Elisabeth was the picture of a virtuous young lady, the kind of girl he would marry if he was lucky enough to find his match, but he wasn't naive. Or at least not *completely* naive. The plague had changed everyone, like she'd said. When it felt like you were the last person left, you clung to other survivors like lifeboats in a stormy sea. It didn't matter that Colin was a chimney sweep, or Crane was Nico's master now, or that Branson was insufferable. The Bloody Three had made them family.

"What is it like out there?" he asked, to change the subject. "Is there any commerce? Are things…" He didn't want to say *normal*; *normal* had no meaning now. "Are they better?"

Her eyes met his, and for the first time he could tell that she was haunted by the things she had seen. "The plague is gone," she said quietly. "As far as anyone can tell. I left Glendale alone, but I met others on the road. We were a small group by the time we reached Esmoor. They weren't nobles, but they were good, kind folk. I started to feel hopeful. But

Esmoor was…" She swallowed thickly. "The people who are still there live like rats in the shadows, scurrying about, fighting over scraps. We didn't stay long. It wasn't safe."

Nico hung on her every word, trying to imagine Esmoor so changed. He'd only been a few times as a child, but it had been a lovely city. He should have gone back himself, seen these things with his own eyes. *Helped* someone.

Before he could ask more questions, Lord Crane entered the library. "There you are, Miss Talbot. I was afraid we'd lost you."

Nico hurried to his feet. "Apologies, sir. I was just finishing up in here."

Crane's smile crept across his face lazily, like wine down the bowl of a crystal goblet. If Miss Talbot was the quintessential lady, then Crane was everything Nico imagined a nobleman should be: handsome, generous, powerful. He was also the most intimidating man Nico had ever met, other than his father.

"Miss Talbot has good taste," Crane said, still smiling at Nico. "The library is one of my favorite rooms in the manor."

Elisabeth rose and took Crane's arm, casting an unreadable glance at Nico. "The sun is finally out. I should like to see the gardens before I go."

"It would be my pleasure." He tossed the next words over his shoulder like salt. "Mott, I believe the silver needs polishing. See to it, would you?"

"Polishing the silver?" Colin asked when he found Nico in the dining room, sweating over an elaborate candelabra. "Whatever have you done?"

Nico puffed his hair out of his face and bent back to his

task. "Lord Crane found me alone with Miss Talbot. I made the mistake of sitting on the sofa."

Colin let out a low whistle. "Can't say I haven't let a pretty face get the better of me in the past, but Miss Talbot is the master's guest."

"I wasn't trying to woo her. I was trying to console her. She thinks her brother is at Eldridge Hall."

Colin raised an eyebrow. "Alive?"

"So it would seem. I was trying to tell her that the odds of that are..."

"Nonexistent?"

"I put it a little more delicately than that."

Colin picked up a silver dish and a rag. "Hardly seems worthy of punishment, then."

"He didn't catch the conversation, I don't think. Just me sitting down like I own the place."

"You *are* a gentleman."

"Not in this house. And I'm glad of it. I don't think I could handle the responsibility of all those lives. But it is hard to remember sometimes."

"And Miss Talbot?"

"What about her?"

Colin smoothed his bushy brown hair off his forehead as he bent down to pick up a cup. "Do you think she likes you? Perhaps the master was jealous."

"Of me?" Nico laughed. "Don't be a fool. He's a decade older and infinitely wealthier. I'm hardly a threat."

"Don't underestimate the power of a pretty face," Colin said, flicking Nico on the chin. "I'll finish up here. Branson's on digging duty today."

Nico sighed. "I should lend him a hand."

"Why? He wouldn't help you."

"That's what separates the men from the beasts," Nico said with a wry smile.

"What is?"

"Generosity. Kindness. The ability to rise above petty differences."

"Really? I thought it was our fancy clothes." Colin plucked at his waistcoat for emphasis.

Nico laughed. "You're polishing the silver for me, you realize."

"Only so I don't feel obligated to help Branson."

Nico arched an eyebrow as he backed out of the room. "And so the wheel turns."

He changed into his digging clothes and headed out to the fields, following the deep ruts in the mud left by Branson's wheelbarrow. If nothing else, it was nice to be outside, enjoying the fresh air. When the plague first came, everyone had stayed hidden inside, just like those poor fools at Eldridge Hall.

Something rustled in the trees ahead and Nico froze. Since the plague, predators had come down from the mountains, their fear of hunters forgotten. He'd seen a wolf only once—on its own, fortunately—sniffing around a corpse. Even the animals wouldn't touch the plague-ridden bodies, but they had found other evidence of predation: deer and sheep with their throats torn out, along with desiccated squirrels and rabbits.

"Help!" someone called, and Nico sprang forward, wishing he'd brought a weapon with him. He broke through the brush and into a clearing, where two men were wrestling on the ground.

"Where is she?" one of the men demanded, his hands wrapped around Branson's throat.

"I don't know," Branson sobbed. "I swear it."

Nico rushed forward without any real plan. "Unhand him!"

It had sounded more gallant in his head. The man on top of Branson turned to look at him, and Nico immediately recognized the stranger who'd come to the door so unexpectedly the other evening. Adrien Arnaud. There was a wild look in his eyes that made Nico feel far less brave than he had seconds before.

"You!" the man shouted, dropping Branson and moving swiftly toward Nico. "Tell me where the girl is!"

"I'll do no such thing." Nico leaped out of his grasp, heading for the wheelbarrow. The shovel was the closest thing they had to a weapon, and Branson didn't seem inclined to help.

"You don't understand," Arnaud said, a note of pleading in his voice. "I need to find her."

Nico looked closer and saw that the man was clad in the same fine clothing as their last encounter, though it was now tattered and filthy. Nico imagined it was close to what he himself had looked like when the master found him. Thank goodness Crane had taken pity on him, because he hadn't spared any for this gentleman.

"I'm sorry," Nico said, "but the lady is a guest of Lord Crane. Even if I knew where she was at the moment, I couldn't tell you. I suggest you leave these lands before he sees you again. I don't think he'll take kindly to your presence."

"I can't leave without the—"

A scream sounded at the same time as the gunshot. Nico covered his head on instinct, but Crane was an excellent marksman. The bullet had gone straight through the man's back. He fell forward into the mud, dead.

"Good heavens!" Nico cried. "What did you do that for?"

"The man was raving," Crane said coolly, dismounting from his stallion. Miss Elisabeth sat astride Locket behind him, her mouth a little O of surprise. "I put him out of his misery. It was a favor, believe me."

Nico wasn't sure anyone could call a bullet in the back a favor, but he did his best to compose himself. Another reason he couldn't be a master; he didn't have Crane's resolve. But at least he wasn't cowering on the ground like Branson.

"Get up, Branson," Crane said, toeing the dead man with his boot. "The good news is you already have everything you need to bury him. Hurry up and see to it. Mott, you'll come with me."

"Don't leave me alone out here," Branson whimpered. "Please, sir."

Crane waved his gun at the body. "There's nothing to fear now. I need to get Miss Talbot to the manor." He glanced back at her, a strange expression on his face. "She's had quite a shock."

Elisabeth was indeed pale, and Nico noticed there was a small trickle of blood coming from her nose. He passed her a handkerchief, explaining how to tip her head forward to encourage clotting, but he was reeling a bit himself, trying to understand how a man who had saved him from certain death could be so unfeeling toward a stranger.

The first time Nico ever saw Crane, he'd been lying on the forest floor, sure he was hallucinating again. Crane had been riding his black stallion, Bane, with a hunting rifle across his lap. Bane snorted, likely at the discovery of Nico's half-unconscious form, and the man dismounted, his polished boots winking in and out of Nico's vision.

The next thing Nico remembered was Crane's strong hand on his wrist, checking for a pulse.

"Lucky I found you when I did," he muttered, picking Nico up as though he were a child. "Another few hours and you'd be finished." Crane had helped Nico into the saddle, then mounted behind him. He slept for most of the trip to Crane Manor, but Crane spoke to him quietly as they rode, telling him that he was safe now, that there was a warm bed and plenty of food waiting for him. It had all felt like a dream, one Nico was astonished to find was real once he recovered.

When Nico's duties were laid out for him by Colin, he had accepted his new position gratefully. It was only right that he should repay Crane for saving him. And when the occasional traveler passed by Crane Manor, Crane always treated them just as kindly as he had Nico. Surely, it was concern for Elisabeth that had prompted Crane to kill Arnaud. Still, it left Nico unsettled to see his benefactor behave so violently. Once again, he had the feeling that the two men had a history.

At the manor Nico was asked to escort Elisabeth back to her chambers, fetch Abby, and to keep Elisabeth there until Crane sent for her. He disappeared into another wing of the house as soon as they returned. As Nico and Elisabeth walked down the corridors together, he couldn't ignore her muffled sobs.

"Don't cry, Miss Talbot. You're very safe here in the manor." He gently pulled her hand, which was still pressing the handkerchief to her nose, away from her face. He was glad to see that the bleeding had stopped.

"That's just it," she said, sniffling. "What if I encounter another lunatic in the woods when I leave tomorrow? I won't have anyone there to protect me."

"Perhaps someone could escort you, at least part of the way."

"Oh, would you?" Elisabeth embraced him suddenly, burying her face in his chest, the light reflecting off the crown of her dark, silky hair. "I would be forever indebted to you."

"Oh." He stood frozen for a moment, unsure what to do. Bloody noses he could deal with, but he'd never learned the remedy for a weeping maiden. "I doubt I'd be permitted to leave. But perhaps Lord Crane could take you."

"He makes me uneasy," she whispered as they reached her chamber. Before he could turn and leave to fetch Abby, she grabbed his arm and pulled him into the room, closing the door behind him.

"Miss Talbot, please. This is most inappropriate. Lord Crane is a gentleman, I assure you."

She scoffed. "Does a gentleman go shooting men in the back? I think not."

A prickle of unease crept down his spine, but he shook it away. "Arnaud was raving, begging to know your whereabouts. He'd already pretended to be your husband. Lord Crane was *protecting* you."

She dropped to her knees and took one of his hands. "Please, Mr. Mott. Nico. I'll never make it all the way to Eldridge on my own. I need you. The way Crane looks at me…"

Nico felt the flush creeping up his neck and willed it back down. "You're a lady, so perhaps you don't understand—"

She shot him a cutting look that made him feel like a child.

"I know what desire looks like. This is different. There's a hunger in his eyes that frightens me."

There was no stopping the blush now. Hunger, desire—weren't they one and the same? "What do you mean?"

She rose to her feet, now only inches away from Nico. Her eyes reached to the hollow of his throat, and he swallowed audibly. Gently, she laid her palm on his chest, her fingers fanning out across his shirt, just above his heart. There was no chance she didn't feel how fast it was beating.

"That, Mr. Mott. That's desire. But Crane... It's like he's a wolf and he wants to..." She bit her lip and looked up at him, her brown eyes huge in her blood-streaked face. "Like he wants to devour me." Her fingers trailed down his chest to his stomach, where they gripped the fabric of his shirt and pulled him closer still. "Please, help me."

Nico glanced at the closed door, convinced Crane was going to enter any moment and shoot *him* in the back. If Elisabeth was sick or injured, he would do everything in his power to help. But even if he was allowed to escort her home, he would do a miserable job of it. He wasn't a good marksman. He didn't know the roads. He had barely survived on his own out there.

Besides, if Crane thought Nico was overstepping, he could exile him from the manor. Nico didn't want to go back to living alone in a house full of ghosts. He wasn't sure his sanity could withstand it.

"I can't, Miss Talbot. I'm sorry." He broke free of her grasp and moved to the door. "I'll send Abby right away. Try not to worry. You've had a scare, but everything will be all right."

He found Abby and sent her to Elisabeth's room, warning

her that the lady was distraught. Crane had told him to wait outside her chambers, but Nico didn't think that was wise, given her behavior. Instead, he went to his room and tried to clear his head. He couldn't go with Elisabeth; that much was clear.

But he also hated the idea of sending her out into the woods on her own. Perhaps if he spoke to Crane, he could convince him to escort her at least part of the way. Nico and the others could take care of the manor in his absence.

He was heading toward the kitchen when he heard the master speaking with another servant, a young boy named Gavin who worked in the stables.

"Miss Talbot and I will leave at first light," Crane said. "Tell Mrs. Horner to prepare enough food for ten days of travel. I don't think I'll be gone that long, but it's better to be safe than sorry. We'll take the carriage."

"Yes, sir," the boy said.

Nico sighed in relief. Elisabeth would be taken care of, and he hadn't even needed to intervene. He kept to his room for the rest of the night, avoiding Elisabeth. It was best for everyone that she left.

CHAPTER 5

It wasn't until she'd been at Eldridge Hall for nearly a year that Seraphina learned why Giselle despised her so much. Their mother, Queen Aurora, had died giving birth to Imogen when Giselle was five years old—old enough to remember her mother, yet young enough not to understand the inherent dangers of childbirth. According to Jocelyn, Giselle refused to acknowledge Imogen as a baby. It didn't help that King Stuart seemed to channel all his sadness at the loss of his wife into love and affection for baby Imogen.

Still, this charade had been Giselle's idea, and she was bound and determined to see it through. Even if it meant watching her own father dote on a commoner. A *Jewish* commoner, no less.

Today the king was feeling nostalgic and had asked all his daughters to join him for an afternoon of cards and music. The real Princess Imogen had been a talented piano player, but Seraphina had never touched an instrument in her life. Her sisters had explained this to their father as stiffening in Seraphina's finger joints that made it difficult to play. But she had a fine singing voice, so she entertained the king in her own way.

"Lovely," Lord Greymont said as Seraphina returned to her seat after accompanying Nina for three songs. Nina was twenty-six and the heir to the throne, though she didn't have a "sovereign's temperament," per Giselle. Indeed, Nina didn't seem bothered about the fact that she'd have to marry to produce an heir one day. "Flirtation keeps me young," she'd once told Seraphina with a wicked grin.

Seraphina inclined her head at Lord Greymont and took up her embroidery. "Shall we resume our game?"

"I had a different game in mind."

She glanced at the king, who was snoring softly on a sofa with his head on Giselle's shoulder. She was undeniably beautiful, with her bright green eyes and dark chestnut hair, but she wore a perpetual scowl that hinted at the ugliness inside her.

Rose, who was just twenty-two, was equally lovely, with a pair of dimples that could make the most cantankerous lord smile. She was also the only one of the princesses engaged to be married, though whether or not the prince she was betrothed to was still alive was unknown.

"And what game is that?" Seraphina asked finally.

"Hide-and-seek."

"That is a children's game, Lord Greymont."

He grinned. "Not the way I play it."

"Regardless," she said quickly, "we can hardly play hide-and-seek in one room." She didn't like the way his grins made her belly flutter. Or rather, she *did* like it, and that was the problem. She pinched her wrist beneath the pillow.

"Then we shall have to leave."

"I have been asked to spend the afternoon with my father."

Lord Greymont leaned so close his hair brushed her neck. "Part of the fun is sneaking out without getting caught."

Seraphina chewed on her lip for a moment. She didn't want to do anything improper, but she also didn't want him to tire of her before she'd determined his usefulness. "And I assume you expect me to hide?"

"Naturally."

She had been snared like a rabbit once and forced into this gilded cage, but Imogen didn't have to play by the same rules as Seraphina. "I think not. If we're to play, you will be the one hiding. I can claim I was searching for something I lost, should anyone ask."

"Very well," he said. "I'll need a five-minute head start. The castle is quite large, after all."

"Personal chambers are off-limits. As are the servants' domains. You know how they love to gossip."

Greymont twisted his lips in thought. "What does that leave?"

"The great hall, the library, the old armory, any of the unused apartments, and the cellar. I think that should suffice."

"Indeed. Happy hunting." He rose and began to step away, but Seraphina caught his sleeve.

"What do I get if I find you?" she whispered. "The prize must be very great, to make it worth such a risk."

His eyes sparked with mischief. "What would you have of me, Princess Imogen?"

She knew what he was hoping for: something he was eager to receive, like a kiss. But she was a princess; she didn't bestow kisses for free. "A favor of my choosing, whenever I ask it."

He raised his eyebrows. "Any favor?"

She nodded. "As I said, this is a great risk for me, to be seen cavorting around the castle when I'm meant to be spending the afternoon with my father."

He raised one corner of his mouth. "Very well, then. A favor of your choosing. I do hope you find me."

"As do I," she said with a bat of her lashes. "Otherwise, it could be a very long day for you."

Seraphina waited a bit longer than five minutes, just to make sure no one connected her departure to Lord Greymont's. The king was still sleeping when she slipped out, claiming she needed to relieve herself, and though Giselle had narrowed her eyes at Seraphina, she hadn't moved for fear of waking her father.

She tried the apartments and the library first, as they were on the way to the great hall. The cellar was a last resort because there was a much higher likelihood of running into a servant there. Not that any of them would dare to question her, but even still. She didn't like to give them any reason to gossip.

One of the only good things to come of her imprisonment was access to the castle library. Her father was a scholar who'd taught her to read at an early age, but he studied Torah and historical texts, not necessarily subjects that interested young Seraphina. Now she entered the library and inhaled the warm, musty smell of old books that had become as familiar as friends. She often settled down here to read away the afternoon, as did some of the other lords and ladies. They had all been trapped for years, and reading was one of the few means of escape left to many of them. Yes, there was gambling, the elaborate meals, hours spent dressing and preening, sordid affairs in dark corners, or wandering around the many halls of the castle, as she was doing now. But there was no opportunity for outdoor amusements like riding, hunting, archery, or any of the activities that might have interested her in her former life.

She checked the empty apartments next. There were more now than there had been when this whole charade began because people had died during that time. Not of the plague, but of natural causes and accidents. Several people had gone missing according to Nina, who was the most attuned to the castle's gossip. No one knew how they'd escaped, though it certainly supported Jocelyn's theory about a hidden tunnel. But Seraphina's unattended moments were rare. In fact, she realized as she checked behind a canopied bed, this was the first time she'd been alone outside her tower in ages.

She sang to herself as she walked, one of the ballads she'd been performing for the king. But as she allowed herself to get lost in her thoughts, the words began to change to a nursery rhyme, which was sung to the same tune as the ballad.

Old King Stuart's lost his head, hoping he won't end up dead.
Lock the windows, bar the door; the plague will come for rich and poor.
If you want to stay alive, there are three ways to survive:
Run away across the sea; pray for blood immunity;
Or die and be reborn again, and drink the blood of living men.

Dalia had sung it to Seraphina, just a few days before the princesses came for her. Dalia had a sweet singing voice, like her beloved songbirds, which somehow made the words even more unsettling.

King Stuart had already begun to hoard crops and supplies by then, and other cities in Goslind had closed themselves off to outsiders. Giselle had taken a risk in bringing a stranger into the castle; although she now knew that the plague had not yet arrived at Esmoor when she'd been taken away, at the time there'd been no way to know for sure, and Seraphina could theoretically have been in the early stages of the mori roja. But then, Giselle had no experience with plagues. Her father's temper, on the other hand… That, she'd known all too well.

The last line, about the reborn, was pure nonsense. But it gave Seraphina a chill every time she sang it. Why were children's rhymes always the ones to make your skin crawl?

She spun around as she entered the great hall, sure she had heard someone call her from one of the apartments. But she'd checked them thoroughly, and Lord Greymont wouldn't be so foolish as to call her by her first name out in the open like this. She was about to pass through the hall to the cold fireplace at the far end when the ebony clock began to chime.

She turned to face it slowly. The clock was as tall as two men standing on top of one another, and as broad as five. It was solidly, impenetrably black, from the lion's feet pedestals at the bottom to the eagle finial—or was it a raven?—at the very top. Even the face was black, making it difficult to read the golden filigree hands. Not that it mattered, considering they were always positioned at three. She guessed the real time was closer to five o'clock in the evening.

She stepped toward the clock, noticing for the first time that there was a little keyhole in the door carved into the front. She smiled to herself. It would be a very clever place for Lord Greymont to hide, probably too clever. If she had never noticed it before, she doubted he had. She lifted her hand to the door, curious if the space inside really was big enough to house a grown man. If so, she would keep it in mind when it was her turn to hide.

When her fingers brushed the surface, she shuddered. Slowly, she brought her other palm up to the door. The clock was cold, far colder than a wooden clock should be. She pressed her cheek to the surface and listened, expecting to hear the *tick-tock* of the pendulum inside. Instead, she heard the steady whine and whoosh of wind. That was the sound she'd heard before: not a voice calling her name, but the wail of wind through a tiny opening.

She was lowering her eye to the keyhole when something clamped down on her shoulder.

"There you are," Lord Greymont said as she whirled around.

Her heart pounded in her chest as she took a step back, pressing against the cold face of the clock. He was smiling, his white teeth almost too bright in the unlit hall. Seraphina had been forced to bleach her teeth with lemon juice when she arrived, to try and undo some of the damage from drinking strong coffee without milk for years.

"You're trembling." He brought his other hand up to her shoulder, grasping her tightly. "I'm so sorry. I didn't mean to frighten you."

She wanted to pull away from him and run, but she forced her muscles to relax and smiled. "Startled. Not frightened. You're *supposed* to be hiding."

"I'd been gone so long I was worried my beard was coming in and you wouldn't recognize me when you found me."

She smirked at his smooth cheeks. "It's been less than half an hour."

"Is that right? I swear an age had passed. What century is it, Princess?"

Before she could answer, Lord Greymont tucked a loose curl behind her ear, leaned forward, and brushed his lips against her cheekbone. It was brief and could hardly be considered a real kiss, but she was a princess, as far as he was concerned. Even as Seraphina, she would never allow a boy to take such liberties without permission.

"I'm sorry," he said when he saw her furrowed brow. "I shouldn't have—"

"No. You shouldn't have."

There was a panicked look in his eyes. "Forgive me, Your Highness."

As much as she would have liked to see him squirm a bit longer, she didn't want to scare him off entirely. "I suppose we'll just have to pretend this never happened." She grinned and stepped around him, away from the clock. "Where were you hiding, anyway?" She heard his sigh of relief behind her and her grin broadened. As long as he was afraid of offending her, she still had the power.

"I was in the cellar. That's part of the reason I came looking for you. I found something there I thought might be of interest."

She let him take her arm and lead her toward the cellar. Not once did she let her gaze return to the clock, or to the dust on the floor surrounding it. She especially didn't look at the footprints she had seen there, leading away from the door inside the clock, and the sliver of sunlight—as fine as one of the golden hairs on her head—coming from the floor beneath it.

★ ★ ★

Seraphina and Greymont stood staring at the cellar, the uninvited kiss forgotten. It was empty. Utterly, disastrously empty, aside from a few sagging sacks of grain and jars of pickled vegetables.

"Have you ever been down here before?" Seraphina asked when she finally found her voice.

He shook his head. "No, never. I know it sounds foolish, but I almost didn't want to know where the food was coming from."

"I know the feeling. But this... We'll never last the winter."

"No, we won't." He turned suddenly, grabbing her arm and pulling her into a corner of the cellar where the light from the doorway didn't reach.

"What are you doing?" she demanded, struggling against his grip.

He dropped her arm immediately, but she was trapped in the corner by his body. "No more games," he hissed.

"I am not *playing*," she said through gritted teeth. If she screamed, a servant would probably hear her. But she wasn't eager to explain to the king what she was doing alone with Lord Greymont, potentially putting her "virtue" in peril, something the king often advised her against.

"It's been nearly four years. The plague is gone. We all know it. When is the king going to let us out?"

Seraphina's breath came fast against the laces of her corset. He had done it, broken the illusion, said the forbidden words. She half expected the ceiling to fall down around them.

"When?" he demanded, slamming his palm against the wall next to her head.

Seeing the fear in his eyes helped her to shake off her own.

She stood taller and barked a wry laugh. "I don't pretend to know the inner workings of my father's mind, Lord Greymont."

Greymont dropped his arm and collapsed against the wall next to her. "I'm sorry. I know this isn't your fault."

At his apparent exhaustion and desperation, her anger began to dissolve. For the first time in years, she felt a little less alone. Even Jocelyn wouldn't discuss the possibility of the food running out. But more than that, Greymont might just be her key to surviving once she did get out of here—because she *would* get out. "I'm sorry, too," she said, softening her posture and her tone. "Perhaps there is something I can do, to help matters along."

They stood there, both breathing heavily, and Seraphina wondered what calculations were going on in his mind. Greymont was right about one thing. They were all going to starve, and meanwhile the king was expecting a feast for her birthday. What would happen when no food materialized on the nobles' gilt-edged plates, when the clock wound down and the music stopped? These weren't people accustomed to fending for themselves. Would they be rendered impotent by fear? Or would they shed their civility like snakeskins, revealing their true natures beneath?

"I assume others talk about this, how the plague is over?" she asked finally.

He nodded. "Never where the king might hear, but yes, there is talk. More and more lately."

"I do have my father's ear, of course. I could try to reason with him," she said, though the very idea terrified her. She had seen him lose his temper before, and it was not a pretty sight. Once a servant told him they had no fresh cream and he had backhanded the poor woman, knocking her to the floor in front of everyone. Seraphina could still picture the gleaming crimson blood on the dull gray stone.

The color in Greymont's cheeks rose. "Would you? He would listen to you, I think. Tell him there is no more food. He has to let us out. He must. There are people willing to risk it out there, who *want* to."

People. Meaning him? Who else did Greymont conspire with? She felt a cold sliver of worry lodge in her chest. Throughout her time at Eldridge, she had struggled to separate farce from reality. Was Jocelyn her friend, or simply playing a part? Did everyone suspect she was an imposter, going along with the lie to preserve the king's fragile mental state, or did they really believe she was Princess Imogen?

And when Greymont took her hand in his and pressed a kiss to the back of it, did he care about her, or was she simply a means to an end? She'd assumed he wanted her because she was a future queen, but she was starting to feel more like a pawn.

All she knew was that the game *was* still in play, only the stakes were higher than ever now. If there was no food in the cellar, then perhaps any possible outside source had also run out. If the servants had the ability to escape, why did they return to Eldridge Hall? Was she still safer in here, even if the plague was gone? She had never been on her own before.

She told herself she stayed in Eldridge Hall for her own protection, that her safety was what her parents—what *God*— would want. But it wasn't just devoutness that kept her here. Deep down she knew it was fear. And as much as she hated to admit it, even with a way out, the truth was that she didn't know what awaited her out there. How would she even get home, to see if her family survived? Here, now, was someone who could help her, someone who could make the terror of the unknown just a little less frightening.

She made her eyes as big and doleful as possible and found it wasn't difficult to conjure tears. "And where would you go, if you were to leave Eldridge?" she asked softly.

He brushed his finger along her cheekbone, catching her tear. "I do know of a lovely vineyard..."

She turned her head away to hide her smile. "Then I hope these years cooped up in the castle haven't harmed your sailing abilities, my lord."

"Impossible," he replied.

She looked back up at him to see him grinning down at her. "I wish—" she began.

"What do you wish?"

She wished to be far away from Eldridge, on a ship across the sea to a place where the Bloody Three never existed. She wished she was still in her safe, loving home with her parents, or next door at Dalia's house, waiting for a fresh loaf of Dalia's mother's famous challah. She wished that she was Seraphina again, not Imogen the Worthless, Imogen the Shy. Imogen the Impotent.

Her wishes beat against her chest like trapped birds, aching to be free. She wanted to feel anything other than the deep pit of terror in her belly, to forget for one moment who and where she was, so she blurted, "I wish you would kiss me."

He laughed, a soft rumble in his chest. "You are nothing like the other ladies at Eldridge, Princess Imogen."

She reached up and gently pushed a lock of hair away from his forehead as he started to lean toward her. *Oh*, she thought as his lips brushed hers. *You have no idea.*

CHAPTER 6

In Crane's absence, Nico found himself thinking of Elisabeth often. Had Crane gotten her all the way to Eldridge Hall? What had they found there? Would he return with Elisabeth if her brother was dead? Marry her? She was young, but not too young to marry, and Nico imagined she would appreciate the security. That was what she had asked him for that night in her room, after all: safety, someone to protect her.

At night, in the small hours when he couldn't sleep, something chewed at his insides like a rat in a corpse. He couldn't stop thinking of Arnaud and his seeming desperation to find Elisabeth, and the ease with which his master had shot a man in cold blood.

"Stop moping," Colin said to him as they cleared the dead shrubs from the garden under a cold, gray sky. "Miss Talbot was never meant for you."

Nico narrowed his eyes, hoping Colin would get the hint and drop the subject.

"Don't get me wrong, she's a lovely girl, but she's too dependent. She needs someone like Crane, who can provide—"

Subtlety was wasted on some people. "I don't want to talk about it."

Colin ignored him. "—a comfortable life. You need a partner."

Nico had always imagined meeting a girl who shared his interests in literature and medicine, someone with whom he could have meaningful conversations. But he wasn't jealous of Crane and Elisabeth. He just wanted to know that she was safe.

"When are *you* going to tell Abby how you feel about her?" Nico asked.

"When I've made something of myself, I'll ask her to marry me. What have I got now to tempt her?"

Nico waggled his eyebrows. "Charm and good looks, of course."

"I'll leave that to the likes of you and Branson. Well, the good looks, anyway. I've got more charm in my little finger than Branson has in his entire body."

Nico snorted in agreement. "Speaking of which, where is Branson? I've hardly seen him since that day the master shot the trespasser."

"I think he's avoiding leaving the manor in case we find any more bodies. He was always a bit squeamish, but now he seems downright spooked."

"I suppose burying a man you've seen killed is different than an anonymous corpse in the woods."

They both looked up at the sound of jangling tack and hoofbeats. The master's carriage was coming up the road, pulled by one of the dependable cart horses.

Nico's eyebrows lifted when he saw that Crane was alone.

"Good day, sir," Colin said, taking hold of the horse's harness. "I take it Miss Talbot got home safely."

"She did indeed." Crane climbed down from the carriage and dusted off his coat. "Fetch Gavin, would you? The horse needs to be cooled down. It was a difficult journey. Nico, help me with my trunk."

He hurried forward and lifted the trunk from the back of the carriage. "Did you make it to Eldridge Hall, sir?"

"We went straight to Miss Talbot's home. It was a more direct route."

Nico was unable to keep the surprise out of his voice. She had seemed determined to find her brother. "Her parents survived? How fortunate."

"Just her father. But yes, it was a very happy homecoming." Nico couldn't help noticing how healthy and refreshed he looked, as if he'd just come back from a holiday. It must have lifted Crane's spirits to see survivors. It was certainly buoying Nico's to hear about them. "Shame about her mare, though."

"Locket? Did something happen to her?"

"We had to ford a river at one point. The cart horse had no trouble with it, but Locket absolutely refused to cross. We had no choice but to leave her behind."

"Miss Talbot must have been distraught," Nico said, thinking of the way Elisabeth cared for the mare, more than once asking Nico to pilfer an apple from the stores. They didn't have enough to spare, but he found he couldn't say no to her. "She loved that mare so much."

"It was difficult, of course. But she understood that it was the only way to make it back to her family. What is a horse compared to being reunited with her father?" Crane seemed to put the matter to bed, though Nico's heart still ached at the thought of Locket all alone in the forest, at the mercy of the wolves. "How have things been here?"

Nico hefted the trunk with his knee. "Good, sir. Just one body, and it was quite old. I think we've covered all your land now."

"Excellent. We may move on to neighboring lands soon, but for now you can see to the storeroom. Winter will be here before we know it. Take my trunk up to my chambers." He paused and ruffled Nico's hair affectionately. "You're a good lad."

Nico was annoyed at the way the words warmed him. There was a part of him that craved Crane's approval, his own father having withheld it until the day he died, but he was a grown man now. He wanted to hear more about Elisabeth and her reunion with her father, not be dismissed like a child.

A wave of guilt washed over him for thinking her deluded. In fact, she'd been incredibly brave to venture out into the world on her own. He should have left Crane Manor himself ages ago; should have found physicians doing the work of searching for a cure for the Bloody Three and *helped*, for God's sake.

He took the trunk upstairs and unpacked the clothing, then carried it downstairs to the laundry, his heart heavy despite the good news that the plague was gone, that Elisabeth was safe.

"The master is home?" Abby said as she took the armful of clothing from him. "Miss Talbot?"

"Happily reunited with her father." He knelt down to pick up a shirt that had fallen on the floor and frowned at a splatter of dark stains on one of the sleeves. Crane was usually fastidious, but he had been on the road for over a week. "Looks like this one will need extra washing," he said as he handed it to Abby.

She scraped at one of the small spots with a fingernail. "Blood. Should come out with enough scrubbing."

Nico's stomach gave a slight twist, though it had nothing to do with squeamishness. "Blood? Are you sure?"

"It's not wine," she said, though she sniffed it anyway. "Not to worry. The master cuts himself shaving sometimes. I'll see to it."

"Thank you, Abby." Nico left the laundry room and headed toward the storeroom, but something was nagging at him. The master hadn't shaved on his trip; he had the beard to prove it. More likely the master had caught a rabbit for dinner one night. He was an excellent hunter, and he wouldn't want to go so long without fresh meat. The stain looked like blood spray.

He shivered. The animal must have struggled.

Nico entered the storeroom and frowned. It was more barren this year than last, and even worse than the year before. There were still fresh vegetables and fruit in the gardens, but there was no wheat or barley, or any of the other field-grown crops that the surrounding farms would have produced. Mrs. Horner had preserved what she could, but there were more people living at Crane Manor than there had been when Nico first arrived. They would have to decrease their rations yet again.

Before he left his family home, Nico had taken what he could from the surrounding abandoned houses and managed, but the fresh food only lasted so long. He shuddered at the memory of wandering through one particular country manor, where he'd found three bodies rotting on their blood-soaked mattresses. He had buried them, alone, knowing he'd want someone to do the same for his family.

Now it fell to Nico to alert his master to their lack of food. He found him in his study, writing what looked like a letter. "Sorry to disturb you, sir, but—"

"Hello, Mott. Come in. How are the stores looking?"

He scratched at the back of his neck, not sure how truthful he should be.

Crane looked up. "That bad, eh?"

"We'll have to ration, sir."

"With the bodies cleaned up, you and Colin can spend more time hunting. We'll cure what we can't eat, though I do prefer fresh meat. How many sheep are left?"

"I believe seven, sir."

"Good. That should ensure us some lamb come spring." His tongue darted between his lips, as if he was tasting a lamb chop that very moment. Crane set his quill down and turned around. He had black hair that brushed his shoulders and dark, deep-set eyes. His clean-shaven skin practically glowed in the lamplight. "You're looking well, Mott. Much better than when I brought you here. How old are you now?"

"Nineteen, sir."

A wistful look passed over the master's face. "When I was nineteen, I toured the continent with my best friend. We had a wonderful time. Have you traveled much?"

"No, sir. I was sixteen when the plague hit. My father was already dead."

"Mmm. You have brothers, correct?"

Nico swallowed down his apprehension. Crane had never

asked him so many personal questions before. "Had. They died in the plague."

Crane rubbed his chin. "Yes, that's right. Very unfortunate." He picked a small framed portrait off his desk and held it up for Nico. "I lost my beloved wife, as you know. She was only twenty-five."

The portrait was too small to see any detail from where Nico stood, but he smiled politely. "She was very beautiful, sir."

"She was. And so sweet. I doubt I shall ever find her equal. Although the first is always the most special, don't you think?"

Nico had no frame of reference for such things, but he nodded anyway.

Crane chuckled. "I see. What about our Abby? She is a pretty girl."

Nico's cheeks warmed and he found himself staring at his toes. "I believe she prefers Branson, sir."

"Women. They always prefer the villain, eh?" He shook his head and returned the portrait to his desk. "Never mind that. I'm sure you'll have your chance. And with more immaculates coming out of the woodwork, it's entirely possible someone new will come along. It might even be time to go to the city and see what we can find, now that we know the plague is truly gone. I get first pick, of course." He flashed a vulpine smile, one Branson would have cheerfully returned, but one Nico found as off-putting as his master's words. Something dark and cold oozed through his belly.

He remembered what Elisabeth had said about the way Crane looked at her. Up until her arrival, Nico had only ever seen Crane behave like a gentleman, but maybe that had more to do with the fact that their last few guests had been men. He recalled a young woman when he'd first arrived at Crane Manor, but he'd been so enamored of Crane then, too awestruck by his master's magnanimity and the comfort of a properly run household full of other warm bodies to notice anything amiss.

"Was there something you wished to tell me, Mott?"

Nico cleared his throat, aware that his master was expecting some sort of response. "Hunting, sir. Should Colin and I go tomorrow? I've seen quite a few pheasants in the forest, and rabbits."

"I actually had something else in mind," Crane said. "For all you boys. Meet me in the library in one hour—and tell Chambers and Branson to join you." He turned back around to his letter, though to whom he was writing, Nico had no idea.

"I'll leave you to it, then," Nico mumbled, still unaccustomed to being dismissed so abruptly after all this time. As he passed the large four-poster bed, he noticed a ruffle poking out from underneath. It was delicate lace, just like the collar of Elisabeth's dress. Nico stumbled, unable to pull his eyes away from the fabric.

"Steady on," Lord Crane said with a laugh. "No wonder you haven't caught yourself a woman yet."

Nico had no time to talk to Colin before they made their way to the library, but his mind was still racing from his interaction with Crane. Had the master always been this repugnant? Or had something changed in the past week?

He relaxed slightly when he saw Crane lounging on one of

the sofas in the library, a pleasant smile on his face as he read a book with a burgundy cover and gold lettering.

When they entered the room, Crane clapped the book closed and set it down on the cushion next to him. "Good evening, lads. Thank you for coming. Please, take a seat."

Colin and Nico exchanged a glance, but Branson didn't hesitate to lower himself onto the sofa, taking up far more than his share of the space and glancing around him in a way that said, "Ah yes, *this* is where I belong." Nico couldn't blame him entirely; in a past life, it was exactly where they belonged.

When they were all seated, the master lowered his legs and turned to face them. "As you know, we've cleared the lands for miles in every direction. You've done a remarkably good job, and I commend you for your hard work."

Was the lord finally going to pay them for their work? Reward them in some way? Nico leaned forward a bit.

"And now I have another favor to ask of you."

Nico deflated a bit. *Of course.* But Colin and Branson were still leaning forward, eager.

"When I was returning from taking Miss Talbot to her father, I decided to go past Eldridge Hall, to see if her brother was still alive."

"What did you find, sir?" Branson asked.

"Very little to give Miss Talbot encouragement, which is why I didn't go back to her. However, I had decided to camp for the night nearby, and just as I was settling down to sleep, I saw what looked like a candle in the highest window of the highest tower. It was just a glimmer through a crack; all the windows have been boarded up. But unless my eyes were

playing tricks on me—and I have excellent night vision—
there is someone living at Eldridge Hall."

"You didn't try to enter, sir?" Nico asked, because he already had a feeling where this conversation was leading.

"No. I was alone, and if I was wrong and there were people inside the castle, including a mad king, it could have been
very dangerous. But three strapping young lads like yourselves
will be safe together."

Nico arched an eyebrow. "You want us to, what, exactly?
Storm the castle?"

Colin elbowed him none too gently in the ribs.

"I don't mean to be impertinent, sir, but if the castle is indeed boarded up, how are we to enter?"

"If someone is alive inside, there is a way of getting in and
out. They couldn't possibly have had enough food to last this
long. I didn't have the luxury of staying there for days to
watch and wait. My people needed me here, of course. But
you have all done such a marvelous job of clearing my lands,
as I said, and the other servants are perfectly capable of running the manor without you. I'll hunt while you're away, to
be sure we have plenty of provisions for any immaculates who
may be inside Eldridge Hall."

A chill crept up Nico's spine into his hair. "Immaculates,
sir?"

"Immaculates, immunes, you know what I mean. Any survivors." There was a sharp edge to Crane's voice that hadn't
been there a moment earlier. Nico was sure of it.

"Of course, sir," Colin said. "We are happy to do it. And
if we do find any survivors, are we to approach them? Or
should we return home and tell you first?"

"If you're spotted, then of course you should introduce yourselves so they know you mean them no harm. But if not, then yes, one of you should return here to tell me and I will join you. We will inform them that it is safe to come out, and that they have friends here at Crane Manor."

Nico was about to question why anyone living in the castle would want to come to Crane Manor, but Colin cut him off.

"Yes, sir." He rose, dragging Nico up with him. "We'll leave tomorrow morning."

"Excellent," Crane said with another one of his toothy smiles. "I knew I could count on you boys. You're like sons to me. And one day I hope to leave all that I have to you. Continue to serve me loyally, and one of you could be the lord of Crane Manor."

Branson flashed an oily grin, and Colin stood a little taller, squaring his shoulders. It hadn't escaped Nico what the master had said: *one* of you. He was pitting them against one another, goading them into seeing who could be the most loyal. The unspoken words his friends couldn't hear chilled his blood: *Find me immaculates, and you will be rewarded.*

CHAPTER 7

Seraphina didn't talk to the king that night, or the next night, or the next. Every time she thought she might do it, something got in her way. The king was in a foul temper, or one of her sisters called her away to help with birthday planning. She avoided Greymont's questioning glances, not wanting to admit to him that she hadn't even broached the subject of leaving Eldridge Hall.

"You seem pensive tonight, my dear," the king said as they passed into his room. "Thinking about your birthday masquerade?"

She nodded, wondering if this was her opportunity. "It's in less than a week. I'm anxious that everything should go right. The food—"

"Nothing to worry about at all," he said, patting her hand. "Your sisters have been working day and night to make sure it's as perfect as you are. Is there something else troubling you?"

She chewed her cheek for a moment, hesitating. The king looked harmless enough now, but he could be so volatile. A memory came to her of her early days at Eldridge, one so bitter she'd put it out of her head for years. She had been home-sick and angry, resentful at being plucked and groomed to the point where she didn't recognize herself anymore, exhausted from sleepless nights crying for her family. She missed Dalia, who hadn't yet begun to appear at the edge of the forest. She'd never felt so alone.

When a servant placed a dish in front of her at dinner one evening—something soft, gray, and unidentifiable that reeked of unfamiliar spices—she wrinkled her lip in disgust without thinking. The king's hand had come down so hard on the table that she screamed.

Who is this spoiled, selfish girl? the king had shouted, his pale face flushing an alarming shade of scarlet.

The king had been escorted to his chambers by Giselle, who mumbled soft, soothing platitudes and cast furious glances at Seraphina. Later, she had taken Seraphina roughly by her arm and dragged her up to her tower. She'd glanced around the cramped space, her mouth twisted in a sneer. "Even this is too good for you," she spat, leaving Seraphina crying on her narrow bed.

"There is something wrong," the king insisted now. "What is it, my dearest daughter? You can tell your father anything."

Seraphina felt a stab in her chest, something between af-fection and despair. The king's love for Princess Imogen was so powerful it had transcended death. Meanwhile, she could hardly remember what her own father looked like. He came to her in dreams, sometimes, but when she woke up she found she couldn't recall his features beyond the facts: his eyes were brown, like hers; his hair was graying at the temples. But had his nose, which had been broken years ago in an accident, crooked to the right or the left? Were his cheekbones high, like hers, or had she inherited those from her mother? She hadn't paid enough attention to the things that truly mattered back then. If she could do it all over, she would memorize every detail of her family.

"It's nothing, Father. Only..." She toyed with the ribbons she'd tied around her wrists to cover the bruising, casting him a sidelong glance.

"What is it, Genny?"

"Only I would so like to watch the sunrise on my twentieth birthday." She said it in a rush, not realizing she was going to say those words until they'd spilled out of her like dice from a cup. The windows at Eldridge Hall had been boarded up when the gates were closed so that no one from the outside would see that the castle was still inhabited. King Stuart had been worried that desperate people would attempt to seek refuge here, and he hadn't been wrong. In the early days, the people had revolted, after they realized all the food and livestock they had turned over were to be stockpiled for the sole use of the nobility and royal family.

Shortly after she was taken from her family, Seraphina had been in her chambers with Jocelyn, Nina, and Rose. Jocelyn had been helping Seraphina practice her courtly etiquette: curtsies, proper table manners, how to speak to a gentleman. As the true Princess Imogen's ladies' maid, Jocelyn had only been spared traveling with her on that fateful trip because she had terrible motion sickness. Jocelyn was far too perceptive not to notice an imposter, though she hadn't voiced any surprise upon seeing Seraphina for the first time, playing along from the start without missing a beat. Of course, it was in her interest as much as everyone else's that Seraphina perform well as Imogen's stand-in, but Jocelyn was a genuinely kind person. Eventually, Seraphina would tell her everything, but she hadn't trusted anyone at all in those earliest days.

Suddenly, a rock had burst through the window, sending glass shards raining down on Nina and Rose, who had been seated closest to it. Nina had sustained several cuts on her bare arms and shoulders, while Rose, who was always cold, had been protected by her shawl. She screamed far louder than Nina, however, who only looked from the blood on her arms to the broken window and said, "Shit."

Guards had come running at the sound of Rose's screams, while Seraphina stood midcurtsy, trembling. She was so afraid of making a mistake and being punished, while at the same time wishing the king would let her go. She didn't understand then that the king would *never* let Imogen go. The windows had been boarded up ever since.

"The sunrise?" the king said, blinking, as if he had never considered the idea in nearly four years. "That seems simple enough."

"Really?" She clapped her hands the way Imogen did, annoyed to find that the habit came easily now.

But seeing her smile lit up the king's face. "A wonderful birthday present, I think. Of course, there will be more, but a perfect one to start the day."

It wasn't anything close to being released from the castle, but it was a step in the right direction. She could imagine the king flinging open the curtains in the great hall on her birthday morning, the guards rushing forward to pry away the boards. The entire castle would be there. They would see that the world outside Eldridge Hall was peaceful. *Then* Seraphina could tell King Stuart about the empty cellar. Then everything would be fine.

She just had to ensure Greymont would take her with him when he left.

She said good-night to the king and went straight up to her bedroom without joining her sisters for cards or gossip. For the first time since she had come to Eldridge, there was the spring of promise in her step. Even the cold stone stairs biting her bare feet didn't reach her heart tonight. She changed out of her dress into her nightgown, combed out her hair, and walked to her window as she did every night, wishing she could somehow project her good news through the crack in the boards.

But though she waited until the moon was high in the sky and longer, until the dark night began to seem not so dark, for the first time in nearly four years, Dalia never came.

The next morning Seraphina stood frozen while a seamstress placed pins in the hem of her birthday costume, her head and heart heavy. She knew in her bones that it was almost impossible Dalia had survived the plague. If history was any guide, the Jews of Goslind would not have fared well. They always made the perfect scapegoats whenever tragedy befell the kingdom. And if Dalia *had* somehow survived, she would have wanted to get far away from the city—not stand outside Eldridge Hall every night in plain sight.

So every night when she saw the girl at the edge of the woods, Seraphina half believed she was seeing Dalia's dybbuk, wandering in the spirit world until she found a body to inhabit.

The other half of her, however, had become quite adept at denial these past few years, and she'd told herself that it was really Dalia she was seeing. It made the guilt of surviving—and worse, assimilating—less painful, so long as she believed she was going to see someone she loved again one day.

"Your Highness?"

She glanced down at the seamstress, who indicated that she was finished. Seraphina raised her eyes to her reflection.

The gown was simple enough, white muslin trimmed with lace, but so thin it must have taken hours and hours to get just right. Even with the requisite petticoat underneath, it clung to her body when she moved, revealing the curve of a hip one moment, the length of her thigh the next. On top of her head was a golden circlet, an early birthday present from her father, and the seamstresses had fashioned a pair of wings out of real feathers. They were attached to her shoulders with gold velvet ribbons. She imagined they would be heavy by the end of the night, but the whole effect was rather beautiful.

"We'll curl your hair," Nina said, standing behind her as the seamstress adjusted the hem.

"And pin it up, of course. Your gold comb with the seed pearls would be just the thing," Rose added. She was wearing her pink rose gown, which cascaded in tiers of satin ruffles from her waist to the floor. She'd spent most of the morning twirling in circles to watch the layers float up around her.

Nina examined her own plum-colored gown in the mirror. It was tight at the waist, ballooning out a bit around her legs and tightening once again with a ruffle around her ankles. The collar of the dress was high and ruffled at the throat, not revealing even an inch of cleavage. Nina had complained, but

Jocelyn, ever the diplomat, had pointed out that the tight waist accentuated her bust and hips without looking too risqué.

Meanwhile, poor Jocelyn's dress would have been appropriate for a small child. The seamstress had covered it in little white crocheted daisies, with a bonnet to match. But Jocelyn never complained. She understood that this masquerade wasn't about her.

Giselle had completed her fitting before Seraphina arrived for hers, claiming she had important business to attend to.

When they had finished, they went to the dining hall for luncheon. A calico named Pudding jumped into Seraphina's lap, hoping for some table scraps, but it quickly realized there was no meat to be had and went off in search of a better offer.

"Did you speak to the king?" Greymont asked her when he sat down, oblivious to her despondent mood.

"I did. He has agreed to let us watch the sunrise for my birthday." Even as she said it, she knew it didn't sound like much. Hardly the confrontation he'd been hoping for—but she'd waited this long for a chance at escape, and she couldn't rush things now. She hated being dependent on someone else for her escape, that she needed to convince Greymont she was useful. If only *she* had a ship.

"The sunrise?"

"If we can see outside, he'll realize that there is nothing to fear. I know it's a small step, but it's a step." She started to reach for his hand under the table, then thought better of it. She was a princess. She wouldn't beg for his approval like a dog. "After that I'll be able to press harder."

He stabbed at a prune on his plate.

She lifted her chin. "I hardly think you need to take your frustration out on that poor prune."

"You're right. *It* hasn't done anything wrong." There was a growl in his voice Seraphina hadn't heard before, and it stirred a memory she'd long since buried. Before she could respond, the king entered the room. Everyone began to rise, but he waved them back down. "Sit, sit, all of you." He glanced at Seraphina and Greymont next to each other and smiled fondly. "Such a handsome couple," he said to himself, before settling down to eat.

Seraphina glanced at Greymont and found that his expression had changed entirely. He was puffed up with pride, and, unless her eyes deceived her, hope. Of course. He wasn't a fool. He'd told her himself that everyone had ambitions at court. It was good to remember that he viewed her as a means to an end, too. That whatever tension might exist between them, this wasn't puppy love. It was life or death.

"Excuse me," she said, pushing her chair back with a screech. She hurried into a hallway, self-consciously touching the thin scar that ran along her jawline.

It was the work of a man who had broken into her family's home when she was nine. He'd come through the open window and grabbed her, holding a knife to her throat while demanding her father wrap the few valuables they had in a tablecloth. They'd learned later he was a thief on the run, and he had a nasty habit of marking his victims with his knife. After Seraphina's father had placed their good candlesticks and her mother's wedding ring, along with a few coins, into the makeshift sack and handed it to the thief, he had pressed the tip of his knife to the flesh just below Seraphina's left ear.

"Something to remember me by," the man whispered as he ran the blade several inches along her jawline. The knife was so sharp she'd barely felt it.

He was out the door by the time her skin opened like a seam and the blood seeped out, running down her neck and ruining her collar. Her father had fainted. He'd never liked the sight of blood.

It was the first time in her life Seraphina had felt her vulnerability as a girl. It was no accident the thief had chosen her. She was lucky he hadn't ruined her face, her mother said. That would have destroyed any desirable marriage prospects she may have had. She smiled to remember what Dalia had told her, in all her indignant girlishness—that a scar didn't *ruin* a face, it only added character. The doctor had decided against stitches, afraid they'd scar worse than if they let the wound heal itself. Now it was hard to see—it was all but healed over, and any lasting trace was hidden by the pearl powder—but she knew it was there. Another reminder of how little control she had over anything in this world.

"Princess Imogen."

She startled at the sound of her name. Lord Greymont had followed her. He was the last person she wished to see.

"What are you doing here?" she hissed after a servant passed, his eyebrow arched impertinently.

"I upset you," he said.

"Is that a question?" she shot back. She knew getting defensive wasn't going to win his approval, but she couldn't help herself. Fear had kept her small and passive these past few years, but imminent starvation required her to take a more active role in her own survival. The pressure was already starting to get to her.

"My apologies." He looked at her hand for a moment, as though he were contemplating taking it. "I spoke out of turn."

She sniffed and raised her chin. "You seek my father's approval."

He blinked, apparently surprised at her bluntness. "I—Well, yes, I do. He is my king, after all."

She glanced away. "And my approval? Does that mean nothing to you?" Her head whipped back toward him at the sound of his chuckling. "Oh, you find that amusing, do you?"

This time he did take her hand, and she wasn't sure if she was angry or relieved. "I only find it amusing that you doubt my desire for your—" his eyes flicked down toward her neckline "—approval."

She pulled her hand away, refusing to betray the thrill she'd felt run through her at his insolence. "I should warn you, sir. If your pursuits are dishonorable—"

"Forgive me, Your Highness. I assure you, my intentions are as honorable as can be. I have taken liberties..." Something about the way his gaze devoured her made her certain he was imagining said liberties. "It is only because I find you to be the most beautiful woman in the world."

She rolled her eyes to hide how much she enjoyed his flattery. "We should get back. Father will be wondering where I've gone."

"Yes, of course. But please, tell me you forgive me first. I'll never be able to eat until I know you're not upset."

She was impressed with his acting skills. The green flecks in his eyes glimmered, almost as if he was really upset at the idea of offending her. "Hmph."

"I just..." He lowered his voice and stepped toward her.

Her back was already against the wall, bringing him within inches of her. "I want you to know that whatever your father says, I'm behind you. You're not alone, Princess."

His words—words she'd been longing to hear for years—pushed past all her defenses, and she found her legs going a little watery.

The swishing of a maid's skirts brought her back to herself, and she straightened up, willing the color to drain from her cheeks. "You're forgiven," she said, offering him the back of her hand.

He kissed it and looked up at her through his eyelashes. "After you, Princess."

She returned to her seat, ignoring the questioning glances from her sisters and Jocelyn. The king was nodding into his porridge, always so tired lately.

"So," Seraphina said, picking up her fork. "The sunrise?"

Greymont grinned, making her blush again despite herself. "You're right, of course. The idea of watching the sunrise on your birthday *is* wonderful. Though I doubt we'll be allowed to watch it together."

"Nonsense," she said. "I'm sure we can assemble the whole court for such an occasion. We'll open the big window in the hall. The sun rises around seven at this time of year. It's early, but not scandalously so, surely."

He was watching her mouth. "Indeed. Not scandalously so."

Contrite, her left eye. The man was incorrigible. She would need to keep her wits about her if she was going to win whatever game this was.

"What are you two scheming about?" The king, who had woken from his nap when a cat began eating from his plate, smiled at Seraphina and Greymont.

"Noth—" Greymont began, but Seraphina spoke over him.

"We're discussing my birthday sunrise," she said so loudly that everyone in the room would hear.

Now everyone would know, and the king wouldn't be able to change his mind. It *would* set everything in motion. It had to.

"How much we're looking forward to it," she continued as her hand found Greymont's under the table and squeezed it.

CHAPTER 8

Nico stared up at the ceiling in bed that night, where the moonlight through the trees cast strange shadows. He knew it was imperative he get some rest, given the journey ahead of him, but Crane's words were echoing in his head, making his stomach churn with unease. It was foolish to be afraid of the master, he told himself. He would be just another corpse in the woods if not for Crane. But lately, there was something undeniably sinister about him. He knew he wasn't imagining that.

To make matters worse, Abby had started humming that damned children's nursery rhyme from the plague. And though he knew it was ridiculous, he couldn't get the last three lines out of his head:

If you want to stay alive, there are three ways to survive:
Run away across the sea; pray for blood immunity;
Or die and be reborn again, and drink the blood of living men.

"Not you, too," Colin said sleepily, and Nico realized he'd hummed the tune out loud. He wasn't sure if it was right to gossip about the master—loyalty had always kept him from voicing his opinions—but this felt too important to ignore.

"I was in Crane's office earlier. He was writing a letter, and one of Miss Talbot's gowns was underneath his bed."

Colin let out something between a laugh and a whoop. "Is that what this is about? You're jealous that the master bedded Miss Talbot?"

"Of course not," Nico said, though his cheeks were burning at Colin's acknowledgment of what he'd suspected. "I just think it's all a bit strange. The fact that her father is still alive... What are the odds of that? If he's only a few days from here, why didn't we encounter each other at some point over the course of several years?"

Colin looked over at him. "What are you saying? You think the master *did* something to Miss Talbot?"

Nico ran his hands through his hair and squeezed his eyes shut, trying to push away the memory of Elisabeth on her knees, begging him to take her away. The truth was he was weak, and it shamed him. "I don't know what to think."

After a few moments of silence, Colin sat up and turned to Nico with a frank expression. "Look, the master has no reason to harm Miss Talbot. He gets what he wants from these women freely. There's no need to use force, and certainly no reason to murder her. That *is* what you're thinking, isn't it?"

Now that Colin had said it out loud, Nico knew it was. "Yes."

"What purpose would that serve? Unless he's a sadistic madman who kills for fun, and honestly, wouldn't we have figured that out by now? He's saved so many of us. Without him, we'd all be dead."

"But we wouldn't, would we?"

"What do you mean?"

Nico clenched and unclenched his jaw. "Every single person Lord Crane has taken in is an immune. You must have noticed this, too. The immaculates never stay for more than a few days. Why? Why aren't they just as happy to stay and work here as the rest of us?"

"I don't know. They didn't stick around long enough to see who survived, like we did. If you'd been gone this whole time, you'd want to find out if you had anyone left, wouldn't you?"

Nico took a breath. "I suppose. But it still doesn't explain what happened with Arnaud."

"What about him?"

"When Arnaud attacked Branson that day, he was looking for Miss Talbot. That's when Crane shot him, right in the back, in cold blood. Why did he do that?"

"To protect her," Colin replied, exasperation straining his words.

"From what? She was safe with us. There was no need to go shooting the man. And why did Arnaud want her so badly? She certainly isn't his wife. Who is she to him?"

"Damn it, you can be daft sometimes. Miss Talbot is young and beautiful and healthy."

Nico's thoughts were racing toward some conclusion, though he couldn't yet see what it was. "Abby is young and beautiful, too, but Lord Crane has never shown the slightest interest in her, not even for dalliances. If all he wants is someone to share his bed, he'd have no trouble convincing one of the servants. And if he wanted Miss Talbot for a wife, why not persuade her to come back after she found her father? Why simply bed her and send her on her way?"

Colin sighed, but it was wistful, not exasperated. "I don't know, Nico. But I do know we've survived this long by keeping our heads down and our ears open. Don't go making accusations now, when you have no proof."

After a moment Nico turned his gaze toward the woods. He thought of Arnaud, of the desperation in his voice when he'd asked about Elisabeth, the hunger in his eyes the first time he'd seen her. It was the kind of hunger she had described in Lord Crane. Not the hunger of desire, but the hunger of need, of desperation.

The hunger of a starving man.

On the morning that Nico set out with Colin and Branson, Lord Crane bid them farewell from the front porch. The rest of the servants stood beside him on the steps, the girls weeping a little as if the boys were headed off to war. Even the cook dabbed at the corners of her eyes with her apron and pulled the stableboy, Gavin, into her side, ruffling his hair affectionately as she waved goodbye to the men.

Nico, Colin, and Branson left on foot, each outfitted with a gun, a knapsack filled with food and supplies, and the clothing on their backs. If they needed more, they'd have to pilfer it from any houses they passed.

Soon enough, they were deep in the woods, and Nico's thoughts were free to wander. He had told himself he wouldn't dwell on Elisabeth, at least not yet. A half-formed thought had taken root in his mind, that he could find Elisabeth's house for himself once they'd investigated Eldridge Hall. Assured of her safety, he would be able to rest with an easy conscience once again. And from there? For the first time since Crane had found him, Nico was warming to the idea of leaving the manor.

He understood that the world as he'd known it was gone. The king, if he was still alive, no longer seemed to care about collecting taxes or punishing lawbreakers, and without him, the people were like children whose parents had gone away on holiday and left no one else in charge. Nico was a man of order and science. He was afraid of chaos.

But there was also a sense that anyone—even Nico—could find his fortune now. Colin could be a master; Branson could be a servant. And Nico could finally become a physician. In this new world, he might even find redemption.

Branson had quickly fallen behind, so Nico and Colin stopped at midday to eat and give him time to catch up.

"Do you know what I miss most?" Colin asked as he gnawed on a piece of cured meat. "Besides my family, of course. Good cheese. I wish someone at the manor knew how to make it."

"We'd need a cow for that. Or two, I suppose."

Colin sighed. "We had nearly a dozen, at one point. That first winter, nearly half our animals disappeared. We assumed we were being robbed by desperate neighbors, but the master wasn't worried. He seemed to think the plague would run its course quickly and we'd be fine for food. No one thought so many people would die."

Nico arched an eyebrow. "What do you mean, the animals disappeared?"

"Exactly that. They vanished from their pens during the night."

Nico recalled the master's tongue sliding across his lips as he declared his preference for fresh meat and found he no longer had an appetite. "What happened to Crane's wife, Colin? He mentioned she died of the plague, but where did she get it?"

"It was early that same winter. She went down to check on a tenant family, despite the master's warnings, and fell ill. She was already gone when Crane took me in."

"And Crane was immune..." Nico glanced down at his wrists, exposed by his rolled shirtsleeves. The red marks were like mirror-image branches, tracing the course of his veins on either wrist. The telltale sign that though he had encountered the mori roja, something in his blood had saved him.

"What do you miss?" Colin asked, interrupting Nico's thoughts.

"I miss people." He leaned back against a decaying log and looked up at the trees. A few leaves still clung to their branches, a fitting metaphor for the plague and the people it had left behind. Eventually, they would all die, and who would be around to watch them fall?

"Excuse me, but you're with people." Colin flashed his most winning smile, his teeth bright against his dark skin.

Nico's snarky reply was cut off by the sound of something heavy rustling in the brush behind them. At first, Nico thought it was Branson, but then a gray horse emerged into the clearing, wearing a halter and a torn lead rope.

Colin rose first. "Is that...?"

"Locket," Nico finished, standing slowly to keep her from spooking. But she seemed relieved to see them, coming forward and nuzzling Nico's outstretched hands as if searching for treats. "Lord Crane said he had to leave her behind. She wouldn't cross water."

Colin scratched his head as Nico ran his hands down the back of Locket's legs, checking for swelling. "Odd. I wonder how Miss Elisabeth made it so far without ever crossing a stream or a brook. Lucky, I guess."

Just then, Branson himself came crashing through the underbrush, making far more noise than a thousand-pound horse. He collapsed onto the log Nico had been leaning against, groaning dramatically.

"What's for lunch?" he asked.

"Lunch is over," Colin said, gathering up the remnants of their picnic. "Next time, walk faster."

"I don't see why I can't ride it," Branson moaned for the fifteenth time that evening. Nico had known the trip would be long and slow going on foot, especially if it snowed. But he hadn't taken into consideration Branson and his infernal whining.

"I already told you," Nico muttered. "She's got an abscess, probably from standing around in the mud. It's a small one, but she needs a chance to heal."

But Branson was already on to his next complaint. "Blast this weather!" he said as another cold gust ripped through the trees. "We'll be nothing but frozen corpses in a week. What was Crane thinking, sending us off like this?"

"He was thinking at least he wouldn't have to look at your ugly face for a while," Colin said cheerfully. "Maybe you'll get lucky and your nose will fall off from frostbite. It would be an improvement."

Nico was too cold to smile, but he had the decency to keep his misery to himself. His toes were numb in his boots, and the woods were dark and menacing at this hour. Locket's warm body beside him was reassuring, at least.

"Do you really think someone's living at Eldridge?" Nico asked Colin. "A light through a crack in a boarded window could be anything. It seems like a lot of trouble to send us out here just in case one person survived."

"Perhaps the master wants us to confirm if the king survived. If he didn't, things could get very interesting as the kingdom recovers."

Nico had considered that, too. Who would rule Goslind, or what was left of it, if the entire royal bloodline had been wiped out? Maybe there was a distant cousin somewhere, but then maybe they were all dead, too. Did Crane have his eyes on the crown? Was that the source of his strange behavior? Nico shook his head. Who in their right mind would want to rule over a country of corpses?

They finally made camp for the night in an abandoned woodshed. The structure was rotted and barely standing, with a gaping hole where a roof should be, but it provided a little shelter from the wind, which showed no signs of easing that night. It filtered through the cracks in the wooden walls and made its way through their blankets and the seams of their clothing.

Even Colin was starting to show signs of strain as he attempted for the fifth time to light a fire. Every time a spark caught, the wind gusted enthusiastically, extinguishing the flame and their hopes along with it.

"Damn it!" he shouted, dropping another match into the dirt and debris that littered the floor. "I think we'll have to go without a fire tonight. I don't want to waste any more of our matches."

"It's fine," Nico told him, passing around the bread, dried meat, and withered apples they had for dinner. He didn't admit that the thought of a warm fire was what had kept him moving all afternoon. "It's just for tonight. Tomorrow we'll find somewhere better to camp."

Branson started to grumble but Colin cut him off with his raised palm. "Please, no more tonight. I can handle the cold, but I can't take any more of your moaning."

"Who put you in charge, anyway?" Branson snapped. "You're the lowest-ranked man here. In fact, you're so poor you don't even have a rank."

"Branson," Nico warned, but the fool didn't know when to bite his tongue.

"It's true. Why is he even here? He should be back at the manor with the other servants, cleaning piss pots."

Nico sat up. "That's enough, Branson!"

"Your rank means nothing out here," Colin said quietly. His blanket was pulled up to his chin. In the darkness of the woodshed, Nico couldn't see his face, but his voice was as icy as the wind. "I could kill you right now and it would mean nothing to anyone. There's no one to mourn you, no one to bury you. You'd be just another nameless, faceless corpse in the forest."

Just then, a low howl reached their ears from somewhere in the woods, making Branson jump. "What was that?" he whispered.

"Just the wind in the trees," Nico said, though he wasn't sure. It hadn't sounded like a wolf, but it hadn't sounded like a tree, either. It had sounded almost human. He'd left Locket free to graze for the night, confident the mare wouldn't wander far given her abscess and her fondness for apples. Now he worried he should have kept her closer.

"That wasn't the wind," Colin said. They were all sitting up in their blankets now, the cold momentarily forgotten. "Sounded more like a wounded animal."

"Quiet," Branson hissed. "You'll call its attention."

Another howl sounded, this one fading into an anguished moan. "Too late," Colin said. There was a note of glee in his voice, as if he was enjoying Branson's terror. Nico found himself wishing he hadn't removed his boots. He wouldn't get very far in his stockings.

The sound of feet dragging through fallen leaves outside the shed was unmistakable. Nico reached for his gun. So did Colin. Branson was frozen in place except for his chattering teeth. Nico had never despised him more.

Nico crawled to the door and pressed his face to it, peering out through a crack in the wood. The first thing he noticed was the man walking purposefully toward the shed, clad in only trousers, a tunic, and a light jacket.

The second thing he noticed was the ragged hole through said jacket, from where he'd been shot—by Lord Crane.

"Good heavens, it's Arnaud!" Nico hissed to Colin.

"I thought he was dead!" Colin turned to Branson. "I thought *you* buried him!"

"I did!" Branson squeaked.

Arnaud's clothing was filthy, as if he *had* been buried. Nico glanced at his fingertips and gasped. Sure enough, Arnaud's nails were broken and crusted with dirt. Had Branson been stupid enough to bury the man *alive*?

"What in the devil is going on?" Branson whisper-screamed.

Nico realized with an odd sense of detachment that his entire body, which had been racked with shivers only moments before, had gone completely numb. *Devil* indeed. This was wrong, not only from a metaphysical standpoint, but also a medical one. There was absolutely no explanation for how this man was still walking.

The door was barred with a wooden plank, and it rattled in the latch as Arnaud pounded on it.

"Little pig, little pig, let me in…" Arnaud sang. "Come on, lads. It's colder than a witch's—"

Branson whimpered. "I've pissed myself."

Nico had been wrong. *Now* he'd never despised Branson more.

"How is it possible?" Colin whispered. "Crane shot him. Branson buried him."

The infernal nursery rhyme went through Nico's head. "Or die and be reborn again…" he murmured.

"What?" Colin and Branson asked in unison.

Nico pressed his back to the door and turned to the men. "What if the children's song wasn't wrong? What if there are men who contract the plague and die, only they aren't truly dead?"

"Now is not the time for you to go soft in the head," Colin said as the door rattled again after a few moments of silence.

Nico waved him off. "He was looking for Miss Talbot before. Not us. Which means he knew she was an immaculate somehow."

"Or he was looking for a little fun," Branson said. "She was as fine a specimen—"

"Don't you understand?" Nico pressed, talking more to Colin than Branson. "He was looking for an immaculate. *Crane* is looking for immaculates. The three of us are immune."

"So what?" Colin asked.

"So we have to let him in," Nico said. "We have to find out what's going on. There are three of us and one of him. He isn't armed. Or at least he wasn't before."

"Not a chance," Colin said. "My mother always told me to respect the dead, but God bless her, this is *not* what she meant."

"Then I'm going out there." Nico stuffed his feet into his boots. It was quiet outside the shed again as he pulled his coat on. He put his eye back to the gap in the wood.

A bloodshot eye stared back at him. Nico yelped and leaped backward.

"I can hear you breathing," the man said, his voice low and steady now. "I'm not going to harm you."

"How can we trust that?" Nico asked, his gun clutched tightly to his chest. It might not do any more good than Crane's had, but he felt safer holding on to it.

"I can smell immaculates from a hundred yards. You boys reek of sweat and immunity. And piss. I don't stand to gain anything by killing you."

Nico lowered his face back to the hole, forcing himself to meet the horrible red eye. "And what do you want with the immaculates?"

"You already know the answer to that, lad."

Nico swallowed the lump in his throat, unwilling to allow the truth to coalesce in his mind. "What do you want with us?"

"Tell me where the girl is and you'll never see me again. You have my word."

"Miss Talbot left the manor with Lord Crane days ago. As far as I know she's been reunited with her father."

"If you believe that then you're as much a fool as that lordling who buried me. Let me in out of this damned wind and I'll tell you everything."

Nico glanced over his shoulder, where Colin and Branson were both vigorously shaking their heads. "I'm afraid I've been outvoted on that score."

The man's sigh rattled in his chest. He wasn't dead, Nico told himself. Just altered. Hideously, damnably altered. "Just tell me one thing. Why did your master send the three of you out here into the woods alone?"

If Nico had any idea how to kill this creature, he would do it now, but guns had already proven worthless. He said a silent prayer for Elisabeth, though some part of him knew Arnaud was right, that Crane hadn't taken her safely home. And if there really was a survivor in Eldridge Hall, Nico couldn't lead Arnaud to them.

He couldn't lead Crane to them, either.

"Our woods are barren of prey," he lied. "We're looking for new hunting grounds. I suggest you do the same."

The man grunted. A moment later they could hear him shuffling back through the leaves. Nico kept his eye pressed to the door, watching until he had disappeared into the trees.

He turned back to the two men and saw Colin pinching his nose and glaring at Branson. "Please don't tell me—"

"That he shat himself?" Colin said. "Of course he bloody did."

Nico sighed and waited a few minutes, until he was sure Arnaud was gone.

"Where are you going?" Branson whispered.

"To check on Locket." He slipped outside and didn't blame Colin when he heard the bolt slide into place behind him. It took a few minutes of wandering, but he found the mare, her eyes shiny in the moonlight as she watched him from the other side of a creek.

Nico swore under his breath. How on earth had she managed to end up on the far side of the water? He was resigning himself to wet feet when he remembered the apple in his pocket.

He held it aloft. "Come on, girl. I've got your favorite, right here."

Locket didn't hesitate. She stepped into the creek eagerly, not even balking as the water touched her abscessed hoof. A cold pit formed in Nico's stomach as his last hopes for Elisabeth slid away, along with any trust in his master's word.

Elisabeth was dead, and the man he'd once thought of as a father was a murderer.

No, not a murderer.

A monster.

CHAPTER 9

As the days went by, Seraphina found it harder to keep up her flirtation with Lord Greymont. More to the point, she found it difficult to remember it wasn't real. Her plan to persuade Greymont to take her with him when he left hinged on her convincing the king to let them out in the first place. For now, she wasn't necessary to Greymont at all, which meant he needed to *want* her, at the very least. And the more she pretended to desire him, the more she found herself believing her own lie.

Or worse, realizing that maybe it had never been a lie to begin with.

It didn't help that she was exhausted. Every night she waited up until the sun was pinking the horizon, praying to catch just a glimpse of Dalia. But she never came again, which left Seraphina to wonder: If it was possible she'd never been there to begin with, how could she stop coming? If she was just a figment of Seraphina's imagination, then what had changed within Seraphina?

She had once asked Jocelyn if she missed the real Imogen.

She'd been Imogen's attendant since they were both twelve, and by all accounts, Seraphina and Imogen had very different personalities.

Jocelyn had looked wistful for a moment. "I am sad that she died. She was always kind to me. But she was…unusual. She spoke to herself, far more than she spoke to anyone else. It was my duty to keep close to her, but she would disappear in the middle of the night, only to turn up in the morning with the soles of her feet muddy and her hems stained green. Some said she had a touch of her father's madness in her. I wouldn't go that far but I don't know what she would be like now, had she lived. I don't know what this plague would have done to her."

Seraphina sometimes wondered if by embodying Imogen, some sort of madness had crept into her own mind. If the Dalia that Seraphina had seen through her window wasn't real, and she wasn't a dybbuk, then what *was* she?

A few days before her birthday, Seraphina was in her chambers with her sisters while servants decorated the castle for the masquerade.

"I'm so hungry," Rose moaned. She lifted a lock of golden-brown hair and frowned at it. "I think my hair is suffering. Does it look less shiny to you?"

To be fair, they were all famished. The meals had grown smaller and smaller until breakfast consisted of a lump of pickled herring and a radish.

Nina was sprawled on a fainting sofa in her underthings, bored and sullen. "I just don't understand why we have to stay in here all day. I was finally making headway with Lord Basilton. He keeps asking me to meet him in the library."

"Is he very fond of books?" Rose asked.

Nina rolled her eyes. "Yes, that's it, Rose. Books."

"You'll have plenty of opportunities to steal away in dark corners during the ball, and a mask to hide behind," Seraphina said.

"I know Father wants the decorations to be a surprise for Imogen, but he won't keep us out of the dining room for the next four days, will he?" Rose asked.

Nina sighed. "What difference does it make if there's nothing to eat?"

Seraphina was holding her golden birthday mask, inwardly noting the irony of a mask that only covered her eyes and the top of her nose. As if anyone wouldn't know who she was, especially with her hair freshly hennaed. Jocelyn, meanwhile, lifted her own mask to her face and sighed. It was white and covered in more of the ridiculous daisies. A fuzzy little bee affixed to a coiled wire bobbed from one of the temples.

"Lord Greymont told me he's very excited about the ball," Nina said, now hanging halfway off the sofa and looking at Seraphina upside down. *"Very."*

"As is everyone," Seraphina said casually. "It's the most exciting thing to happen here since... In years."

Jocelyn sat down next to Seraphina and stroked her hair. "How are you feeling about all of this? I know it's not your—" she lowered her voice "—real birthday. It must feel strange to celebrate without your family."

"I haven't thought about it like that," Seraphina admitted. Birthdays had never been that important to her family, unlike the High Holy Days. This time of year, autumn, was always difficult. How could she repent for her sins in good conscience, knowing she must continue to lie?

Jocelyn was still watching Seraphina with a strange look on her face. Fortunately, Rose had begun to sing, and her voice was so high and nasal it distracted all of them.

"Dance with me," Rose said, reaching for Seraphina's hands before going back to her wretched singing.

"I think I'll sit this one out," she replied with a laugh. "But I believe Nina would love a dance."

Nina propped herself up on her elbows. "Not a chance."

"Then I suppose Jocelyn will have to do me the honors," Rose sang, wheeling toward her. "Dance with me."

Jocelyn acquiesced and took Rose's hands in her own. It wasn't clear at first who would play the man's role, but Rose clearly had no idea how to dance anything other than the lady's part. Jocelyn cast Seraphina a desperate glance.

Still smiling, Seraphina rose and bowed to Nina. "May I have this dance, my lady?"

"Uggghhh," Nina groaned, but she allowed Seraphina to pull her up and spin her around. They were all in various states of undress, having grown hot with no doors or windows open for ventilation. Seraphina and Rose had their hair unpinned, and it flew out behind them as they spun, all of them singing now, laughing hysterically when Rose hit a particularly high and sour note.

They danced and twirled, colliding with each other or the furniture every few minutes. Seraphina gasped when she took the sharp corner of an end table in the hip, but Nina's momentum kept her spinning, and all she could do was laugh at the absurdity of it.

"I must say," Nina said between breaths, "you are a lively dancer. Have you had much practice?"

Seraphina narrowed her eyes. "Ha ha." Nina knew that she had suffered through countless dance lessons, and even now she didn't have the grace and elegance Nina was apparently born into.

"She learned well," Jocelyn called over her shoulder. "Just don't pick your feet up quite so high, Imogen. There, that's better."

"Can someone loosen my corset?" Rose asked. "I feel like I'm going to faint."

Her cheeks were indeed gleaming with sweat. Seraphina was grateful for a chance to rest, the lack of food combined with all the spinning leaving her light-headed, so she whirled to Rose and untied the corset laces. "Better?"

"Much!" Rose used the opportunity to grab Seraphina's hands, forcing Nina and Jocelyn to switch partners. Jocelyn was so thin she hardly needed a corset, but she looked lovely with her skin flushed and her eyes wet with tears of mirth. Seraphina felt a stab of affection for all of them as they careened around the room, singing a bawdy song completely out of tune. In another world, in another life, they might have been friends. She would have found Rose's frivolity charming, Nina's vanity merely amusing. And she would have known that Jocelyn's loyalty was borne out of love, not duty.

Suddenly, the door to the chamber burst open, admitting a guard, two servants bearing trays, the king, and Lord Greymont.

"What in God's name is going on in here?" the king bellowed.

Rose screamed, covering her torso with a throw blanket

from one of the sofas and retreating behind a curtain. Jocelyn scurried to Seraphina, doing her best to gather Seraphina's wild hair, while Nina merely smirked at the young male servant who was having a difficult time keeping his tray steady.

"The servants have been knocking for five minutes," the king continued. "Have you all gone mad?"

"We're just practicing for the masquerade, Father," Seraphina said, shrugging into a robe Jocelyn had brought to her and tying it closed. Greymont was doing his best to avert his eyes—and failing, Seraphina noticed smugly.

"Really, this behavior is not befitting of princesses. I'm very displeased."

Seraphina dropped her eyes, shame finally settling over her. "I'm sorry, Father."

"Your Majesty, they have been trapped in here all morning," Greymont said. "And you can't blame them for being excited about the masquerade. It's all anyone has spoken of for weeks."

Seraphina glanced up through her lashes. What was he doing here, anyway?

"That's true," King Stuart said. "You make a good point."

"Shall we leave the ladies to their…rest? They'll need to keep up their strength for the festivities. Although it looks like they've got plenty of stamina." Greymont had the gall to wink at Seraphina as he said this. She pulled her robe a little tighter and he grinned.

"Yes, you're absolutely right, Lord Greymont. The ladies need their strength for the ball. Genny, please come and say good-night before you retire for the evening. I have a surprise for you."

"Of course, Father."

As soon as the men left, Rose peeked out from behind the

curtain. "Is it safe to come out now? I can't *believe* Lord Greymont saw me in my knickers."

Jocelyn, Nina, and Seraphina shared a look before collapsing in a fit of giggles.

As directed, Seraphina went to see the king that evening for her birthday "surprise." There had been a time when she'd loved nothing more than spontaneity. Purim was her favorite holiday, when she would deliver treats to neighbors and receive her fair share in turn. Dalia was the best at surprising her with gifts. She'd once brought Seraphina a poppy seed hamantasch, knowing Seraphina hated poppy seeds but would eat the triangular cookie anyway, to be polite. Inside, Seraphina had discovered a tiny hamsa amulet.

"To protect you," Dalia had said, cleaning poppy seed paste off the little silver icon representing the hand of God. Seraphina had worn it every day, until it was taken from her when she arrived at Eldridge Hall.

But here, unpredictability was dangerous. Anything that deviated from the carefully constructed web of lies she'd spun put her in danger of a misstep, of angering the king.

"There you are," he said when she stepped into his chamber. He was in bed already, claiming exhaustion, and Seraphina couldn't help thinking that starvation for a man of his age was dangerous, even more so than for the rest of them. She couldn't see his lips beneath his thick mustache, but the crinkles at the corners of his eyes told her he was smiling. "Excited for your birthday, Genny?"

She nodded. "Yes, Father."

"I imagine you're looking forward to a dance with Lord Greymont?"

She laughed nervously, unsure how Greymont could possibly figure into her birthday surprise. "I suppose."

"He's a good lad. Intelligent. Loyal."

"Yes, Father. I believe he is."

"The fact that he's handsome doesn't hurt, either," he added with a wink, and she looked down at her hands to hide her embarrassment. "You've grown into a beautiful young woman, Genny," he went on. "You should marry the most handsome man in the world. But you are worthy of a prince."

Something about the way he said it made her look up. "What do you mean, Father?"

"I've invited the Prince of Pilmand to come and meet you. You're turning twenty, after all. I think he'll prove an excellent match."

Her thoughts swirled in every direction. A marriage match? *Now?* When she was just beginning to make headway with Greymont? How had the king even gotten in touch with someone in Pilmand? "When?" was all she could manage.

"He'll be here in time for your birthday." The king frowned for a moment. "At least, I hope he will..." He blinked, as if coming back to himself, and smiled. "I thought you might like to know ahead of time, to prepare yourself. Lord Greymont will be disappointed, naturally, but he will understand. You're a princess, after all. Happy birthday, my dear."

This was the part where she was supposed to let him kiss her forehead and go off to bed. She'd done it a thousand times before. But she couldn't make sense of what he'd told her. The king was going to allow a stranger *into* the castle?

Did that mean he believed the plague was over? Or was this part of his madness, a delusion that would come to nothing?

And where in the hell was Pilmand?

A snore startled her so badly she jumped. The king had fallen asleep. She kissed his forehead automatically and left his chambers.

It was time to take another trip to the cellar, she decided. There was to be a birthday feast in just a few days, one apparently fit for a foreign prince, and the king didn't seem the slightest bit concerned. *Someone* had to call him on it. The emperor may have no clothes, but it would be much harder to ignore if he had no *food*, either.

Later that night, after she'd already gone to bed and the rest of the castle was quiet, she slipped on her robe but kept her feet bare. If anyone asked what she was doing out and about at such an hour, she would tell them she'd gone looking for a snack. The chef didn't keep any food in the kitchens at night—a rationing measure from the early days of the plague—so the cellar was logical.

Seraphina took a back staircase that was normally used for servants to make her descent. It was the fastest route, and if she did run into a servant, they weren't likely to question her. At this time of night the castle was almost pitch-black, with only the moonlight seeping through the cracks in the boarded-up windows and a single candle to guide her.

A black cat, possibly Fig, darted past her and she startled so badly that hot wax dripped onto her hand. She took a deep breath and steadied herself, shielding the flame with her hand against any sudden drafts out of habit; there were no drafts here because there was no air coming in from the outside. If she stopped and thought about it long enough, she'd get claustrophobic, so she kept moving.

Finally, she reached the cellar door. The chef locked it at night, but Seraphina had brought a hairpin with her for the occasion. Back in her days in the Jewish quarter, when she was mischievous and resourceful, she had picked the occasional lock just to see if she could. But when rumors of the plague reached Esmoor, the people who could afford to leave did. She and Dalia had broken into the kosher bakery after the baker left, knowing all the bread would go moldy rather quickly. It hadn't felt like a sin then. Neither did this.

The lock was ancient and opened with a few deft turns of her wrist. Seraphina gasped. The room was so full she could barely open the door. She pushed her shoulder against it as hard as she could and wedged her way in, wondering how the portly chef would manage. But perhaps he sent the wasting servants down to fetch food for him. They would have no trouble fitting through.

Seraphina raised her candle and turned in a slow circle in the space at the center of the room. The empty corner where Greymont had confronted her was now stacked high with crates. She peered inside them. Bushels of apples, loaves of bread, and cuts of dried meat assaulted her nose with their aromas. Saliva flooded her mouth, and she couldn't stop herself from plucking a fat, golden apple off the pile.

How had the king managed this? Had the cellar been full all this time, and she and Greymont only happened to find it on an empty day? Where had it all come from? Was the king giving the servants permission to leave the castle, or were they doing it on their own?

A noise in the hall startled Seraphina out of her pondering. She hurried out of the room, closing the door quietly behind her, and gazed down the hall. A maid blinked at her in the light of her own candle.

"Princess Imogen?"

"Indeed," she said haughtily, wondering how best to approach this. "What are you doing out at such an hour?"

"Chef asks one of us to check on the cellar every night. Food was going missing, despite the lock." She glanced past Seraphina, no doubt wondering how she had gotten in, maybe if she was responsible for the missing food. At moments like these Seraphina was keenly aware that she was no better than the servants here at Eldridge. In fact, as a Jew, she would never have even gotten a job at the castle.

"Well, I've done the work for you tonight. Everything is in its place. Except for this apple," Seraphina said with a grin. "I know I can trust you not to snitch on a princess."

"Of course, Your Highness." The maid gave a little curtsy that was far neater than Imogen's early attempts. She was thin, and not just because she was still a girl.

"Here," Seraphina said, handing her the apple, though her stomach cramped in protest. "I'll have more on my birthday." She smiled and the girl smiled uneasily back.

"Thank you, Your Highness. Good night." The maid hurried back the way she had come, and Seraphina breathed a sigh of relief.

Suddenly, the echo of the great ebony clock's chime reached her, causing Seraphina to nearly jump out of her skin. She'd forgotten about the keyhole and the footprints after finding the cellar empty that night. She fingered the pin in the pocket of her robe and decided to make one more stop.

The great hall was cold and dark and foreboding. Her candle had burned down to a stub. But she saw it almost as soon as she entered the room: a tiny pinprick of moonlight, shining through the keyhole in the clock.

She crossed the room quickly, her feet so cold they were numb, and inserted her pin into the lock. Several minutes passed as she wiggled the pin this way and that, wondering if this lock was too sophisticated for her unskilled burgling. But finally, she heard a click, and the door in the clock opened just a crack.

With trembling fingers, she pulled the door wider. A gust of wind hit her immediately, snuffing what was left of her candle. She gasped at the feel of cold outside air on her face. All this time, the key to freedom had been right here. This had to be how the servants who brought food got in and out. It must also be the route the few people who had managed to escape had used.

And if there was flour out there, and sugar and meat and everything else filling the cellar, then there had to be people harvesting the wheat and butchering the animals. There were survivors, and they were thriving, by the look of things.

She couldn't go now. She didn't even have shoes on, for heaven's sake. But for the first time since coming to Eldridge Hall, Seraphina felt something bloom in her chest, a feeling she hadn't known herself capable of anymore. Hope. Maybe there really was a prince coming to take her away. Maybe Lord Greymont could whisk her off to an island if the prince proved unbearable. Maybe there were other Jews who had survived. Maybe Dalia was one of them.

And maybe, just maybe, her *parents* had survived.

She stuck her head into the clock a little farther, sucking in the smell of fresh air through her nose, and reluctantly closed the door. She laid her palm against the keyhole and glanced up at the bird above her. With a smile, she raised one finger to her lips.

"Shhhh."

CHAPTER 10

They found the bodies on the fourth day.

A driver and a footman, or what was left of them, lay beside the coach, which had fallen onto its side, the axle broken. It was a glorious rig, intricately carved and decorated, with plush velvet seats and cushions. It looked like wolves had torn out the victims' throats, though Colin mused out loud that it was odd for wolves to leave so much meat behind.

"Wolves didn't do this," Nico said quietly, his stomach roiling.

Branson, after being sick all over himself, trudged into the woods, insisting he couldn't possibly look at the sight anymore.

They were all weak, hungry, and freezing their bollocks off, but Colin and Nico knew they couldn't leave the bodies like this. Besides, if there was a driver and a footman, there was at least one passenger, and they might still be alive.

They almost gave up looking when Colin called to Nico from behind a large tree. "I found him!"

Nico ran to join him, hoping for the best, but his spirits sank immediately when he got to the tree. For the past two mornings they had woken to a coating of frost on the forest floor, and it appeared the young man had died from a combination of shock and exposure. He was frozen stiff, his ice-blue eyes staring at nothing, his pale eyelashes and white-blond hair laced with frost. He was dressed in fine clothing befitting royalty but not nearly warm enough for the conditions. Probably he had fled the coach while his servants were attacked. Colin made a halfhearted attempt to close the eyelids, but they were too stiff to move.

"Poor fellow," Colin said. "What do you suppose they were doing out here? That coach is sturdy, but awfully fine for a long journey. And judging by the crest on the front of it, not from anywhere near here."

Nico could only shake his head. It was like something out of a fairy tale, a frozen prince in the woods, perhaps on his way to meet a princess.

An idea struck him, but it was so ludicrous he didn't voice it.

"What is it?" Colin asked. He knew all of Nico's expressions by now, including his quizzical furrowed brow.

"It's silly. But do you suppose they could have been heading to Eldridge Hall?"

Colin stomped his feet to keep them from going numb. "We are only a day or so away. I suppose it's possible. But that means—"

"Someone really *is* alive at the castle."

They stood in silence for a moment, shivering.

"What do we do?" Colin finally asked.

Nico blinked. He hadn't expected Colin to defer to him. After all, they were equals now, and Colin was far more resourceful than Nico. "If there are survivors, we need to tell them what happened to the prince. They must have been expecting him."

"All right. But what about Crane?"

They exchanged a glance that said what neither had spoken of in the days since Arnaud came to the woodshed. Crane's interest in survivors—particularly in *healthy* survivors—was not altruistic. It was beginning to make sense now that everyone Crane employed was an immune. Clearly, Arnaud could smell the difference. And whatever Arnaud was, Nico was certain that Crane had recognized it. That Crane *was* it.

Nico blanched at the thought of the two dead men near the coach. Could Crane have done something so horrible to a gentle young woman like Elisabeth? He thought of the few other guests they had entertained, how they had spent a few days at the manor and then resumed their journeys. Only he was sure now that they hadn't. Perhaps they were buried on Crane's own lands. Maybe Nico and Colin had buried some of those bodies themselves, not even recognizing them.

He remembered how Crane had touched his wrist when he found him that day in the woods, and suddenly he knew that he hadn't been checking his pulse.

"We can't lead those people to their deaths," Nico said finally. "We have to warn them."

"Warn them what?" Branson had managed to clean himself up a bit, though there were bits of frozen vomit clinging to his coat.

"Nothing," Nico said quickly. Either Branson was too absorbed in his own misery to put two and two together, or he didn't care what Arnaud and Crane were. Branson wanted

Crane Manor, and once he was in charge, there was little reason to believe he'd do anything to protect the rest of the staff. And while Branson may not be capable of murder, Nico didn't trust him not to sacrifice hordes of innocents if it meant getting what he wanted. For someone like Branson, the end always justified the means, just so long as he came out on top. "We should bury these men and continue on our journey."

Branson sneered. "The ground is frozen solid and we haven't got any shovels."

"Just the same, we can't leave them like this." Nico moved toward the dead prince's head and placed his hands under his arms. "You get the feet," he said to Colin. The corpse was so stiff it remained curled in on itself as they carried it back to the coach. They laid it down next to the other two bodies.

"Now what?" Branson said as if he'd done anything useful up to this point.

"Look." Colin pointed to a large wooden chest still strapped to the back of the coach. "I reckon we could fit three bodies in there, if we're willing to get creative."

Branson was starting to go green again. "Go see if you can find the horses," Nico ordered. "They could still be nearby."

Relieved to be off corpse duty, Branson hurried into the trees while Colin took out his knife and began to saw at the ropes holding the chest to the back of the carriage. It fell to the ground with a heavy thud. Nico found a large rock and banged it a few times against the lock, which was brittle with cold and broke on the third blow.

Inside the trunk were treasures that would have dazzled two young men under ordinary circumstances: jewels, gold, fine gowns and embroidered jackets, soft white breeches and polished leather boots. But they were after two things: winter clothing and food. Of the latter they found nothing. Whatever food they'd been carrying must have been taken, or else they'd run out. But they did find heavy fur cloaks, one of fine white ermine and another of black sable. They threw them on, relishing the warmth immediately.

Colin said a quick prayer to the dead prince as they turned out the rest of the contents of the chest. Just as they were hoisting in the prince's body, Branson returned from the woods leading a black horse.

"I'll be damned," Colin said. "You finally did something useful for a change, Branson."

He glared and turned to Nico. "I found him in the trees. No sign of the other."

"One is better than nothing," Nico said. "Thank you."

Branson stared at the pile of gold and jewels on the ground, then glanced back at Nico. "Where's my cloak?"

"I'm afraid there were only two."

"But fear not," Colin said. "We saved the best for you." He threw a heavy velvet robe at Branson, hitting him squarely in the chest. The horse started, but Branson managed to keep a hold of the reins.

He glanced at the rumpled green velvet, scowling. "This is a lady's robe."

"It's better than nothing," Nico said.

"Easy for you to say."

Nico glanced down at the ermine cloak. It was fit for a king, not someone like him. But he was warmer than he'd been in days, and he'd be damned if he was giving it up.

"You can have mine," Colin said. "If you can get the footman and the driver into the trunk without vomiting."

Nico stifled a laugh. Branson, to his credit, tied the horse to a nearby branch and laid the lady's robe over its flanks. "Very well," he said, rolling up his sleeves. He approached the mangled corpse of the footman. His head had been nearly torn off and several vertebrae gleamed white amid the crimson. Branson hadn't even reached his foot when he turned to the side and retched, spitting up a bit of yellow bile.

"It was a noble effort," Colin said. "Better luck next time."

Branson wiped his hand on the back of his sleeve. "One of these days everything is going to go back to normal, and you'll be nothing but a peasant. And I'll be Crane's legal heir. I'll find a fine young lady to marry, after I've had my way with Abby, of course."

Nico started to argue, but Colin shook his head. "The only thing that distinguishes a gentleman and a peasant these days is our conduct. Abby has seen enough of yours to make her own decisions."

Colin returned to his work, but Nico saw the way Branson glared at his back. He recognized well enough the look of a man with little left to lose, and the desperation of someone willing to do whatever it took to keep it.

CHAPTER 11

On the morning of her birthday masquerade, Seraphina woke with a start. Crocheted daisies drifted off her bed like cherry blossoms in a breeze. It took her a moment to recognize them from Jocelyn's dress, which she had "altered" last night, removing nearly two-thirds of the daisies one by one with a pair of embroidery scissors, keeping only the flowers that accentuated the bosom and hips. The bonnet she hid under her bed, and the mask was stripped of all but one daisy at the right temple. The bee followed the bonnet under the bed. With a needle and thread, she made subtle tucks and adjustments, finally removing two of the lace petticoats that made the gown so unfashionably large.

Today was the day, she realized. The day they'd finally get to watch the sunrise.

Seraphina dressed quickly, wincing at the cold stone on her feet as she flew down the stairs. She donned her slippers and skipped her way to the princesses' chambers, where Rose and Nina sat bleary-eyed and grumpy at their vanities while their maids bustled around them.

"I don't see what all the fuss is about," Rose mumbled. "It's just a sunrise."

"Something you haven't seen in four years," Seraphina reminded her. "And if you two don't hurry up, we're going to miss it."

Finally, after much folderol, they were deemed suitable for company, and they made their way through the castle together.

The king's decorations for Seraphina's birthday ball were bizarre, to say the least. Seven seemingly random chambers were swathed in silks of various colors: cobalt blue, a purple as deep as the skin of an aubergine, a rich forest green, marigold orange, snow white, and a shade of violet Seraphina thought of as twilight.

The final chamber was the great hall itself, and it was enshrouded in plush black velvet. The perfume of black calla lilies and burgundy-black roses filled the air. Seraphina had no idea where any of it had come from, but she couldn't deny its strange beauty. The ebony clock stood at the end of the dark hall like a sentry, counting down the minutes until three o'clock.

It was so dim, even lit by torches, that it took a moment for Seraphina to find the king, surrounded as he was by eager nobles hoping for a front-row view of the sunrise. But others hung back, clearly not as excited about what they might find when the boards came down.

"Ah, there you are! Happy birthday, Genny," the king said when Seraphina reached his side.

"Thank you, Father."

"I must admit I don't see why you're so eager to watch the sunrise, especially when I've taken such care on the decorations..." He gestured to the wall of black curtains obscuring the boarded-up window.

"I know, but it means so much to me," Seraphina said with a sweet smile. When he proffered his cheek, she leaned in to kiss it, pinching her wrist hard below her waist.

He gazed at her adoringly. "Very well, my dear. Guards?" The king motioned for the men to step forward. They pulled back the black curtains, revealing the heavy wooden boards that had been hammered into the large window frame so long ago. Wielding crowbars, the men set to work.

Several minutes passed before they were finished, and a collective hush fell over the crowd. For a moment there was nothing but the reflection of all their pale faces and torchlight in the glass, which had shattered in several places.

And then everyone gasped in unison. Seraphina's own breath caught as the sun peeked over the top of the castle wall, as warm and yellow as freshly churned butter.

Tears filled Seraphina's eyes, and she blinked them away rapidly, not wanting to miss a moment. She didn't realize Greymont was standing next to her until he spoke.

"I'd forgotten," he breathed. "I'd completely forgotten."

They stood side by side, watching as dawn flooded the castle courtyard, chasing away the remnants of the night. The grass was turning brown at the coming of winter, but in the early-morning sun, it appeared golden. Too quickly, the orange yolk of the sun tugged itself free from the top of the wall. It was all over in a matter of moments, and when it was finished, Greymont's hand found Seraphina's among the folds of her skirt. His hand was warm and firm, and fresh tears sprang up in her eyes.

It wasn't a romantic gesture. It was a physical expression of the emotional connection they had just shared: two people watching the sunrise for the first time in nearly four years. But as her tears dried and the sun continued its ascent, Seraphina became conscious of his thumb stroking the back of her hand, and she pulled away.

She turned to find the nobles milling restlessly. Then she noticed the king, standing just a few feet behind her, his mouth pressed in a firm white line while the rest of his face flushed scarlet.

For a moment she was sure he'd seen Greymont touching her, and an explanation was already forming on the tip of her tongue. But then she realized he was staring beyond her, at a skeleton sprawled on the grass, a rock in its outstretched hand.

Oh, God. She'd made a terrible mistake. She was used to the view from her tower to the fields beyond the walls. But the king couldn't see that the outside world was safe from here. All he could see was what lay between Eldridge Hall and the wall separating them from freedom: a courtyard strewn with skeletons and refuse, flanked by the gallows constructed for deserters.

Suddenly, she wished she could take Greymont's hand again. He'd promised to stand behind her, no matter what her father said. But he'd vanished from her side just as quickly as he'd appeared.

"Replace the boards immediately!" the king bellowed, spittle flying from his lips. "Whoever removed them will be hanged for treason!"

The guards shuffled uneasily, not wanting to take responsibility for removing the boards in the first place.

As if on cue, Giselle, who had been conspicuously absent just a few minutes ago, materialized at her father's side. "Don't you remember, Father? This was Imogen's birthday wish." Giselle's green eyes narrowed a fraction as her gaze met Seraphina's. "You did all of this for her."

"Why? Why did she want this?" he asked, blinking at his second eldest daughter like a lost lamb.

"Because it reminds me of Mother," Seraphina blurted, her pulse pounding in her ears. If she didn't phrase this perfectly, she didn't know what the king would do. "Aurora means dawn, after all."

She watched the king's eyes closely, afraid to see the vicious clarity return, but they remained clouded and confused. "My Aurora. Yes, she did love to watch the sunrise..."

As Giselle escorted the king away, the guards made their own hasty retreat, and the relieved nobles began to make their way to the dining room for breakfast.

As the room emptied, Seraphina sniffed back her tears, still searching for Greymont. He'd promised her that other people wanted this, that they would help convince the king it was time to leave Eldridge. But no one had stood beside her, least of all Greymont.

Her silly, pathetic excuse for a plan had failed miserably. All she'd succeeded in doing was reminding everyone how bad things had gotten before the king boarded up the windows; how close the castle had come to being breached. The banquet tonight would be a false reassurance to them all that things here were just fine. They were never going to leave.

Would *Greymont* even want to leave now? If not, she was doomed. She certainly couldn't count on some mythical prince to arrive and save her. No doubt the prince from Pilmand had all been part of the king's delusion.

Jocelyn, seeing Seraphina's distress, took her arm and patted it gently.

Seraphina allowed Jocelyn to lead her to the dining room. The king had insisted they save the majority of the food for the masquerade, so their breakfast was particularly meager. The porridge was thinned near to water and the cuts of cured meat seemed parchment-fine. Even the king himself was gaunt in a way Seraphina hadn't noticed before. She watched him eat, wondering if it was just her imagination that his cheeks seemed hollower. The movement of the joint in his jaw entranced her as he worked on a piece of stale bread.

She was still rattled from her utter disaster of a birthday gift, but at least the king seemed to have forgotten. Giselle sat close by his side, whispering reassurances into his ear.

Seraphina startled when someone cleared their throat next to her. Greymont had taken his seat.

"What happened to you earlier?" she whispered, hoping there was some explanation for his abandoning her.

He remained facing forward. "I didn't think you wanted me there."

"*Why?*" she hissed.

"You dropped my hand. I assumed it was because of your…"

"My what?"

His eyes darted to her. "Your *engagement* to the Prince of Pilmand."

A cold sweat prickled Seraphina's back. She had assumed no one else knew about her betrothal. The only person she'd told was Jocelyn. "Who told you?"

"Does it matter? I thought it was a lie, but then when you dropped my hand before the king, I started to question everything. Perhaps I don't know you at all."

She studied his profile, trying to determine if Greymont was saddened by this news or merely disappointed that his grand plans were dashed. He wanted her, and perhaps he felt he needed her, but she didn't believe that he loved her.

"Do you really think this prince exists?" she pressed. "We just witnessed my father's utter breakdown at the reality of what lies beyond these walls. Even if he did somehow get word to Pilmand, he would never allow a stranger in."

Greymont gave a noncommittal grunt.

"I'm disappointed in you," she said after a moment. Perhaps appealing to his vanity would help. "I didn't think you were the kind of man to give up so easily."

He glanced at her from the corner of his eye. "I'm not. Not if something is worth fighting for."

"Am *I* worth fighting for?" she murmured.

His lips curled in one of his cocky grins as their eyes locked, sparking something low in Seraphina's belly. "Yes, Princess, I think you are."

She released her breath quietly, feeling some of the fear leave her. All hope was not lost, and he hadn't even seen her in her birthday gown yet. She lifted her chin and squared her shoulders just like she'd been taught. After tonight he wouldn't just *think* she was worth it.

He would *know* it.

The masquerade would start just before sunset, but until then Seraphina would stay in her room with her sisters and their ladies. There was no great surprise now; she'd already seen all the decorations, and though bizarre, they were well suited to the madness of the affair. There was an undeniable tension in the air, and even she couldn't help feeling a little thrill of excitement as she joined her sisters.

"Happy birthday, Imogen!" Rose said as Seraphina entered the room. She sat in her chemise and corset, her maid pinning up her hair in long coils. Silk roses lay in a pile on the vanity. "All the real ones are wilting," Rose said with a pout. "But these will look just as pretty, don't you think?"

"Of course," Seraphina said, joining Jocelyn on a sofa. Jocelyn was reading, but she set her book aside when Seraphina sat down.

Jocelyn's dress was still on its form, looking much more fashionable after Seraphina's alterations. Nina was dressed in her chemise, corset, and silk robe, examining her complexion in a hand mirror. A seamstress was attending to her dress.

"Did something happen?" Seraphina asked, nodding at the gown.

"I've lost so much weight in the last week it has to be taken in," Nina said with a frown. "I swear my bosom has shrunk."

Jocelyn smiled knowingly. "She plans on getting an offer of marriage today. Her entire future rests on the size of her bosom, apparently."

"I doubt Lord Basilton will notice," Rose said.

"Then you haven't been paying attention to our interactions." Nina squeezed her corset a little tighter. "His eyes rarely travel above my neck. Which seems such a pity." She blew a kiss to herself in the mirror.

Lord Basilton was rich, or he had been once. He was handsome enough, and not as arrogant as some of the other nobles. But if King Stuart had chosen a prince for his youngest daughter, he was never going to allow Nina, the heir to the throne, to marry a mere duke. Seraphina felt it wasn't her place to remind Nina of that, and with her so happy, Seraphina didn't have the heart to tell her anyway.

"We should start getting you ready," Jocelyn said to Seraphina with a grave expression. "We've only got three hours before your grand entrance."

Seraphina laughed but walked dutifully to her vanity, where a maid was waiting with brushes and cosmetics. When she was finished styling Seraphina's hair, she produced a bowl of pearl- and diamond-studded pins and downy white feathers, which she arranged artfully throughout. The gold circlet from the king was placed on the crown of her head last.

The dress itself was easy enough to wear; the style didn't require all the squeezing and fastening that Nina's did. Seraphina would wait to put on the wings until the last minute. They were quite heavy and would make it impossible to sit.

Finally, the clock struck three o'clock and the ladies finished readying themselves. Seraphina would make her appearance at the top of the stairs leading down to the white chamber, where the king and the rest of the lords and ladies would be waiting. She took one last look in the mirror as Jocelyn tied the golden ribbons of her mask, and started.

Behind her the reflection of a portrait of the real Imogen watched her with mournful eyes. Her gaze flicked back to herself, and for one unsettling moment it was as if she were looking at Princess Imogen's ghost.

What would the king see when he saw her descend the

stairs? His daughter as an angel in heaven, with her halo atop her auburn hair and her wings outstretched behind her willowy, pale limbs? Or simply a Jewish girl in a costume, one in desperate need of a good meal?

Whether or not the prince arrived, or she escaped with Lord Greymont, how long could she keep up this charade outside Eldridge Hall? She had lived as a fraud for nearly four years. Did she mean to die as one, too?

Her sisters began their descent, leaving Seraphina alone at the top of the stairs. She was hidden in the shadows of the hall, but from here, she could see down to the bottom. The white room was a ballroom, with polished wooden floors and crystal chandeliers hanging down from a ceiling painted like the heavens: blue sky, billowy white clouds, pink cherubs trailing flower garlands. The room seemed almost painfully bright from here.

Seraphina's mouth dropped open as she realized that sometime in the past few hours, the boards had been removed from all the windows.

It made no sense, not after the king's reaction this morning. But she wasn't imagining it. Afternoon sunlight flooded the room, and though the early-winter light was beautiful, the lords and ladies themselves were a disturbing sight. How gaunt they all were; how pale and insubstantial. Lord Greymont, standing near the king, was more than thin. He looked sickly. Her sisters, normally so vibrant, were sallow, their limbs as thin as birch branches.

She felt as if a veil had slipped from her eyes. How much had been hidden in the shadows for all these years?

A chill crept over her spine as someone sounded a gong,

heralding her arrival and signaling to everyone assembled it was time to don their masks.

With her right hand gripping the balustrade, Seraphina descended the stairway as slowly and with as much dignity as she could manage. She hadn't realized how weak she was until this moment, when hundreds of eyes in hundreds of upturned faces fell on her. She tried not to let her gaze linger too long on individuals. It helped that everyone was masked and she couldn't recognize most of them from here, but a few expressions bled through: a woman whose upper lip was curled in what looked like a sneer of disgust; a leering man who had changed so much that Seraphina at first didn't recognize him as Pottington, the once-portly lord at whom just weeks ago Lord Greymont had been casting jealous looks; the king, whose eyes shone bright with tears.

Hundreds of men and women, hundreds of different opinions and expectations, a multitude of dreams and nightmares...

All waiting for her.

CHAPTER 12

The men arrived at Eldridge Hall just after dawn on the fifth day of their journey. They'd made better time with the horses, with Colin and Nico riding the stallion and Branson—the slightest of the three of them—on Locket, whose hoof was healing well. The weather had turned even harsher the last couple of nights, but the fur coats helped. Nico had even let Branson borrow his a few times, preferring to suffer the cold than Branson's complaining.

They set up camp in the woods facing the castle walls. They hadn't bothered to try the gates. They could see from here that they had been soldered shut, and they were far too high to climb. But if anyone was alive at Eldridge, there was a way in.

"What's the plan?" Colin asked as they unpacked their bags.

Nico was fumbling with numb hands to start a fire. "Why do you always assume I have a plan?" he asked over his shoulder, wondering if "wait for someone to find us" would satisfy Colin.

"Because you always do. We can't just force our way into the castle. We have to assume they've got ways to keep people out."

"I doubt anyone has tried in years," Branson said. "If there is someone alive in there, they're most likely weak and starving. And probably desperate for company."

"How do you manage to make everything sound sinister?" Colin asked. "If they wanted company, they'd have come out."

"Not if they're alone and afraid."

At last, a spark caught, and Nico carefully stoked the flames until he had a decent blaze going. Then he went to tend to the horses—Colin had named the black stallion Wolfbait, which Nico had promptly changed to Wolfgang to spare the horse's feelings—and made his way to the edge of the woods, to get a better view of the castle.

He found himself searching for the tower Crane had mentioned. There, that had to be it: a tall, spindly thing that looked like it would come crumbling down at any moment. If someone was alive in the castle, what were they doing up there? He was too far away to make out if the windows were boarded up, as Crane had said.

He studied the rest of the castle, impressed by its sheer size. The walls were nearly twenty feet high, impossible to climb. No wonder the king had locked himself up here; it was a veritable fortress. There was no chance of the plague getting to him or his family as long as they remained locked inside. He shuddered at the thought. Anything could be a cage under the right circumstances, even a castle.

"We should split up," Nico said when he returned to the camp to find Branson lounging on his bedroll and Colin attempting to heat water for tea. "The castle is enormous and we'll cover more ground separately."

"I'll stay with the horses," Branson volunteered. "Wouldn't want a wolf to get them."

Nico and Colin rolled their eyes at each other. "Just make

sure the fire doesn't go out," Nico said. He knew Branson likely wouldn't have been useful anyhow.

Carefully, Colin and Nico made their way across the open field to the castle walls. When they reached it, they followed the perimeter, looking for a way in. Every now and then Colin would try his hand climbing the wall, using a promising crack or odd-shaped stone for a foothold, but he never made it more than ten feet up.

They'd rounded the first wall and were headed along the west side of the castle when Colin held a hand up. Nico heard the voices a moment later.

They pressed themselves against the wall because there was nowhere else to go. It was a man and a woman speaking, their voices low but not whispers. The man said something that made the woman laugh, and it was not the laugh of someone trying to conceal herself. Colin pointed forward and began to creep along the wall. Nico followed, crouched low and trying not to breathe too loudly.

Fortunately, there was a bend in the wall here, and they were able to conceal themselves behind it. Colin poked his head out, just far enough to see. He was so tall that Nico didn't have to crouch down to see below him.

"Can't believe the chef asked us to get more swans," the woman said. "As if five wasn't hard enough to come by."

"Princess Imogen must have swans for her birthday feast," the man said in a mocking tone. "Think they'll figure out these are geese?"

"Not a chance," the woman said. "Those people are like vultures at a carcass every time they get fresh meat."

Finally, they came into view, walking toward Colin and

Nico from the forest. Both were carrying large sacks over their shoulders.

The sight of two people walking and talking as if everything was normal stirred something deep within Nico, and for one disorienting moment it was as if he was back in his old life. Then Colin pushed him back farther into the recess they were hiding in and the moment ended.

"He wants to impress the Pilmandish prince," the man said, "as if he could possibly make it here. These royals have no idea what the roads are like, what with all the wolves come down from the mountains."

"This is the last run," the woman said with a snort. "I'm not coming back to the castle after the ball tonight. Now that the plague is gone and we've got the trade established, those pretty lords and ladies can rot in there for all I care. Princess Imogen most of all. What kind of person demands a masquerade ball when most of the country is dead of disease and starvation?"

"If they don't rot here, they'll rot in hell, that's certain," the man said.

The talking faded as the people disappeared. Nico and Colin waited a few minutes before coming out of their hiding spot and walking to where the servants had gone. Sure enough, there was a narrow opening there, as if someone had pried away the stones one by one. From far away, you wouldn't even see it. Colin slid through easily but Nico had to turn sideways and suck in his breath to keep from brushing against the walls.

Colin immediately scurried to an overturned wagon and crouched down behind it, Nico following close behind. The servants were crossing the large open space that separated the castle walls from the keep itself. It was an ancient thing, several hundred years old at least, and looked almost primitive compared to Crane Manor.

As Nico took in his surroundings, a sense of dread washed over him. Hand-painted signs had been hung here and there, warning people to turn around, that the castle had been hit by the plague. Lies, undoubtedly; just a desperate measure to keep people out. The servants walked past the signs, chatting away, and didn't even balk as they passed the gallows, where several skeletons hung, scraps of tattered clothing still clinging to the swaying forms.

Aside from the servants, the entire area was deserted. Crane Manor was practically brimming with life in comparison. There was nothing growing here, no signs that anyone ever left the castle. But the servants had referred to *those people*, which meant Eldridge Hall wasn't deserted at all.

And that Lord Crane was right.

"Did you catch what the man said?" Nico whispered to Colin. They watched as the servants disappeared into an unassuming wooden door. Could it really be that simple?

"Which part?"

"They mentioned something about establishing a trade, which means there are survivors elsewhere. Things really are returning to normal."

"What do you make of the *wolves*?"

"They must have seen signs of predation, but it didn't sound to me as though they understood what they'd really seen."

"What do we do now?" Colin asked. "Should we follow them?"

"I don't think so. From the sound of things, we'll be greatly outnumbered." A wave of pure hatred swept over Nico. To think, all this time, the king was alive and well, holding court over a bunch of lords and ladies who ate swan and held balls while the kingdom lay under a blanket of death and decay. He hoped someone *did* steal the throne, even if it was Crane. He was no more a monster than King Stuart. "But there's to be a masquerade tonight, and they're expecting a prince *we* know is never coming."

Colin arched an eyebrow. "So what are you suggesting? That one of us sneaks into the ball?"

"We know the way in. Once we're there, we can assess the situation."

"We?" Colin laughed. "You may be able to pass yourself off as a prince, but I never could."

"Fine, I'll take Branson."

"And what about telling the master?"

As disgusted as Nico was with the king and the princess and everyone else inside the castle, the idea of telling the master about potential immaculates trapped in one place made his stomach turn over. "I think we should wait until we know what we're dealing with."

A rustling sound caught Nico's attention and he turned to where they'd entered the wall, but there was no one there.

"I'll stay with the horses and keep an eye out, but I won't be able to help you once you're inside," Colin said. "We'll need a story. As soon as they hear you talking, they'll know you're not a foreigner."

"Then I'll try not to speak. At least not until I have to." He knew very little about Pilmand, other than that it was in the north and that their largest export was fur, which helped explain their cloaks.

"Fine. But what are we going to do about a costume?"

Nico glanced around the courtyard. There was a pile of refuse near the gallows that looked promising. After all, the garbage from the castle had to go somewhere.

As they rummaged through the discarded odds and ends, they found plenty of threadbare ladies' gowns, old slippers that were worn through on the soles, and a thousand soiled hand-kerchiefs. With the right materials, they may have been able to create a mask out of some scraps, but they had no needle and thread. Besides, aside from sewing sutures, Nico had no experience as a seamstress.

He sighed. "This is hopeless. I've got the prince's fur cloak, and that will have to be enough."

"You need to play the part of a prince, and you need to blend in," Colin said. "You certainly can't wear that." He jerked a thumb toward Nico's filthy tunic and breeches.

"I think Branson took some of the prince's clothing from the trunk. We can wear those." Nico sat down on the edge of a wheelbarrow and leaned back on his elbows. He was ex-hausted from traveling. The idea of pretending to be a prince right now seemed impossible. He nudged what looked like a dark tarp aside to make room and froze.

At first, he thought it was a massive bird's skull and nearly jumped out of the wheelbarrow. But then his brain caught up with his eyes and he laughed. Beneath what was in fact an oilskin cloak lay a brown leather mask with an elongated, beak-shaped nose and two eyeholes. A plague doctor's mask.

Colin joined Nico as he held the mask aloft. They both shuddered at the sight of it. A few years ago its presence would have meant imminent death. The doctors had all died or fled within the first few months of the plague, but perhaps the king had kept one around just in case the disease managed to find its way into the castle.

"If you show up in that, they'll definitely kill you," Colin said.

"We'll have to disguise it a bit. Paint it black with tar or something." He looked up at the castle again, wondering what he'd find inside. "We'd best get back before someone catches us."

Colin followed him out through the hole in the wall and they hurried across the fields toward camp. Every now and then Nico glanced over his shoulder to look up at the tower where Crane had seen the candle. Who was it up there? Some poor servant, no doubt, trapped by a selfish king and his spoiled daughters. Tomorrow he would find that person and rescue them, somehow.

"Oh, bollocks."

Nico turned to look at their camp. Or what was left of it. There was no sign of the stallion, or of Branson. The white ermine cloak was gone, along with the blankets they'd stashed in the hollow tree. The only thing left was a pair of the prince's breeches and the sable cloak, which Colin had tucked high up in a tree out of Branson's reach.

Nico thought back to the rustle he'd heard inside the castle walls. Branson must have followed them and overheard their conversation.

Which meant he knew there were people living in Eldridge Hall, and that Nico was planning to enter. This was Branson's opportunity to prove his loyalty to their master, to earn himself a place in Crane Manor for the rest of his life.

Nico gazed into the forest, his stomach sinking to his feet. "He's gone to tell Crane."

CHAPTER 13

Finally, Seraphina reached the last step, and the crowd erupted in applause. Surrounded by a room of blank, expressionless masks, she felt oddly exposed and hurried over to the king, who hugged her so fiercely she was nearly thrown off balance by her wings.

He was dressed as a king, but an old-fashioned one, in a full white ermine cloak with black fur tufts and an exaggerated gold crown. His mask covered his entire face in white porcelain. "Happy birthday, my beautiful daughter. How does it feel to be twenty years old, Genny?"

Seraphina had never felt more alone than she did in that moment. Everything he'd just said was part of the beautiful lie she'd allowed to be constructed around her since she left her family. Yes, she had been taken, but she should have refused. She should have died trying to escape and get back to her family, no matter what the rabbi told them. Even if it had only given her one more day with the people she loved, it would have been worth it.

Someone handed her a glass of sparkling wine. The king's

head was cocked, the blank expression of the mask somehow expectant, and she felt like she had no choice but to drink. There, she wasn't even strong enough to resist a sip of wine.

I'll make a game of it, she told herself. *One sip every time someone wishes me a happy birthday.*

Somewhere music began to play, and someone took her hand and whirled her into a spin. She looked up to find a man in a white mask with gold scrolling. She'd always found this the most disturbing style of masquerade mask, the way the area beneath the nose protruded forward like a shovel, but it was practical. The wearer could hide his identity and still eat and drink freely.

"What are you supposed to be, Lord Greymont?" she asked, taking in his elaborate black-and-red costume. "You look like the devil."

"I don't know who this Lord Greymont is, but I hope he's good with a sword, because I plan to fight off any man who attempts to dance with the angel in my arms."

Seraphina couldn't help laughing. "We both know I'm no angel."

As they spun toward the window, he ran his fingers along the edge of her gold mask, where it met her cheekbone. "Happy birthday."

Her breath caught at their reflection in the exposed glass: an angel whirling in the devil's arms, the Danse Macabre personified. They were Life and Death, removed only by a single heartbeat. She hardly recognized herself behind the mask.

When they waltzed past a servant holding a tray of crystal flutes, she plucked one off the tray and drained it in one gulp.

As the evening passed into night, she was handed from one

masked partner to another, always spinning, drinking, laughing. She was no longer Imogen, or Seraphina, but some other girl entirely, one whose wings were heavy but whose feet were lighter than air. The lords were all practiced enough that it didn't matter if she knew the steps; they carried her around the room as if she were as insubstantial as a dove. She gazed up at the ceiling, where cherubs gazed back at her from the Garden of Eden. She'd been taught that everything in this life would be explained in the world to come, that all the hardships her people endured would make sense on the other side. But that was before the plague came and everything was turned upside down. Now she wondered what she could possibly learn in death that would help her to understand a God who would allow so much suffering.

As the sky outside began to darken, she found herself clinging to her partner's arms to stay upright. His dark clothing came into focus and she realized Greymont had found her once again.

"You should eat something," he said as the music slowed to a stop. The musicians were taking a break. "Dinner hasn't been announced yet, but there is bread somewhere. I can get some for you if you like."

"I'm fine," she said, pushing her mask up to her forehead. "Let me see your face."

He clucked his tongue. "That will spoil the illusion."

Her vision blurred, turning him into a two-headed demon. "Please, Lord Greymont?"

"Only if you'll stop calling me Lord Greymont. My name," he whispered, "is Henry."

She smiled and nodded. "Very well, Henry."

He pulled the mask off and shook out his hair. "Happy?"

"You really are handsome, Henry," she mumbled, though it took more effort to form the words than it should have.

He laughed. "You're just now noticing?"

She was about to reply with something snarky when she felt a gentle but firm grip on her arm.

"Come, Your Highness. You need to rest." Jocelyn led her away from Henry with a knowing glance. As they passed a servant, Seraphina reached for another glass of the sparkling wine, but Jocelyn batted her hand away.

"No more of that," she said, replacing Seraphina's mask. "You'll be sick if you keep this up." She led Seraphina to an alcove in a hallway where they had a little privacy. "Here, let me help you with your wings."

Seraphina hadn't realized just how heavy they really were until they were removed. There was a dull aching in her lower back and a sharper pain in her shoulders, where the ribbons had cut into her skin. Jocelyn laid the wings on the floor near her feet. "Drink this," she commanded, handing her a glass of water.

Seraphina sipped dutifully. The partygoers had branched out from the white ballroom into the other colored chambers. From where they sat, she could see into the violet room, where Nina was dancing with her lord. Seraphina wondered if he'd proposed yet. Rose was nowhere to be seen, but Seraphina was confident she was dancing somewhere. Anything that would allow her to twirl in her pink dress. She caught fleeting glimpses of Giselle as she was passed from one would-be suitor to another, though Seraphina couldn't imagine her ever deigning to marry one of the men here.

"It was her idea, you know," Jocelyn said, gesturing toward Giselle. "Removing all the boards from the windows."

Seraphina started. "What? Why?"

"I think she was hoping it would turn the king against you, after what we all witnessed this morning. You know what she's like. She hates that all this fuss is being made on your behalf."

Giselle *had* reminded the king that the sunrise had been Seraphina's idea earlier. But why would she want to tamper with the king's fragile mind now, when all these years she'd done everything she could to protect it? Especially when it came to Seraphina?

Could *Giselle* want to leave Eldridge Hall, finally?

"Did Lord Greymont propose?" Jocelyn asked, interrupting Seraphina's thoughts.

It took a moment for her friend's face to come into focus. "I beg your pardon?" Seraphina said with a hiccup.

"You've been spending so much time with him lately, and you've seemed so much happier. I assumed a proposal was coming, if it hasn't already."

She drained the glass of water and handed it back to Jocelyn. "No, of course not. If he'd proposed, do you really think I wouldn't have told you?"

Jocelyn lowered her eyes to her lap, where she plucked at one of the crocheted daisies. "We haven't spoken as much lately."

"Don't be ridiculous. We talk every single day."

Jocelyn lowered her mask. "I mean about the world outside Eldridge." She dropped her voice to a whisper. "You haven't mentioned your family in weeks."

Seraphina untied her mask, too, revealing the tears in her

eyes. They seemed to come so easily lately. "Every time I mention them, I'm reminded of how much I miss them. Of how wicked I am for leaving them behind." She held up her hand when Jocelyn began to protest. "I know you're going to say it wasn't a choice—"

"That's because it wasn't." Jocelyn wiped the tears from Seraphina's cheeks with a handkerchief. "Please, try not to cry. It's your birthday."

"But it's not, Joc. You of all people know that."

"I know." She held on to Seraphina's hand, though she didn't meet her eyes. "If you're determined to leave, I know of a way. I think it's safe now, or at least safer than it was." She bit her lip, as if unsure if she should continue.

"What is it?" Seraphina asked.

"I don't want you to hate me."

"I could never hate you, Jocelyn."

Finally, she looked up, her own eyelashes damp with tears. "There's a way out of the castle. A door in the keep's wall, and a gap in the wall surrounding the castle. One of the servants told me. He owed me a favor."

For a moment Seraphina wondered how long Jocelyn had known, but she decided it didn't matter. The truth was she hadn't been brave enough to leave on her own before now. Maybe she'd needed this—to have her hopes stoked by Greymont, and then dashed by the king—in order to rise to the occasion. "I know," Seraphina said. "I discovered it myself recently."

Jocelyn blinked. "Then what are you still doing here? Why haven't you left?"

Seraphina took a deep breath. "You're going to think me a fool, but I'd devised a plan."

Jocelyn arched an eyebrow. "A plan?"

"It involved Henry."

Jocelyn's other eyebrow rose to meet the first. "Oh, he's Henry now?"

Seraphina rolled her eyes. "*Lord Greymont* has a ship, and an island. I thought if I could make him fall in love with me, he would agree to take me away from Eldridge Hall, after we all watched the sunrise and saw that it was safe to leave."

Jocelyn was quiet for a long moment. "You were going to leave with Lord Greymont?"

Seraphina sighed. "I was afraid I couldn't do it on my own. I don't know what's waiting for me out there. But it's become clearer with every passing day that the king is never going to let me leave. This morning was the final proof."

"But you wouldn't have been alone. You would have had *me*."

Seraphina was surprised by the vulnerability in Jocelyn's voice. "You always tell me how fortunate we are to be here. I assumed you wouldn't want to leave."

A single tear slipped down Jocelyn's cheek. It was the first time Seraphina had seen her cry. "You're the only family I have left."

Seraphina placed her hand over Jocelyn's, her heart swelling with gratitude to have even one person in Eldridge who accepted her exactly as she was. "Of course you can come with me. I'd be a mess out there on my own. And I think it's safe to say there's no 'Prince of Pilmand' coming to save us." She paused as a couple walked by, their heads nearly touching as they whispered to each other. Behind their masks, Seraphina could feel their eyes on her, judging.

Jocelyn wrapped an arm around Seraphina, and she rested

her head on Jocelyn's thin shoulder. "You're right. You *would* be a mess out there," Jocelyn said with a laugh. "You can't even dress your own hair."

Seraphina gasped in mock offense. "I can so." She smiled to herself. "I just like it better when you do it."

"So it's settled, then? Whatever happens, we'll leave here together?"

Seraphina nodded, stifling a yawn. They sat in silence so long that Seraphina wasn't entirely sure she hadn't fallen asleep. She sat up, pressing the heels of her hands to her tired eyes. "Would you mind finding me some tea, Joc? I promise not to drink any more wine tonight, no matter how many people wish me a happy birthday."

"So that was the game you were playing?"

Seraphina laughed wryly. "Among many others."

Jocelyn nodded and rose. "Do you want help with your wings?"

She ran her hands over the feathers and frowned. "No, they're too heavy. Besides, the king seemed to be matching me glass for glass of the wine. I doubt he'll notice now."

"Very well. Think you can stay out of trouble for a few minutes?"

"I'll do my best." She waited for Jocelyn to go before rising. The time off her feet seemed to have helped. Her head was clearer, though the dim light made her feel as if she was floating as she walked down the corridor. Surely, they would be called to eat soon. Food would do her good. Food and strong black tea.

She hadn't realized she was heading toward the great hall until she heard the *boom-boom-boom* of the clock, striking what she guessed was ten o'clock. She'd lost count of the hour. The only light in the midnight chamber came from the crescent moon through the open window, swathing Seraphina in silver. There was no one here, of course. Why the king had even bothered to decorate the room was a mystery.

The wind whistled through the keyhole in the clock, and Seraphina could have sworn she smelled a whiff of decay on the breeze. Perhaps it was only the flowers decorating the hall. They were already beginning to droop in their black porcelain vases. But that was the beauty of darkness: it obscured what shouldn't be seen. By moonlight, death could masquerade as slumber.

She turned back toward the great hall's entrance, where a faint glow of candlelight beckoned her back to the hallway, and to the promise of Jocelyn's warm tea. She would be looking for Seraphina by now.

Just as she was about to leave, she heard a soft scraping noise behind her. A shiver ran up her spine. She was mere feet from the hallway. She could hear the laughter of the party coming toward her; could feel the warmth of the bodies in the other rooms. Somewhere, a dinner bell chimed, calling everyone to the feast. But something made her turn.

She didn't see it at first. It stood in front of the clock, so black it was nearly indistinguishable. Then the moonlight caught along the edge of something long and curved, like a beak. An enormous raven, as if the bird on top of the clock had grown into a giant and descended from its perch. Its black feathers were coarse and oily, and its shiny black eyes stared at her, unblinking.

A memory came to her of one harsh winter, when a raven

would come to her window every morning and peck at the glass. When she woke, she would bang on the window, but the raven wasn't afraid of her. It would continue to strike its strong beak against the glass, cocking its head at her and making a terrible noise in its throat. *Let me in*, it seemed to be saying. *Let me in or I'll break the glass myself.*

Seraphina gasped and turned, her feet tangling in her thin white skirts. The next thing she knew, she was falling.

CHAPTER 14

Nico entered the castle walls around dusk, making sure there were no servants coming in and out. As the sun began its descent toward the horizon, he crept into the clock and waited there, sweating in his cloak, itching underneath his mask, watching through the tiny keyhole in the door. No one had entered the great hall in all the time he'd waited, and he could understand why.

Someone had draped black curtains along all the windows. Black flowers filled ebony vases, sending a putridly sweet smell to him in the clock. He'd heard tales of men being buried alive, and he couldn't help imagining their final moments now, the terror of that impenetrable darkness. Every hour the clock struck three—which he found particularly disorienting—and the great chimes seemed to shake his entire body. He would have liked to have a look at the gears, clockwork being something of a fascination of his, but it was too dark to see anything beyond his own beak.

Finally, when he was beginning to doze off, the clock had chimed again, scaring him half out of his mind. He was about to burst out of the clock, entrances be damned, when he saw someone come into the room.

For a brief, disorienting moment, he thought he had died in the clock. How else to explain the angel before him? In the moonlight she seemed to glow in her simple white gown, her skin nearly as pale as the fabric. Her hair was curled and pinned half up around a gold circlet, while the rest hung in gleaming spirals nearly to her waist. Nico had never seen any of the royal family before, but he had heard about Princess Imogen's infamous auburn hair. He wanted to hate her. But she was the most beautiful thing Nico had ever seen in his life.

Nearly as quickly as she had appeared, she saw that the room was empty and turned to leave. She seemed a bit unsteady and lost, and before he knew what he was doing, he had pushed open the clock door. It made a horrendous scraping noise as it went, and he winced as the girl turned back toward the clock. It took a moment for him to register the horror on her face. Of course she was afraid! He must look like a monster in the dark. He was about to go to her when she gasped and spun away, her bare feet tangling in her skirts. She went down almost in slow motion. By the time her head hit the black marble floor, Nico was beside her.

And she was unconscious.

It was only hours ago that they had returned to their abandoned camp, where Colin had cursed Branson so creatively Nico might have been impressed under other circumstances.

"Look, nothing's changed," Nico had said as he joined Colin near their fire, which Branson hadn't even bothered extinguishing. "We didn't have a chance to assess the situation before going after Crane, true, but Branson hasn't a clue how to navigate. If anything, we're lucky to have him off our hands. I doubt he'll even make it back to the manor."

"He took Wolfbait," Colin grumbled, his chin tucked deep into the collar of his coat. Perhaps the thing that had angered him even more than being down a horse was that Branson had taken the white sable cloak. That left them with only the black cloak, which they'd agreed Nico needed for his costume.

"We didn't have any horses when we started this journey, so we're no worse off than when we began. Besides, I didn't like the way Wolfbait was eyeing Locket," he added with a smile.

Colin glared at Nico for a moment before nestling back into his coat. "What if he does make it home? Then what?"

"It's four days by horseback for a strong rider, which Branson is not. And then another four or five days back. We can certainly come up with a plan in that amount of time!"

But in the great hall, as Nico removed his mask, which they'd covered in a combination of dark mud and charcoal from the fire, he knew that their meager plan wasn't going to cut it. Underneath the cloak, which was shabby enough from days of riding that it was starting to look like feathers, Nico could never be mistaken for royalty. He touched one of the princess's bare feet with a work-worn hand and recoiled. They were as cold as ice. Where on earth were her slippers? He pulled the fur cloak over her and tapped her cheeks delicately.

Nico had spent his hours in the clock imagining hordes of frightened people to whom he would deliver an eloquent and forceful diatribe on what had been going on outside the castle walls for the past four years. He would talk about how he'd had to witness his entire family bleed to death; had spent years burying the bodies of the dead; how people who hadn't died of the plague had starved to death; how vandals and looters had destroyed homes all throughout the country.

Instead, he leaned down and whispered, "Hello? Are you all right? Please don't be frightened."

For a moment he was worried she was dead, but he leaned closer and felt a small puff of warm breath against his face. He should run and find help, but how would he explain himself? Her halo had been knocked askew in the fall and he carefully removed the few remaining pins and set it aside, checking her scalp for any lumps. Remarkably, there were none, but he smelled wine on her breath. She was probably more drunk than injured.

He removed his coat, placed it underneath her head, and rose. She was so much smaller than he would have imagined; not just petite but thin, as if she wasn't getting enough to eat. Her skin was pallid, highlighting the few freckles spattered across her nose. Her eyelashes were long and dark against her cheeks. A small, thin scar ran along her jawline on the left side of her face. *How does a princess get a scar like that?*

One of her fingers twitched. He picked up her hand, turning it over so he could check her pulse, but he needed to move one of her gloves to expose it. He pushed it back carefully and caught his breath at the bruises there. It looked as if someone had grabbed her or restrained her. Could this really be Princess Imogen, the spoiled, selfish girl the servants had described?

He checked her other wrist and noted that there was no telltale branching mark there, either. But then, no one here would have been exposed to the plague. It would be impossible to know who was an immaculate and who was immune.

He was scanning the rest of her body, or what little he could see of it, for more injuries when suddenly he had the feeling he was being watched. He turned toward her head and saw that her eyes were open. And they were the saddest eyes he'd ever seen: wide and downturned at the corners, fringed with those long lashes.

"Who are you?" she asked.

And Nico, the fool who had once fancied himself a poet, found he had no words.

CHAPTER 15

Seraphina had been awake for several minutes, but she hadn't opened her eyes, afraid of what might happen if she did. It seemed safer to pretend to be unconscious; maybe he'd get bored and leave.

But then the stranger had taken her wrist and pushed back her glove with such gentleness, touching a tentative fingertip to a bruise there so softly it didn't hurt, that she was no longer afraid. She was as vulnerable as a person could be and he hadn't tried anything malicious. If anything, he'd been astonishingly thoughtful, covering her in his cloak and placing his coat beneath her head.

The question was: Who in the bloody hell was he? She'd thought he was a monster when she first saw him, a giant, hulking crow-beast. But now she could see it was just a plague mask covered in mud—clumps of it had gotten in his hair, and there were sooty smears on his face—and a fur cloak. He didn't look anything like a prince, but then, he'd just made a long journey to get here. Who knew what horrors he'd faced? Because it had to be the prince, didn't it? Who else would even know to come here?

When his eyes began to travel over the rest of her body, she lifted her head and opened her eyes all the way.

"Who are you?" She sifted through her mind for the name of the Prince of Pilmand. "Prince Martin?"

He stared back at her blankly, and for a moment she wondered if he spoke English. What language did they speak in Pilmand? Pilmandian? Pilmandish? Was she expected to spend the rest of her life with someone she couldn't talk to?

But finally, he cleared his throat and offered her a hand. "I'm so sorry I frightened you. Can you stand?"

"I think so." She took his hand and let him help her to her feet, because she was still a little wobbly from the wine and the fall. She waited for him to say something, but he only looked around the room anxiously.

He seemed awfully unsure of himself for a prince. "I'm Princess Imogen," she said. As she curtsied, she realized her halo was missing and bent down to retrieve it. "Where is your retinue?"

"I'm afraid there was a terrible accident. We were set upon by wolves. Everyone else was killed."

She gasped and threw a hand over her mouth. "That's terrible! Have the animals gotten so bold over the years?"

"Indeed they have. The woods are not as safe as they once were. The world has changed very much in your absence, Your Highness."

He didn't look at all how she'd imagined, but underneath the soot and soiled clothing, she could see that he was handsome, with dark, intelligent eyes, a strong jaw, and the healthy complexion of someone who had spent time out of doors. "You must be exhausted. Come, meet the king. He'll be so delighted to find you here. We had all but given up hope that you'd make it."

"I can't present myself to the king like this," he said, gesturing to his clothing. "And if my costume causes maidens to faint, I should probably do something about that as well."

She laughed. "I didn't faint. I was frightened, but it was the wine that caused the fall."

"I nearly forgot. You're celebrating. Happy birthday, Your Highness."

She searched his brown eyes until he looked away. "Thank you." She realized they were still holding hands and she slipped free of his grasp, getting her bearings. The room didn't look so frightening anymore. "Come with me. I'll find you a costume and a proper mask. Then we can introduce you to the king."

He followed her to her princess chambers, where she left him in a room full of half-drunk wineglasses, discarded petticoats, and an embarrassment of fainting sofas. She returned a few minutes later with new clothing to find him rummaging through a little glass dish full of mismatched buttons.

"I see you've found my button collection," she said. She set the pile of clothing on a sofa and came to stand next to him. "They're silly, I know." She held out her hand and he placed a small wooden button he'd been examining into her palm. The bruises on her wrist were garishly green in the candlelight, but there was no sense in covering them now, when he'd already seen them.

"What are they from?" he asked, indicating the buttons.

But she was staring at his hand. "You're bleeding."

"It's nothing. Just a scratch from a nail by the window. They were boarded up, I take it?"

"Until today." She went to a dresser and pulled open a drawer, returning a moment later with a fine hand-embroidered handkerchief. She pressed it to his wound, and he stared at her with his mouth slightly agape. A princess was probably supposed to be squeamish.

When she was satisfied the bleeding had stopped, she dipped the kerchief in a water basin and wiped away the excess blood. "I found you something else to wear." She gestured to the folded pile of dark clothing. On top was a proper mask of black porcelain, though one with a long nose reminiscent of his plague doctor's mask.

"Thank you." He picked up the mask, turning it over in his hands. "How have you all managed to survive in the castle for so long, Your Highness?"

Seraphina sat down on one of the sofas. If there was any way to respond without making them all sound cruel and selfish, she didn't know it. "My father collected supplies from all his subjects, then barred the doors."

"And the subjects? What of them?"

She shook her head and lowered her eyes, images of her parents and Dalia flooding her mind. "I imagine they suffered greatly."

He was silent for a long moment. "Yes, I imagine they did."

Her cheeks heated at the implication in his tone as guilt, shame, and defensiveness welled within her. She couldn't bite her tongue fast enough. "Things are not what they seem at Eldridge Hall, Prince Martin. I implore you to remember that."

He started. "Is that a threat, Your Highness?"

"A warning."

"Then I should warn you, Princess, that things are not what they seem outside the castle, either. The world is greatly changed since you locked yourself inside these walls."

She rose, lifting her chin despite the shame still washing over her. "Please, get changed and I will take you to the king. He will be eager to meet you, and I am eager to get something into my belly other than sparkling wine. They're serving swan, I believe."

Seraphina thought she knew what noblemen's hands felt like: as smooth as her butter-soft leather slippers. But the stranger's hands were rough and callused, his skin browned in the places where the sun would have touched it. As they neared the dining room, he tensed beside her. She placed a reassuring hand on his forearm and felt that it was corded with muscle beneath his shirt. Whatever life in Pilmand had been like these past few years, it was very different from Eldridge Hall. Perhaps nobility in Pilmand weren't afraid of a bit of hard labor.

She wished she had asked him more about the world outside, but that would have to wait until the king was tucked in bed. He may have been willing to invite a stranger to the castle to marry his favorite daughter, but that didn't mean he was ready to hear about the man-eating wolves and suffering outside the castle walls. If, in his fantasy world, the plague had never existed at all, then Prince Martin himself would need to tread carefully. She was just grateful she'd recovered her own wits by the time the prince found her—or that her fall had knocked them back into her. If they'd crossed paths earlier in the evening, before she'd sobered up, she would have told him anything he'd wished to know, including her secrets.

When they entered the room, the clinking of cutlery and hum of chatter came to a halt as everyone stopped to look at them. Seraphina beamed brightly and walked straight to the king.

"Look, Father. I've found my birthday surprise. Prince Martin has made it to us. It's a true miracle."

She could feel the prince's eyes on her, but she had no idea what was going through his head.

The king rose and the prince bowed smoothly. "Your Majesty," he said as he straightened. "I am so pleased to meet you, finally."

"Prince Martin! We are delighted to have you!" The king pulled him into an embrace. "Please, have a seat. You must tell us about your journey. We were beginning to think you wouldn't make it."

King Stuart gestured to the two empty seats beside him, saved for the prince and Seraphina. "Please, sit."

"I'm afraid the journey was not a pleasant one," the prince said. "We were attacked by a pack of wolves. The rest of my party was killed. It's a miracle I made it here at all, as Princess Imogen said."

Seraphina steeled herself and watched the king closely, to see how he would react to such news, but he only nodded. "Well, we are certainly happy you did make it," the king said. "We held this masquerade as much for you as we did for my darling Genny. I'm so glad she found you first. I'm sure you're already as enchanted with her as the rest of us."

He glanced at her from the corner of his eye. "Oh yes, Your Majesty. She is charming, indeed."

Something in his tone rang of insincerity, though the king was as oblivious as always. She turned to her other side, where

Henry was sitting. "Allow me to introduce you to Prince Martin," she said. "Prince Martin, Lord Greymont."

Henry inclined his head, but he barely managed to suppress the scowl twisting his mouth. Seraphina almost felt sorry for him, after she'd offered him hope. But nothing was set in stone yet. She wasn't sure the prince would *want* to marry her, once he got to know her better. Clearly, he disapproved of the court's behavior, though she couldn't blame him for that.

"Please, Prince Martin, tell us about Pilmand. I had heard yours was a pale and fair-haired people, owing to the climate in your country." Henry stared pointedly at the stranger's dark hair.

"Like Goslind, our people vary in appearance. Tell me, have you studied Pilmand much?"

"No more than any other country."

Prince Martin smiled. "Ah, I see. That explains your confusion."

"You misunderstand me. I have studied the history and geography of our continent quite thoroughly. We've had four years with not much in the way of diversion. Aside from our company in the castle, of course," Henry added with a smirk at Seraphina.

The prince's lip curled in barely concealed disdain. "I beg your pardon. *Diversion* hasn't been high on my list of priorities lately."

Seraphina had been enjoying watching the men posture while she ate the delicacies brought to her by the servants, but she didn't appreciate Henry's insinuation that she was merely a recreational activity for him. She cleared her throat loudly.

Henry deflated a little and turned back to the prince. "I

wonder if you can tell us more about the world outside the castle walls, Prince Martin."

Seraphina wanted to kick him under the table, her gaze darting pointedly to the king, but fortunately, he was dozing.

The prince fixed his dark eyes on Seraphina, and for some reason she flushed. His words, and his glances, were more frank than any she'd experienced here in the castle, including Henry's. "We can talk about that another time. It's Princess Imogen's birthday, after all. We should be celebrating."

The king perked up suddenly. "Celebrating! Yes! Come, let us return to the ballroom for a while. My daughter only turns twenty once."

Seraphina almost laughed at the irony. She had misplaced her mask, and her wings were long forgotten, but she took the prince's arm and escorted him to the white room. She was glad he didn't don his own mask. Every time she saw it, she remembered the moment she'd first encountered him in the great hall and shuddered.

Why didn't he come through the front door? she wondered. Most men here would have sauntered right up, expecting a retinue to greet them upon arrival. And he was a prince. Why sneak in like a thief in the night? Unless he was afraid of them, too. Perhaps he'd wanted a chance to suss them out before revealing himself.

She was surprised he'd even found the door to the clock. Was it so obvious from outside the castle? If so, they were fortunate no one else had snuck into the castle all these years.

"Tell me, Princess Imogen," he said as they took their places on the dance floor. "What is it like to be the king's favorite daughter?" His eyes traveled to Giselle, who was preparing to dance with the king. She was glaring at Seraphina, not even bothering to hide her annoyance.

Seraphina arched an eyebrow. "How do you know I'm his favorite?"

"Rumors."

"All the way in Pilmand? I had no idea I was so famous." Seraphina placed her hand on the prince's shoulder, once again noticing with a shock how much bigger he was than Henry, who had always seemed so solid and strong to her; his transformation, like all of theirs, had been slow.

She scanned the room and found Nina giggling at something Lord Basilton whispered in her ear. Rose was standing with her attendants, gossiping, no doubt. "My sisters are happy so long as the king is happy," she said finally.

"And what about you?" the stranger asked, his eyes meeting hers. "Are you happy?"

Seraphina blinked. In four years not a single person had asked her if she was happy. What a ridiculous notion, that she could be happy in circumstances such as hers. She remembered his finger against her bruised wrist and wondered what he'd made of it, what he'd made of a spoiled girl having a ridiculously lavish birthday party while the outside world rotted.

Henry watched her from across the room, his eyes large in his too-thin face, and she wondered, if she stood next to the girl she'd been four years ago—the last time she'd been happy—would she even recognize herself?

"Why wouldn't I be happy?" she asked Prince Martin as the musicians began to play. "I'm a princess."

CHAPTER 16

Princess Imogen's hair was so long it tickled Nico's hand as he placed it on her narrow waist. From here he was looking down at the top of her head, where the roots of her hair were a golden-blond. It must be the light from the chandelier reflecting off her crown. He remembered Elisabeth's shining hair when she'd embraced him and swallowed down the bile in his throat. He almost shuddered to think of how defenseless these people would be to the likes of Crane, or Arnaud. "The king seems very happy tonight. Of course, I've never met him before, but he is rumored to have a temper."

"The king is…unpredictable," she said, choosing her words carefully. "None of us even dare to mention the plague in his presence. You are lucky he is in a good mood tonight." She turned her face up to his. "Tell me, Prince Martin. Are we to leave for Pilmand at once? I am eager to experience the world outside."

He swallowed. When he'd decided to impersonate a dead prince, he hadn't thought things through beyond getting inside and warning the inhabitants. Now he was to take the princess to Pilmand? How, exactly, would he manage that? It was seeming more and more likely that the late Prince Martin had been invited here as a marriage match for Princess Imogen. Rather unfortunate, then, that she'd landed herself a grave digger instead.

Deflect, he thought. *Deflect and distract. If you tell her who you are now, you'll end up dead without warning anyone about Crane.* "That depends, Princess Imogen. I assume you'll want to be married first."

A sly grin curled her soft lips. "Eager to experience things *inside* this castle, are you, Your Highness?"

He glanced around the room, his entire face on fire—she couldn't possibly be suggesting what he thought she was—where dozens of masked nobles watched them. There was something menacing about them, pale and thin as they were, swathed in their finery like a ballroom full of ghosts. He despised them for their willful ignorance, their useless manicured hands and silken frippery, but to allow them to die wouldn't bring back all the good people lost to the plague. It would only add more suffering to a world drowning in sorrow.

The king, who had made it through half a song before returning to his throne, was also watching them behind his blank white mask. The music was coming to an end, but he was reluctant to let go of Princess Imogen. Spoiled though she may be, she seemed safer than the rest of them.

"You said your entourage was attacked by wolves," Imogen said, sparing him from answering, all the while giving him another equally perilous test. "How did they manage to overtake you? Surely you had weapons to defend yourselves with."

"We weren't expecting it, I'm afraid. Pilmand...ian wolves

are far more interested in caribou than men." He hoped he sounded convincing, and thought of what the servants outside the castle had said about "predators." They were the people he really needed to speak to.

"Please, tell me more about Pilmand. If it is to be my new home, I should like to know what to expect."

"It's cold," Nico said, beginning to sweat in his fancy tunic. "Except for the summers, which are short."

"And the plague? How did your people fare?"

He swallowed. "We were fortunate. The mori roja didn't make it quite so far north," he said, thinking of the real prince and his retinue. They had appeared well fed, not starving like the people here. He imagined Pilmand would have had enough warning of the plague to close its borders, but that was pure conjecture.

"How did my father contact you? I didn't realize he was in communication with anyone outside the castle all this time."

Nico was saved from the princess's interrogation by the dance finally coming to an end. He stopped and bowed to her, grimacing as a drop of sweat rolled off his chin. He had to extricate himself from the situation before he blew his cover. "I've just realized how tired I am," he said as the musicians began to play a waltz. "Would you—could you show me to my room?"

Her eyes widened and he realized what he'd just asked of her. But before he could apologize, Lord Greymont appeared at his shoulder.

"I'll be happy to take you," he said. "The princess has had a very long night."

"We all have," she said, bowing her head. Her sad brown

eyes met Nico's, and he found himself unable to reconcile the bruises and the scar, the bare feet and thin frame, with the girl he had heard the servants describe outside the castle. "Good night, Your Highness."

For a moment his mind was a complete blank. Without missing a beat, the princess raised her wrist to him, and he took it, pressing a swift kiss to the back of it. "Good night, Princess."

He turned and bowed to the king, his mouth as dry as cotton gauze. "Your Majesty."

"Good night, Prince Martin! Tomorrow you'll get to know my darling Genny better. We'll play chess. But be warned, I'm a formidable adversary."

Before Nico could respond, Lord Greymont took a hold of him a little more roughly than necessary. "Follow me."

Of all the people who could have offered to help him, Lord Greymont was the last person Nico would have chosen. He was obviously jealous, though he must have known about Prince Martin. Maybe he hadn't believed the prince would come, and that he could marry the princess himself. And why not? The real prince was dead. Nico would clearly not be marrying her. But of course, he couldn't tell Lord Greymont any of that.

"Your journey sounds harrowing," he said to Nico as they walked down a corridor past several other colorful rooms. "You must be grateful to have made it here, and to find such a beautiful bride waiting for you."

Nico didn't like the possessive tone in Greymont's voice. "She is beautiful, yes. And clearly beloved."

"By the king, you mean," Greymont said pointedly.

Nico let the silence answer for him. "I do wonder, however, what kind of person demands an elaborate masquerade when so many are going hungry."

At this, Lord Greymont whirled on his heels and thrust a finger into Nico's chest. He'd clearly touched a nerve, and Nico was thankful he had a good twenty pounds on the lord. "You don't know her at all."

"And you do?" Nico asked, keeping his tone neutral, though his meaning was anything but.

"If you're implying that any impropriety occurred between Imo—" Lord Greymont cut himself off abruptly. "Between the princess and me, you are wrong. I am fond of her, yes, but so are we all."

Nico knew that, at least, was a lie. He'd seen the way the middle sister, Giselle, glared at Imogen. The way some of the nobles whispered every time the princess passed by.

Greymont stopped in front of a room and opened the door. "I take it this will be good enough for Your Highness."

Nico poked his head in. The room was far grander than anything at Crane Manor, with a large four-poster bed covered by a plush comforter that practically begged Nico to dive into it. "It will do nicely, thank you."

"If that will be all, I'll leave you to your rest." He seemed to have recovered some of his composure, though he ground out his words through clenched teeth.

"Thank you so much for your hospitality, Lord Greymont. I look forward to getting to know you, and the princess, better in the days to come."

Greymont gave a quick, perfunctory bow and disappeared into the hallway. As soon as he was gone, Nico closed the door and locked it. Part of him wanted to leap onto the bed—

somehow, someway, he'd done it! But another part of him was terrified. He was trapped inside the castle, with no friends, no way to communicate with Colin, and no real way out. Someone would surely notice if he disappeared.

He undressed and settled himself in what was without question the most comfortable bed he'd ever slept in. He thought of Colin, out there in the cold and dark, and wished that he were here, too. But Imogen might not have trusted him if he hadn't been alone. As it was, if she continued to pepper him with questions, his story would fall to pieces. Especially with Lord Greymont watching him like a hawk.

The quiet was disconcerting. Nico hadn't slept alone in a room in years. The nocturnal stirrings of the forest were better than this silence. He tossed and turned, his thoughts returning to Crane again and again. Nico estimated that they had at least a week before he arrived, but eventually he'd have to tell the king that Crane was coming. Somehow. And what could he say that wouldn't reveal his true identity, or worse, make him seem insane? Crane was just one man against hundreds, and so far all Nico really knew was that he had killed Elisabeth, though he strongly suspected he'd killed other people as well.

Nico suspected he'd killed other *immaculates*, anyway. Like himself, and everyone else who lived at Crane Manor had been, the immunes in the castle, if there were any, would be safe. For the moment, at least, the inhabitants of Eldridge Hall were far better off than anyone Nico had encountered outside it.

As the downy comforter swaddled him like a baby, he thought of Imogen's room with its mirrored vanity and fainting sofas, and the feast in the dining room below. There was a tempting illusion of safety here, but it was just that: an illusion. A beautiful, elaborate lie. If he'd had the same opportunity to hole up here while the world around him crumbled and fell, would he have been brave enough to leave? Deep down, he knew the answer was no. He hadn't even ventured beyond Crane's lands until now, and no deluded ruler was keeping him prisoner.

At some point he would have to tell Imogen and the others the truth about the world outside the castle walls, that though the plague might indeed be eradicated, there were other dangers lurking. Dangers like Arnaud and Crane, and God only knew what else.

There were no swans at Eldridge Hall; only sitting ducks.

CHAPTER 17

When Henry led the prince away, Seraphina granted a few more men dances before thanking the king for the party and excusing herself. Henry hadn't returned, but she had a feeling it was better not to see him again tonight. His jealousy of Prince Martin was undeniable, if unfair. The prince couldn't have known what he was walking into, and she'd only known of his existence for a few days.

She walked upstairs to her tiny room, some part of her wishing he could see where she really slept, knowing that he thought her an overindulged child. His presence made her feel guilty for things she knew she hadn't chosen, but which she hadn't fought hard enough to deny. Even if he saw the ways she punished herself, even if it made her a little less odious in his eyes, she still had to live with herself. Besides, blowing her cover wouldn't help her get out of here. For now she had to remain the spoiled princess.

She removed the white gown and the rest of the jeweled hairpins. Now that all the windows of the castle were open, the one in her tower didn't feel quite so special, but she went to it anyway. At first, she thought she was seeing things when she noticed the tiny yellow light near the trees. But no, it was definitely there. A campfire.

Worry twisted her already wine-soured stomach. The prince had said his retinue was dead, that he was alone. So who was camping outside the castle walls? Some other stranger? Now that the windows were open and there was an apparently discoverable way into the castle, were they suddenly exposed to anyone who might desire entrance?

She'd barely had a moment to talk to Jocelyn after discovering the prince, and Jocelyn had peppered her with questions about him, questions Seraphina had no answers for. Now a sliver of doubt burrowed beneath her skin. The plague was gone, according to the prince, but that did not mean its survivors were all honorable, or—if the prince's attitude was any indication—that they'd take kindly to those who'd sat out the plague within the castle walls in relative comfort.

In the morning she went downstairs for breakfast to find the prince already there, wearing a fresh set of clothing a servant must have provided.

When she took her seat next to Henry, he leaned in, his expression inscrutable.

"Good morning, Princess."

She inclined her head. "Lord Greymont."

"I trust you slept well?"

"As well as can be expected. I'm afraid I had a little too much to drink last night."

He smiled blandly. There were dark circles under his eyes and his hair was disheveled, and she wondered if he'd slept at all. She remembered the kiss they'd shared in the cellar with a pang, then glanced at the prince, who was watching her with a curious expression.

"Good morning, Prince Martin."

He nodded. "Your Highness."

"Genny," the king said suddenly. "Why don't you show Prince Martin around the castle? I'm sure he'd love a tour."

"From me, Father?" Seraphina asked softly. She remembered the fire she'd seen in the woods last night and felt a small flicker of doubt. The prince didn't *seem* dangerous, but she of all people knew better than to trust appearances.

"Of course, my dear," the king said. "You can't very well marry him if you can't even show him the armory."

She rose, indicating that Prince Martin should follow her. She could feel Henry's eyes on her as they left the room.

They walked in silence to the library, Jocelyn trailing several feet behind. At least they wouldn't be completely alone, and the library, which hadn't been decorated for the masquerade, was the same warm, inviting room it had always been.

The prince turned in a slow circle, marveling at the shelves and shelves full of books. He reminded Seraphina of the first time she'd been to the library. She remembered thinking that Dalia wouldn't believe her if she told her that all these books were unique, that every single one she opened was full of words on every subject under the sun and beyond. History, science, philosophy, art. The sheer amount of information in the world was overwhelming sometimes.

He pulled a book off a nearby shelf and scanned the pages. She thought she heard him inhale as he flipped through. "How fortunate you are, to have access to all this."

She wished she could explain what this room represented

for her. She never would have had the opportunity to read—not out of necessity, but for the sheer pleasure of it—if she hadn't come to Eldridge. Her education was the only good thing about her life here. "Extremely fortunate," she said instead. "But you must have a similar library in Pilmand?"

He cleared his throat. "Of course. I just haven't had much time for reading of late."

He couldn't resist taking shots at her, could he? She sat down on a leather sofa and gestured for him to sit in one of the armchairs facing her. Someone must have provided him a bath; his hair was clean and combed, hanging nearly to his shoulders, and he had shaved away the week of stubble on his strong jaw. He looked younger now, probably only a few years older than her real age. He had the straight-backed posture she would expect of a prince, but his eyes were bright and guileless, so unlike the haughty half-lidded gaze of men like Henry.

She fiddled with one of the ribbons on her wrist, remembering the way he'd touched her there. Once again, she found herself wishing she could tell him the truth about who she was. She hadn't felt judged by the other nobles at the castle these past few years; they were all complicit in the same lie. But Prince Martin clearly hadn't left his people to die, and his innocence made her guilt all the more painful.

"What is the world outside the castle really like, Prince Martin? Aside from man-eating wolves, which we will clearly need to arm ourselves against, what can we expect?"

He settled back into the armchair as if he was about to tell a story. "Very well, Princess. I will tell you. Please, close your eyes."

She scoffed. "What?"

"Close your eyes. You won't be able to picture it fully if you're gazing at a grand library in a castle." He grinned and closed his own eyes, and once Seraphina was sure they would stay closed, she did the same. "Now, imagine the world as it was before the plague. That should be fairly easy for you, since you haven't been out of the castle since."

She rolled her eyes beneath her lids. "Yes, we've established that."

"Good. Now imagine your subjects' fields turned fallow, corpses left to rot, nearly all the domestic animals slaughtered for food long ago. Imagine a world without people, or very few. The villages have all been abandoned. Cities are even worse."

"Why?" she asked around the lump forming in her throat.

"Because the survivors are fighting for whatever scraps are left. The infrastructure is crumbling with no one to care for it. The sewers..." He cleared his throat. "Well, I'll leave that to your imagination."

She wanted to ask him about the Jews, but she couldn't, and not only because she was too afraid of the answer. In her mind's eye, she saw her mother, her father, Dalia, as the corpses that Prince Martin asked her to imagine. She saw her own home, once warm with candlelight, barren and combed over. "Does anyone survive?" she asked softly.

"Yes. There are people who have immunity to the mori roja. No one understands why, but they survive. They witness horrible, devastating things, but they live. Life is not what it once was, of course. Everyone has lost someone, and that trauma leaves an indelible mark. Joy feels selfish, unearned, so people repress it. They keep their dark thoughts to themselves; everyone has enough pain of their own."

The way he spoke, it was as if he'd experienced these things somehow, but the plague hadn't reached Pilmand. Had he seen all this on his travels here? She may not have been around to watch everything fall apart, but she knew about loss and trauma. She knew what it meant to feel guilty for every positive emotion. She'd felt it every day here for the past four years, because although no one had ever spoken these things aloud to her with such candor, she'd known the world outside here had been burning, and likely her family along with it.

The king hadn't just invited a prince to Eldridge Hall. He'd invited the truth. And like death, there would be no escaping it.

"Though humans are remarkably adaptable, in the end," he continued. "Eventually, the people who were in hiding start to come out. They find each other. The lucky few might even find their loved ones alive."

He stopped speaking suddenly and Seraphina blinked her eyes open. The prince was staring at her, his brow furrowed.

She dried her tears with a handkerchief and nodded for him to continue.

"I…" He seemed at war with himself, and for a moment she had the sense he was going to reveal something personal. But then he straightened, his jaw clenched. "You've been living in a fantasy these past few years, Princess Imogen. I know that isn't what you want to hear, but it's the truth. Your father has cost thousands of people their lives. *You* have cost them their lives."

His eyes met hers, and there was no trace of the man who had found her passed out on the hall floor. No more sympathy or compassion. Only resentment.

She could have accepted his disapproval, or even ignored it. But his words stirred up resentment of her own. This *fantasy* hadn't been her choice. She would have taken the horrors of reality, even her own death, over this, if anyone had ever bothered to ask.

She lifted her chin, forcing herself not to look away.

"Tell me, Prince Martin. What have *you* done to help?"

CHAPTER 18

For a moment Nico had considered telling Princess Imogen the truth. Spoiled though she may be, she was at least capable of compassion, given the tears in her eyes. She'd been, what, sixteen when the plague began? Not a child, but not an adult, either, and it wasn't her fault she'd never known hardship. Nico hadn't, either, before the plague.

At the same time, she hadn't seen the bodies or the devastation. She hadn't lost the people she loved. His bitterness toward a woman he was supposed to want to marry was seeping through his facade, and she had grown defensive, just as he was now. If he was to continue this charade, he had to behave like a prince who'd spent the past four years largely removed from the mori roja, not like a grave digger who'd been in the trenches. He wasn't being careful enough. He wished Colin were here to encourage him. Even Branson would have played this role better.

He decided to change the subject. "Do you know if anyone in this castle has immunity?"

She softened a bit at his tone. "You mean blood immunity? I don't know. The plague hadn't reached the J— Hadn't reached here when the king locked the gates."

"I see. For all we know, no one here is immune."

"Or maybe we all are. I don't see how we could know, one way or the other. Tell me, how can we be sure the plague is really gone if the only people still out there all have immunity? If, as you say, some of us in the castle aren't immune, how can we know it's safe to emerge?"

"You misunderstand. Everyone who encounters the plague dies from it, unless they are immune. But there are immaculates as well. People who never encountered the plague at all—either because they were sequestered someplace, as you all have been, or because it never reached their land, as with my people. There are immaculates out there now, living, and in good health. The plague is gone."

"Immaculates," she said as if she'd never heard the term before. "Isolated people like those of us here in Eldridge." She seemed far away for a moment, and then she blinked and sat up straighter. "Then if there are these so-called immaculates out there, there's no reason to remain locked up here in the castle."

But there was. He should tell her about Crane. He had a week at most before the monster descended upon the castle. But once he revealed that he had impersonated a dead prince to gain access not only to the castle, but also to *her*, he would lose her trust entirely. Right now it was extremely fragile, and he needed her help if he was going to persuade the entire castle that they were in danger.

"Do you really think your father will let everyone leave?" he asked, sidestepping her question. "He seems rather content here. Everyone does. You yourself said he won't tolerate any mention of the plague."

She stared down at her hands and played with the ribbons wound around her wrists. He thought again of the bruises there. Had Lord Greymont done that to her? Had the king? "He will not like it."

"But he'll want to leave, too, won't he? Once he knows the plague is gone?"

"I don't pretend to know the king's mind." She swallowed and looked up at Nico. "But I will go with you when you leave, if you'll take me. I will marry you."

For the second time since encountering her, he was rendered speechless. Why would a girl who lived in relative luxury and safety be willing to marry and leave with a complete stranger? Whatever she thought of Nico—and she certainly didn't seem enamored so far, not that he blamed her—she apparently thought less of her life at Eldridge. But bruises or no, there was no way she could understand what things were like outside the castle. He obviously wasn't going to marry her, but that didn't mean he wanted to leave everyone here to die at the hands of a monster.

"Don't you think you need a little more time to make that decision? You hardly know me."

"I was planning to leave Eldridge Hall anyway, after my birthday." She raised her chin as if to challenge his disbelief. "I'm resolved to go. Even if I have to do so on my own."

There was clearly more to her situation than he understood. But no matter what her reason for leaving was, she wouldn't survive out there alone. He shook his head adamantly. "No, Princess. You can't do that."

"Why not?"

"I've already told you. There are wolves. Thieves. It's not safe."

She pursed her lips. "If it's safe enough for everyone else who doesn't have the good fortune to be locked in a castle, it will be safe enough for me. After all, I have enough blood on my hands, as you so bluntly pointed out. Staying will only sully me further."

He ran his hands through his hair, surprised when his fingers didn't catch on a snarl. He hadn't been this clean in years. "I can't guarantee your safety beyond these walls."

"I *am* leaving, one way or another. With you, with Lord Greymont, or alone."

The thought of Imogen at the mercy of Arnaud or Crane, who would stop at nothing to get their hands on someone like her, made his stomach turn with disgust. However much he disapproved of King Stuart and his court, he could never live with himself if he failed to protect yet another innocent.

And there were hundreds of other innocent people here at the castle. It would be wrong to spare her and abandon all of them. He needed to at least tell King Stuart the truth; after that, it would be up to him to decide what to do with it.

"I will take you, Princess Imogen. But not just yet. Can you spare a few more days?"

She watched him for a moment, but he couldn't read her thoughts. Part of him wished she would leave with Lord Greymont and take the decision away from him. He wouldn't abandon her, but he was still daunted by the prospect of being responsible for another person's life. He was happy to treat a broken fingernail or a twisted ankle, but he'd never done anything more serious than that. When it came to everyone in his family, he'd failed them all miserably. His mother most of all. He could still remember how she'd clung to him as she died, begging for mercy.

Do I even still want to be a physician? he wondered. If so, he would have to assume responsibility for someone's life. For many lives, if he was any good at his job. You couldn't cure a plague if you weren't willing to face its devastation. And you couldn't save a life if it was never at risk in the first place.

Imogen finally seemed to come to a conclusion and nodded. "I've waited nearly four years," she said. "I suppose a few more days won't kill me."

As much as he hated to admit it, Nico was beginning to understand why Lord Greymont hadn't left Eldridge Hall. Why *none* of them had. Nico was treated like the prince the king believed him to be. There were no graves to dig, no silver to polish. Imogen's sisters fawned over him to the point of such ridiculousness, he almost wished Branson were there to see it. He felt terribly guilty, knowing Colin was out in the forest freezing, but so far he'd hardly had a moment to himself. Reporting back to his friend was proving more difficult than he'd imagined.

Imogen sat back with a wry grin while her sisters flirted with him, ever the haughty, aloof princess. Once, when Princess Nina had insisted on playing a game of cards with him, Nico had looked to Imogen helplessly. She had laughed and whispered in his ear, "Don't worry, Prince Martin. Nina doesn't bite…much."

Nico had gone scarlet to the tips of his ears, and Imogen had laughed until she snorted, earning her admonishing glances from everyone else in the room. Nico, on the other hand, had found it almost…endearing.

But other times he found her intolerable, like when she laughed too loudly at Lord Greymont's jokes, or clapped her hands like a child when her father praised her. And though she obeyed King Stuart every time he asked her to spend time with Nico, her behavior in his presence was strange. When it was just the two of them—and Jocelyn, for Princess Imogen didn't seem to go anywhere without her—her posture softened, and even he had to admit she disarmed him with her kindness to her lady-in-waiting. The moment another servant entered, however, she would sit up straight, raising her chin and making demands without looking the poor soul in the eye.

On his third full day at Eldridge, Nico and Imogen found themselves playing chess while the king and their attendants looked on. Fortunately, the best that could be said of either of them was that they were competent players, and the game didn't last long.

"Genny, won't you sing something for Prince Martin?" the king asked. "He should get to know all of your finest qualities."

Imogen bowed her head and made her way to the pianoforte, where Rose, the golden-haired beauty with the somewhat blank expression, had been playing softly.

Nico turned to watch as Rose and Imogen agreed on a song. Rose played well, as was expected of a woman of her pedigree, but it was Imogen he couldn't take his eyes off. Her voice was soft and tremulous at first, but there was a sweetness to it, coupled with her sad eyes, that stirred something in him.

The song was about young lovers separated by their families. Imogen sang of wilted roses and nights of dark despair, her own eyes shiny with tears, as though she were that girl.

Just before the song finished, Imogen's eyes met Nico's, and the lump that had been forming in his throat became almost painful. Nico hadn't wept in years, not since his mother died, but if he'd been alone, he might have wept then.

The final notes of the song were as melancholy as the words, something about "never to be seen again," and Nico noticed that even the king was teary-eyed.

When Imogen finished, she curtsied to her father and returned to her seat next to Nico. Nina had taken Imogen's place and as she and Rose began to perform an uplifting song to lighten the somber mood, he leaned toward her.

"That was lovely," he murmured.

Her lips twitched in a small smile. "I'm glad you think so."

"Why did you choose that song?" he asked after a brief silence.

She released a sigh and turned to face him, as though she had no interest in conversation with him. "It was my mother's favorite."

"Ah yes, the queen. I've heard she was a great beauty."

A strange look passed over Imogen's features, but it was so brief that Nico couldn't read it. "Yes, I believe she was."

Suddenly, a cat jumped onto Imogen's lap, startling both of them, and she let out a surprised laugh.

"Fig, really," she said as the black cat curled into her lap. "You'll shed all over me." But despite her feigned annoyance, she stroked the cat's head and scratched behind its ears while it purred contentedly. She turned her face to Nico. "Do you like cats, Prince Martin?"

"My mother was allergic to cats. The only one we had lived in the barn." He smiled. "I'm more of a dog person, to be honest."

"We had a dog when I was young. Her name was—" She cut herself off so abruptly Nico wondered if the cat had scratched her, but he was still purring blissfully in her lap.

"Yes?" Nico prompted.

"Excuse me," Imogen said, setting the cat on the floor. "I'm not feeling well."

Nico didn't see her for the rest of the day, which finally gave him the opportunity to explore the castle on his own, making sure there wasn't some other entrance he didn't know about. Now, at last, was his chance to talk to Colin. He decided at dinner—the princess still markedly absent—that he would have to sneak out in the middle of the night to report what he'd learned and pray that he was able to get back into the castle without being caught.

After everyone had gone to bed and the halls were quiet, he snuck out of his room with a single candle and made his way to the great hall. The infernal clock boomed out its three chimes, nearly scaring the wits out of him, but he managed to slip out without incident. He breathed in the fresh night air, realizing for the first time how stuffy the castle was, despite its massive size. It was a cold night, dipping toward freezing, and he hoped he wasn't going to find Colin's frozen corpse when he arrived.

To his relief, he found his friend sleeping next to the dying embers of a fire. Gently, he nudged Colin awake.

He sat up with a start. "Bloody hell, you scared the wits out of me, Nico!"

"I'm sorry," Nico said, sitting down on the ground next to him.

"I thought you were dead. You've been gone four extremely cold nights."

Good God, had it really been so long? He had to tell the king about Crane tomorrow. It couldn't wait. And yet, the idea of telling the king terrified him. "I couldn't get out in the daytime. I'm under too much scrutiny."

"So you've done it?" Colin asked, his eyes wide with amazement. "They bought the whole *prince* scheme?"

Nico laughed at the impossibility of it. "I suppose they did. The only problem is they believe I'm alone—I told them the rest of my retinue was mauled by wolves—so I've got no way of getting *you* in."

Colin brushed some leaf litter off his hair. "I've been all right. I went hunting yesterday and caught a rabbit. But it *is* getting cold, and Branson will be back at Crane Manor by now."

"I know. I just haven't figured out how to tell everyone that they're in danger." He let out a deep breath. "To be honest, I'm not sure they're *in* danger from Crane. The castle is well fortified. If we lock the door in the clock, he won't get in. It might be best for everyone if they stay hidden."

"I'd be inclined to agree with you, if I hadn't caught Arnaud sniffing around my campsite while you were off playing prince."

"What?" Nico's stomach turned with involuntary fear as he remembered the man's bloodshot eyes.

"I didn't actually see him," Colin explained. "But I heard him last night. I think he wanted me to know he was there."

"How can you be sure it was Arnaud?"

"Just a hunch, I suppose. But I can't help thinking there are more of them, Nico. And everyone who isn't immune is in danger from them. You saw what happened when we tried to kill him."

"Nothing," Nico conceded. "I keep searching for a scientific explanation, but—"

"I think maybe you just have to accept that this time, there isn't one."

Nico nodded, though inside he still felt certain there was an underlying disease responsible for this, along with every other plague. Because if there wasn't one, there could be no cure, and Nico refused to live in that world.

"What do we do in the meantime?" he asked finally. "It doesn't seem fair that I'm in there eating like a king and sleeping on a cloud while you're out here."

"I'm all right," Colin assured him, and Nico was once again grateful for such an easygoing, amiable friend. "Maybe next time you come, you can bring me some of that king's food, though."

"Oh, that reminds me." Nico reached into his pocket and pulled out a fresh roll and a small pat of butter. "It's not much, but hopefully it tides you over till I can make it back."

Colin smiled and took the food. "I don't suppose there's any king's whiskey to go with it?"

Nico laughed, feeling lighter than he had in days. "I'll bring that next time, too."

CHAPTER 19

For the first few days of Prince Martin's visit, Seraphina managed to put on her Imogen act rather brilliantly, if she did say so herself. She pretended to find him interesting, though not *too* interesting, and she pretended to find him handsome, though not *too* handsome. Neither was particularly difficult, if she was being honest. Henry, for his part, acted appropriately jealous—although perhaps he wasn't acting. And her sisters, who should have been delighted that she'd be leaving soon, seemed appropriately jealous, too.

She'd only slipped up once, when she nearly revealed the name of her childhood dog, Gittel. She would never have been able to explain how a gentile princess happened to have a dog with a Yiddish name. Still, Prince Martin had seemed smitten enough with her singing performance that she hoped that was what he'd taken away from their conversation.

On the fourth night, when dinner was served and the portions were noticeably smaller than they had been following the masquerade, Seraphina glanced at the prince to see if he noticed and found him already looking at her. They both blinked and turned away, Seraphina's cheeks heating in embarrassment. Henry, seated beside her, pursed his lips but didn't say anything.

The decorations from the party had come down, at least, and the castle was as "normal" as it ever was. King Stuart seemed more tired than he had been before the ball, but that was to be expected. All the excitement had clearly exhausted him.

Seraphina was in the king's chambers for her midday visit, playing the world's longest chess game, when he placed his hand over hers.

"Genny, now that you've had some time to get to know Prince Martin, I want to know what you think of him."

His hand was soft and dry, and as delicate as a young girl's. He'd never done physical labor, had never even been to war. He had inherited a prosperous kingdom from his own battle-hardened father, and until the mori roja, he'd never faced a moment of adversity.

"I like him," Seraphina said, but inside she hadn't entirely worked out how she felt about him. He was clearly intelligent, and funny in an accidental sort of way, but he wasn't witty and flirtatious like Henry. He was frank and thoughtful and a little shy. In fact, it was hard to imagine him ruling a kingdom, small though it may be. She'd asked Jocelyn what she made of him, but Jocelyn had been oddly quiet on the subject. Seraphina assumed it was because Jocelyn was being protective of her.

But she supposed she didn't need to like him. She just needed to trust him to keep her and Jocelyn safe when they left Eldridge Hall.

The king's eyes lit up. "Delightful! A wedding will be just

the thing. There will be another feast to plan. Another masquerade, perhaps. With jesters this time…" He trailed off, and Seraphina wasn't sure if he was remembering that both the court jesters had been hanged for trying to escape in the early days of the plague.

She bit her lip to keep from groaning. The last thing they could afford was another ball. Hadn't the king noticed how meager their meals had become once again? "I was thinking a small, simple ceremony, Father. It will be more romantic that way." She'd always imagined being married by the rabbi under a beautiful chuppah, surrounded by her family and friends. Dalia would help with her hair. Of course, she'd also planned to marry someone she loved, but she'd given that dream up a long time ago.

"Hmm. Small and simple," he mused as if the very words were foreign. "I suppose, if that's what you'd prefer. But you must have an exquisite gown, at the very least."

"I wondered if I could wear Mother's." Seraphina had never known the queen, of course, but there wasn't time to wait for some elaborate gown to be made. Prince Martin had persuaded her to give him a few more days, but she'd gone back to the cellar in the middle of the night and found it as empty as it was before the ball. And this time she didn't think anyone would be replenishing it. She'd noticed that her usual maid was gone, replaced by a girl who was barely thirteen.

"Oh, that's a lovely idea. You're such a thoughtful girl, Genny." He patted her hand and moved his queen into a position so obviously perilous Seraphina wondered if all this time he'd been losing on purpose, just to see if those around him would continue to let him win. "Now," he said, taking a sip from a glass of water, "why don't you go and tell Prince Martin the plans. A month should be enough time to prepare for a wedding."

A *month*? "But, Father, that's so long. I was thinking a week, perhaps?"

He chuckled. "My, aren't we eager. Very well, then. Anything to make you happy."

She held in the sigh of relief she wanted to release. There was enough food to last until then. There had to be. "Thank you, Father."

He smiled. "Of course, my dear. And then you can get to work on bringing me grandchildren."

Seraphina laughed. "Prince Martin and I will have to get to Pilmand first, Father."

The king's smile faltered. "Pilmand? Were you planning to honeymoon there?"

Seraphina was glad she was sitting, because suddenly the room felt like it was tilted sideways. "I'll have to move there, Father. Prince Martin has to return if he's to rule his own country."

One of the king's watery eyes began to twitch, a warning sign that made Seraphina's blood run cold. She had never really understood the king's mind. She wasn't sure anyone did. He was generally pleasant and calm, just as long as everything around him went the way he wanted it to, which they had all become experts in predicting. But the moment something was out of place, his temper emerged in the form of what would be deemed a tantrum in a small child. In a king, it was downright terrifying. Was he truly mad, she wondered, or merely manipulative and cruel?

"Father?" she pressed, taking his hand. "I'll come back to visit," she said. "All the time."

Suddenly, the king rose and swept the chess board off the table with a roar. "Liar!" he screamed. "Ungrateful, selfish girl! Guards! Get her out of my sight!"

Seraphina gasped and pressed back against the wall, though the king's outburst had now reduced him to a trembling old man. Maids and guards came running in, confusion and alarm written on their faces.

"He's had a fit," Seraphina managed. "He's unwell. He needs to be in bed."

A maid nodded and hurried to the king's side, just as Princess Giselle entered the room. "What happened?" she demanded, her eyes immediately finding Seraphina. "What did you say to him?"

"N-nothing," she stammered. "We were playing chess and…"

"Get out," she spat. "Get out, you filthy *Jewess*." She hissed the word, too quietly for anyone else to hear, but Seraphina felt as though she'd been slapped across the face. Giselle hurried to the king's side, platitudes and nonsense already falling from her lips like he was a baby. Seraphina left before her anger could resurface.

She hurried down the hall, past the physician and several other servants, who barely glanced at her, as if they, too, knew who she really was. As if the echoes of Giselle's cruel whisper were following her down the corridor. By the time she reached her princess chambers, her entire body was racked with tremors. She collapsed onto the nearest fainting sofa, which was finally living up to its name after all these years.

"What is it?" Jocelyn asked, hurrying in from another room. "I heard screams."

"The king," Seraphina managed.

"Good God," Jocelyn said, kneeling down and taking Seraphina's hands. "You look like you've seen a ghost. What happened?"

She recounted what the king had said, then Giselle's even crueler words. She'd always known Giselle was antisemitic, but Giselle hadn't dared voice her thoughts in years, lest she give Seraphina away. "She hates me," Seraphina whispered. "*She* brought me here. *She* ruined my life. And still, she hates me."

"Giselle hates everyone," Jocelyn said gently, "including herself. But no one deserves to be treated that way. Especially you."

"Is that what Nina and Rose think of me? Have they been pretending all this time?"

Jocelyn shook her head. "Perhaps, at one time, they thought of you as less than them. But Nina and Rose have come to love you. So many people have."

Seraphina barely heard her friend's words. "*So many people—* only because they don't know who I am. *What* I am." She laughed bitterly. "What was I thinking? That the king would actually let me leave, even with a prince? Of course he won't. I'm going to die in here. We all are."

Jocelyn shook her head. "Don't say that. There's still a way out."

Seraphina swiped the tears off her cheeks with the back of her hand. "Even if I were to marry Prince Martin in secret and he agreed to get us out of here, he's alone, unarmed, and unguarded. I don't think he's capable of protecting us."

Jocelyn was quiet for a moment, thinking. "That's not true. He's been out there. He knows what to expect. He can ride, maybe even drive a coach."

Seraphina sank back against the sofa. "But can we trust him? What if he discovers who I am? He doesn't know that we have no food left, or that the king is utterly mad, or that I'm a... A *Jew*," she whispered, in the same hateful, disgusted tone as Giselle.

To be a Jew surrounded by gentiles was something Seraphina had never been prepared for, aside from brief ventures into the city beyond the Jewish quarter. Among her friends and family members, she was simply herself. Judaism informed every aspect of her life, but it wasn't something she'd had to explain or defend.

And the bitter irony was that there *was* no inherent difference between Jews and gentiles. If there was, she would have been discovered a long time ago. How could Giselle not see that, after all these years?

"Hush," Jocelyn said, stroking Seraphina's hair. "He isn't going to find out you're not a princess. Not until we're well clear of Eldridge."

"And then what? Where will we go?"

"We'll sort that out when the time comes."

"It's coming, sooner than you think. Before the king's outburst, we'd agreed to set the wedding for a week from now. I'm determined to see it through, so you and I can leave. The food is almost gone. The servants are leaving. The king is unwell, and if something happens to him, who knows what Giselle will do to me. We have to get out of here, Joc. Before it's too late."

Seraphina woke early to weak sunlight filtering through her window. She lay there for a moment, not wanting the day to begin yet. Maybe if she waited long enough, every-thing would go away.

Eventually, she crawled out of bed and splashed cold water on her face. She released her hair from its braid and let it fall over her shoulders. It was becoming annoyingly long, and the henna was fading, with more and more of her natural blond showing through. They would need to reapply the dye soon. She trailed her finger along the scar on her jaw. She knew the prince had seen it that first night. His eyes kept return-ing to it unconsciously.

She imagined telling Prince Martin the story of how she got it. It might strike some chivalrous chord in him, making him want to protect her. But she was tired of relying on men to do what she wished she could do herself. If she were bigger, stronger, if she hadn't been raised her entire life to be docile and restrained, if she had been born a man…if she weren't a…

She cut off her thoughts with another splash of frigid water. Wishing to be someone else was no more useful than wish-ing for someone to save her.

Seraphina had managed to miss dinner last night, but she couldn't hide in her tower forever. And though she knew the king's fit yesterday had been serious, she was surprised to find that he was still in bed.

"He's unwell," was all Giselle would say, with a look that could kill a man where he stood. "No thanks to you."

Prince Martin, oblivious to what had happened earlier, sat down next to Seraphina with a hesitant smile. "How are you feeling?" he asked as a servant placed a small pastry on her plate. Seraphina was about to reach for it when she no-ticed the flaky pastry crust was furred with gray mold. She grimaced, and the servant, who hadn't yet stepped back, gave a horrified gasp and quickly removed the offending pastry.

But a moment later there was another gasp, followed by a grunt of displeasure, and suddenly the servants couldn't keep up with all the moldy pastries. This was what they got for hoarding food for a stupid ball, when they could have made the flour last for months.

"Thank goodness the king isn't here," Seraphina murmured, more to herself than anyone.

"Is this really the first time you've had moldy food in nearly four years?" the prince asked.

Seraphina nodded and waited for the servant to put fruit on her plate. It was fresh, but the serving was almost laughably small.

"I think the chef is putting me on a diet," he said as a single sausage was placed before him with a flourish.

"Is this the first time you've had a meager meal in four years?" she asked, unable to keep the acid out of her voice. She let her eyes linger on his, to see if he would catch her meaning, but he cleared his throat and picked up his utensils, unable or unwilling to meet her gaze.

"I spoke with the king yesterday," she continued. "The wedding is set for Friday." She didn't know if this was true anymore, but she had decided last night that she wouldn't wait around for the king to decide. For her sake, and for Jocelyn's.

Prince Martin choked on a bite of sausage until a servant stepped forward and patted him roughly on the back. "Friday?" he finally managed, his eyes watering.

"You asked for a few days. You've got them."

"A few days to *decide*," he hissed. "Not to get married."

She plastered a beatific smile on her face and leaned closer to him. "In case you haven't noticed, we don't have the luxury of waiting." This time he glanced around at all the other empty plates. "This is going to be a cabbage soup diet if we wait much longer."

He took a long sip of his watered wine. "I see."

"I'm not sure you do." Seraphina was staring at her plate, but she could feel Prince Martin's eyes on her.

The prince leaned closer. "Then why don't you show me."

CHAPTER 20

Nico followed Imogen and Jocelyn on their "stroll" through the castle after breakfast, avoiding Greymont's flinty gaze. It seemed the meager servings and moldy pastries were indicative of a grave food shortage at the castle. Now she was taking him to the cellar, apparently so he could see for himself.

Whatever the case, he knew he had to tell King Stuart about Crane and Arnaud. And he was going to have to do it fast, before he ended up wedded to a princess.

"How many staff do you have here at Eldridge?" he asked as they continued down long corridors, past closed doors that had the air of abandonment, though he couldn't see inside.

"We had over a hundred at one point," Jocelyn said. "I think we're down to fifty or so now, though the numbers keep dropping."

Fifty people to run a castle of this size was woefully inadequate. He estimated, from the night of the masquerade, that at least five hundred nobles resided here. It was a miracle anyone was being fed at all. Somehow, the nobles all dressed immaculately every day, so he supposed there must

be enough servants for general tasks like cleaning and laundry, but he wondered if some of the nobles were having to
fend for themselves for once. He imagined Lord Greymont
darning his own socks and snickered to himself.

"Here we are," Imogen said, stopping in front of the cellar. There was a large padlock on the door, Nico noticed, but
Imogen managed to open it with a hairpin and a few deft
turns of her wrist. He didn't have time to question how a
princess had learned to pick locks before the true severity of
their situation hit him.

"Where is everything?" Nico asked. "Did we eat it all at
the ball?"

"It would appear so," Imogen said with a sniff. "So now
you see that staying here isn't an option, and you'll need to
take Jocelyn and me with you when you go."

Nico snorted. "And what about everyone else here? What
are they going to eat?"

"That's not my concern," Imogen said, before Jocelyn
placed a gentle hand on her arm.

"What Princess Imogen means to say is there isn't anything
we can do for such a large number of people. Most of the lords
and ladies here have land of their own they can return to."

"That may be true, but I'm willing to bet that most of them
haven't traveled unattended before. They'll be extremely vulnerable."

Imogen took a step toward him. "You keep saying that,"
she said, her eyes narrowing as she looked up at him. "And
yet, so far you've told us there's nothing worse out there than
wolves and thieves."

"Ruffians, too," he grumbled.

"Still, it seems we don't have a choice but to face our odds outside. That, or starve to death."

"I don't understand," Nico said, shaking his head. "The servants who brought in the food for the ball said something about trade."

"You spoke with the servants?" Imogen asked, her eyebrows lifting.

"No, no," Nico muttered. "I overheard them when we were trying to get in..."

"We?" Now Imogen's eyebrows lowered menacingly as she took another step toward him, bringing her within just a couple of feet of him.

"I—erm..." Nico could feel his cheeks going red as apples. "The royal we," he said, wincing at his own pathetic attempt at a lie.

Imogen's brown eyes bored into his. "You've never used the royal we before."

"I might have," he replied, trying to match her tone.

"I remember everything you've said—" She cut herself off when Nico arched his eyebrow, a coy grin spreading on his lips. Now she was the one to blush, and Nico found it rather gratifying.

Suddenly, Jocelyn squeezed between them, sending Nico stumbling backward. For a moment he'd forgotten they weren't alone. "Princess, it's time for your visit with the king. You should go, before you're missed," Jocelyn said.

"But—"

"You already missed your visit last night. People will notice if you don't go now. I can see Prince Martin back to his chambers."

Imogen's eyes darted to Nico's, and for a moment he thought

she'd refuse. But apparently, she decided the king was more important than this conversation. "Very well. Jocelyn, please come and speak to me when you're finished here."

Jocelyn flashed a strained smile as Imogen disappeared, leaving them alone at the entrance to the barren cellar. In an instant, her entire demeanor changed, and Nico suddenly wished he'd followed Imogen out.

"I lied before," she said in a low, forceful tone. "We are down to less than thirty servants. Only the kitchen staff and some of the maids who don't have family outside the castle stayed after the ball."

"Does the princess know?" Nico asked.

"Not the full extent of it. I do my best to protect her, but…" Jocelyn shook her head. "It's getting quite desperate, Your Highness. We will need to leave soon. And Princess Imogen will require a little more…protection than the others."

Nico had to fight to keep from rolling his eyes. "Let me guess. Her delicate constitution?"

Jocelyn's shoulders stiffened. "She has been through far more than you can possibly imagine."

Nico scoffed. "How? She's spent her entire life pampered and primped, her every whim catered to."

"As have you," Jocelyn said. "Being a prince and all." She met his eyes and suddenly a cold chill washed over him. Lord in heaven, she knew.

"Right," he managed. "As have I."

Without warning, Jocelyn took his arm and yanked him into the cellar. A knife appeared out of nowhere, and she was brandishing it with all the skill of a lady-in-waiting who'd never done more than cut her own butter-soft meat. But the look in her eyes was enough to entice him to raise his hands.

Before he could say anything, Jocelyn stepped forward. "Listen here, you…imposter! I know you're not who you say you are. I don't know what you want with the princess, but I can tell you this. You won't get within ten feet of her without me watching. Without me there to protect her." She seemed to remember the knife in her hand and waved it around for emphasis, mere inches from his face. "She's the best person I've ever known, and unfortunately, she needs your help."

Nico waited for Jocelyn to catch her breath before he carefully placed his hand on top of hers and lowered the knife. She didn't resist, and he knew he'd never truly been in danger. The knife was so dull it couldn't cut through a boiled carrot, let alone flesh. "There's no need for violence," he said. "I already told Princess Imogen I would get her out of here. But I can't just abandon everyone else."

"You wouldn't be abandoning them," Jocelyn said. "They've as much chance out there as anyone. They have access to weapons. I'm sure some of the few remaining guards would be willing to escort them in exchange for land. But the king isn't going to leave Eldridge, even if he gets well again."

"Is he that ill?" Nico asked. He'd heard mutterings about the king having some sort of spell yesterday, and he hadn't been at breakfast, but he'd been fine the day before.

Jocelyn nodded. "He's taken a sudden turn. And he is extremely possessive of Imogen. He won't let her go on her own."

"Will he let her go with me?"

"Willingly? I doubt it. But as the princess's betrothed, it

will be difficult for him to stop you. Especially once you're married."

Nico ran his hands through his hair and slumped against an empty shelf. He didn't want to reveal the truth, not without a plan. Not without Colin. But Crane could be here any day, and they could starve in a few more. It was now or never.

"You were right, Jocelyn. I'm not… I'm not who I said I am." Jocelyn didn't look surprised by his words, so he carried on. "My name is Nicodemus Mott. I'm the third son of a butcher. My entire family died of the Bloody Three. A lord who lives about a week from here by foot took me in. He saw a light in the castle tower and asked three of his servants to come and investigate."

Jocelyn was quiet for a moment as she processed his words. "I see. And where is this lord now?"

"Likely on his way here."

"And you're waiting for him?"

"Not exactly." Nico began to pace the cellar, unsure how to phrase any of this. "I came here to warn you of his plans."

"And what are his plans?"

To drain you of blood, he thought and almost laughed at the absurdity. "They're…they're not honorable. I think people here could be in danger from him."

"Is he bringing an army with him?"

"No, no, nothing like that."

"Then I fail to see how much harm one man can inflict."

Nico erupted, unable to maintain his composure any longer. "Of course you do! Everyone does! But that's because you haven't seen *Crane*. You haven't seen Arnaud, what he endured. What he's capable of."

Jocelyn placed her hands on Nico's shoulders, steadying him in place. He hadn't even realized he'd been pacing again. "What are you talking about, Mr. Mott? What have you seen?"

It was now or never, Nico knew. Even if she thought him mad, even if saying it out loud would be to accept that he might actually *be* mad.

Nico looked into Jocelyn's kind eyes, sighed, and told her everything.

CHAPTER 21

Jocelyn and Seraphina sat in her tower, the only place they could speak privately without worrying about Nina and Rose overhearing. The bed seemed even more tiny with two people on it. Seraphina wondered why she wasn't more surprised as Jocelyn explained who "Prince Martin" really was—an aspiring physician turned grave digger, as improbable as that seemed—but began to realize that the man she'd initially met in the great hall probably was his true self. No wonder he thought she was spoiled and selfish, given everything he'd been through.

"Well, this certainly changes things. I should tell him who I really am," Seraphina said when Jocelyn was finished. "He might be more apt to take us with him."

"Perhaps. But that's your decision to make, not mine. As far as he knows right now, you're still Princess Imogen."

Seraphina nodded and rose, walking to the little window. She could just make out the campfire through the trees. It belonged to Mr. Mott's friend, Colin Chambers. Or so he'd told Jocelyn. No one else in the castle would be able to see it over the high walls; the advantage of living in a lookout tower.

She was just about to turn back to Jocelyn when something caught her eye in the moonlight. "What's that?" she asked.

"What?" Jocelyn rose and came to stand beside her. A dark shape was streaking across the wide field that stretched beyond the castle wall to the forest. "I have no idea," Jocelyn said, just at the same moment that Seraphina said, "There's another!"

"I think they're people," Jocelyn said.

"I'd gathered that. But who are they?"

It was too hard to tell in the moonlight. But as they drew nearer, Seraphina could make out more details. The man in front was dark-skinned, dressed in work clothing. The man behind him was unnaturally pale, with clothing that appeared tattered and torn.

"I think that must be Colin," Jocelyn said.

"Who's the other man, then?" When Jocelyn didn't answer, Seraphina turned to look at her. Jocelyn's face had gone white as a sheet, and her eyes were as round as two Hanukkah gelt. "Jocelyn? What's wrong?"

"There's one part of Mr. Mott's story I didn't tell you," she said, her voice strange. "Because I didn't know if I believed it myself."

"Believed what?"

Colin was nearly to the wall, but the man behind him was gaining. Was he some kind of madman from the woods, trying to rob Mr. Mott's friend? Jocelyn had said Colin was armed. Why didn't he just fire at the man?

"There's no time to explain," Jocelyn said, turning abruptly from the window. "I'm going to find Mr. Mott. You stay here, with the door locked. Don't come out unless you hear me on the other side."

"What in God's name are you talking about?" Seraphina

asked, but Jocelyn was already out the door, flying down the stairs at an alarming rate. "You're going to hurt yourself!" Seraphina called, but Jocelyn was gone.

Seraphina sighed. She was grateful Jocelyn had managed to get the truth out of Mr. Mott, but now she was holding back information that seemed rather relevant at the moment. She returned to the window and looked out. Colin had disappeared from her view. He must know about the door in the clock. If the madman saw him, surely he would follow. That must have been what Jocelyn was worried about. But there were still a few guards at Eldridge, and by now she would have gotten their attention. There might only be a handful remaining, but they were well trained. She knew this because they had shot down anyone who tried to breach the walls when the king had first locked the gates.

She remembered hiding in her room with Jocelyn and her sisters when it happened, Rose whimpering next to her, Jocelyn stroking Rose's hair, Giselle sitting steel-faced in a corner, pretending not to be afraid. Nina had continued with her embroidery, not even flinching when the shots were fired. She was so self-possessed—truly brave, unlike Giselle—it was unnerving at times. Seraphina hadn't cried, but she certainly hadn't been comfortable. What if her parents were among the people trying to get in? Her father was a soft-spoken scholar, but she could still hear her mother's screams as the royal coach had rattled away from her home. She might have tried to get her daughter, especially if they were starving and had nothing left to lose.

Her thoughts turned to Dalia. In that moment, while whoever it was out there Jocelyn was so afraid of closed in on the castle, and the real Prince Martin and his retinue lay ravaged by wolves in the forest beyond, she knew that Dalia had never really been there, looking up at Seraphina's tower every night from the woods. She'd been an illusion all along. Madmen, man-eating wolves… No young girl could survive out there on her own, not for all these years. Seraphina's loneliness, her homesickness—it had made her see what she'd wanted to see.

She picked up a crocheted daisy that had been sacrificed to her sewing scissors before the ball. There was a time when she would have done almost anything to get her hands on something as fine as this silly adornment. She twirled it in her fingers, thinking of the little dish of buttons on her vanity, the ones Mr. Mott had noticed his first night at the castle. They were the buttons off the clothing she had worn when she first came to Eldridge.

Her first day here, Giselle had the guards bring her in through the servants' entrance. She was stripped down to her undergarments in a maid's room, scrubbed until her skin was raw, as if Giselle believed they could wash away who she really was. They had stuffed her into her first corset, commenting on her appearance throughout as if she were livestock. She'd never felt less human than she had that day.

After a few moments of feeling sorry for the girl she'd been, Seraphina dropped the daisy and went to the door. It wasn't like her to just sit by while anything could be going on below. Mr. Mott had finally promised to take them away from Eldridge Hall. She didn't even need to marry him.

The madman downstairs might ruin everything.

Seraphina made an exception to her usual no-shoes rule and put her slippers on before descending the stone steps. If she needed to run, she didn't want to be barefoot. There were no men shouting or ladies screaming as she'd feared. She peeked into the royal rooms at the bottom of the stairs. Nina, Giselle, and Rose were playing cards with their ladies, barely glancing up when Seraphina poked her head in. Everything was as it should be.

Without saying anything, she slipped away toward the great hall. The silence was eerie. Where was Jocelyn? Where were the guards?

Finally, when she was nearly to the hall, she heard muffled shouts and scuffling. She rushed forward, afraid Jocelyn was in trouble, and froze in the entrance. Mr. Mott and his friend Colin were holding the door of the clock closed with all their might, but something was on the other side pushing back against them, and it seemed to be winning.

Where the hell was Jocelyn? Seraphina wasn't sure how much help she'd be able to provide if sheer strength was what they required. She ran across the hall to a wall decorated with weaponry and reached for the nearest sword. It was so heavy she nearly toppled over once she'd removed it, but she managed to drag it across the room.

"Here," she said to Mr. Mott.

He turned, startled. "What are you doing here?"

"Helping you," she grunted, forcing the pommel into his hand.

The moment he turned to take the sword, the man on the other side of the clock overpowered Colin, who went flying backward onto the marble floor.

"Run!" Colin shouted, but Seraphina was too horrified to move.

The man who stood in the entrance to the clock might

have been handsome once, but he was preternaturally pale, his hair hanging in unkempt locks around his gaunt face. Though his chest heaved, there was no sweat on his brow. His clothing was filthy and tattered, but they were the garments of an aristocrat. For a horrible moment Seraphina thought he had the bloody plague.

Suddenly, the man's head jerked up, his gaze finding hers. The whites of his eyes were bloodshot, but the irises were nearly black. His nostrils flared and he smiled, revealing teeth that were much too long. "Oh, boys. You've been holding out on me."

Seraphina took a step back, and suddenly Jocelyn was beside her, holding out what appeared to be a butter knife. "Where were you?" Seraphina hissed.

"Getting help," Jocelyn whispered back.

Fortunately, Mr. Mott stepped in front of both of them, the sword aimed at the man's chest. "Don't move," he said, his voice remarkably firm considering the circumstances.

"Come now, lad. You can't deny a dying man a last meal. You've already deprived me of one."

Seraphina's blood froze in her veins. The man's eyes had never left hers. She had a terrible feeling that when he said *meal*, he was referring to her.

"Go!" Colin shouted to Seraphina and Jocelyn over his shoulder as he came to stand next to Nico.

She started to back away. She would go and find the guards. They would take care of this horrible creature.

Mr. Mott stepped forward with the sword, trying to drive the man back out of the clock. But he held his ground until the blade was inches from his waist.

Seraphina screamed as the stranger took the sword by his bare hands and impaled himself. Mr. Mott stood stunned on the other side of the threshold until he was nose to nose with the stranger and the hilt of the sword was pressed against his belly.

"Can't kill me that way, boy," the man purred.

Mr. Mott stumbled backward, releasing the sword and shielding Seraphina and Jocelyn with his body. It was a noble thought, but useless. The man was still standing, and there was nothing preventing him from entering the castle. So why didn't he?

He licked his lips, his eyes still roving over Seraphina. "It's been so long since I've tasted a maiden. The driver and footman slaked my hunger for a bit, but there's nothing like untainted blood."

Bile burned the back of Seraphina's throat. Jocelyn had said that Mr. Mott discovered the real Prince Martin's dead retinue in the forest on his way to Eldridge—that was how he'd known to impersonate the prince when they'd first met, in this very room. She'd left out how they died, however, only saying that it hadn't been wolves after all. Another scream was building up in Seraphina, along with a watery feeling in her limbs that made her want to run and faint at the same time. With a concerted effort, she turned her back on the men, gripped Jocelyn's hand, and started to run.

A moment later she skidded into the arms of Henry. He gathered her against his side, but his eyes were on the stranger.

"Who are you?" he demanded. He glanced from the man to Mr. Mott and jerked his head toward Colin. "And who is he?"

"My name is Adrien Arnaud. I followed these two here," the stranger said, gesturing to Colin and Mr. Mott.

"From where?"

"From the woods, of course. They're drifters."

Henry looked down at Seraphina. "What the hell is going on?"

"We'll explain everything later," Mr. Mott said. "Right now all you need to know is that this man wants to kill the princess."

Henry scoffed, his eyes darting between the men. "Have you all gone mad?"

"Look," Seraphina said, pointing to the gaping wound in the man's belly. The sword had fallen out, taking some of the man's entrails with it, but there was no blood. "Prince Martin stabbed him to protect me. He didn't even flinch."

Henry seemed to finally grasp the absurdity of the situation, his face going a little green. Seraphina could feel him swallow thickly. "Sir, I'm going to have to ask you to leave."

Arnaud laughed, a rich, throaty sound completely at odds with his appearance. "Now, I've come a long way to get a hot meal. It doesn't have to be this one," he said, glancing at Seraphina. "If you've got a young scullery maid, that will do just as well for my purposes."

"Good heavens, man! What kind of a monster are you?"

The man grinned and began to hum, so quietly at first that Seraphina couldn't make out the tune. But as he continued, he got louder, until by the end Seraphina could practically hear the children from the quarter singing along to it:

Old King Stuart's lost his head, hoping he won't end up dead.
Lock the windows, bar the door; the plague will come for rich
and poor.

If you want to stay alive, there are three ways to survive:
Run away across the sea; pray for blood immunity;
Or die and be reborn again, and drink the blood of living men.

He wasn't a monster at all. He was a man, or he had been once, and now he was here to literally drink her blood. Seraphina felt her knees go weak and braced herself against Henry. Mr. Mott's gaze had turned to her, and she saw in his eyes the truth he'd known all along. This was why he wasn't eager to leave Eldridge. This was why he didn't want Seraphina to go. Why he didn't want any of them to go. This was the part Jocelyn had known, too, and hadn't wanted to tell her.

Whoever Arnaud was, he clearly could not be killed with bullets or swords. They had to keep him out of the castle.

She stepped away from Henry, forcing her back straight and her chin up. "I am Princess Imogen, fourth daughter of King Stuart, and I demand that you leave Eldridge Hall immediately and never return."

The man had the audacity to roll his eyes.

"The princess was very clear," Mr. Mott said, coming to stand beside her. "You should leave now, before the guards arrive." Colin came to her other side, so tall she had to crane her neck to see his face. She could feel Henry breathing heavily behind her.

For a moment Seraphina was afraid Arnaud was going to make a break for her. He didn't seem any worse for the wear, despite the wound in his gut. Whatever he was, he was strong.

But perhaps not stronger than three healthy men.

"I'd suggest you lock the door up good and tight," he said

finally. "I'm not the only one hunting in these woods, and when word gets out that there's an entire castle full of immaculates here, you can bet the others will come." His gaze landed on Seraphina a final time. "I could have made it gentle for you, Princess. I could have made death a sweet release. I doubt the others will be so generous."

With that, he turned and climbed back out through the clock, disappearing into the night.

CHAPTER 22

Nico stood outside Imogen's chambers, pacing the hall while Imogen explained everything to Lord Greymont. There was more to tell her, of course, but the lord had been ready to tear Nico apart, and Imogen was the only one who could calm him. Colin was in Nico's room, hidden away until they could decide what to do with him.

Lord Greymont's voice was rising on the other side of the door. But a moment later he heard Imogen's voice, just as sharp and angry as Lord Greymont's, and he knew that there was nothing he could say to help the situation now. He thought back to the way Imogen had clung to Lord Greymont for support in the great hall and felt an unfamiliar burning sensation in his chest. This looked like a lover's quarrel, and he needed to stay out of it.

Finally, the door opened and Lord Greymont emerged.

"Everything all right?" Nico asked.

"All right?" He jabbed a finger into Nico's chest. "I should kill you for putting the princess in danger like this. For putting *all* of us in danger."

"I am *trying* to help you," Nico said, slapping his finger away. "I've suspected what Arnaud is for weeks, but I didn't know for certain. And if I'd come in here as myself, claiming that there were blood-sucking monsters roaming the forest, do you think anyone would have believed me?"

Lord Greymont glared at him for a moment, then deflated a bit with resignation. "No, of course not. But what are we to do now? King Stuart isn't going to believe any of this."

"Not even coming from you?"

"Please. He'd be more likely to believe the mythical Prince Martin than me. And telling him the truth isn't going to make him want to leave Eldridge. If anything, he'll take it as more reason to stay. And we can't."

"Because we're out of food," Nico added grimly.

"And staff. I went to fetch the guards when Jocelyn told me what was happening and I realized we were down to half a dozen. They all refused to help. This place will devolve into panic the moment word of this gets out."

Nico nodded. "We're truly between a rock and a hard place. But the good news is that Arnaud appeared unable to enter the castle."

"What do you mean?"

"I'd thought nothing of it at the time, but it all came together tonight. Arnaud came to Crane Manor a fortnight ago, and Lord Crane forbade me from inviting him in. When Colin and I spent the night in an abandoned shed on our way here, Arnaud threatened us from outside but never broke in, even though he easily could have. And tonight, even after I was unarmed, he never crossed the threshold of the clock. For some reason I think he simply couldn't without permission. And Crane knew that, somehow."

"So you think Crane wouldn't be able to enter, either?"

Nico shrugged. "I don't know for sure. For now we just have to make sure no one else tries to leave."

Greymont nodded. "I'll bribe the guards to keep watch at the clock. That should work for the rest of the night. I'm going to my room to think. Don't let anyone see your friend Colin until I've figured out a plan."

"Understood."

Lord Greymont turned into the hall, leaving Nico outside Imogen's door. Everyone was asleep except for Jocelyn, who was in a small adjoining chamber for propriety's sake. Nico stared at the door for a moment, sighed, and turned toward his room.

A few strides later he stopped, turned back around, and entered Imogen's chamber.

She was sitting at her vanity, fishing through the tray of old buttons. They looked like something a servant would have, not a princess. And for a moment he wondered if he'd been wrong about her all along.

But as soon as she saw him, she sat up, her posture going rigid, her chin tilted at a haughty angle. She looked remarkably calm, given everything they'd just witnessed. "Yes?"

"I wanted to make sure you were all right," Nico said. He remembered the foul things Adrien Arnaud had said and struggled to keep a blush from his cheeks. No young lady should have to hear such talk.

"I'm fine," she said. "Well, as fine as can be expected. Please, sit."

He sat down on one of the fainting sofas and she turned

in her vanity seat toward him. She was still wearing her pink evening dress, but she'd removed her slippers. Her bare toes peeked out from beneath her hem. She must have caught him looking, because she tucked them back under her skirt, her cheeks going as pink as her dress.

"Jocelyn told you about me," he said finally. "Who I am, why I came here."

"She told me some. She failed to mention Mr. Arnaud, however."

Nico grimaced and lowered his gaze. "I suppose there's something to that whole 'seeing is believing' thing."

She laughed, a soft puff of air. "I suppose so."

"Lord Greymont said he's going to come up with a plan."

"Did he? Well, I'd be very much surprised if he does. The man isn't exactly a master strategist. No one here is."

"Surely, the king—"

"The king is the least strategic of all. He's never been to war, never faced hardship."

Nico was surprised to hear her speaking so coldly of her own father. "But he must have had training. All kings do."

"Perhaps. But Giselle will have my head if she discovers what we've brought to Eldridge. We'll have to solve this problem on our own."

The thought struck him so suddenly he jumped up, causing Imogen to flinch.

"What is it?" she asked.

"It's nothing."

"It's not nothing. You get a little crease between your eyebrows when you have an idea."

He paused, surprised that she had noticed. "It might be

something. Arnaud said we couldn't kill him by stabbing him. But he did say he was dying."

"Right. So you believe he can be killed?"

Nico nodded. "Yes. And I think I have an idea how. But there's only one way to test my theory."

"How?"

He swallowed, already dreading what he was about to suggest. "By leaving Eldridge Hall."

Nico searched for a clean tunic in his wardrobe while Colin stretched out on the enormous feather bed and sighed. "I don't suppose you've got any food in here?"

Nico emerged with a white shirt and tossed it to Colin. He would have to ask Lord Greymont to find breeches that would fit someone with Colin's scarecrow build in the morning.

"I'll bring you something after breakfast, assuming there's anything to eat. I'm afraid if I go sneaking around now someone will catch me."

Colin stripped out of his filthy tunic, throwing it into the corner. "Thank you," he said to Nico as he slipped into the clean shirt.

"What the hell happened out there?" Nico asked finally, fighting to keep frustration out of his voice. "I thought you were going to wait for me."

"I was! I had no intention of running into the castle, believe me." He sighed and leaned back amid a pile of pillows. "Arnaud was still sniffing around camp, but he'd never shown himself, and I knew I wasn't who he was after. Eventually, I got bored and decided to do a little hunting myself. I figured maybe I could learn something useful. And I found him, all right. He was perched in a tree like a goddamn owl, his eyes wide open. I expected him to leap down and attack me, but he didn't even flinch. It was like he was asleep with his eyes open."

That must have been why his eyes were so red, Nico thought with a shudder.

"Then I heard voices, like people were approaching, and I hid behind the tree. Two servants from the castle were walking past, carrying large bundles. One of them said that they'd never gotten word from the last two escapees, and that eventually they'd realized something had happened to them. There was talk of a strange predator in the forest that was draining its victims of blood. And then they said they'd left the door into the castle unlocked, so they could return if they needed to. When I looked up at Arnaud, he was staring straight down at me, a horrible grin on his face.

"That's when I realized he knew where the door was all along. He'd just been waiting for his opportunity. I took off running. I thought he'd come after me, but then I heard screams… I think he killed the servants before chasing me to the castle. I knew if I didn't get in before him, you were all doomed."

Even with Colin's head start, Arnaud had nearly caught him. Nico doubted Arnaud had gone far tonight, knowing that eventually he'd have another chance to get into the castle, or someone else would leave through the clock. He remembered the way Arnaud had looked at Imogen, like an animal with cornered prey. It was the same way Crane had looked at poor Elisabeth. He tried not to imagine what her final moments must have been like. Maybe, like Arnaud had said, he'd made it gentle, but something told him that his master enjoyed the hunt.

"We've got to get out there and take care of Arnaud before Crane arrives, Colin. Branson knows the way in. And Arnaud said something about *others*. I don't know how many of these reborn there are out there, but it wouldn't take many to overpower us. In the meantime, I think one of us should be posted at the clock at all times to ensure that if Arnaud makes another attempt at entry soon, he doesn't get lucky and arrive when an unsuspecting servant or noble is in the great hall. Without clueing the rest of the castle in to the situation, it's only a matter of time before he's inadvertently invited in."

"But how do we kill Arnaud? Bullets and swords aren't working, Nico."

"There are tales of creatures like this, undead men who drink the blood of the living."

"Those are ghost stories," Colin said. "This is real life."

"Trust me. No one knows that better than I do."

Colin threw his hands up when he realized Nico was serious. "All right, so how do people handle these *undead* in your tales?"

Nico felt foolish even thinking it, but what else did they have? "A stake through the heart while the creature is sleeping. Or beheading." He ran his finger along his throat for emphasis.

"Beheading," Colin said quietly. "That's going to require a damn big knife."

"Or a sword."

"I've never handled a sword, Nico."

"Well, neither have I! You think I spent my childhood practicing swordplay with my brothers?"

Colin's voice rose to the same pitch as Nico's. "I don't know! But I can't behead someone. I just don't think I've got it in me."

Nico settled onto the floor next to the bed. "I watched my father butcher countless animals. I reckon I could do it, if it came to it."

"And you want us to go out there and look for Arnaud?"

Nico shrugged. "We've got to test the theory before it's too late."

Colin rustled around on the bed, as if he couldn't get comfortable on the soft mattress. "Why don't we just tell everyone here what's coming and let them decide how to handle it?"

"First of all, there's no *we*. The king can't know you're here. And second of all, we risk a panic if word of this gets out. But if we can kill Arnaud for good, we can kill the others."

Colin's eyes appeared over the edge of the mattress. "You're serious about this, aren't you?"

"Of course I am. I failed my family. I failed Elisabeth. I can't fail everyone else." He set his jaw, pushing away the thought of his mother's final words. "I won't."

CHAPTER 23

Seraphina slept in her princess chambers for the first time in years that night, with Jocelyn next to her in bed. Neither of them was particularly keen on being alone, and besides, they needed to talk. Suddenly, their plans to leave with Mr. Mott— or, even more impossible to imagine now, on their own— were dashed. But while leaving immediately was no longer an option, they still didn't have a solution to their equally pressing concern of the lack of food in the castle. Their choices were almost comically horrific: don't eat, or be eaten.

Eventually, Jocelyn fell asleep, and Seraphina lay awake, thinking. Arnaud hadn't seemed interested in Jocelyn or Greymont, so according to the rules Mr. Mott had explained to her, they must have immunity. Given his clear desire to drink her blood, Seraphina now knew that she didn't. But the thought of hiding in the castle until she slowly starved to death was just as untenable as Arnaud's alternative. By the time she fell asleep, she'd made up her mind: it was time to act. She couldn't wait for someone else to do it for her any longer.

She just didn't know what that action should be.

Breakfast the next morning was a meager affair of porridge and dried fruit. The nobles exchanged worried glances, and since the king wasn't there to admonish them, a few even complained out loud. Everything felt like it was at a boiling point, and Seraphina had no idea what it would look like when this pot boiled over.

"The king is asking for you," Princess Giselle said to Seraphina as she passed her chair after breakfast. Giselle had been so careful for all these years, but now she was openly expressing her disdain. A few of the nobles looked their way, no doubt picking up on the fact that Giselle hadn't said "Father."

On the one hand, Seraphina had no desire to visit a man who, the last time she'd seen him, had cast her away so violently. But she'd spent the past four years as two different people, and deep down she knew that the king had, too. Every now and then, the real Seraphina surfaced under Imogen's mask, and she told herself that was what had happened with the king. The madness had bled through, but it wasn't who he truly was at heart.

The king was sleeping, so Seraphina sat gently on the edge of his bed and waited. Finally, he seemed to notice her presence in his sleep and blinked his eyes open. For a moment she was terrified she'd see the king as he'd been the other day. Or worse, that he'd see *her* as he had then—an unrecognizable, ungrateful stranger.

But his eyes were placid this morning, his voice soft and gentle. "Genny. I told your sisters not to worry you."

"I wasn't worried, Father. I simply wanted to see how you were feeling."

He smiled, and Seraphina felt something resembling real

affection squeeze behind her ribs. "I'm fine, dear, as you can see." He struggled to sit up a little against his pillows. "How was breakfast?"

She couldn't tell him the truth. What good would it do? "Delicious, as always. You were missed."

"I'll be out of bed in no time. It's just a little indigestion. Nothing serious at all."

But Seraphina wasn't so sure. He looked thinner and paler than usual, and there were creases of pain around his eyes. Was it possible his eruption the other day had caused this much weakness? Or had a disease been introduced to the castle somehow? "How is the wedding coming?" he asked.

Seraphina blinked. She'd almost forgotten that they'd decided to hold the wedding. With everything that had transpired since, it didn't matter anymore. Prince Martin was dead, and marrying his impersonator wouldn't save her. But the king looked so hopeful that she lied anyway.

"Everything is perfect," she said, placing a kiss on his forehead, trying not to grimace at the smell of illness.

Jocelyn was waiting for her outside the king's chambers. "Mr. Mott and Lord Greymont asked us to meet them in the library," she whispered as they walked down the corridor.

Seraphina nodded at a guard, whose eyelids were droopy with sleep. Henry had said they refused to help last night. She wondered why they stayed here at all.

The two men were talking when she approached the doorway, and she stopped for a moment to study them. The contrast was almost startling. Henry was the handsomer of the two, at least by conventional standards among the nobility, but Mr. Mott glowed with health and vitality, his hair long and curling against his collar, his skin tanned from the sun. She had gotten used to the nobility's elegant clothing and sophisticated way of speaking, but she'd never found it particularly appealing. Mr. Mott, despite his disdain for Imogen, was the kind of man she would have been drawn to in her past life.

Not that it mattered. He likely wouldn't deign to speak to her once he knew what a fraud she was.

Mr. Mott cleared his throat and Seraphina realized she'd been staring. Henry was giving her an odd look. She glanced down to hide her blush and walked to the nearest bookshelf, pretending to be looking for something.

"How is the king?" Henry asked.

"Not well," she said, her back still to both men. "I'm afraid he has something serious, though he says it's just indigestion."

Mr. Mott cleared his throat. "I have some medical training. I would be happy to look at him, if you think I might be able to help."

Seraphina turned to face him. "Would you? We have a physician in the castle, but he prefers…old-fashioned methods." Leeches, bleeding, concoctions that sedated a patient until they were unconscious. The doctor in the Jewish quarter seemed far more practical and scientific, but in the end she supposed it hadn't mattered. According to Mr. Mott, no one had been cured of the Bloody Three.

"I would never pretend to have the kind of knowledge a true physician has, but I learned a few things over the years. I tended to the people at Crane Manor."

"I'm sure the king would be grateful for your help."

Henry motioned for Seraphina to join them, clearly more concerned about their own predicament than the king's.

"Jocelyn," Seraphina said. "Come sit with us. She's as much a part of this as we are," she added to Henry before he could object.

"Very well. Mr. Mott and I have discussed it, and we'll leave at midnight to look for Arnaud. Mr. Chambers believes he can track Arnaud relatively easily, and Mr. Mott thinks he's discovered a way to…" He paused to clear his throat. "To put an end to his shenanigans."

Seraphina couldn't help snorting at Greymont's delicate description. "All right, then. Where are we meeting?"

Henry shook his head. "You misunderstand me, Princess. You won't be *joining* us. It's far too dangerous."

Seraphina had anticipated this, but she'd already made up her mind. "I want to help."

Henry softened his tone to a patronizing coo. "Come, my dear. You know you'd only be a liability out there. Mott agrees with me."

To his credit, Mr. Mott glanced up, his face scarlet. "I didn't say that."

Henry chuckled without mirth. "Come now, Mott. Be serious."

Seraphina rose, her own face flushed with indignity now. "I'm a princess, and I make my own decisions."

Jocelyn reached for her. "Perhaps Lord Greymont is correct."

Seraphina cast her a pointed look, but Henry closed his eyes and tipped his head back in exasperation. "You're acting like a child. Mott, tell her she's being ridiculous."

Mr. Mott glanced between the two of them, his gaze finally settling on Seraphina. "I agree that you'd be far safer here in the castle," he said. "But you are a grown woman capable of making your own decisions." He turned to Henry. "It's up to Princess Imogen."

Henry opened his eyes and stared at Mott in disbelief. "You aren't serious. What is this, some ploy to get into her—"

"Lord Greymont!" Seraphina stared at him in shock. "That is entirely inappropriate."

"I was going to say good graces," he muttered, but they all knew that was a lie.

Seraphina's eyes drifted to Mr. Mott, who looked like he wanted the floor to swallow him whole. "I think I should take my leave."

"Oh no you don't," Seraphina said, grabbing his sleeve as he started to retreat. "Have you given Lord Greymont reason to believe something untoward has happened between us?"

"Of course not! I would never presume—"

"Let me be very clear to all of you," Seraphina said, her voice far steadier than she felt. "I alone of the four of us have the king's ear. I alone have access to his carriages, his horses, his guards. If you think cutting me out of your plans will increase your odds of survival, you are sorely mistaken." She rounded on Mr. Mott, dropping her voice to a whisper only he could hear. "And if you think I will ever let you anywhere near my...*good graces*, you're *very* sorely mistaken."

She cast one more furious glance at Henry and stalked from the room. "Come along, Jocelyn. I'll see you both at midnight, near the clock."

"Don't you remember the way Arnaud looked at you?" Henry called after her. "He wants to *eat* you, for God's sake."

She stopped, turned slowly on her heels, and smiled icily at him. "Then think of me as your bait."

CHAPTER 24

Nico had managed to convince a servant that breakfast hadn't been nearly enough food, though he'd hated seeming like a spoiled prince. A tray was delivered to his room in the late morning, after his disastrous meeting with Imogen. His face was still burning from the things she'd said to him.

Colin laughed when he recounted everything. "I've got to give her credit. She's spunky, for a princess."

Nico grumbled and flopped back on the bed. They had hours before they were supposed to meet at the clock, and while he thought Imogen's joining them was a royally foolish notion, he felt begrudging respect for her bravery. She was the only one of them who had thought to take a sword down in the great hall, and she was willing to face Arnaud, even knowing that she was the only one of them he wanted. He thought again of Elisabeth's lace collar beneath Crane's bed and felt rage course through him. There was something horrifically carnal in the way they looked at their prey.

A knock on the door startled both men.

"Who is it?" Nico called. Colin was already climbing into the wardrobe.

"Greymont," came the muffled reply.

Colin unfolded his long legs and Nico went to open the door. "I thought we were meeting at midnight," he said as Lord Greymont slipped into the room. He was clad in dark clothing and boots suitable for hunting.

"We need to go now, before the princess realizes we've gone."

"What?"

Greymont crossed his arms. "Don't tell me you actually thought I'd allow her to come with us. She's a girl. She'll get herself killed out there, and us, too."

Colin reached for his coat, but Nico stayed where he was. "I agree that it's dangerous to bring her, but I won't agree to deceit. She believes we're meeting at midnight, and that's when I intend to go."

"I hate to say it, but his lordship is right," Colin said. "If all goes well, we'll find Arnaud, chop off his head, and be back through the clock before the princess notices." He shook his head with a dry laugh. "Now, there's a sentence I never thought I'd say."

"What about using her as bait, like she suggested?" Nico asked. "That wasn't a bad idea. It was a bloody good one, in fact."

"She may just be bait to you," Greymont said, "but I was as good as engaged to marry her before you showed up."

Nico noticed that he hadn't said he loved Imogen, merely that they were engaged. "She's not just bait to me. She's a human being, and that's why I don't feel right lying to her."

"Suit yourself, Mott. We're going."

Colin gave an apologetic shrug, but it was clear he intended to follow Lord Greymont, and Nico couldn't very well stay behind while they went off to fight Arnaud. He hesitated, torn between respect for Imogen and not wanting to leave his best friend to deal with Arnaud without him.

In the end, loyalty won out. Besides, he didn't want Imogen getting hurt any more than Lord Greymont did. He pulled the heaviest coat he had out of his wardrobe and walked quickly to his writing desk, where he scrawled a note to Imogen, explaining where they'd gone.

The others were already through the clock by the time he made it downstairs. He grabbed a small sword off the wall, tucked the note for Imogen in a nook below the clock's upper door, and followed the others out into the night.

They'd been tromping through the woods for what felt like hours, though Nico was sure it wasn't midnight yet. They'd found Colin's old camp readily enough, and Colin was following what looked like signs of Arnaud through the trees, but Nico was starting to wonder if he was just pretending to know what he was doing. Lord Greymont was muttering obscenities under his breath and Nico's right arm was numb from clutching the sword.

"This is ridiculous," Greymont said finally. "We'll never find him in the dark. We should come back again tomorrow, during the day, when we actually stand a chance of finding him."

"I thought we decided we'd have better luck at night," Colin said, his voice as strained with frustration as Greymont's.

"You don't get to have an opinion. This is your fault. If you hadn't led that madman to the castle, we wouldn't be out here in the first place."

"He already knew the way in. If he had gotten there before me, he could have asked an unsuspecting castle dweller to invite him inside, and that would have risked all of you. Not to mention that he has a distinct advantage over me, being already dead, and I needed to get to safety. I had no choice."

"This is no one's fault," Nico cut in. "It's a rotten situation and we all need to keep our heads straight, so we don't do anything stupid."

"We're hunting a dead man in the middle of the night," Greymont said. "I think that ship has sailed."

Suddenly, Colin froze and held a finger to his lips. "Look," he whispered and pointed to a mound up ahead.

He motioned for them to follow, and they crept slowly forward, none of them wanting to be the one who stepped on a twig and gave their position away. As they approached, Colin's posture relaxed a little.

"It's just a deer," he said. "Or what's left of it."

Greymont peered down at the carcass and recoiled instantly. "Its throat's been ripped out. And its..." He pressed his fist to his mouth. "Its viscera."

Nico held his breath and knelt down next to the body. "The aorta and the liver, specifically," he said. "That's where the most blood is."

"He took more than blood." Colin pointed to the deer's haunches, which had been ripped to shreds. "How is it even possible for a human to do that?"

"It's not," Nico said. "Our teeth weren't designed for it.

Neither were our stomachs. But I don't think we can call whatever Arnaud is *human*. He's become something else. *Reborn*, like the song says."

"I know you think Lord Crane is one of them, but I still can't believe it," Colin said. "He's been good to us. He's a gentleman. He wouldn't rip a woman's throat out and eat her liver." He stopped, turned to the side, and vomited. "Apologies."

"Perfectly understandable," Greymont said. He was looking rather green himself.

Nico touched the deer's head. It was warm, and steam was still rising from the carcass. "He killed this animal recently, which means he can't be far from here. Let's go, before midnight comes and *someone* notices we're missing."

At least they had a trail to follow now. There was blood leading away from the carcass farther into the woods. They found a puddle a few minutes later, next to a rock. The blood was congealing in the cold air, but it looked like Arnaud had rested here, possibly to consume the liver.

"We're close," Nico whispered. "Come on."

They all raised their swords and moved forward, their senses on high alert now that they were finally making progress. Nico could hear his own blood pounding in his ears. If he wasn't able to get near enough to Arnaud to cut off his head, or if he was wrong about this, they could all be in grave danger. But he had promised to protect Imogen, even if she didn't want him to. He wouldn't let everyone down again.

Especially himself.

CHAPTER 25

A little before midnight Seraphina changed into the trousers and tunic she'd taken from a young male servant, pulled on her leather-soled slippers, and tied her hair into a long braid down her back. She wished she had boots like the men, but this would have to do. She felt guilty for lying to Jocelyn, who had made her promise not to follow the men, but this was something she had to do for herself. Jocelyn would forgive her once Arnaud was dead. As she made her way downstairs, she marveled at how freeing the trousers were and made a mental note to find some more when it came time to leave Eldridge for good.

When she arrived at the hall, the clock was just striking three o'clock/midnight. The men must not be down yet. She paced for a few minutes, matching her stride to the *tick-tock-tick* of the clock. She was frightened of Arnaud, but it felt good to take matters into her own hands rather than wait around for something bad to happen. Besides, she was going to leave the castle for the first time. She could practically taste the night air on her tongue.

When five minutes passed, Seraphina began to worry that the men had been detained. It was risky, what they were doing, and three men wouldn't move as quietly as she did. But as she passed the wall of weapons, something caught her eye. Several swords were already gone.

"Damn it!" she cursed, running back to the clock. Then she noticed the little white card on a shelf built into the clock's ornate body. She pulled it down and tore it open.

Princess Imogen,
I tried to convince Lord Greymont to wait for you, but he in-sisted on leaving early. I know you'll be furious, but I hope you'll forgive us. He only wants you to be safe.
So do I.
—Nicodemus Mott.

Damn, damn, damn! Seraphina stomped her feet and flapped her arms as silently as she could manage. How dare they leave without her? Even if she was in danger, wasn't that her deci-sion to make?

No. Not in Henry's eyes, anyway. And the truth was she was partly to blame. For the past month all she'd done was act the coquette, flirting and playing along with his insipid games. She had used her feminine charms to her advantage, appeas-ing or coercing, whichever was most convenient at the time.

And as for Mr. Mott, he clearly didn't think she was as ca-pable of deciding for herself as he'd claimed. Of course, he couldn't let the other two face the danger without him. That would be *ungentlemanly*. No doubt they hoped to be back be-fore Seraphina even noticed they'd gone. Then they could tell her that she didn't need to worry; they'd protected her like gentlemen ought to.

Well, they weren't back yet, and she was leaving Eldridge whether they liked it or not. After all, they weren't here to stop her.

Seraphina found Colin's camp quickly and strode into the woods behind it. Why hadn't she come out here years ago? If she'd tried harder, been more resourceful, she would have noticed the door in the clock. In the past four years she'd built up the outside world as something terrifying, but the sky was enormous and full of stars, and the ground was so much softer beneath her feet than the stone floors of Eldridge. She almost wished she could take her shoes off and dig her toes into the earth.

She had considered taking one of the swords with her, but she knew she wouldn't make it far trying to lug it through the woods. Instead, she'd taken a small decorative knife she'd found on the wall. It wasn't going to chop anyone's head off, but it might buy her some time if she were to come across Arnaud alone. That seemed unlikely, however. The woods were quiet and peaceful, not nearly as foreboding as she had imagined. He was probably far away by now, terrorizing someone else.

She stubbed her toe on a rock and swore. How could the men have done this to her? Mr. Mott and Henry had both agreed to take her away from Eldridge. Did they think it would be easy, setting off into the unknown? Had they planned on doing everything themselves? It wasn't like they'd have servants with them, except for Jocelyn, and once they left Eldridge, she wouldn't be a servant any longer. She would be an equal. They all would.

But perhaps that was unrealistic. She had this notion that the world was starting over in some way, but she had to consider Mr. Mott's situation. He'd gone from a life of relative luxury before the plague to being a grave digger and a footman. And who would she be out there? Not Princess Imogen, clearly. But she couldn't go back to being Seraphina, either. Not even if she managed to find her family alive.

"Madam?"

Seraphina whirled toward the voice. She couldn't see anyone among the trees, but she knew she hadn't imagined it. "Who's there?"

Her question was met with silence. An owl hooted somewhere in the distance. She pulled the knife out of its enameled scabbard and held it in front of her.

"Such a lovely thing you are," the voice said. "But alone?" He clucked his tongue. "Some men can be so careless. If you were mine, I'd never let you out of my sight."

If she screamed, the men would probably hear her. If she ran, she might be able to escape Arnaud, given the severity of his wounds. No doubt that was what he expected, what he *wanted* of her. She was the damsel in distress, the frail, meek creature who ran from the villain with no thought to what lay ahead.

Not tonight, Seraphina thought bitterly. She was through with waiting around for someone to save her.

"You're not going to harm me, Mr. Arnaud," she called into the darkness. "You're going to leave these woods, before the others arrive, and do what should have been done back at the castle."

A soft laugh was his only reply, so deep and rumbling she felt it in her chest. It was oddly seductive, but she reminded herself whom the laugh belonged to: a dying man with several bullet holes and a stab wound through his abdomen. This laugh was a bluff. It had to be.

A puff of air on her neck, as cold and stale as a tomb. "I'll scream," she breathed, knowing it was a lie. All the air in her lungs seemed to have left her in a rush of utter terror.

A hand closed on her shoulder, and the voice that had moments ago been far away whispered in her ear, "Hush, my darling. It's much too late for that."

CHAPTER 26

When they came upon Arnaud, he was sitting on a fallen log at the edge of a small clearing, his face and hands drenched in blood. He slurped it noisily from his fingers like a child savoring the remnants of a bowl of pudding.

Nico's stomach turned, but he lifted the sword and motioned to Lord Greymont and Colin that he was going to sneak around from behind. Arnaud was so absorbed in his meal that he hadn't even noticed them.

As Nico took his place behind a tree near Arnaud, Greymont and Colin stepped into the clearing. Arnaud glanced up almost lazily, as if he'd been expecting them.

"Good evening, gentlemen," he said. "I'm sorry to eat in front of you when I have nothing to offer, but something tells me you wouldn't accept it if I did."

Greymont scowled. "You're disgusting. We're doing you a favor by killing you."

"Killing me?" Arnaud smiled. "Come now, I think we established that's not going to happen. Where's the princess, eh? Did you leave her behind with the other young man? Not a good decision on your part," he said to Lord Greymont. "I saw the way he looked at her. Mind you, I've seen him fight, and it was nothing impressive. But—"

Now seemed like as good a time as any for Nico to test his theory. He stepped forward and swung the sword in an arc with all his might.

A moment before the sword made contact, Arnaud caught the path of Lord Greymont's gaze and swiveled his head toward Nico. It turned out all that grave digging had been good for his strength, and his aim. The sword passed through Arnaud's neck cleanly. His head toppled to the ground a moment later, landing face up in the dirt. His mouth was open midsentence. He hadn't even had time to scream.

"Good heavens, Mott!" Greymont cried. "You might have given us some warning."

"Don't be a fool," Colin said, bending over the severed head. It wasn't moving, which seemed to be a good sign. The headless body slumped slowly over onto the log. There was hardly any blood on the stump of his neck.

"It worked," Nico breathed, dropping the sword. "I can't believe it actually worked."

Greymont's eyes widened. "What do you mean, you can't believe it?"

"It was a theory. For all I knew the sword could have gotten lodged somewhere in his flesh. He could have stood up and danced a jig. I wouldn't be surprised if he did it without a head, to be honest." He wiped the sweat from his brow.

Colin grimaced. "We should bury the body."

"I wouldn't be against driving a stake through his heart, just in case," Nico added.

"I thought you were a man of science and reason," Colin said with a nervous laugh.

"I just beheaded an undead man. I've become much more open-minded in the past few weeks."

"What are we going to dig with?" Greymont asked, looking extremely uncomfortable. He flicked a piece of dirt off his velvet coat, realized it was gore, and retched.

Nico glanced down at his hands, flexing them. He'd done it. He'd actually done it. And that meant he could kill Crane. He could avenge Elisabeth. He could save the people in Eldridge Hall.

Colin kicked at the dirt. "The ground is rock solid. We won't be able to dig without a shovel. We'll need to go back to the castle to get one."

"Let's bury the head at least," Nico said. "The sword will do the trick." He got to work digging a hole a few feet deep while Colin and Lord Greymont dragged the headless corpse far enough away that it wouldn't be able to reunite with its missing piece. When they had finished burying the head, Nico hefted his sword and drove it through Arnaud's chest. The body twitched, probably from the force of the sword, and Greymont shrieked. Nico could barely smother his smirk.

They headed back through the woods toward the castle, all feeling smug with accomplishment. If more of the reborn decided to attack Eldridge Hall, at least they had a defense. And if King Stuart refused to evacuate, they wouldn't be leaving the people there completely vulnerable. Without proper guards, it might be difficult to defend themselves, but Nico had managed it. He thought with enough preparation, someone like Greymont could do it, too.

Colin's long legs had carried him farther ahead, and Nico found himself walking next to Greymont. Once upon a time, they might have been friends. True, Greymont likely wouldn't have associated with the son of a butcher, no matter who his mother had been, even if, ranking-wise, they were equals. But the past four years had changed Nico so much that he could scarcely remember the boy he'd been.

"Thank you for your help tonight, Greymont. I'm sorry I wasn't honest with you earlier, but I truly was at a loss."

He glanced at Nico from the corner of his eye. "I understand. Many of us in the castle tried to envision life outside of Eldridge Hall, but all we thought of was death and destruction. The idea that there were literal monsters out here... Well, I doubt even the most imaginative among us could have conjured this."

"No, I don't believe they could have." Nico thought for a moment and decided to press ahead. They may know how to take care of Crane, but that still didn't answer the question of what they would do when the food ran out. "I imagine you'll be leaving the castle soon," he ventured.

"I suppose I'll have to."

"Do you have lands to return to?"

"In theory, yes."

"Family?"

"I don't know."

Nico cleared his throat. "And Princess Imogen?"

Now Greymont stopped and turned toward him. "What about her?"

"Well, if I'm not mistaken, you two are...sweethearts? I

imagine you'll want to marry her, now that there's nothing to stand in your way."

"You mean nothing but the king himself?" He laughed bitterly. "I might have, if 'Prince Martin' hadn't arrived just in time."

"I'm sorry. I didn't mean to cause any trouble for you."

"You didn't. Not in the way you're thinking, anyway. She thinks I have access to a ship. That's all she really wants of me—transportation. My father owned a fine ship, before the plague, but I have no idea where it is, and without someone to sail it, it won't do us any good. Let's be honest. Any of us could get a ship now if we wanted one. There are probably dozens in the port with no one to claim them."

Nico nodded. He'd never really considered leaving Goslind. Where would he go? But he supposed for Imogen, who hadn't known that the plague was gone, and had perhaps worried that she'd need to go far to get away from King Stuart, a man with a ship would seem mighty appealing.

"Have you told her any of this?" Nico asked.

"No, of course not. Our first step was to get out of Eldridge. She was the one who discovered the door in the clock. I'm not sure how I didn't see it, to be honest."

"And now?"

"Now I don't know what I'll do. At least we know the monsters can be killed. If the plague is truly gone, and we can start collecting our own food, I'm less inclined to leave Eldridge than I was before."

Nico could understand that. They were relatively safe in the castle now that the only enemy with knowledge of the secret entrance was dead—assuming Arnaud hadn't told anyone else—at least until Branson and Crane returned. Though Arnaud had claimed there were others like him nearby, they'd seen no evidence of it in the forest.

"What will *you* do now?" Greymont asked.

"I haven't decided."

"You asked me about Princess Imogen. Why?"

Nico was grateful for the darkness, which helped cover his embarrassment. "She asked me to take her away from Eldridge, before she knew about Arnaud. But if you're in love with her..."

"In love with her?" Greymont shook his head. "Princess Imogen is beautiful, of course, and I suppose in another world I could have come to love her. But the only person I've truly thought about these past few years is my sister. She went abroad just before the plague reached Eldridge, but once the king closed the castle gates, I had no way to get word to her. At least not any way I was aware of."

"You think she's still alive?" Nico asked.

"I can only hope. For all I know she could have come home by now. Our family estate is only two days from here. My plan when we leave Eldridge is to look for her there."

He knew it was none of his business, but he couldn't help asking. "And what were you planning to do with the princess? If you don't love her, and you were going to leave Eldridge Hall either way...?"

"She's the king's favorite daughter, Mott. As long as she was protected, *I* would be protected, if I married her."

"But now?"

Greymont ran his hands through his hair. "The king is ill. If he dies, Princess Nina will be queen in name, but Princess

Giselle will do the ruling. She despises Imogen. Always has. I'm afraid now is not the time to tie myself to Imogen after all."

Nico felt a pang of sadness for Imogen. Yes, she had readily agreed to marry "Prince Martin," meaning her allegiance to Lord Greymont hadn't been particularly solid, either, but she must have thought he had some sort of feelings for her. Nico certainly had.

"At any rate, if Elisabeth is still alive, I'll stay with her."

A chill ran over Nico's scalp at the name. "Elisabeth?"

"My sister."

"You said your family lives nearby?"

"Yes. Have you been listening at all?"

Nico swallowed. "I'm sorry. It's just that a young lady named Elisabeth came to Crane Manor a few weeks ago. She said she was going to find her family, who lived near the castle. She said she had a brother at Eldridge Hall."

Greymont's face lit up with hope. "Where is she?"

"It's probably a different lady," Nico said.

As they came to the clearing near the edge of the forest where Colin and Nico had set up their camp, Greymont stopped.

Colin turned back to look at them. "Everything all right?"

"We just need a moment," Nico called.

"Did she give her surname?" Greymont asked. "What did she look like?"

Reluctantly, Nico described her. "Brown hair. Olive skin. Wide-set brown eyes. She was petite. Her surname was Talbot."

"That's Elisabeth! Talbot was our mother's maiden name. Where did she go after she left the manor?"

Nico suddenly wished he were anywhere else. Even Imogen's fury would be better than this. He considered lying to spare Greymont. Nico didn't know for certain what had become of Elisabeth, so it wouldn't even really be a lie. "Lord Crane took her to find her family. He told us he'd dropped her off with her father."

A relieved smile split Greymont's face. "Then they're alive? Elisabeth is home?"

Nico glanced down at his feet. If he'd helped her when she asked, she might still be alive. Maybe she would have made it here to Eldridge and reunited with Greymont. His guilt was as heavy as his father's gaze whenever Nico disappointed him. He looked at Colin, who was standing a few feet away, and knew he couldn't lie. "I don't think she ever made it."

"Why? What could have happened?"

"Crane is like Arnaud," he said softly. "Elisabeth was an immaculate. He returned without her, claiming he'd taken her home. But there was blood on Crane's shirt when he returned, and I saw one of Elisabeth's gowns beneath his bed. And then we found her mare, Locket, in the woods. Crane claimed she wouldn't cross water and had to be left behind, but…"

"My sister loved that mare." Greymont's face was bloodless in the moonlight. "What are you saying, Mott?"

Tears pricked Nico's eyes. He hadn't let his imagination go that far, but now that he'd seen the deer, it was impossible not to. She had died a horrible death, the same death Arnaud had intended for Imogen. "I'm so sorry." He reached forward for Greymont's arm, but the man turned and vomited, retching so hard he collapsed to his knees.

"Oh, God," Greymont moaned. "It can't be true. Please, tell me it isn't true."

"She told us she had a brother here," Nico said gently. "I never imagined it was you."

"My God," Colin breathed. He went to pat Greymont on the back, but he shook Colin off.

"Leave me alone." Greymont stumbled out of the forest, wiping his mouth on his sleeve.

"Should we go after him?" Colin asked.

Nico shook his head. "Let's give him some time. He knows the way back."

Colin nodded, and they were both quiet for a moment. "We should find a shovel. I can take care of Arnaud if you want to talk to the princess. She won't be happy when she discovers what you've done."

Nico grimaced. "No, I imagine she won't."

They crossed the field to the castle wall, which rose to an imposing height above them. It was hard to imagine that for the past four years, the people inside had lived on as if nothing had changed. He'd spent enough time with Imogen now to catch glimpses of a conscience, but she had stayed. She had danced and sung and drunk wine, while Elisabeth, no doubt as sheltered as Imogen had been before the plague, had braved the wilds to reach her family.

Nico was about to slip through the gap in the wall when he saw Greymont standing over someone, his sword pointed at the man's head.

Nico and Colin exchanged a glance and ran forward. "What happened?" Nico asked as they approached. "Are you all right?"

"He says he knows you." Greymont's eyes were bloodshot from being sick, and the tendons in his neck bulged in fury.

When the man turned his face up to Nico, he suddenly understood why. He'd recognize that oily grin anywhere. "How the hell did you get back here so quickly, Branson?"

"So you do know him," Greymont said.

Colin nodded. "Let him up. The man can't defend himself against a horse fly."

Nico expected Branson to scowl, but instead a smile curled his lips, causing Nico's skin to crawl with unease. "You couldn't have made it all the way to Crane Manor and back by now," he said to Branson. "Where is Lord Crane?"

Branson's grin broadened into that leering smile Nico despised. "I met him halfway back to the manor. He had already left to come looking for us. With the horses and the master's knowledge of the forest, we made good time getting back here."

Nico grabbed the sword out of Colin's hand and pressed it to Branson's weasely throat. "Where is he?" he bit out.

"He's already inside the castle." He rose slowly, but Nico kept the sword to his Adam's apple. "The fox is in the henhouse," he said in a reedy, singsong voice. "I think he's already found himself a hen."

Princess Imogen. Nico turned and ran through the gap in the wall with Colin and Greymont at his heels. He threw open the clock door and darted inside, his heart pounding in his ears. It could have been a servant, he told himself. It could have been anyone.

But as soon as he entered the great hall, he froze. Imogen was seated on a chair, her wrists and feet bound with rope. Behind her, Crane rested his hands on her shoulders. Her jacket had been removed and her tunic was wrinkled where

Crane's fingers dug into her flesh. He leaned down to whisper something in her ear and she flinched. Even in the dark he could see the color in the man's lips and cheeks. He'd fed recently, Nico guessed, though not on Imogen at least. She was terrified, but she was whole. Her eyes darted from Greymont's to Nico's.

I'm sorry, she mouthed.

Nico shook his head gently. He was the one who should be sorry. He should have known she'd come after them. If they'd stayed together, this wouldn't have happened. Beside him Greymont was trembling with fear, or rage, or maybe both. Colin had his sword held in front of him, though there was clearly nothing he could do to Crane with Imogen between them.

Crane was staring at Nico, his eyes glimmering in the dark. Without dropping his gaze, Crane tipped Imogen's head to the side, nuzzling her neck. He inhaled sharply and shuddered in ecstasy.

"Do you remember what I told you, Mott? Back in my study? I told you the first was the most special, that I doubted I would ever find my wife's equal."

Nico felt his gorge rising. Crane had killed and eaten his own wife.

"I was wrong, Mott." Crane smiled at Nico's horrified expression and ran his lips along Imogen's scar. She no longer looked terrified. She looked furious. "I believe I've found her equal. And I am going to savor every moment of her death."

CHAPTER 27

As Seraphina felt the man's breath on her cheek, all she could think about was how she was going to murder him once she was free. At first, she'd thought he was Arnaud, until he asked if she knew a Mr. Mott and a Mr. Chambers. He'd taken the knife from her easily and held it to her throat, just like the thief had when she was a girl. She hated how easily she succumbed to him, but she had no idea what his intentions were, and getting herself killed in a struggle might be premature.

It wasn't a matter of showing him the way into the castle. He already had that information, thanks to the other man, who must be the third servant Nico had mentioned when he told Jocelyn the truth. She hadn't told him she was a princess yet, not sure if that was information that would help or harm her. She hadn't told him anything, only allowed him to drag her back to the castle.

And then he had forced her to invite him in.

After she was restrained, he leaned down and whispered his identity in her ear, but by then she'd already surmised that this was Crane, Nico's master. He told her he'd just killed a maid he'd seen leaving the castle earlier in the day. Even having gorged on human blood, she could feel the amount of restraint he needed to resist her, especially when he put his lips to her flesh.

She struggled against his iron grip, but the man was unnaturally strong.

"Let her go," Mott said. "She's a princess, for God's sake."

Crane chuckled. "What would a princess be doing out in the woods in the middle of the night? And dressed like a man? You're a terrible liar, Mott. Always too honest for your own good. I thought I told you women always go for the villain. They want the dangerous man, the cruel man. Not the scholar, or the nurse."

Henry managed to keep his voice calm considering how furious he looked. "Princess Imogen is King Stuart's youngest daughter, and if you harm even a single hair on her head, he will have yours on a stake before the night is through."

"If she's so precious to King Stuart, what was she doing out in the forest all alone?"

"That's a good question," Henry murmured, turning his gaze on her. She couldn't help feeling chastened. He had tried to prevent this, and she had walked right into Crane's trap. But from what Mott had told Jocelyn, he shouldn't have been back here so soon.

"Is it true?" Crane said, tipping Seraphina's head back to meet her eyes. "Are you a little princess, playing pretend in the woods?"

"I am a princess," she said. "But I am not little, and I was not playing."

"No? What were you up to, then?"

"I was hunting monsters."

Crane smiled. She might have thought him handsome if she had met him under other circumstances. He was strong but graceful, his skin luminous in the dark. His lips were seductively red, like he'd just eaten a bowl of strawberries. God, how she loathed strawberries.

"If she's a princess, she'll be able to prove it to me in the morning," Crane said. "For now I think we should all get some rest. Mott, why don't you show me to your room. I'll sleep there."

"You know I can't do that," he said.

"Do what?"

"Let you stay here."

"*Let* me? Don't forget who has provided you food and shelter all these years. You would be dead and *un*buried if it weren't for me."

Seraphina could feel Crane's anger in the way he gripped her shoulders. How could Mott have failed to see what a cruel master he'd worked for all this time? Had he been that good at disguising it? And did Mott really think he would be able to prevent Crane from doing anything at this point? He was in the castle. They hadn't warned King Stuart about the reborn, and seeing Crane was a completely different thing than seeing Arnaud. Crane looked healthier than anyone at Eldridge Hall. Who was going to believe he was *dead*?

But what was Crane planning to do now that he was here, if he didn't intend to eat Seraphina immediately? If the king didn't believe Mott now, he would certainly believe him when she had been killed. And Crane had to know that while he might be able to take on three or four men, he couldn't take on every man at the castle.

Mott seemed to be asking himself the same questions. That little furrow between his brows had appeared, and he was chewing thoughtfully on his lip. *Please let him be formulating a plan*, she thought.

"You, sir," Crane said, turning to Henry. "You look like an intelligent young man, one who knows how to make the most of a difficult situation. One who isn't going to throw away everything good just to be a hero for a pretty lady."

Henry's eyes darted between Seraphina and Crane, and she felt her stomach sink. Crane was right. Henry was a man who put himself first no matter what. He had certainly managed to make the most of his situation in Eldridge Hall, nearly engaging himself to the king's favorite daughter. If it was his life versus hers, she no longer believed he would choose hers. How could she have been so foolish? She had told herself it was a game, had pinched her wrists until they were purple, had convinced herself that she was using Henry as much as he was using her. But she could see now that wasn't the case at all. She had trusted him against her own better judgment, and now she was going to pay the price.

"What is it you want, Lord Crane?" Henry asked. "We've seen what your kind is capable of. You knew what you were doing when you convinced your men to investigate Eldridge Hall, with the plan of entering it, clearly."

Henry was right. Crane was no Arnaud—he wanted Seraphina's blood, yes, but he was calculating enough to consider his next meal, and the one after that. He had an entire castle's worth of potential victims at his disposal now.

Crane brushed Seraphina's cheek possessively as he strode past her. "My plans are my business, sir. All I ask is a room for the night. Tomorrow you can introduce me to the king, and he can decide what to do with me."

Henry raised his chin. "Then I will ask you to kindly untie Princess Imogen. If your intentions are so innocent, you can have no reason to treat her like this."

Crane raised his hands and shrugged. "You can hardly blame me for mistaking her for a servant. I am unaccustomed to seeing ladies in trousers. Or cursing like sailors."

"You should be wary of untying me, sir," Seraphina growled. "I'm afraid my manners are as indelicate as my language."

Crane turned to her and grinned, his dark eyes gleaming. "Oh yes, we're going to have some fun later," he murmured. He looked back up at the men. "I can't very well give up my hostage. I'm afraid the princess will have to stay with me tonight. Otherwise, what's to stop you from setting the guards upon me in my sleep?"

Henry and Nico had both started to protest when Colin stepped forward. "I will guard your room tonight, sir. I'll make sure no one harms you. You have my word."

Crane narrowed his eyes at Colin. "And what's to stop you from letting your friends in to kill me? How can I have any certainty you'll protect me?"

"Promise me Crane Manor."

Seraphina glanced up at Colin in surprise. She didn't know the man, but she would never have expected him to be so disloyal to Mott. But Nico remained silent, regarding Colin with a furrowed brow.

Crane considered for a moment. "I've already promised it to Branson."

"We both know you're not going to leave anything to him. Promise it to me, and I will make sure you come to no harm tonight."

After a long moment Crane nodded, eliciting a mewl of protest from Branson. "Very well. Mott can come for us in the morning, and then we can all pay a little visit to the king."

Seraphina watched in silence as Henry escorted Crane and Colin to one of the guest chambers. Just as they were leaving the great hall, Colin turned and nodded at Mott.

Mott nodded back. Colin hadn't done this to protect Crane, she realized; he had done it to protect his friends from Crane. He had saved her by offering himself up as a guard. He would not betray Mott for a house, no matter how grand.

"Come on. Let's get you to your chambers." Mott untied the ropes binding Seraphina's wrists, pulling them away with that same tenderness he'd used when he felt for her pulse the night of her masquerade. She rubbed at them for a moment, wincing as her hands brushed over the already bruised flesh.

Mott escorted Seraphina to her chambers without asking, and she was grateful for it. Though they walked in silence, she expected that at any moment he would chastise her for her stupidity. And she would deserve it. All her righteous anger at the men for abandoning her had vanished when she realized the danger she'd put them in.

"Mr. Mott?"

He glanced down at her. "Yes, Princess Imogen?"

She was trying to formulate some sort of apology when the

door opened. A red-faced, clearly irate Jocelyn stood with her hands on her hips. "Where the hell have you been?"

"You could have been killed," Jocelyn said when Seraphina finished explaining, apparently more concerned about Seraphina than the fact that they had a man-eating monster staying in the castle. "How could you have gone off on your own like that? I would have gone with you."

"I know," she said gently. "And I would never put you in harm's way."

Jocelyn's lips pressed into a bloodless line. "Then you know exactly how I feel."

Seraphina nodded and tucked a strand of Jocelyn's hair behind her ear. "You're right. I'm sorry. From now on we do this together."

"Promise?"

"I promise." She rubbed her shoulders where Crane had held her and turned to Mott. "At least tell me you got Arnaud."

He sighed. "That's the only good news to come from tonight. The beheading worked."

"Then it will work on Crane, too?"

"I believe so, yes."

Seraphina took what felt like her first full breath in hours. "Thank God."

She'd barely had time to take another breath when the door swung open and Henry entered the room without so much as a nod. "How could you?" he asked in a low voice as he strode to Seraphina. "Dressing as a man and running off into the forest alone? Have you gone mad?"

"You were supposed to wait for me," she said, but his scornful gaze at her legs made her blush with shame.

To her surprise, Mott stepped in front of Greymont, placing a steadying hand on his shoulder. "Lord Greymont, please. Princess Imogen has been through a terrible ordeal. There's no use in recriminating anyone now. We've got to figure out what to do with Crane. It's not safe having him here, even with Colin watching him. Do you realize how many vulnerable people there are in this castle?"

Henry ran his hands through his hair and took a deep breath, stepping away from Mott. "We just need to make sure we talk to King Stuart first, before Crane gets to him."

"But what is his aim?" Mott asked, beginning to pace the room. "The man is no fool. He knows he can't just start slaughtering people. There will be a mass panic, and at most he'll be able to kill a half a dozen people before the rest escape."

"He could take us all prisoner, eat us one by one," Seraphina said, shuddering at the thought.

"He could. But I think he wants more than that. I think he wants power. *Real* power. And the king could give him that."

"Especially if he believes his favorite daughter is in danger," Jocelyn said.

Henry shook his head. "We should leave. Tonight, while we still can."

"We can't just leave everyone here," Seraphina said, gaping at him. It had been one thing to expect people to find food on their own, but to not tell them there was a monster in their midst was unthinkable.

"We did our best to prevent this, and we failed," Henry said. "Crane is here now."

Mott exhaled heavily in frustration. "And so is Branson. For all we know, he's gone for reinforcements. He has no idea what he's brought to this place. With Crane in the castle, we might as well have let in the Bloody Three itself."

Henry groaned, shook his head, and walked to the door.

"Where are you going?" Seraphina called.

"To talk to the king. We can't wait until morning."

"All right. I'll come with you."

Henry frowned and lowered his voice. "I spoke with Princess Giselle earlier. The king is apparently still angry about whatever transpired between you. I think it's best if I go alone."

The words struck Seraphina in an oddly painful way. The king had been angry with her before, but he'd never held on to his grudges. Once an episode passed, she went back to being his favorite daughter. "Are you sure?"

"I'm sure. Get some rest," he added, before nodding to Mott and ducking out the door.

Seraphina was weary to her bones, but she wasn't quite ready to go to bed. "Mr. Mott, would you leave Jocelyn and me for a moment?"

He nodded. "Of course. I should get some sleep, too."

"Can you wait, please? I have something I'd like to discuss."

His brow furrowed, but he nodded again and left without question.

"What is it?" Jocelyn asked when they were alone. "Did something *else* happen?"

She shook her head. "No, it's not that. It's just... I think I should tell Mott the truth about who I really am."

Jocelyn studied her for a moment. "Are you sure?"

Seraphina sighed, absently rubbing her raw wrists. "I'm tired of lying, Joc. Tired of pretending. Tomorrow... Well, we don't know what's going to happen tomorrow, but I don't think it's going to be pleasant. And if I'm going to die—" Jocelyn started to cut her off, but Seraphina continued. "I want to die as *me*."

Jocelyn was silent for a long moment. "All right, then. We can tell him together."

Seraphina shook her head and kissed the back of Jocelyn's hand. "I'm sorry for everything I put you through tonight. But you need rest. Crane doesn't know I sleep in the tower. He has less reason to search for me there than here. And Mott can stand guard."

"Are you sure? We still don't really know him. How do we know if he can be trusted?"

"I think I do know him now." Seraphina rose and placed her hand on Jocelyn's thin shoulder. "I promise we'll leave this place together, no matter what. I just need you to trust *me*."

After a moment Jocelyn nodded. "I trust you."

CHAPTER 28

Nico waited in the hallway outside Imogen's room as she had asked him to, though his eyelids were heavy with exhaustion and his body felt weak and shaky now that the adrenaline had washed out of his system. When Imogen finally stepped into the hallway, she surprised him by asking him to escort her.

He blinked in confusion. "To where, Your Highness? You need some sleep."

"I do. But this is not where I sleep, Mr. Mott."

A blush crept up his neck at the very idea of her in bed, particularly after Greymont's insinuation earlier. "Does Jocelyn know you'll be alone with a stranger, Princess?"

She arched an eyebrow. "Are we really still strangers, Nicodemus Mott?"

"Please, call me Nico. The only person who ever called me Nicodemus was my father. And he didn't say it kindly."

"Very well. Nico, there's something I'd like to show you."

He frowned but trailed her as she walked to a narrow stairway. "What is this?" he asked, but she started to climb, and he felt he had no choice but to follow.

When they reached her room, she held the door open for him, as if there was no question that he would enter. He paused on the threshold, unable to hold his tongue any longer.

"I don't understand," he said. "This is the tower where Crane saw the servant with a candle…" He trailed off as realization dawned on him. "You sleep here?"

She nodded, motioning for him to come in. When he hesitated, she laughed. "Don't worry. I'm not going to take advantage of you."

He could feel the blood heating his cheeks, but there was no hope of hiding it in this small space.

"Have a seat," she said.

He looked around the room for a chair, and the way she giggled at his confusion left him baffled. "I'm afraid you'll have to take the bed," she said.

He shook his head in mortified amusement. "I'm scandalized already."

"Surely this is not the first time you've been in a woman's bedroom, Nico."

"It's the only time I've been in a princess's bedroom," he said, clearing his throat to hide the tremble in his voice.

She sat down on the bed and looked up at him. "Then perhaps it will help you to know that I'm not a princess."

He stared at her blankly for a moment, sure he'd misheard. "I beg your pardon. I must be more tired than I realized. I think I misheard you—"

She smiled. "You heard correctly. I'm no more a princess of Goslind than you are a prince of Pilmand."

He took a seat almost without meaning to. "I don't understand."

"Then let me explain."

She told him everything, about how the princesses had taken her from her family, about how she'd been forced to pretend to be Imogen for nearly four years, about why Giselle despised her. His eyes grew rounder with every word, his emotions shifting from shock to horror to empathy to anger. By the time she finished, her eyes were wet with tears, though she managed to keep them from spilling over.

He was silent for several minutes, trying to process her words. "And the real Princess Imogen?"

"She was exposed to the plague while traveling," she said. "Giselle was afraid that news of her death would be too much for the king to bear, so she went in search of someone who looked like Imogen. I was that unfortunate someone."

He nodded slowly. "I see. And the rest of the court?"

"They believe the lie. Or at least they pretend to. It's a delicate balance here, to live in fear of what waits outside the castle walls, while also knowing what dwells within. I think we all got so good at pretending everything was fine to keep the king happy, that we started to believe it ourselves at some point. But I need to know what happened to my family and the rest of the community." She held her breath for a moment. "The rest of the *Jewish* community."

The way she said it, Nico knew she was bracing for some sort of attack or insult, or at the very least, revulsion. But all he felt for her was compassion. This poor girl had been through hell. "I wish I had answers for you. I haven't been to Esmoor since the plague broke out. All I know is that there were…pogroms."

Such a small word for such an unspeakable atrocity. To

slaughter Jews out of pure hatred, ignorance, and prejudice. He paused for a moment and then rose swiftly to his feet. "I've been such a fool!" he said, smacking himself in the forehead. "I can't *believe* the way I've treated you all this time. You must have thought me the most arrogant, selfish, pigheaded *ass!*"

A snort of laughter escaped her, and he glanced up, feeling a strange relief that she wasn't screaming at him in agreement. "I should have known then," he said, unable to keep from smiling. "When you snorted. I'd never imagined a princess to snort before."

"I truly am the worst princess," she conceded. "I'm amazed I managed to fool you at all."

"*Fool* being the operative word," he said with a laugh, and he felt in that moment that they were making a genuine human connection, and it reminded him of why he'd been so reluctant to admit the truth about Crane—to Colin, to himself. Why he hadn't accompanied Elisabeth into the woods when she'd asked him to. Why he couldn't let the idea of Crane go, and why he couldn't let the idea of Elisabeth in. He was terrified of being alone, of never feeling this sort of connection again.

"I admit I had an ulterior motive in asking you up here," she said finally. "I need rest, but I didn't want to put Jocelyn at risk by staying with her. Would you sleep here tonight? There's an extra straw mattress in the corner," she added. It was leaned up against the wall, with an old gray blanket draped over it, so drab it blended in with the stone.

"Of course I'll stay," he said when he regained his faculties. "It's the least I can do, after all the danger I've put you in."

"Considering I'm the one who let Crane into the castle, I'd say we're even."

Nico stared at her for a moment, reliving all the horrible things he'd said in the past several days, how judgmental he'd been, accusing her of sitting idly by while others suffered. "I'm so—"

He realized she'd already started to remove her stockings and spun around to face the window. He tried to imagine her up here every night, preparing for bed by the light of a single candle, completely unaware of Crane waiting below like a wolf with his prey up a tree.

"You can look now," she said behind him.

He turned slowly, trying to prepare himself, and still caught his breath at the sight of her. As much as he had resented her privilege these past few days, she was still the most beautiful thing he'd ever seen.

Her lips curled in a small smile. "Thank you for escorting me."

His eyes flicked to his feet. "You could have asked Lord Greymont."

"Would you have preferred that?"

His eyes shot up to hers. "Would you?"

She was silent for a moment, studying him. He tried to see himself through her eyes and failed. All he'd ever been was a burden to his father, a joke to his brothers. The only person who had truly loved him had died in his arms, and since then he'd catered to the whims of a madman, all for the sake of company.

But she wasn't who she appeared to be, either, he reminded

himself. She had also done things she was ashamed of to survive. Who hadn't, these past four years?

Her sad eyes softened and she sat back on her bed. "No. I'm glad you're here instead of Greymont."

"Why?"

"Because he can never understand what I've been through. Even if I told him the truth. Perhaps *especially* if I told him the truth."

"You don't believe he would care for you if he knew who you are?"

She shook her head. "No, Nico. I don't believe he would."

He hadn't planned to tell her, but Nico thought she deserved the truth. "He told me he was hoping to find his sister when he left here."

Her face was pale in the light of the single candle. "His sister?"

He explained what he'd learned tonight, and how Crane had killed Elisabeth. He didn't tell her how Elisabeth's death was part of the reason he'd come to Eldridge. He was too ashamed to admit he'd failed her.

She sat impassively for a few minutes, considering his words. "Poor Henry. That must have been very difficult for him to hear."

Nico nodded. "It was. It's clear that he loved her very much."

She sighed and shifted. "While we're in a confessional mood, the truth is I was using Henry, too. I thought he could take me away from here. That was all I wanted. And then I thought that maybe I could go on my own, that I didn't need anyone's help." She laughed bitterly. "But I only made it a mile from the castle before being kidnapped."

"That wasn't your fault—"

"Crane doesn't look like Arnaud," Seraphina continued, lost in her memory of the monster. "He looks healthy, virile."

"Arnaud looked that way, too, before Crane shot him. And Branson buried him. And I stabbed him."

She grimaced. "I see. But how did they get like that? How can mortal men have become *immortal?*"

"I think it must be some strain of the disease, or a mutation, perhaps. Just like immunes, who clearly have something in their blood that *protects* them from the plague. We believed everyone who contracts the plague dies from it, and we were almost right. But clearly there are a few exceptions. And those exceptions, for whatever reason…come back." He exhaled, not realizing just how exhausted he was until that moment.

"Sit back down, for God's sake," she said, making room for him on the bed. "We're long past the point of propriety now, don't you think?"

He could feel another blush creeping up his neck and turned his face away, but she nudged him with her shoulder.

"I think it's endearing, your blushes. Most men don't show emotion the way you do."

"Something my father never failed to point out." He glanced at her sideways, sheepish. "He thought it wasn't masculine to be emotional, that feelings were strictly in the feminine domain."

"That's ridiculous. Why should women feel things more strongly than men?"

"Not more strongly, perhaps. But differently. I was very close to my mother. My older brothers were always stronger, more prone to violence than I was. I liked helping my mother with domestic things, tinkering with clocks, helping to nurse anyone who needed tending. Even my interest in medicine vexed him."

"He was threatened by your intelligence and ambition."

Nico shrugged, feigning indifference, but something about her words warmed him. No one had ever defended him before, aside from his mother. "I never thought of it that way. But I suppose you could be right. My mother's family never let him forget that he was beneath them."

"I know a little something about that myself," she said.

Of course. She was a Jew in a castle full of gentiles. He couldn't imagine how hard it must have been to give up not only her home and her family, but her beliefs and traditions, too. "I'm sorry for what you've been through, and for the part I played in it."

"I'm sorry, too." She yawned, barely managing to cover it with her hand. He caught a flash of her wrist, raw now in addition to the bruises there, and without thinking he reached for it.

"I think I can help with this, if you'll let me."

She hesitated a moment before allowing him to take her arm in his hand and turn it over, palm up. She had wrists as slender as a girl of thirteen, not nearly eighteen, but he could still see the traces of calluses on her palm from carrying water from the well. "Tomorrow I'll get some honey and some gauze and wrap these. That should help treat the burns from the rope. The bruises…"

"Those won't heal on their own," she said. "Not unless I stop causing them."

He looked up at her, his heart clenching at the pain he saw in her eyes. "You did this."

She took a deep breath and released it slowly. "Yes."

He didn't ask why, because suddenly he knew. It was the same reason she slept in this freezing tower. The same reason she had cried when he described the world outside the castle. The same reason she knew Henry could never understand her. Survivor's guilt was the price you paid for living, and sometimes the cost was too high.

Slowly, his eyes never leaving hers, Nico lifted her wrist to his lips and brushed the softest kiss against the delicate skin there. A little shudder went through her, but she never tried to pull away from him. He repeated the same thing with her other wrist, then laid it gently in her lap.

"I forgive you," he said, and closed his eyes as she whispered the words he'd needed to hear for four years.

"I forgive you, too."

CHAPTER 29

When Seraphina awoke, the room was still dark. Something had disturbed her in her sleep, a dream perhaps, or a noise. She sat up and blinked, willing her eyes to adjust. Nico was still there in front of the door, lying prone on the straw mattress, but he seemed to sense that she was awake and sat up a moment later.

"What is it?" he whispered.

"I'm not sure. I thought I heard something."

He rose, tucked his shirt into his trousers, and reached for his boots. "I'll check."

"No!" she hissed. "Please. I don't want you to leave."

It was an hour or two before dawn, and she thought she could see his cheeks pink even in the darkness. She found she took perverse delight in making him blush. It was almost too easy.

"All right." He sat back down on his mattress, but he pulled his boots on anyway. "Just in case," he said with a reassuring smile.

She snuggled back under her blanket, her pulse already returning to normal. There was something oddly comforting about Nico's presence; a protectiveness about him that made her feel safe. Even when he'd disliked her as Imogen, she had known he wouldn't let anything happen to her. There was no game here, and that made him easier to trust.

She settled her head on her pillow, facing Nico, who sat with his back against her door. They stared at each other, both with small, introspective smiles on their faces, and she felt her own cheeks heating under his gaze. She remembered the feel of his lips on her wrists, how the gentleness of his touch had been more healing than any balm. She hadn't realized how badly she needed absolution until she felt it.

Her thoughts were cut off by a scraping sound outside her door. Nico was on his feet instantly, a knife in his hand. Seraphina leaped up, threw her robe over her shoulders, and rushed to his side. She watched in horror as the doorknob twisted, caught on the lock, and twisted slowly back.

She released a small, relieved breath. It was a flimsy door, but no one was going to break it down.

The knob twisted again, this time with more force, and the person on the other side rattled it against its hinges.

"Who is it?" Nico asked, placing himself between Seraphina and the door.

"Is that you, Mott?" someone whispered.

Nico exhaled loudly. "Greymont." He opened the door, admitting Henry. There were dark circles under his eyes and he looked more than a little miffed to find Nico in her room.

"What are you doing here?" he asked Nico as he walked past him. "This seems highly inappropriate."

"He's *guarding* me. Did you speak to the king?"

Henry ran his hands through his hair and paced around the small room. "No. He was too ill to receive visitors. At least according to Giselle." His eyes met Seraphina's. "She won't admit anyone, Imogen. I get the feeling she's hiding something."

Seraphina sighed and sat back down on her bed, frustrated and weary to her bones. "It wouldn't surprise me. But we don't have time for her games. We need to see the king at first light, no matter what."

Henry nodded. "Agreed. I should get some rest." He looked pointedly at Nico. "We all should."

Nico, to his credit, merely nodded and opened the door for Henry, who cast one last glance at Seraphina before leaving.

"He's possessive of you," Nico said when Henry was gone. There was a hint of jealousy in his voice that made her heart go a little melty around the edges.

"He's possessive of Princess Imogen," she corrected him. "Not me."

"You never told me your real name." She must have looked surprised, because he corrected himself immediately. "Not that you need to tell me. I just thought…"

Not even Jocelyn dared to call her by her real name. She hadn't heard someone else say it in so long, she felt oddly possessive of it now. Like it was the last vestige of her previous life, and by revealing it, she was somehow giving that away, too.

But they were leaving soon, if God was on their side, and she wasn't going to take Imogen's name beyond these walls. If they died…well, she wasn't going to take Imogen's name to the grave, either. She took a deep breath and released it slowly. "My real name is Seraphina. Seraphina Blum."

"Seraphina," Nico repeated softly, like he was trying it on for size. He must have decided it suited her, because he smiled.

The rest of her heart softened like molten metal, so warm she could feel it all the way in her bare toes. "Say that again, please."

He arched an eyebrow. "Seraphina?"

"Yes," she breathed. "No one has called me that in so long."

A shadow of sadness passed over his eyes. "Do you know what it means?"

"My mother said something about angels."

"The seraphim were angels, yes. But the origin of the name means 'fiery ones.'"

She let the words settle into her for a moment. She'd been fiery, once. But that flame had been suppressed for the past four years, and though she'd felt a spark of it when she left the castle on her own, she was afraid to let it kindle. After all, it had nearly gotten her killed.

"It suits you," Nico said when Seraphina didn't respond.

"You think so?" she asked, meeting his eyes just to see him blush.

He nodded, tugging his collar away from his neck. "Things tend to get heated in your presence."

She grinned at that and crawled back under the covers. Nico must have been cold, too, but he sat back down in front of the door without a word of complaint. She knew she wouldn't be going back to sleep now. It was nearly dawn, and they needed to get to the king before Crane did. But part of her wished she could stay curled up in her bed forever, with Nico watching her from the door, her stomach fluttery and warm, remembering for the first time in many years what it felt like to be safe.

When day finally broke, they dressed quickly and made their way downstairs. The castle was quiet, almost eerily so, until they grew closer to the king's chambers. The sound of someone crying reached them, and they hurried forward to find a maid sobbing in a hallway. A moment later Nina appeared, her face pale and stricken.

"What happened?" Seraphina asked, gripping Nina by the shoulders. Terror coursed through her at the thought that they were too late, that Crane had already wreaked havoc in the castle.

"Father is dying," she cried, her body shaking with her sobs. "I don't know how he became so ill so quickly, but the doctor says he's not likely to last the day."

Seraphina's eyes met Nico's over Nina's shoulder. "Do they know what it is?" she asked.

"They're not sure," she said, attempting to compose herself. "I'm going to fetch Giselle and Rose."

She hadn't expected half of the castle to be up already. She had no idea if the princesses were immune or not, and with Crane in the castle, it seemed foolish to let them run around unguarded.

"Prince Martin has some experience with medicine," Seraphina said, her voice as calm and soothing as she could manage. "Perhaps he could meet with the king for a few minutes. In the meantime, why don't you return to your room and stay with Rose. There's no need to upset her prematurely."

Nina nodded, as if all she'd wanted was someone to tell her what to do. "That's a good idea." She turned to Nico. "Thank you, Prince Martin. We're fortunate to have you here."

"Where is Giselle now?" Seraphina asked.

"She finally went to bed to get some sleep. She was up with Father all night."

Seraphina nodded and led Nico down the hall to the king's room. A servant let them in, her nose red from crying.

Seraphina stepped quietly into the king's candlelit bedchamber, where someone had lit incense to stifle the scent of illness. The king lay on his bed with his eyes closed, but he was moving restlessly, not fully asleep.

"Father," Seraphina said, going to his side. "What's the matter? Nina tells me you're unwell."

He opened his eyes at the sound of her voice and tried to smile, though she could see it pained him. "Not unwell, child, just a bit tired."

Despite his madness and cruelty, Seraphina couldn't help the throb of affection that went through her. She couldn't be there for her own parents, but as she stroked the king's hair, she told herself she was doing this for them. And maybe, just a little, for herself. Maybe she could find closure in a goodbye, even if it wasn't the one she wanted.

Nico entered the room and stood behind her, peering over her shoulder at the king.

"Your Majesty," he said, bowing to King Stuart. "I am sorry to hear you haven't been feeling well."

The king made a brief show of effort to sit up, then collapsed back against his pillow. "It's my stomach, mostly."

"Have you been vomiting?"

King Stuart glanced at Seraphina. "I prefer not to discuss such matters in front of Genny."

"Of course." Nico turned to her. "Will you wait in the hall for me?" he whispered.

She nodded and left the room, grateful for the fresh air as the faint boom of the clock striking three reached her ears like a memory.

It seemed like ages passed while she waited, and as the minutes ticked by, a terrible feeling began to wash over her. Where was Henry? Was Colin still guarding over Crane? They should have checked on him before going to see the king. She hadn't even checked on Jocelyn.

She was turning to go when the door to the king's chambers opened quietly. Nico emerged, his brow looking even more furrowed than normal.

"What is it?" she asked.

"The king is far worse than I imagined."

"What's the matter with him? Is it the mori roja?"

"No, not that, thank God. I'm not sure what's ailing him, but I have an idea. I need to check the cellar and the kitchen. But first we should make sure everything is all right with Crane. He'll be angry if we don't let him out, but we can't very well take him to see the king right now. Do you know the way to the guest chambers?"

Seraphina nodded. "This way." As they walked, she began to realize how much danger they were in if the king should die. Nina would be queen, inheriting an absolute disaster that she currently had no knowledge of. The nobles would have no reason to stay once they realized they were completely out of food. Which meant they needed to alert everyone in the castle about the reborn, all while keeping Crane locked up away from them.

"Where have you been?" Colin asked when they found him and Henry standing outside a closed door.

"Visiting the king," Nico explained. "He's gravely ill. The doctor thinks he might not last the day, and I'm inclined to agree. He wants to bleed him, but I fear that would kill him. Any word from Crane?"

"Silent as the dead," Colin said. "He hasn't stirred all night."

Nico nodded. "Good. I need to visit the cellar and the kitchen."

"What for?" Colin asked.

"Just following a hunch. Can you and Greymont stay here until we get back?"

Both men nodded.

"Princess Imogen! Thank goodness you're all right!" Seraphina turned to find Jocelyn running toward her, panting. "I was worried sick."

"Why? What's the matter?" Seraphina took Jocelyn's hands. "Is someone hurt?"

"It's Rose. Nina and I can't find her anywhere. I saw her last night, before she went to bed. She seemed fine. I thought perhaps she had gone..." She lowered her voice and whispered in Seraphina's ear. "I thought perhaps she had gone to visit a gentleman."

"Are you sure she hasn't?"

"I've asked all the likely suspects. No one has seen her."

Seraphina turned to Colin. "Are you sure Crane didn't leave during the night?"

"I was awake the entire time. I would have seen him. Besides, I have the key."

"We can look for Rose on the way to the kitchen," Seraphina said to Jocelyn. She turned back to Henry and Colin, her eyes landing pointedly on the sword at Henry's hip. "We'll be back as soon as we can. Whatever you do, don't let Crane leave this room."

CHAPTER 30

Nico glanced behind him every now and then to make sure the women were all right. The idea of Crane harming Rose, who was as delicate as her namesake flower, made him sick with worry. But he trusted that Colin wouldn't have fallen asleep and lied about it, and there was no reason for Crane to leap out a window or attempt some other means of escape. Everything he wanted was *inside* Eldridge Hall.

Seraphina's brow was dimpled with concern, and he tried to keep his own face calm and composed. She needed him to be strong, not panicked. Last night he'd tossed and turned on his straw mattress, reliving all the awful things he'd said to her, and—perhaps even worse—the way her skin had smelled when he'd kissed her wrists. Then he had imagined what it would be like to really kiss her, which only proved to be an exercise in futile desire, especially when she exhaled softly in her sleep.

Given the king's symptoms, which included pain in his stomach and vomiting, Nico had a very strong suspicion of what might be ailing him, but he didn't want to make any accusations until he was certain. Poisoning would not only implicate someone close to the king; it would mean there was almost no hope of recovery.

When they reached the cellar, they all stopped at the threshold. There was nothing there. Everything, down to the last breadcrumb, was finally gone.

Nico walked to a corner of the cellar and peered down at one of the shelves. As he'd suspected, a white powder was sprinkled along the wall.

"What is it?" Seraphina asked.

"Arsenic. It's a poison used to keep rats away."

"I know what arsenic is," she said. "But I'm surprised it was necessary, with all the cats. I haven't seen a rat since before the plague."

Nico's stomach sank farther. He had studied poisons while at Crane Manor, thanks to Crane's extensive library. Arsenic was known as "the king of poisons" for good reason; it had been used throughout history to dispatch countless rulers, being odorless, tasteless, and easy to administer. "We need to search the kitchens. Any idea where the chef lives?"

"The kitchens are barren as well," Jocelyn said in her typical frank manner. "We are almost entirely out of food and staff. It seems a whole swath of them left in the night and took almost all the food that remained with them. But I can take you to the servants' quarters—where the chef lives."

They walked for some time to a far wing of the castle, where people of lower rank lived in older, less richly appointed chambers.

Nico knocked on the chef's door, noting how cold and drafty it was in this wing, which explained why the nobility didn't live here. After several minutes, the chef appeared.

He looked like he'd been woken from a nap, and he wasn't pleased to see Nico.

"What do you want?" he demanded in a heavy accent Nico couldn't place.

"I'm Prince Martin, Princess Imogen's betrothed. I was wondering if we could ask you a few questions."

The chef, who Nico noticed was far less emaciated than the nobles, only sniffed.

Nico glanced over his shoulder at Seraphina. She nodded and stepped forward.

"Good morning, Chef."

Upon seeing Seraphina, he ducked his head, finally realizing the gravity of the situation. "Good morning, Your Highness."

She lifted her chin in a way Nico had previously believed came naturally, but now he could see she was slipping into the role like an actor in a stage production. "I need to know what my father has been eating recently. He's quite ill, as you may have heard."

The chef remained standing inside the door to his chamber, shifting his body as if to block their view of the room. "I have heard, yes. A problem with his stomach."

"Indeed. Hence our inquiry into his diet."

The chef's eyes darted to Nico and back to Seraphina. "For the past few days, he's only sipped on broth. He isn't able to keep anything else down."

"And who prepares the broth?"

"I do. I make all the king's meals."

Seraphina smiled magnanimously. "Excellent. He's always been such an admirer of your skills, as have the rest of us. Would you mind telling me what's in the broth?"

"Mostly chicken bones and vegetables. And seasoning, of course."

Nico was tempted to remove the bottle of arsenic from his trousers, but he was afraid the chef would stop answering their questions the moment he realized they knew he was guilty. "Which seasonings?" he asked. "We'd like to inspect them, to make sure nothing has gone rancid. The king's symptoms seem to be limited mostly to his stomach, leading me to believe the cause could be something he's eating."

"Are you a physician?" the chef asked, eyeing Nico suspiciously.

"He is," Seraphina cut in before Nico could respond.

The chef avoided Nico's eyes after that. "The doctor said the king is ill because he is old. Everyone's health is poor these days."

"And yet you appear rather robust," Nico said with a glance toward the chef's belly, which was straining against his tunic. The man had somehow managed to gain weight while everyone else was starving.

"I have always been a large man. I do not take extra food, if that is what you're implying. Anyway, I'm busy at the moment. Excuse me." The chef shut the door abruptly, causing Nico to stumble backward into Seraphina.

"That wasn't helpful at all," Jocelyn said behind him. "Now what?"

Nico folded his arms over his chest. "Oh, we have our man, all right. And I think I know who his accomplice is."

"Shouldn't we be looking for Rose?" Jocelyn asked as Nico led them back down the hallway.

"This will only take a few minutes." They stepped into an alcove and he pressed a finger to his lips. There were few lanterns here, and the corridor was dark and drafty. Nico suddenly had the feeling that Eldridge Hall was as full of secrets and scandals as it was halls and chambers. Hundreds of people meant hundreds of lies; everyone told them, even Seraphina. Even him. And he was sure the chef had more than his share.

As he'd hoped, the door to the chef's room opened several minutes later. A figure emerged, wrapped in the burgundy velvet cloak he'd seen hanging near the door to the chef's room. The woman glanced both ways before turning away from them and hurrying down the hall. After she'd gone around the first corner, Nico waved Jocelyn and Seraphina forward. They followed as swiftly and silently as they could.

The woman led them away from the old wing toward the royal chambers. At first, Nico was worried she was heading for the king's room, but she continued on past. Nico held out his hand and stopped Jocelyn and Seraphina. He knew where the woman was going, and there were servants here who would no doubt notice the three of them following her.

"What is it?" Seraphina whispered, her breath tickling his neck and heating his cheeks, which was definitely not what he needed at the moment.

"I know where she went, but I'm afraid this is as far as we should follow her."

"Who?" Seraphina asked.

"Princess Giselle."

"*Giselle?*" Seraphina blurted. Nico put a finger to his lips to quiet her. "How do you know?" she whispered.

"I recognized her cloak," Nico said. "And she's certainly the most...well rounded of your sisters."

"My God," Jocelyn said, pressing a hand to her mouth. "I knew she was cruel, but she's always been so protective of the king."

"Has she?" Seraphina asked. "Or has she been protecting herself this entire time?"

"The chef is a fool if he thinks he has anything to gain by aiding her," Jocelyn said. "She won't elevate his station. She isn't even next in line for the throne."

Suddenly, Jocelyn and Seraphina shared a look of fear. "Nina," they said in unison.

"I'll go," Jocelyn said. "You two should find Rose and make sure everything is all right with Lord Crane."

"I don't want you to be on your own," Seraphina said. "It's not safe."

"I'll be careful." Her lady kissed her on the cheek. "Just... promise me?"

Nico wasn't sure what she was alluding to, but it was clear Scraphina did. "I promise."

"Tell Princess Nina we need to gather the entire castle," Nico said. "Everyone needs to know about the king, the food, and Crane."

When Jocelyn was gone, Nico turned to Seraphina. "And then we have to get as far away from Eldridge Hall as possible."

CHAPTER 31

Crane's room was empty. The only thing out of place was a scrap of red fabric that had been hastily tied around an old nail in front of the window.

"I hadn't heard Crane inside for hours," Colin explained. "I assumed he was asleep. But as the morning wore on, I got worried. Henry and I broke in, but this is all we found."

Seraphina glanced between the two men, trying not to panic. They still hadn't found Rose. "What does the red fabric mean?"

"It's a signal of some kind," Henry said. "It must be."

"To Branson?" Nico asked.

"I don't know who else it could be," Colin said. "I'm sorry. I didn't leave this doorway all night."

"It's all right," Seraphina started to say, but she was cut off by Jocelyn.

"He has Rose. I know it."

Her stomach sinking at Jocelyn's words, Seraphina returned to the king's chambers, relieved to see the two guards there hadn't abandoned their posts. "Admit no one but the doctor," she told them. "And whatever happens, don't let Princess Giselle feed him anything—detain her and send for us immediately if she returns to these chambers."

The guards, who were trained to remain expressionless, glanced at Nico as if for confirmation. Seraphina let out a huff of exasperation and walked away before she could say anything unprincessly.

Jocelyn had found Nina, at least. She was with Lord Basilton, who had proposed last night. Servants had been sent to round up all the lords and ladies to gather in the great hall at true three o'clock. At least then they'd have everyone together and—God willing—accounted for.

"How did he get out if the door was locked from the outside?" Seraphina asked, going to the window to tear down the piece of fabric. If it was a signal, it could only mean there was someone out there Crane was communicating with. Branson seemed likely, but it was certainly possible there were others. She peered out the window. There was no way Crane had climbed out. They were several floors up and the walls of the castle were practically sheer. Perhaps a reborn man didn't have to worry about broken bones, but the dust on the sill had not been disturbed.

"There must be a secret passage," Jocelyn said quietly.

Everyone turned to stare at her. "A what?" Seraphina asked.

"The first kings built passages between the rooms, particularly the chambers for people of higher rank. It allowed the king to visit whomever he liked, whenever he liked."

Seraphina noticed Nico blushing from the corner of her eye. "How do you know about this?"

"From another servant. I've never heard of them being in any of the guest chambers, but I suppose it's possible."

Seraphina arched an eyebrow but didn't question Jocelyn further. She had a distinct feeling that Jocelyn had used the passages herself, and there was no point in embarrassing her. Whom had she visited? The person who told her about the door in the clock?

"Does that mean Crane's room leads directly to the king's?" Nico asked sharply.

"Possibly," Jocelyn replied.

He shook his head. "How could Crane have known this?"

"It's not uncommon in castles, especially ones as old as this. There's usually a triggering mechanism somewhere hidden."

Henry walked to the walls and began pressing on random bricks. He pulled a few books from the bookcase, then stopped in front of a tapestry hung on the wall. "It's probably behind here." He threw back the tapestry dramatically and frowned at the blank wall beneath.

"What about here?" Seraphina asked, lifting the corner of a fine woven rug. She pushed it back several inches and nodded. Sure enough, there was a trapdoor built into the floor.

"Well done," Nico said as he crouched down next to her. "Now the question is should we go looking for Crane, or stay here until Princess Nina has a chance to gather everyone?"

"We're going to have to split up again." Henry returned to the window, peering outside. "I think the women should stay here with me. You and Chambers know Crane best, and my presence will be missed if I'm not at the gathering."

Seraphina started to protest—Henry wouldn't be missed more than Prince Martin—but Nico nodded. "I agree with you, as much as I hate to leave."

"You can't go down there," Seraphina said, too softly for the others to hear. "It's too dangerous."

Nico's serious brow softened. "Lord Greymont is right. If we can find Crane and kill him, it will make the news of the king's illness less terrifying for everyone. Princess Nina will explain the food shortage, but we can send servants out to get more. Anyone who wants to leave Eldridge Hall should be allowed, with the warning that there are dangers outside the walls and people are safer remaining here."

"Be careful out there, and hurry back," Henry said, handing his sword to Nico. "Let's hope you don't need this."

Seraphina pushed the carpet out of the way and lifted the trapdoor. "Nico," she said as he started to descend the steep staircase leading down.

He paused and gazed up at her. "Yes?"

"Don't do anything foolish, all right?"

He grinned. "I promise not to, if you'll promise the same."

She nodded and watched him disappear into the floor, feeling strangely bereft as he went.

As soon as Colin was through, Henry closed the trapdoor and reached for the bolt that would lock it from this side.

"What are you doing?" Seraphina asked, moving to stop him.

He glanced up at her. "We don't want Crane coming back this way."

"But you could be trapping Nico and Colin along with him."

"They can look after themselves. My charge is to guard you and Jocelyn, and I plan to do just that." He slid the bolt into place. "Come on. We need to look for Rose."

Jocelyn and Seraphina shared a glance as they followed Henry out of the room. A pit formed in her stomach as she took one last look over her shoulder and closed the door behind them.

"We should go to your room first, just in case Rose has gone there to look for us," Jocelyn said to Seraphina. "And pack whatever belongings we want to take with us."

Seraphina squeezed her hand. Whatever happened, they were in this together. "Henry, stand guard outside of my rooms while Jocelyn and I prepare."

At least he didn't argue with her about this. "Very well. Hurry, though. It's nearly three and I'd like to locate Rose before the gathering."

In her rooms Seraphina used her warmest cloak to tie up a bundle of clothing, including the men's trousers and tunic she'd worn into the woods. She changed out of her muslin gown into a simple woolen one that was not only warmer but also less likely to tear, and she traded her slippers for her more sensible leather shoes.

"Here," she said, thrusting a similar dress at Jocelyn. "This will be better for the forest. Escaping won't do any good if we freeze to death the first night."

Jocelyn nodded and began to change, but there was a sense of sadness to her that Seraphina didn't think had anything to do with leaving Eldridge Hall.

"What is it?" she asked, quickly filling a small silk purse with her most expensive jewels and hairpins.

"You spent the night with Mr. Mott, didn't you?"

Seraphina sighed. "Mr. Mott is a good man. And a gentleman. Nothing happened between us, Jocelyn."

She lowered her eyes. "I don't want you to get hurt. That's all."

Seraphina tied a knot in the silk cord on the purse and set it among her belongings. She loved Jocelyn, and she knew Jocelyn loved her.

"Come here," Seraphina said, opening her arms to her friend.

They embraced for a long moment, long enough that Henry knocked on the door and called in an impatient voice, "What's taking so long?"

"Almost finished," Seraphina said, releasing Jocelyn. "Whatever happens between me and any man won't change my friendship with you."

Jocelyn sniffed. "I'm frightened. I don't know what my place will be once we leave Eldridge. I've been your helper and companion for nearly four years. Before that I worked for Imogen, and before that I was my parents' daughter. I've never been independent like you are. I've never been on my own."

Seraphina shook her head. "I wasn't independent before I came to Eldridge. I was a child, too. I didn't know anything but my own family. When I came here, I was determined to shut myself off from everyone, to guard my heart because it belonged to the people I left behind. But slowly, you became my friend, and I couldn't close myself off completely. If it weren't for you, I wouldn't have survived here."

"But the most shameful part of me is afraid once we leave here, Mr. Mott *won't* leave you. You'll have him, and you won't need me anymore. And the thought of not being needed is terrifying."

Seraphina sat with Jocelyn's confession for a moment. She'd

been so focused on the needs of those around her these past few years, she had never even considered what it would be like to find herself free of those tethers. The king was desperate for her love and attention. Giselle, Nina, and Rose needed Seraphina to be the sister they'd lost. Henry had needed her as a means of escape.

Meanwhile, Seraphina hadn't thought of herself as *needing* anyone at Eldridge. But she did need Jocelyn, now more than ever. She pressed a kiss to Jocelyn's forehead and pulled her to her feet. "Come on. We have to find Rose. Right now *she* needs us."

CHAPTER 32

Colin and Nico had been following the staircase down for quite some time when it finally leveled out. It was so dark they couldn't see anything and had to rely entirely on their other senses to make their way. Nico remembered how Crane had once referred to his excellent night vision. It must be a side effect of whatever had made him this way, or perhaps it was simply part of what he was now, like a predator with the ability to hunt at night.

"I don't think this leads to the king's chambers," Colin said as they walked. "We've got to be underground by now."

"I agree. Which means this tunnel likely leads outside. So what's our plan for when we get there?"

Colin was quiet for a moment. "Well, we've got to kill Crane, haven't we? And Branson, if it comes to it."

Nico's stomach soured at the thought. He despised Branson, but killing a man was not the same thing as killing a monster. "Agreed."

Eventually, they could feel a draft of cool air coming toward them in the tunnel, and finally bars of slanted daylight cut through the darkness. The tunnel ended in a grate at the rear of the castle. Colin pushed on the metal bars and the grate swung away on its broken hinges, a sure sign that Crane had come this way.

They emerged into the daylight, their swords held aloft, but there was no one here. Cautiously, they followed the wall surrounding the castle until they reached the gap where they first entered. There was no sign of Crane or Branson.

"I can't help feeling Crane has the advantage the moment we step outside these walls," Colin said. "He's stronger than us, and I hate to say it, but I'm fairly certain he's cleverer."

"You're right on both counts. But we have no choice. We're out of food. We can't stay at Eldridge Hall, and we can't let anyone leave until we know it's safe."

"But what if it's never going to be safe for the immaculates? What if that's just the way things are now—immunes and reborn? Once all the immaculates are killed off, the reborn will have nothing left to eat besides deer and squirrels, and perhaps we can kill them off one by one. But how can an immaculate ever survive out here?"

Nico shook his head. "I don't know. I guess those of us with immunity will just have to do whatever we can to protect the ones who can't defend themselves."

Colin arched a brow. "Are you possibly referring to a certain auburn-haired girl?"

Nico hadn't told Colin about Seraphina yet. It didn't feel like it was his place to reveal her secret. "Princess Imogen hardly needs my help." But even as he said it, Nico knew he *had* been thinking of Seraphina. She might not need him to defend her, but God knew she needed *someone* on her side.

Jocelyn was clearly a loyal friend, but she didn't know anything about the outside world, either.

Or perhaps Nico just wanted to believe he could be useful to someone like Seraphina.

Finally, he took a deep breath, hefted his sword, and slipped through the alcove. The woods loomed on the other side of the open field, dark and foreboding.

They crossed the field side by side, silently making their way through the dead grass. Nico's thoughts kept returning to Seraphina, to what was happening in the castle. It had bothered him that Greymont insisted he stay with the ladies, but he couldn't argue with his logic, and he still felt responsible for Crane's presence in the castle.

He knew that Seraphina could take care of herself, but every time he remembered Crane's promise to kill her, he couldn't keep the dread from washing over him. Crane may be a monster, but he was a monster of his word.

As Nico and Colin approached the first trees, Nico hefted the sword up to his shoulder, ready to swing at any neck that might appear. But it was quiet in the woods, with only the occasional sound of a bird or small creature rustling in the bushes.

They were deep among the trees when Nico felt the presence of something else. Colin must have sensed it, too, because he froze beside Nico.

The girl had come upon them so quietly he wasn't sure how they'd noticed her at all, save for the way she was watching them. Something about her gaze made Nico's skin crawl. But he lowered his sword when he saw that she was only a girl of around thirteen or fourteen, clad in a filthy dress. Her cheeks were smudged with dirt and her hair was long and stringy, but she was unarmed and obviously frightened.

Nico set his sword on the ground and gestured for Colin to do the same. "Are you all right?" he asked the girl. "Have you lost your way?"

She shook her head and responded in a sweet, clear voice, "I was only looking for food, sir. Have you come from the castle?"

Nico peered around with the sinking feeling that there must be someone else here. Perhaps Crane had been using the girl as a distraction. But the woods were quiet. Almost unnaturally so.

"We did," Nico said finally. "We've come looking for a man named Crane. Have you seen him?"

The girl's eyes widened in fear, as though she recognized the name. But she replied, "No, sir."

"Where is your family?"

"They're all dead, sir."

A chill crept up Nico's spine. "You live alone here, in the woods?"

The girl shook her head. "I live in a cottage just over there." She pointed off into the woods. "Would you like to see it?"

She was just a girl, Nico told himself. There was no reason to be concerned. But something about her frightened him. The fact that she'd invited two strange men to follow her didn't make sense. "Not at the moment. What's your name?"

She licked her lips and glanced nervously to the side. "I'm Dalia."

Nico smiled to show her he meant no harm. "I'm Nico, and this is my friend Colin. Do you need help?"

"No, sir. But I was wondering if you could tell me how to get into the castle."

The hairs on Nico's neck pricked as goose bumps spread over his arms. He cast a worried glance at Colin. "Why do you want to get into the castle?"

"I'm looking for someone," the girl said, her eyes darting between the two men. "Her name is Seraphina."

CHAPTER 33

Seraphina, Jocelyn, and Henry found no trace of Rose in her chambers, not that Seraphina had expected to. They went to the library next, where Nina, Lord Basilton, and a sizeable group of other lords and ladies had gathered. Giselle, on the other hand, was nowhere to be found.

"Do you understand what you have to do, Nina?" Seraphina asked as she took a seat on a sofa next to her.

Nina nodded. To her credit, she'd taken everything as stoically as she had when the window shattered around them all those years ago. "I'm to explain that Father is ill, and that we are out of food. And I should warn everyone that there are wolves outside the castle in the forest, and it isn't safe to go out alone."

"Exactly," Seraphina said. "No one should go into the forest alone. Anyone who does must be armed, preferably with swords as well as guns. And anyone who wishes to stay will be responsible for themselves. The remaining servants are free to go if they so wish. We can no longer expect them to care for us when there is no food, although they are welcome to remain at the castle, given the dangers outside."

Nina's lady-in-waiting was not so impassive as the princess. She looked as if she was going to be sick. "I don't understand. Where did all the food go?"

"We ate it," Nina said. "It's all gone. We knew this would happen eventually. We just didn't want to admit it."

The lady twisted a kerchief in her trembling hands. "Who will keep us safe? Most of the guards are gone now."

"Lord Basilton will protect us," Nina said, glancing across the room at him.

"But you'll be queen. You'll be queen with no one to rule. Where will we go?"

"Hush," Nina said, patting her hand. "The castle is still safe. It's been here for hundreds of years, through wars and sieges. We're going to be fine."

The lady blinked, looking slightly relieved. She tried out a small smile, apparently found that she preferred it to her tears, and smoothed out the kerchief.

Seraphina squeezed Jocelyn's hand but kept silent. The idea of staying at Eldridge made her queasy, but it wasn't her home. She hadn't spent her entire life here, the way Nina had. Besides, Nina was going to be queen. It made sense that she would stay in the castle.

Finally, the clock struck three, and the crowd of people gathered in the library began to make its way to the great hall. Murmurs of the king's illness were everywhere, but no one had mentioned the food. Seraphina watched Nina rise with as much dignity as she could muster, but her lips were pressed together in a grim line.

When they reached the great hall, it was brighter than Seraphina had ever seen it, and she found that in full daylight

it was just a room like any other, albeit one with a massive ob-
sidian clock at one end. She would not miss Eldridge Hall. She
would not miss any of the people here. But she also couldn't
imagine it falling into ruin. Seraphina hoped Nina would be
a better queen than she, or Giselle, had given her credit for.

Princess Nina walked to the front of the hall and cleared her
throat. "Good afternoon. I'm afraid that we are not gathering
under the best of circumstances, but I have an important an-
nouncement that I must make. Most of you know that the king
is very ill. He is not improving as quickly as we had hoped,
but I am still praying for his full recovery, as should we all."

Nina glanced at Seraphina. This wasn't part of the script,
but Seraphina couldn't blame her for holding on to hope.

"What you may not know is that Eldridge Hall has finally
run out of provisions." She only paused for a moment, ignoring the gasps and shouts from the gathered crowd. A baby
cried and a woman shushed her. "This was an eventuality we
all should have prepared for. I know you have noticed our
dwindling numbers. Many servants have already left without permission."

This elicited a few curses and jeers from people, probably
other servants. If Nina wanted anyone to stay loyal, this was
the wrong way to go about it.

"Unfortunately, it seems that we will all have to learn to
care for ourselves now. And it's true that we have been fortunate to survive as well as we have for so long. We have our
king to thank for that. Surely, many of us would have per-
ished if not for him.

"I ask you to please remain calm and make your decision
about how you will move forward with as much care and

thoughtfulness as possible. Once you leave Eldridge, you will not be able to return. I have received word that there are many dangers in the woods, including man-eating wolves." As Nina went on to explain what she had discussed with Seraphina regarding weapons and precautions, Seraphina noticed a small disturbance from the corner of her eye. There was milling in the crowd as someone pushed their way through.

Henry noticed it at the same time and hurried toward Nina as if to protect her, a new sword he'd gotten from the armory held close to his side. Was Crane still here? Seraphina reached for her knife with one hand and Jocelyn with the other.

But a moment later Princess Giselle emerged at the front of the crowd, flanked by two guards—the same men who had stood guard in front of the king's chambers. Seraphina ground her teeth in frustration. They hadn't been able to find her, and now it was clear the guards hadn't given her order an ounce of consideration. Giselle must have bought them off. The chef, however, was nowhere to be seen.

"Giselle," Nina said softly. "Is everything all right?"

Giselle stepped in front of her sister without acknowledging her. "I'm afraid I have some sad news. King Stuart has died, after naming me his chosen heir."

Nina reeled as if struck. "What?"

Giselle leaned toward Nina and spoke in a low voice. "Come now, sister. You should be thanking me. We both know you can't rule." Then she turned back to the crowd. "I am queen now, and no one is leaving this castle."

Seraphina couldn't hold herself back anymore. "You don't understand what you're—"

Giselle signaled to someone in the crowd, and yet another

guard stepped forward, along with the chef. "Arrest this imposter," she said in a voice that rang out loud enough for everyone to hear. "That's right. This girl is not my sister. She's a
charlatan who murdered Princess Imogen and took her place."

"Impossible," someone called.

"How could you mistake your own sister?" someone else
shouted.

Seraphina barely heard them. Her corset was too tight; her
vision was tunneling. And the guard was nearly upon her.

"Black magic," Giselle said. She didn't even have to shout,
as she had everyone's attention now. "This girl is a Jew. We
all know what they're capable of."

Seraphina could feel the eyes of everyone in the room move
to her. Jocelyn's grip tightened. Henry, who was at her other
side, faltered, and she braced herself for his reaction.

But to her surprise, he put his arm around her waist, steadying her. "We have to get you out of here."

Giselle was about to turn back to the crowd when something hit the window behind her with a sharp crack. The
object fell to the floor in a rain of tinkling glass. It had come
from outside the castle.

There were more gasps and screams from the crowd, and
the baby began crying again with renewed vigor. But Nina,
who remained remarkably unperturbed, bent down and
picked up the object: a stone wrapped in cloth. "It has your
name on it," she said to Seraphina.

Henry took the stone and unwrapped it. His face went pale
before he handed it to Seraphina. Suddenly, she was wide-
awake.

I promised you some fun, Princess Imogen. Now it's time to play.

Seraphina folded up the scrap of cloth with the message and went to the window, looking down at the courtyard. Everything appeared as empty and deserted as ever, but then a movement caught her eye near the gallows.

"There's someone out there," she said quietly to Jocelyn and Henry.

"Tell everyone to go to their rooms and lock the door," he said to Giselle.

Giselle's gaze hardened in outrage. "Who are you to tell the queen what to do?"

"You are not the queen," he snarled. "And you can either do as I say, or you can die."

For a moment her expression faltered. "What?"

"There are monsters outside this castle as we speak. They are preparing to hunt you down, rip your throat out, and drain you of blood."

The crowd began to mill restlessly, unsure what to believe.

"Careful," Seraphina said quietly, but her eyes were still scanning the courtyard. "There, by the gap in the wall."

A dark-haired man darted into view, most likely Branson, the troll who worked for Crane. He motioned with his arm and a moment later a person Seraphina didn't recognize slipped through the wall, then another, and another.

"There are many more than we thought," she said over her shoulder to Henry. She glanced at Giselle, who seemed to finally grasp the seriousness of the situation, given the way the blood was draining from her face. "Hurry. Lock your door. Don't open it for anyone."

Giselle blinked at her for a moment, then shook her head

as if to clear it and turned to the crowd. "Run to your rooms! Lock the doors!"

Henry shouted to Giselle's three guards. "This clock leads to the outside. Guard it with your lives. Do not let anyone enter. If they do, cut off their heads. *And you'd do well to heed our words this time.*" He ran to the wall of weapons and waved at others to do the same. "There are more swords in the armory," he shouted.

Another rock hit a window and bounced off. A woman screamed.

"It's starting," Jocelyn said, her voice hollow.

Seraphina swallowed the bile rising in her throat. This could only mean that Nico had failed. Crane was still alive, and he was coming for her.

CHAPTER 34

"Who's Seraphina?" Colin asked Nico, who was staring at the girl, wondering how she knew Seraphina. It was clearly from before the plague, but how old would this girl have been back then? Nine? Ten?

"Princess Imogen is Seraphina," Nico said, receiving confused looks from both Colin and the girl. "She was kidnapped by the princesses to impersonate their dead sister." He turned to the girl. "Are you related to her?"

She glanced to the side again. "I don't…"

"It's all right," Nico said, stooping a bit to look her in the eye. "She's safe. For now. Did you know her before the plague?"

The girl nodded, but she didn't say more, and Nico realized that if she was also Jewish, she might be too afraid to tell him. "I see. And you're sure you don't know who Crane is?"

"It's important," Colin pressed. "You need to tell us, for Imo— For Seraphina's sake."

Now her eyes began to fill with tears, and Nico felt more certain than ever that she knew more than she was letting on. "He promised if I helped him, he wouldn't hurt her."

Nico's stomach turned over. "Who? Crane?"

She nodded, tears streaming down her cheeks. "I'm sorry. Will she be all right?"

Shit. Now Crane was using children to accomplish his aims. How much lower could the man stoop? "What did you help him with, Dalia?"

"He found me in the woods one night when I was... He found me, and he said that he was friends with people inside the castle, and that he had other friends living nearby. They were all going to surprise his friends inside the castle, he said. He just needed me to go tell the others. He sent me to find them."

"What friends?" Nico asked, his heart starting to hammer in his chest.

"Friends like Lord Crane. They live in a large house not far from here."

"Whose house?"

"I don't know exactly." Dalia licked her chapped lips nervously. "You're not like Lord Crane."

"You mean...reborn?"

Dalia nodded.

"No, we're immunes. But Seraphina is not, and that's why it's so important you tell us everything we need to know to stop Crane from hurting her."

"But he promised he'd keep all the ladies inside the castle safe."

"He lied!" Colin threw up his hands in frustration, and now Dalia devolved into complete hysterics.

"Stop it, Colin," Nico hissed. "You're upsetting her more." He pulled Dalia into his arms and held her for a moment. "It's all right now. We'll help you, but you have to tell us what you know. Can you do that?"

Finally, after a few shaky breaths, Dalia nodded. "I think so."

"Good. Then tell us everything, as fast as you can. Seraphina is counting on you."

Nico and Colin sat in wordless contemplation, taking in everything Dalia had told them.

Crane had been in contact with other reborn. That was whom he'd been writing to that afternoon in his study when he had shown Nico the portrait of his wife. And Elisabeth's house, where he'd supposedly left her, was still inhabited, though not by her family. There was a group of reborn there. Adrien Arnaud had been with them for some time, but he was a loose cannon, a messy hunter who didn't always share his kills with the group. Though they could survive on live animals, they grew weaker and weaker the longer they went without human blood.

Dalia sat on a log before them, her face pale where tears had streaked through the dirt and grime. "My entire family was killed in a massacre, not long after Seraphina was taken," she explained. "Almost all of the Jews were slaughtered, except for a few of us who managed to escape."

Nico did his best to keep his expression calm, but inside he was simmering with rage. So many senseless deaths amid so many others.

"I ran as far as I could, but after a few weeks, I came back to look for survivors. I knew Seraphina had been taken to the castle, but I didn't know why. Everything had been boarded up by then, and I thought she was either dead or would be soon. But then I saw the light in the tower."

Nico's heart stuttered as he realized what she was saying. "You knew it was Seraphina?" he asked.

She shook her head, causing her matted hair to fall in front of her eyes. "No. Not for certain. But I couldn't imagine who else would be up there, other than a prisoner. So I came every evening, at sunset, just to be sure they were still there. At least I knew *someone* was alive, as long as I saw that light."

"It was her," Nico said, still unable to believe it. "She was there. She may have seen you."

Dalia sniffled, her eyes glimmering with hope. "Crane found me not long ago. I was living in an abandoned house alone, and at first I thought he'd come to kill me. But then he promised me there were others like me. Jews who had escaped pogroms in other cities," she added hastily. "So I went with him."

Nico sighed. "Colin was right. He lied to you. He's trying to get into the castle to access the immaculates living there." Nico's eyes darted unconsciously to Dalia's wrists, but her sleeves covered her pale skin. "Seraphina will be overjoyed to discover you are alive and well."

Dalia worried her raw lower lip with her teeth. "She must be worried, since I stopped coming."

"Where is Lord Crane now?" Colin asked, more gently this time.

"He went to the castle," Dalia admitted. "He took his friends with him. He said they were going to free the people, that King Stuart was holding them prisoner. I knew that was true, at least, because of the boards on the windows and the locks on the gates."

"How did we miss them?" Nico asked Colin. "Did Crane send her as a distraction?"

"They move quietly when they want to," Dalia said. "Will you take me with you? Lord Crane will kill me if he finds out I told you all of this."

"Crane isn't going to hurt you," Nico promised. "And yes, you will come with us. But right now we have to rescue Seraphina. Has everyone left the house where you've been living?"

"All except for the other children. I was supposed to stay with them, but I wanted to be the first one to greet Seraphina when she came out."

Nico sighed. If there were other immune children living with Crane, it was going to complicate everything. "I want you to return to the house and wait there for us," Nico said. "We'll come get you as soon as we have Seraphina. Can you tell us the way?"

Dalia nodded and drew a quick map in the dirt. When they were sure they would be able to find the house, they said goodbye and she headed back into the forest.

"If all of the reborn have converged on Eldridge Hall, we're in a bad situation, Nico," Colin said.

"I know. But all we have to do is get to Seraphina. If you don't want to go back in, I understand. You could wait here in the forest."

Colin laughed. "As if I'd ever allow you to go in there on your own."

It was late afternoon, and the sun would be setting in a couple of hours. The reborn would have a distinct advantage in the dark. How he wished they'd brought Seraphina with them. But seeing as she was trapped in the castle and he was out here, he was going to find a way to rescue her, whether she liked it or not.

CHAPTER 35

"Where do we go?" Jocelyn asked as they ran after Henry through the castle. Leaving wasn't an option. The entire castle was surrounded by now. At least fifty people had swarmed through the gap in the wall. They had to assume they were all reborn.

"It has to be somewhere we can lock from the inside," Seraphina said. "Somewhere with heavy furniture we can use to barricade the door. And preferably somewhere with an alternate escape route."

"We could go back to Crane's room," Henry called over his shoulder.

"But he knows about that tunnel. For all we know, they'll try to get in that way."

"It's a good thing I locked it," Henry said smugly.

"Really? *Now?*"

"If any room has an escape route, it has to be the king's," Jocelyn said.

Henry flinched. "But the king's body is in there."

"We don't even know for certain that he's dead," Seraphina

panted. "I won't believe anything Giselle said until I see for myself."

"But if he is?" Henry pressed.

"Then the scent of death will be all over the king's room. Maybe that will mask my scent. You and Jocelyn appear to have immunity."

They turned down the hall leading to the king's chambers. Most people seemed to have returned to their own rooms. Frantic men and women who probably lived farther into the castle were running down the halls, checking doors and screaming in frustration when they found them already locked.

Fortunately, no one had been brazen enough to try the king's chambers, despite the guards having deserted them. The doctor was inside, his head bowed over the king. He looked up when they entered, oblivious to what was happening elsewhere in the castle.

Seraphina froze. "Is he...?"

The doctor nodded, and Seraphina felt a hollow ache in her chest. She approached slowly, not sure she wanted to see a dead body, but feeling that she needed this closure.

King Stuart looked frail and insubstantial on the massive bed. But someone had closed his eyes, and she could imagine that he was sleeping. In fact, she realized that this was the first time in weeks she'd seen him without lines of strain around his eyes. He must have been in constant pain. She only hoped that Giselle had let him die believing Seraphina was Imogen, that she hadn't attempted to take that from him, too.

Seraphina placed one kiss on his forehead, as he'd done to her so many times, and turned away.

Jocelyn explained everything to the doctor while Henry and Seraphina started to barricade the doors.

When they'd moved every piece of heavy furniture they could find, Seraphina began to search the room for an escape route. The doctor agreed there had to be at least one.

"If invaders ever attacked the castle, there would be a way for the monarch and royal family to escape, probably through a tunnel." Dr. Lemin was checking behind books, paintings, and tapestries with Henry and Jocelyn. Seraphina threw back every rug on the floor, but so far she'd found nothing.

She went to the king's sitting room, still decorated in green from her birthday masquerade. No one had boarded the windows up again after her party, and she wished now that they had. She crept over to the largest window and peeked out from behind a curtain. People scurried around below, but they were several stories up and would be impossible to reach without a very tall ladder.

Just as she was retreating from the curtain, someone stepped into view. He was far away, but there was no mistaking Crane's dark hair, pale skin, and full lips. She ducked back too late. He had smiled at her. And now he knew exactly where she was.

Heart pounding, she ransacked the green room in her search for an escape route. There had to be one here somewhere. Finally, as tears of panic welled in her eyes, she threw back a small rug and squealed with relief.

"I found it!" she shouted. The others hurried into the room. There was a trapdoor here, similar to the one in Crane's room.

"Do we leave now?" Henry asked.

Seraphina shook her head. "There are so many of them

out there, and we don't know where this leads. I think we should wait here as long as we can."

The doctor, who was more a man of God than of science, seemed unable to grasp the concept of the reborn, which Henry had already explained to him several times. Jocelyn alternated between pacing around the room and trying to attend to Seraphina's appearance. It was the last thing she cared about at the moment, but it was less distracting than Jocelyn's pacing.

A shout from the hall broke the silence, and Seraphina bolted upright, forgetting that Jocelyn was in the process of braiding her hair and nearly losing a chunk of it with her sudden movement.

"Oh, God, they're here," Jocelyn said. "What do we do?"

There was another shout and Seraphina reached for her knife. In the corner the doctor began to pray quietly.

The door rattled so suddenly they all jumped. "Steady now. The barricade will hold," Henry said quietly.

The door rattled again, but it didn't budge. It was locked and bolted. It would take a battering ram to get it open.

"Princess," a voice called. "I know you're in there. I saw you through the window."

Henry shot her a furious look over his shoulder, but even he could see now wasn't the time for a lecture. "Is that Crane?" he whispered.

"So the king really is dead," Crane continued. "Shame I couldn't have eaten him, but then, he's so full of arsenic, I doubt it would have made for a satisfying meal."

Jocelyn started to weep next to Seraphina, who put an

arm around her thin shoulders. "It's all right," she whispered. "We're going to be fine."

"I haven't found the other princesses yet, but I will. I promised myself I'd have a princess before the day is through."

Seraphina sighed in relief. Rose and Nina were still alive, at least. There was a pause.

The door shook, harder this time. "You may as well let me in. One way or another, you're going to die, and starvation isn't a good way to go. I'll make it quick, tearing through your jugular first, so you bleed out quickly."

"Is that what you did to Elisabeth?" Henry called, his voice strained. "Did you make it quick for her?"

Another momentary pause, as if Crane was trying to remember which victim Henry was referring to. "Ah yes, Miss Elisabeth! She mentioned a brother, come to think of it. Shame you were hiding in the castle instead of protecting her."

Henry moaned in anguish and Jocelyn began to cry louder.

"Shhh!" Seraphina snapped her fingers to get the doctor's attention. "Keep her calm, please." Dr. Lemin looked relieved to have something to do besides pray. He nodded and led Jocelyn away.

"Who else is in there with you? I can smell two immunes, and I can smell fear. But underneath all that I can smell you, Princess. Such a lovely scent."

Seraphina felt her gorge rising, but she swallowed it down. She wouldn't give him the satisfaction of her fear. "You're wasting your time here."

Another long pause. She and Henry exchanged a worried glance, but several minutes passed by with no more from Crane.

"Where has he gone?" she asked.

"Maybe he believed you." He took a seat on a sofa and rubbed his temples. "I don't know how long I can stand this."

She took his hand and squeezed it. "Can we make one promise to each other? One we'll actually keep?"

He glanced up at her, skeptical. "What?"

"That we'll leave this place together, one way or another? We won't abandon each other, as long as we're still alive?"

"Just so we're clear," he said, tilting his head to meet her eyes, "I can't actually sail."

She smiled wryly. "I know."

He was quiet for a moment. "I have to admit you continue to surprise me."

"You mean because I'm not Imogen? Or because I'm a Jew?"

He shrugged. "Both, I suppose."

"Let me guess. I'm the first Jew you've ever known."

"Yes."

"What were you expecting? A hooked nose? A foul odor? Cloven hooves?"

He winced, and she wondered if he'd actually believed such ridiculous propaganda about Jews. He certainly wouldn't be the first. "I've been a fool, Seraphina. But the fact is that the circumstances of our birth don't really matter, do they? You and I may come from different worlds, but we're both here in this one now."

She nodded.

"What do we do?"

"We stay here. We stay calm. And we pray that Nico is coming for us," she said, leaning back against the couch.

"How do you know he isn't dead already?"

She closed her eyes and sighed. "I just know."

He leaned back next to her, pressing his hands to his thighs. "I may not understand what you see in the man, but for all our sakes, I certainly hope you're right."

CHAPTER 36

Dalia had been right about the reborn. They had moved so silently in the woods Nico and Colin hadn't heard them pass. As they approached the castle, a man ran out of the gap in the wall, screaming. Another man wasn't far behind.

"Help me!" the first man shrieked. He was dressed in fine clothing, while the man behind him wore homespun, the cloth tattered and old.

Nico raised his sword and ran to intercept them, but the reborn caught up to the man first. He tackled him to the ground, and though the man had a knife, which he used to repeatedly stab his attacker, it was no use. By the time Nico reached them, the man's throat was torn out and the reborn had buried his face in the massive wound. Without hesitating, Nico brought the sword down on the undead man's neck with all his strength.

The reborn collapsed on top of his victim, his severed head still attached to the dead man's flesh by his teeth.

Colin gagged behind him. "Good God, Nico. Is that what we're facing inside the castle?"

"I'm afraid so," Nico said, wiping his blade in the grass. "The reborn are greatly outnumbered, but unless people decapitate them, they'll be able to do massive damage in a short amount of time. Come on." He charged through the gap in the wall and ran toward the door in the clock, which had been torn from its hinges.

As soon as he burst through, Nico was immediately attacked by another man.

"It's me, Prince Martin!" Nico cried.

The man, who had no weapon, paused and frowned. "What were you doing outside the castle?"

"We'd gone looking for help," Colin said behind him.

"Who are you?" the lord asked.

Colin huffed in exasperation. "I'm a friend. Now get yourself a sword."

He nodded and picked up a sword lying next to a woman whose throat had been torn out, just like the man outside. Unfortunately, she had been eviscerated as well, reminding Nico of the deer in the forest. His thoughts turned immediately to Seraphina.

Crane's room was as good a place as any to start, so they began to make their way down one of the castle's many corridors. They found half a dozen bodies as they went, all human, all with their throats torn out and their bodies drained of blood. If the reborn had any sense, they wouldn't kill so indiscriminately. There were enough immaculates here to feed them for months, and they were wasting so many lives. But they appeared to be in some kind of feeding frenzy.

As they rounded a corner, they came upon a woman clutching at the skirts of a fallen maid, bared teeth snapping at her ankles while the girl struck at her attacker with a butcher knife. This reborn appeared to be around forty, and though she was missing an arm, it didn't seem to be slowing her down.

Colin ran forward, sword raised, and decapitated the reborn while the maid screamed bloody murder.

"Quiet!" Colin said, kicking the reborn woman's head away from the maid's ankles. "You'll only draw more of them."

She wiped her tear-streaked face on her sleeve and nodded as Colin helped her to her feet. "I don't know where to go. All the rooms are already locked. The lords and ladies won't let the servants in."

"Shocking," Colin drawled. "You might as well leave now. Take a sword if you can find one, and a few other people if possible. You'll have better luck in numbers."

"Leave? You want me to go out there?" she asked, glancing back the way they had come.

Colin took her by the shoulders. "It's all over, don't you see? This lie you've all been living is over. Now you've all got to find your way out there, like the rest of us have."

The maid stared up at him, wide-eyed. "Can't I stay with you?"

"We're looking for Princess Imogen. You're better off out there," Nico said, shoving past her. Colin joined him a moment later.

"We should have taken her with us, Nico."

"We can't save everyone. You know that."

"I know."

They were approaching the corridor leading to the library when the sounds of muffled screams and groans reached their ears.

Nico raised a hand, slowing Colin. Together, they peered

around the corner. The hallway in front of the library was piled with at least a dozen bodies, but the library doors were still closed. These people must have tried to get in and been slaughtered when they found the doors locked.

"Do we leave them there or clear the library?" Colin asked.

"I think they're safer where they are," Nico said. They entered the hallway cautiously and approached the pile of bodies.

"Hello!" Nico called. "Is everyone all right in there?"

"We won't come out!" a man shouted back.

"This is Prince Martin. I'm going to try to clear the castle. I'll come back when it's safe."

"Please hurry, Prince Martin!"

Nico recognized Princess Nina's voice immediately. "Is that you, Your Highness?"

"Yes, it's me! We're all right in here, but some of the ladies have swooned."

"How many of you are there?"

"It's Lord Basilton," a man replied. "I did a head count. There are forty-three of us here."

"Good. Stay there until I return."

"Have you found Rose?" Nina called.

"I'm sorry. I was hoping she was with you."

Nina began to sob and they could hear Lord Basilton consoling her. "What about Jocelyn and Princess Imogen?" Nina asked through her tears.

"We're looking for them now."

"Princess Imogen is smart. She'll have found somewhere good to hide. Somewhere she won't get trapped, like we did."

"Come on," Nico said, stepping over the bodies piled in the hall. Nina was right. Seraphina wouldn't allow herself to be trapped. Which meant instead of looking within the castle, they needed to find where the escape routes led.

Nico and Colin had checked every grate on the castle's perimeter, everywhere in the courtyard that might possibly be a secret exit. They had killed seven reborn in the process and helped several people escape, but there was no sign of Crane, or of Seraphina.

"I was so sure she'd try to escape," Nico said.

"Maybe she's already gone." Colin was sitting on the edge of the wagon where they'd found the plague doctor's mask what felt like a lifetime ago. "What now?" he asked. "I'm not sure I can bring myself to go back inside."

Nico was about to join him on the wagon when they heard a scream coming from the castle, through the clock door.

They were on their feet before they'd even had time to question their decision. Colin made it through the clock first, followed almost immediately by Nico. A reborn had Princess Giselle in his arms, curled toward her as if she were asleep. He glanced up when Nico and Colin came into the room.

The man was young, around their age. There was only a speck of blood on his lips, but his shirtfront was soaked with it.

"I'm so sorry," he said, and from the pain in his eyes, his words were genuine.

Nico approached him slowly. "Put her down."

"I didn't mean to do it. Lord Crane told us to get the princesses for him. I saw her and she was so young and beautiful. I thought I could save her, but instead I…"

Nico reached toward Giselle, and the man's eyes narrowed greedily. "She's dead," Nico said as he came closer. Giselle's neck wound was so severe she was nearly decapitated. "And if Crane sees what you've done, you'll be next."

The man's bloodshot eyes filled with tears as he reluctantly lowered Giselle to the ground. "He'll know it was an accident. I would never do it on purpose."

"Crane is not a forgiving man," Nico said. "I know because I used to work for him."

"But you're...alive."

Nico nodded. "How did you meet Crane?"

"I was living at a house with other men like me. Lord Crane knew our leader."

"Where is your leader now?" Colin asked.

"He's dead. Lord Crane killed him when he came. He told us about Eldridge Hall, how there were immaculates living here. He said if we followed him, we'd never have to live off deer blood again."

Nico glanced over his shoulder at Colin, then turned back to the man. "Whatever he intended, I think you can see that there will be no immaculates left when all of this is over. You'd be better off not going back to your home."

"But what will I do now?" The young man rose to his feet, leaving Giselle in a crumpled heap on the floor. "I don't want to be like this. I'm a good person. There has to be some way to fix this."

"You mean a cure?"

The man nodded eagerly. "Yes, a cure."

"What's your name?" Nico asked gently.

"Morrow. George Morrow. I was an apprentice to a black-smith before the plague."

"Can you tell me how this happened to you?"

George looked at the princess's body, winced, and looked away. "I don't know exactly. I contracted the plague a few days after my employer died. There was no one to care for me at that point. Fled or dead, you know. I was in bed, bleeding everywhere, sure I was dying. And then one morning I woke up. All of my sores were healed. It was as if I'd never been ill at all."

So Crane was the one who had contracted the plague, then gone on to kill his wife. Nico hated himself for helping such a despicable excuse for a man. How could he have been so ignorant? "What happened after that?" Nico asked.

"I went in search of more survivors. My village had been completely abandoned while I was sick. I found some food, took shelter where I could, and then one day I found myself hungry for...blood. Not just hungry. Ravenous. Starving. I'd never known anything like it." George glanced up at Nico, his face red with shame. "I caught a squirrel with my bare hands and sucked it dry. But my hunger only grew worse."

"No more," Colin groaned, but Nico waved for him to be quiet.

"Go on," he said to George.

"I met a man in the woods. I could tell immediately there was something different about him, that he was like me. He told me there was a group of survivors living in an abandoned country house and that I could join them. That's when I met the rest of them."

Nico rubbed at his jaw. He had to mean Crane. "Are there any children with you?" he asked, thinking of Dalia.

"Not many. They're too small to hunt humans. They eat what we feed them."

"God help us," Colin breathed, and Nico felt a chill rise from the base of his spine all the way to his scalp.

After a few moments of silence George reached for Nico, who recoiled on instinct. "Can you help me?" George asked.

Nico shook his head. "If there is a cure, I don't know what it could be."

"You mean besides the obvious?" Colin said quietly.

George reached a shaking hand to his neck. "You mean decapitation?"

"I'm afraid so."

"But I don't want to die. I'm only twenty."

"And Princess Giselle was only a few years older than you," Colin said. "You murdered her. And I'm willing to bet she's not the first person you've killed."

George seemed to notice their swords for the first time and began to back away. "Lord Crane promised everything would be fine if we helped him take over the castle. These people got to live here in luxury while the rest of us scraped by in the forest. Now it's our turn."

Nico's stomach twisted at George's words. So that had been Crane's plan: take over the castle and rule the country. That was why he wanted Giselle. But Nina was the legitimate heir, unless Giselle had been telling the truth about the king naming her his successor.

Either way, Nico knew it wasn't enough just to escape with Seraphina. He had to make sure Nina survived, for the sake of the kingdom. If all the legitimate heirs died, anyone could lay claim to the throne, including someone like Crane.

Which meant above all else, Crane had to die.

CHAPTER 37

Seraphina was so exhausted she'd fallen asleep on Henry's shoulder, despite her fear. She startled awake from a nightmare to find him asleep, too. She extricated herself from him gently and went to the green room. The doctor was snoring in an armchair.

Jocelyn rose from her settee and came to Seraphina. "What is it?" she asked.

"I don't know. I think it was the silence that woke me."

She walked to the window cautiously and looked out over the courtyard. There were bodies scattered around the yard, some lying in pools of blood, including several decapitated corpses. She shuddered and turned back to Jocelyn. "It will be dark soon anyway. We're better off staying the night here."

Jocelyn's stomach responded with a growl. "Excuse me," she said, embarrassed. "I haven't eaten all day."

"Neither have I. There has to be some food here somewhere."

"We can't eat it. Everything could be laced with arsenic."

"You're right. Well, we won't die of starvation in one day. We'll just have to—"

It happened so suddenly that it was almost impossible to process. One minute she was standing with her back to the window, and the next moment she was surrounded by shattering glass. Jocelyn screamed. Seraphina stepped forward, away from the window, and found that she couldn't. She glanced down. A hand was wrapped around her ankle. The next thing she knew, she was falling.

Seraphina scrambled frantically for purchase. Jocelyn stood before her, reaching, her face a mask of shock. Seraphina's fingers met fabric and she grabbed hold of the green velvet curtain. The hand on her ankle pulled harder.

"Come on, Princess," a voice below her said. She looked down to see a man clinging to the windowsill, his hands shredded by broken glass, leering up her skirts. "Lord Crane has asked for you."

She kicked out with her free foot, tangling her hands in the curtain, but she was slipping backward. The curtain wouldn't hold.

"Let go of me!" she shouted.

Jocelyn took hold of her free hand and started to pull, but the reborn was far stronger. "Lord Greymont!" Jocelyn screamed.

As Seraphina clung to the sill with one slippered foot, she looked at her arm and saw multiple gashes, probably from the shattered glass. The sight of the blood made her vision tunnel, and her grasp on the curtain started to weaken. She felt something warm on her ankle and gazed down. The reborn had bitten into her calf muscle and was sucking fervently at the wound.

She started to swoon, her body going limp. She let go of the curtain, falling backward, when suddenly a hand grasped the front of her dress and yanked her so hard her neck snapped forward.

The reborn, startled out of his feeding frenzy, gasped, then fell backward off the ladder he'd used to climb the wall. Henry released Seraphina and she stumbled into Jocelyn's arms. Her calf had started to burn and she looked down to see a raw, bloody wound where the reborn had bitten her, taking a mouthful of her stockings along with him.

The doctor, who had been watching everything in horror, rushed forward with a bandage and began to wrap up Seraphina's leg.

"It's all right," he said. "It's only a flesh wound. We'll have to sterilize it later."

She nodded, trying not to cry. Behind her Henry grunted, and she turned to see him swinging a sword at another man's head. It was an odd angle to try to decapitate someone, and the reborn, though wounded, dropped away before Greymont could complete the process.

"There's too many of them," he said, looking over the windowsill. "At least a dozen."

"Is Crane with them?" Seraphina asked.

"No, I don't see him. But we have to get out of here. Go through the trapdoor. I'll hold them off as long as I can."

"Can't we push the ladder off the wall?" she asked as Jocelyn and the doctor ran to open the trapdoor.

"I can try. I promise I'll be right behind you."

"Just because you're immune doesn't mean they won't kill you!" Seraphina shouted at him. "Come with us. I'm not leaving you here."

"The least I can do is give you a head start." He turned away from the window just long enough for their eyes to meet. "For once, just listen to me. Go, now. I don't intend to die today."

She nodded, her eyes welling with tears. "Good."

Seraphina followed Jocelyn into the trapdoor. Dr. Lemin came behind her, still muttering prayers to himself. Her calf ached, but she didn't have time to worry about that now. The tunnel was pitch-dark, and she reached for Jocelyn's back so they wouldn't get separated. As they walked, she could hear muffled sounds coming from all around them.

It felt like they had been walking forever when they heard a sound from behind them, like a door closing.

"Doctor?" Seraphina waited for his response, but nothing came. "Dr. Lemin?" she called again, louder. Still nothing.

"When did he fall behind?" Jocelyn asked, a note of panic in her voice.

"I have no idea. I thought he was there." Seraphina could feel the fear creeping into her own throat and took a deep breath. "It's fine. He's old and slow. He probably just stopped to rest."

"Let's keep going," Jocelyn said.

Seraphina took her hand and led her forward. Their pace quickened almost unconsciously. In her own imagination Seraphina could sense something coming behind them. She began to jog, every footfall bringing a throbbing to her calf. She dragged Jocelyn behind her, going faster and faster until she was running.

"I have to rest," Jocelyn said after several minutes. "I'm taller than you and crouching down is difficult while I'm running."

Seraphina slowed to a stop, pressing her hands to her thighs as she caught her breath. She was letting her own mind trick her into thinking they were being chased. As her heart rate slowed and her breathing became shallower, a noise like footsteps sounded from far back in the tunnel.

"That must be the doctor," Jocelyn said.

The little girl inside her was still imagining a monster in the dark. *What if it's not him?* she wanted to say. But that would only frighten Jocelyn.

"Doctor?" she called, her voice softer than she intended. "Is that you?"

The footsteps were coming closer. "Why didn't we bring a light?" Jocelyn moaned.

"Let's keep going," Seraphina said, but it was no use. They were both rooted in place, their energy spent from being in a constant state of fear for hours on end.

"Who is it?" Jocelyn shrieked. "Answer us!"

A moment later someone slammed into Seraphina, sending her sprawling on the tunnel floor. She opened her mouth to scream and felt a hand clamp down on her mouth. She was about to bite the hand when a voice whispered in her ear, "It's Henry. They're right behind us. Now get up and run!"

Seraphina picked up her skirts and ran, no longer worried about what was ahead but keenly aware of what was behind.

"They swarmed the window," Henry said between breaths. "I fought off as many as I could."

"Where's the doctor?" Jocelyn asked, her breathing ragged.

"I passed him in the tunnel. I tried to get him to run but he was too tired. We can only hope he has immunity."

The words were barely out of Henry's mouth when they heard a guttural scream from somewhere far back in the tunnel.

Jocelyn choked on a sob and Seraphina dug her fingers into her arm. "Don't waste your breath crying. We can pray for him later."

"I don't know how much farther I can go!"

"It can't be much more now," Henry said. "We've been running for ages."

Seraphina was beginning to feel her own legs give out, the throbbing in her calf reaching a point of unbearable pain, when Henry let out a grunt and they all landed in a heap on top of him.

Scrambling to his feet, Henry felt along the wall that had appeared out of nowhere in front of them. "It's a dead end," he said as they felt all around the wall with him.

"That can't be right," Jocelyn said. "Why would a tunnel from the king's chambers lead to a dead end?"

"Maybe it was a diversion. We took the wrong tunnel." Henry gripped Seraphina's wrist. "I left my sword behind. I knew I could never run with it."

"This isn't a dead end," she said. "Lift me up."

He reached in the dark for her legs and she bit down on a gasp as he grazed her wound. "The other leg."

With Jocelyn steadying her, Seraphina reached up with both hands and pushed against the ceiling. She knew there had to be a trapdoor somewhere. She refused to believe they had come all this way only to die now.

Finally, her fingers grazed a small metal loop. When she wrapped her fingers through it and pulled, the door didn't budge. Though her arms burned from holding them above her head, she continued to fumble around, searching blindly for the latch.

"Hurry," Henry said, just as scuffling sounds came down the tunnel toward them.

"I've got it," she said, her fingers gripping the latch. Thank God it wasn't locked. She pulled it open, grabbed the ring again, and pulled down. They all felt the blast of fresh air through the darkness as the door fell toward them.

"Push me up," she said, grasping for the edges of the doorway. Together, Jocelyn and Henry pushed her through the hole. She didn't pause to get her bearings. She reached down for Jocelyn's hands and pulled with all her might while Henry pushed her up. Together, Jocelyn and Seraphina reached down for him.

A shout echoed down the tunnel toward them. It was hard to tell how far away it was. "Hurry," she grunted, grabbing hold of Henry's arm and yanking as hard as she could.

"They're coming," he said, and sure enough a faint glow began to pulse in the tunnel behind him, growing brighter. "Pull!"

Seraphina pulled so hard she collapsed backward into the small space, but it was enough. Henry scrambled the rest of the way out and Jocelyn burst into sobs of relief.

"There's no time to close the door," he said. "We've got to run."

To her left was a door frame leading outside, with the door torn off its hinges. To her right Seraphina saw a pinprick of light. She pushed with all her might, gasping as the door gave way and she rolled into the great hall. The tunnel had let them out *inside* the clock. And standing in front of her, his mouth open in surprise, was Nico, his sword dripping with blood, the decapitated body of a young reborn at his feet.

Jocelyn and Henry pushed out of the clock behind her as Seraphina felt her body go weak with relief. "You're alive."

"You're bleeding," Nico said, stepping away from the reborn toward her.

Henry held up a hand. "There's no time. There's a large group of reborn just behind us."

Colin and Nico ran to the clock and stared up at its massive wooden frame.

"We'll have to push it over," Seraphina said. "Hurry."

All five of them crowded around the clock's left side and began to push, but it was useless. There was no way they were going to be able to topple the clock.

Seraphina glanced at the wall of weapons, where several large battle-axes hung. She ran toward them, Nico right behind her. They were so heavy it took them both to remove one from the wall. Colin and Henry grabbed another. Nico was the strongest, but it took all his effort to heft it over his head and bring it down on the clock's solid wooden face. It barely made a dent.

Henry hefted the other ax and brought it down above the door in the clock, where it was hollow and weaker. "If we can take down the base, the upper part of the clock will collapse and cover the trapdoor," he said.

Nico nodded and went to the side of the clock, where he immediately began swinging at the wood. Colin found a smaller ax and did the same on the other side. The seconds seemed to pass so slowly that Seraphina was convinced a reborn would burst through the door at any moment, and she looked away, afraid she might scream in frustration.

That was when she noticed Princess Giselle's torn and

bloodied body on the floor near the decapitated reborn. She walked slowly to the body, the sound of splintering wood dull in her ears. Though Giselle's throat was completely torn away, her face was still perfect, her wide green eyes staring up at Seraphina.

She had been cruel beyond words to all her sisters in the end, but no one deserved to die this way. Seraphina leaned down and gently pressed her eyelids closed.

Behind her came the sound of creaking wood, followed by a massive groan. She turned just as the clock struck once, twice—and collapsed to the ground with such force Seraphina felt the floor tremble beneath her feet. The ebony clock lay in a shattered heap before them, never to strike three o'clock again.

CHAPTER 38

Nico stared at the pile of black wood and glass for a moment, while below them shouts and screams of fury sounded, muffled by the rubble.

"How are we going to get out now?" Jocelyn asked.

Nico, Colin, and Henry blinked at her, as if they still couldn't believe they had destroyed the clock. Unfortunately, the rubble was also blocking the exit to the outside.

"We'll use the front door," Seraphina said. She stepped around Giselle's body, somehow staying upright despite the wound in her leg, and shuffled through the great hall to the castle's main entry. The massive wooden doors had been barred for nearly four years, but they had been designed to prevent people from coming in, not out. Henry and Nico were able to break a hole in the door with their axes, large enough for them to squeeze out one by one.

It was nighttime, but Nico could see the bodies scattered around the courtyard in the moonlight.

"We need somewhere free of reborn that we can easily defend," he said.

Seraphina pointed across the courtyard. "What about the guardhouse? It's large enough for all of us and easily defendable."

Nico nodded, grateful that someone else still had control of their faculties. She took a step forward and gasped as her injured leg gave out. Nico reached her just before she hit the stone steps.

"Come on," he said, scooping her up. She weighed little more than a child in his arms. "We'll get settled and I'll take a look at your wounds."

She nodded, allowing her head to rest against his chest, and he felt a sudden pang of protectiveness that made him want to clutch her tighter.

Colin and Henry opened the door to the guardhouse, a round structure in the castle wall that hadn't been used in years. There was a small bed inside, a table with two chairs, and a pile of straw in one corner.

"It looks clear," Henry called, stepping into the doorway.

A moment later he backed out, with a knife pressed to the center of his chest.

Nico took a step forward, but Branson held his free hand out in his direction.

"Not another step, Mott."

Colin scowled, spitting into the dirt at Branson's feet. "You dirty, rotten, good-for-nothing pile of—"

"That's enough, Chambers." Branson sneered at Colin, his greasy black hair falling over one eye. "I can't say I'm surprised to see you here. The cockroaches always manage to weather the storm."

Colin, to his credit, laughed. "If that's not the pot calling the kettle black. Look at you, hiding away while innocent people die because of your actions. Drop your weapon."

Branson, perhaps realizing he was outnumbered and useless with a knife, nodded. "Fine. But you have to promise to let me leave, unharmed."

"Coward," Colin growled.

"Where will you go?" Nico asked. He'd have throttled Branson himself if he wasn't holding Seraphina.

"Back to Lord Crane."

Colin glanced at Nico. "You know where he is?"

Branson nodded. "I saw him leave."

Nico felt Seraphina sag with relief in his arms. Crane wasn't here.

"Fine," Nico said. "Run to your master like the cur you are. But after tonight I make no promises."

Branson turned in a circle until his back was aimed toward the gap in the wall. With one last oily grin, Branson turned and sprinted for the hole, as if they were going to chase after him. As if they were the ones who had no honor.

Henry ducked back into the guardhouse, waited a moment to be sure there were no other intruders, and motioned for the others to follow. Once they were inside, Nico laid Seraphina onto the small bed while Henry locked the door behind him. There was a lantern with a stub of a candle and a few matches. Jocelyn lit the lantern, revealing just how much Seraphina was suffering. Her face was pinched with pain, and a sheen of sweat covered her brow, but she'd never complained.

Nico brought the lantern closer and knelt down next to her. He took a hold of the hem of her skirt and looked at her for permission. She nodded and he lifted it just far enough to see the wound. The hastily applied dressing was soaked through with blood, which wasn't surprising, considering how much running she'd done.

"Are there any supplies in here?" Nico asked Colin.

"I'll look."

As Colin and Henry rooted through a trunk and a few cupboards, Nico delicately unwound the bandage, taking care not to disturb any clotting that had taken place. He noticed absently that his own hands were covered in blood, probably from decapitating the reborn. Not ideal circumstances to treat a wound, but he didn't have the luxury of sterile working conditions.

"There's not much," Colin said, passing a small flask to Nico. "Maybe you can use that to clean the wound."

"I need a fresh bandage. And I'll have to remove your stocking," he said to Seraphina.

"You can use my petticoat for bandages," Jocelyn said. "It's still clean."

When he blushed at the mention of petticoats, Nico could see Seraphina grinning at him, even through her pain. Jocelyn tore a few strips of cloth from the hem of her dress, and Seraphina squeezed Nico's hand.

"Pass me the flask," she said. "I'd like a drink before you clean the wound."

He nodded and she took a long swig before handing it back. She looked exhausted; if she was lucky, she'd pass out before things got too painful.

Nico removed the rest of the bandage and grimaced. "What happened?"

"A reborn bit my leg."

He grunted, though he wanted to curse. "I'm afraid I can't stitch this up. Not without proper medical supplies."

"I'm not afraid of scars," she said quietly.

He winced inwardly, remembering how terribly he'd thought of her just yesterday. "I'll do my best."

"Just do what needs to be done." She hissed once as the alcohol hit her raw skin. Within seconds, she was unconscious.

Nico slept on the floor next to Seraphina. Colin and Greymont had both fallen asleep in their chairs, and Jocelyn was curled up on an old blanket on top of the straw. No one was comfortable, but they were all so exhausted it didn't matter.

When he'd finished cleaning and dressing Seraphina's wounds, Nico had washed his hands with the remainder of the flask and grimaced as the whiskey seeped into a deep cut in his hand he hadn't noticed amid the chaos and blood. It wasn't ideal to have his own open wound touching Seraphina's, but there was nothing that could be done about it now. He'd have to hope the whiskey had done the job of disinfecting her wound. She would have a scar on her calf for the rest of her life, but he didn't think she'd be impaired in any way.

Now, as the first rays of sunlight came in through the guardhouse window, Nico sat up and found Seraphina watching him through half-lidded eyes.

"How are you?" he asked quietly, not wanting to wake the others.

"Better. You?"

"Better."

"When you didn't come yesterday, I was afraid something had happened to you," she said.

"So was I. I'm sorry I took so long."

She gave a small shrug. "You did what you could."

He dropped his eyes. Why did Nico's best never feel like enough?

"What now?" she asked when he didn't reply.

Nico winced as he stretched his arms overhead, sore in every part of his body.

"Here," she said, scooting over on the small bed. She saw his eyes widen and smiled. "Don't worry, Nico. I promise I'll be good."

Carefully, he climbed up next to her, glancing down at her calf to see that only a little blood had seeped through the bandage. They were rolled toward each other on their sides, and Nico felt the overwhelming urge to brush a strand of hair from her face.

"I have something I need to tell you," he said instead.

"All right."

He told her about Dalia, how they'd found her and where she was now. Seraphina's face was so bright with hope and happiness that he didn't have the heart to tell her his concerns about her friend. "Getting to Crane will be difficult," he said finally.

"Yes. But we're together now. We'll kill Crane, rescue Dalia, and reunite with Rose and Nina."

He smiled, hoping it was more reassuring than it felt. "That sounds like an excellent plan. Now we just need to figure out how to make it happen."

Someone stirred behind him and Nico reluctantly left the warmth of the bed to crawl back down onto the floor, but as he went, Seraphina took his hand. He startled at the contact, the intimacy of the gesture. But even when his hand had gone completely numb, he didn't try to take it back.

CHAPTER 39

In the morning, Seraphina rose from the bed, testing out her weight on her injured leg. It was still painful, but it would heal. She had fluttered in and out of consciousness as Nico tended to her wound, pushing away the pain by focusing on the feel of his hands on her, steady and confident, yet as gentle as a caress. She remembered how he'd kissed her bruised wrists, how the pain in her heart contrasted with the butterflies in her stomach at the tenderness of the gesture.

She gazed down at him, curled onto his side in sleep, his brown hair falling over his jawline and brushing the edges of his lips. She wondered what it would be like to kiss him and laughed to herself. As if she didn't have a million other things to consider.

Dalia was alive. She could hardly believe it when Nico told her, that she hadn't lost her senses after all. She really *had* seen Dalia from her tower. Why had she stopped coming?

The last time she'd been in these woods, Crane had kidnapped her and threatened terrible things, but somehow, in the light of day and surrounded by people she cared about, she didn't feel so frightened. She woke the others one by one, all of them cursing softly as they stretched cramped limbs and grimaced at the wounds that had gone unnoticed in the chaos of yesterday.

Nico, Henry, and Colin were armed with swords. Seraphina carried the same small knife from before, and Jocelyn had a hatchet they'd found in the guardhouse. They all agreed the manor Dalia told them about belonged to the Greymont family, which meant even without Dalia's hand-drawn map, Henry knew the way. It would take them all day on foot, especially given Seraphina's injury, but it gave them time to plan.

"Branson will have warned Crane by now," Nico said as they ventured out of the guardhouse. "If there are other reborn left, they're likely following Crane."

"We'll be terribly outnumbered," Henry said. "Perhaps we should free the trapped noblemen. Some of them might be willing to help."

"Or they might run off into the forest and get themselves killed," Seraphina countered. "We should kill Crane and as many of the reborn as we can first."

From the look on Henry's face, it was clear he didn't relish the idea of dying while everyone else cowered in safety, but he would never admit as much in front of the other men.

Eventually, they reached a road, which made the going easier, and they found a clear stream to drink from in the late morning. But no one had eaten in two days, and all of them had experienced some sort of physical strain or shock. Seraphina had nicks and scrapes all over her arms from when the window had shattered around her. Nico's hand was bandaged. He didn't even know when he'd hurt it.

Finally, when darkness was descending through the trees, they reached the end of a long gravel drive.

"We're here," Henry said, his voice strained. "The last time I came here was just before Elisabeth went abroad. We had a going away party for her."

Seraphina felt a pang in her chest for Henry, and she knew then that she considered him a friend. She was glad they were all here, together. If they died, they'd all die knowing the truth about one another.

"The house is at the end of the drive, about a mile long. It's a country manor. No fortifications. We'll be approaching uphill, which means they'll have a good view of us. If we keep to the trees along the drive, it might buy us more time."

They all nodded. Seraphina didn't like the fact that the reborn could use guns against them, from long distance, when all they had to protect themselves were their various blades. But she had to get to Dalia, and Crane must be killed. Hiding in a tower or behind a mask was no longer an option. One way or another, this ended tonight.

Together, they started up the long drive.

Darkness had descended fully by the time they reached the top of the hill. The manor was mostly dark, aside from a few candlelit windows. All was quiet. There was no armed party waiting to cut them down. There weren't even guards at the front door.

"This feels like a trap," Nico whispered, though they appeared to be completely alone.

Colin shuddered. "You don't say. So what's our plan?"

"I hate to suggest splitting up, but we have better odds if we do." Nico glanced at Seraphina, as if waiting for her permission. "I need to find Crane."

She nodded. "And I need to find Dalia."

"I'll go with you," Colin said to Nico. "This is personal for me."

"What about you, Henry?" Seraphina asked.

"I'll stay with you. You'll need someone capable of killing a reborn."

Seraphina didn't argue. She had no desire to be alone here.

"I still believe Crane has Rose," Jocelyn said. "I'll keep close to you, Nico."

"If that's true, she's as good as dead," Henry said gently.

"Crane was specifically interested in a princess. I think he believes he'll have a legitimate claim to the throne if he marries one. He'd want Rose alive."

"Crane wants to *marry* one of the princesses?" Seraphina asked, stunned.

But Nico was nodding thoughtfully. "The young reborn who killed Giselle had mentioned that he wasn't supposed to harm her. I thought it was because Crane wanted to eat her, not marry her. But this makes more sense."

"Then I'm not just bait," Seraphina said, an idea taking form in her mind. "I'm potential collateral."

Jocelyn and Nico glanced at Seraphina, questioning.

"If Crane has Rose, then he might be willing to trade her for me."

Jocelyn shook her head. "You can't—"

"He doesn't know I'm not a princess. As long as he believes I am one, he won't kill me, no matter how tempting my blood is." At least, she hoped not.

"Can you wait here?" Nico asked. "Just until we've established that Crane is here and Rose is alive?"

Seraphina hesitated. "Dalia..."

"I'll find her. You're the only one of us here who's an immaculate, Seraphina. Please?"

Their eyes met, and she knew then that he was asking because he cared. Once again, she had to rely on other people to do what she wanted to do herself, but with Nico, it didn't feel like a demand.

"All right," she said, and she saw Jocelyn, Henry, and Colin all breathe a sigh of relief. Even knowing who she really was—without what little she'd once offered, her sham title and counterfeit crown—they cared about her and her safety.

Nico's gaze lingered a moment longer, as if there was something more he wanted to say. But then Colin was moving, and Nico nodded at her once before turning and disappearing into the night.

CHAPTER 40

Nico and Colin approached the house from the side, where there was only one window on each floor. They had the advantage of darkness, although the reborns' keen night vision might be a problem. They tried a servants' door first, but it was unsurprisingly locked. Next, they crept to the back of the house, making sure to stay close to the structure so no one could see them from above. Colin rose up to peek through a window.

"It's a parlor," he said. "No one here."

"We must have killed more of the reborn than we realized," Nico whispered.

"Or they're somewhere else."

As swiftly as they dared, they made their way to the back of the manor. It was a smaller country estate, but enormous by a peasant's standards. They found another servants' door, also locked, but there was a small window next to it that Colin was tall enough to reach. He pushed it open as quietly as he could, then climbed up and slid through. His head popped up a moment later.

"Come on," he said, offering Nico a hand.

Nico's entrance was far less graceful, and he thumped to the floor on the other side, freezing for a moment to be sure no one had heard. When it remained quiet, they made their way through the servants' area and crept into the parlor they had passed earlier. There was a fire in the fireplace, but no other sign of life.

"Where in the bloody hell is everyone?" Colin hissed.

"They must be upstairs."

"They wouldn't just go to bed knowing we're coming, would they?"

The sound of footsteps came on them so suddenly it was too late to hide. A young boy, no older than eight or nine, walked into the room rubbing his eyes. When he saw Nico and Colin, he froze, his mouth open in surprise.

"Who are you?" he asked. He was a redhead, covered in freckles, but he wore a patch over one eye. The other was as bloodshot as Arnaud's. A reborn child.

"We're looking for Lord Crane," Nico said. The fewer people who had to die, the better, especially when it came to children.

"He's upstairs," the boy said. "Are you Mr. Mott and Mr. Chambers?"

Nico and Colin glanced at each other and nodded.

"He said you'd come. Follow me."

There was nothing to do but follow the boy, even though there was no doubt they were walking directly into a trap. As they passed through halls and chambers, they saw several more young children doing various tasks, everything from cleaning out the fire grates to dusting. If Dalia was living here, then Nico's worst suspicions had to be true.

"Where are the adults?" Nico asked the boy.

He glanced over his shoulder. "They never came back, sir."

A lie? Or could the boy possibly be telling the truth? He led them upstairs down a long hallway to what appeared to be the master's chambers. The house, to Nico's surprise, was in excellent condition. He wasn't sure why he'd expected a house full of reborn to be looted and destroyed, but they clearly weren't living as squatters. And Crane had managed to find himself a new group of servants. All reborn, all children.

Nico reached for his sword, which he'd tucked through his belt for lack of a proper scabbard. He was lucky he hadn't stabbed himself with it. The little boy glanced behind him and gulped audibly, then knocked on the door in front of them.

"Who is it?" a man called.

"It's Eugene, sir. I've brought Mr. Mott and Mr. Chambers."

"Very good. You may go, Eugene."

Eugene gave them a wide berth, but Nico reached for his shoulder at the last second. The boy squeaked.

"Do you know a girl called Dalia?" he whispered.

Eugene nodded.

"Is she one of you?"

He nodded again, and Nico cursed softly under his breath. "Where is she now?"

"She left the manor a couple of hours ago to hunt. She should be on her way back soon."

Nico's entire body erupted in goose bumps. He had to get back to Seraphina, before Dalia did. He released Eugene, who quickly scurried away.

"Let's go," Nico said to Colin. He took a breath and opened the door. They both held their swords aloft, but Crane was seated at the far end of the room on a sofa. Beside him, a girl was curled up; asleep or dead, it was hard to say.

"Good evening, gentlemen," Crane said, not bothering to stand. "Branson told me I could expect you."

The girl on the sofa stirred and turned her face toward them.

Nico was relieved to see the girl was still alive, that Jocelyn's hypothesis had been correct. "Princess Rose. Are you all right?"

She blinked and sat up. "Prince Martin?"

Crane chuckled to himself. "Prince Martin, eh? I must say, Mott, you have certainly come up in the world since you left Crane Manor."

Rose was twenty-two but looked younger, with her soft, dimpled cheeks. She was also the shortest of the princesses, barely reaching Nina's shoulders. She gathered her skirts around herself and sat up straighter, perching closer to the edge of the sofa. Just as she made a move to stand, Crane grabbed her shoulder and shoved her back down next to him.

She broke into loud sobs, burying her face in her hands, and Crane rolled his eyes toward the ceiling. "For heaven's sake, girl. I thought we'd come to an understanding about the tears."

She shook her head, still sobbing.

"What are you doing with her?" Nico demanded.

"As much as I would have liked to kill her, I'm afraid I need her if I'm going to make a legitimate claim to the crown. I imagine you've figured all of that out by now. So what are you doing here, Mott? Come to kill me, have you?"

Nico lifted his chin. "That's the general idea."

Crane rose suddenly, once again reminding Nico just how imposing he was. For a moment Nico was the boy he'd been before the plague, small and scrawny and afraid of everyone. But then he caught his reflection in a standing mirror and was surprised to see a man staring back at him, not the boy he felt like on the inside. He was nearly as broad shouldered as Crane, if not quite as tall, and he was nearly ten years younger.

"I'm not interested in killing you," Crane said, taking a step toward them. "You were good servants, and I'm happy to keep you on. You'd even make a decent adviser, if you play your cards right."

Nico scoffed. "Are you mad?"

Crane tapped his chin. "Am I? No, I don't think I am. In fact, I think I'm being quite reasonable." He turned to Colin. "What about you, Chambers? There are quite a few chimneys at the castle. I'm sure we can find plenty of work for you."

"I'm my own master now," Colin said evenly. Nico had never been more grateful to have him at his side.

"Very well. I'll see you both out." He took Rose by the sleeve and dragged her in front of him, procuring a knife from his belt and pressing it to her neck as he walked, almost as an afterthought. He knew they wouldn't attack him as long as the princess was vulnerable. She broke into a fresh round of sobs as they disappeared into the hallway.

"What now?" Colin whispered.

As they followed Crane through the main hall of the house, a group of children gathered around them. Their nostrils opened wide as Rose passed, and Nico noticed that several were salivating. How did Crane expect to keep an immaculate in this house surrounded by reborn?

"Please, master," one of the children called. "I'm ever so hungry."

"I just fed you," Crane shot back.

"But it were already dead," another boy cried. "You promised us warm blood."

"Warm blood!"

"Yes, sir, warm blood!"

Nico stared at the children in horror. Was Dalia truly like them? It seemed naive to hope she was out hunting rabbits at this point.

As they stepped onto the porch, movement caught his eye near the trees. In the moonlight Nico could see a woman embracing a younger girl, and it felt as though his heart stopped beating in his chest. Dalia had found Seraphina. And he was too late to save her.

CHAPTER 41

Seraphina, Jocelyn, and Henry had only been waiting about half an hour when the front door to the house opened and a girl slipped through. At first, Seraphina didn't recognize her. From her room in the tower, Dalia had seemed small, but Seraphina could at least blame that on distance. Now, as she walked toward her across the front lawn, she knew it hadn't been a trick of the light. Dalia looked almost exactly as she had when Seraphina was taken from her home. A "late bloomer," as her mother had called her, Dalia had never reached womanhood. She was still that girl of fourteen, thin and a little gangly, her dress hanging off her straight torso.

Seraphina understood then how it was possible that her best friend had survived the horrors of the world beyond Eldridge's walls for all these years.

Dalia froze when she saw Seraphina. Seraphina tried to imagine what she must look like in Dalia's eyes: almost four years older than when she'd last seen her, a woman now. Her hair still had enough dye in it that the color would look unfamiliar to Dalia, and her gown, though one of her plainest—not to mention sullied by dirt, blood, and other things Seraphina didn't care to dwell on—was still far finer than anything she'd had in her past life.

And though Seraphina should have been terrified of the girl she'd once thought of as a sister, she found she couldn't resist the chance to hug her once more. "Dalia," she called softly. "It's me, Seraphina."

"Is it really you?" The sound of Dalia's voice stirred so many memories that tears were spilling over her lashes before she even realized she was crying. As she stepped forward, she heard Henry caution her, but she didn't falter. She and Dalia ran to each other, their arms stretched out for an embrace.

Dalia felt both familiar and tiny, her shoulder blades like two wings jutting from her back, the crown of her head barely reaching Seraphina's chin. But somehow, despite everything, she smelled like home.

Dalia inhaled, too, and for a moment Seraphina's blood ran cold. But then the moment passed, and Dalia wasn't trying to harm her. She was hugging Seraphina back, her small body racked with her sobs. Either Dalia's love for Seraphina transcended her nature, or something in Seraphina had altered.

"I'm so sorry," she said when she found her voice. "I should never have left you. I should have fought to stay with you, with my parents."

"It wasn't your fault," Dalia whispered through her tears. "We all knew it wasn't your fault."

As the last of the guilt she'd been holding on to for all these years fell away, Seraphina wept harder. And this time she wept for herself, for the girl she'd been, for the burden she'd been made to carry. Because while the absolution Nico and Dalia had given her was something she'd prayed for for years, the person she really needed forgiveness from was herself.

Their time was limited, and even though she wanted to hold Dalia forever, she needed to know what had become of her mother and father. "What happened after I left?" she asked, drying her cheeks on her sleeve.

"We were all right, for a while," Dalia said, taking Seraphina's hand. "But when the gentiles realized we weren't dying at the same rate they were, they started to say we had poisoned their well. That we were the cause of the plague."

"Your family?"

Dalia shook her head, her eyes welling with fresh tears.

Seraphina swallowed the lump in her throat. "My mother and father?"

Dalia lowered her gaze. "They were taken by a mob, along with many of the others."

Seraphina had known it was foolish to hope, but the well of grief she felt in her chest told her she'd held on anyway. She wasn't surprised, but she was still gutted. "And you?" she asked finally. "Who looked after you when everyone else was gone?"

"No one," Dalia whispered. "I looked after myself, for a while. And then I got sick, and there was no one to care for me." She wept openly then, saying incoherent things, that she was bad, evil, a monster, and Seraphina pulled her close once more.

Over Dalia's shoulder, the front door to the manor opened. A large man stood silhouetted in the doorway. Crane. A girl stood in front of him, sobbing. It wasn't until they had stepped off the porch and onto the lawn that Seraphina recognized Rose. Her stride was so short Crane was forced to walk slowly.

Nico and Colin were behind them, their expressions impossible to read from here.

"What are you doing outside the house, Dalia?" Crane called when he saw her standing with Seraphina. He grabbed hold of Rose's hair and yanked her head back. "Come back here, now."

"Tell me quickly," Seraphina whispered into Dalia's ear. "Is there any way to kill them besides beheading?"

Dalia was nearly in tears again, but she pointed to her heart.

Seraphina squeezed her hand gently. "Go to him," she whispered. "I promise everything will be all right now."

Dalia hesitated, her face white with terror, but Seraphina nodded. After a moment Dalia squeezed her hand back and released it. She made her way up the hill to the manor, her back straight despite her fear.

"Thought you'd have yourself a little snack, did you?" Crane smiled down at Dalia. "Back into the house with you."

Dalia walked to the porch and Crane turned his attention on Seraphina and Jocelyn. "Now, this is an interesting turn of events," he said as he walked closer, Rose tripping along in front of him, hiccupping with sobs. "I already have one princess, and here comes another. What are you doing here, Princess Imogen? I imagined you'd be halfway to the shore by now, if not dead."

"I have unfinished business," she ground out.

"With me? Oh, that is wonderful news. Now I get to have my cake and eat it, too."

Seraphina glanced at Nico, who was trembling with barely restrained rage. But she caught his eye and shook her head slightly, hoping he would understand. She needed him not to do anything gallant at the moment. "I'm afraid you're wrong there, sir. If you want me, you'll have to release my sister," she said, her voice calm and steady.

"Seraphina," Henry whispered, stepping forward. "I don't think this is a good idea."

"For once in your life, trust me," she hissed. She raised her voice for Crane. "Princess Rose is an innocent girl. She shouldn't be punished for my mistake. Release her, and I will go with you willingly."

Crane seemed to deliberate for a moment. It was clear he could not eat a princess and marry her. But he could call Seraphina's bluff by killing Rose here and now. Seraphina knew she'd never be able to outrun him.

As if on cue, Rose began to wail, a sound so nasal and grating that Crane rolled his eyes. "Very well. That's more than a fair trade. Now, come to me slowly." He glanced at Jocelyn, who started to follow automatically. "Stay where you are," he said to her.

Seraphina glanced back at Jocelyn once before striding forward purposefully, her fingers clenched tightly around the knife hidden in her skirts. This would work. It had to.

She looked to Dalia, standing among several other reborn children. *The things she must have seen and done over the years*, she thought, her heart clenching with sorrow. The loneliness and fear. The guilt and horror. Dalia would never become a woman, would never marry or bear children. But Seraphina would care for her until she was an old woman herself, and together, she and Nico would find a cure. She had to believe that. Or else what had all this been for?

Crane towered above Rose, whose eyes were wide with

terror. In his excitement, Crane gripped the knife too hard, and Rose screamed as a thin line of blood opened on her neck.

"Let her go," Seraphina said, watching as Crane's pupils dilated at the scent of blood. It wouldn't be long before he lost control. "If you kill her now, you'll never be king."

Crane licked his lips and removed the knife from Rose's throat, letting it drop to the ground as though the temptation were too great. "Come to me," he said, reaching for Seraphina.

As soon as she was within arm's length, Crane shoved Rose forward and grabbed the front of Seraphina's bodice, pulling so hard she felt something tear.

She glanced at Nico once again, and the fear on his face gave her another burst of strength. Because if Henry could trust her despite his prejudice; if Jocelyn was loyal outside the walls of Eldridge; if Dalia could forgive Seraphina for leaving her behind; and if Nico would risk his life for hers, then she wasn't alone. She didn't have to trick anyone into loving her. Even if her parents were dead, her community slaughtered, she would find a place out in the world. She was cunning, and brave, and she was never going to hide who she was again.

She tore her gaze from Nico's and looked up at Crane, who was staring down at her imperiously. He had underestimated her.

There was blood on his hand from Rose's neck. His pupils were so wide his eyes were black. She stepped closer to him, sliding the blade up toward her waist.

"I told you that I would have you," he said, his voice low. "Men like me always get what we want."

"Yes, my lord," she said, not bothering to hide the tremble in her voice. It would help distract him.

He leaned down, his lips dangerously close to hers. "You know, girl. Once I'm king, I'll be able to do whatever I like to you." She forced herself not to move, despite the revulsion coursing through her. She had to time this just right. She would only have one chance.

"My wife was beautiful like you, but she didn't have your spirit. Even when she knew what I was, she didn't struggle."

"You killed her?" Seraphina asked, everything in her body urging her to run.

"I was ill, and she nursed me," he said. "Neither one of us expected me to recover. And when I awoke…" He curled his lips back, revealing teeth so long and sharp they reminded her of the castle cats. "I was just…so…hungry."

She ignored the acrid taste of bile in her throat and raised the knife slowly, letting her knuckles brush Crane's ribs as if she were caressing him. He shuddered against her.

"Careful, my lord," she whispered. "My life is in your hands."

"I know," he growled.

She kept her gaze fixed on Nico's, whose expression changed as he caught sight of the blade. She raised her hand above Crane's back. Nico tipped his head slightly to the left, guiding her to the correct spot.

"There's just one thing you should know," she said as Crane fingered the lace edging of her collar.

"Hmmm? What's that?"

"I am not a princess."

He raised his head to stare at her. "What?"

"My name is Seraphina. There is no royal blood in my veins. In fact…" She raised her free hand, deliberately passing a scratch on her wrist in front of Crane's nose.

Something *had* changed in Seraphina. She knew it as soon as she saw Crane's expression morph from lust to confusion to disgust. Nico might understand why it had happened. Maybe the bite of a reborn had somehow altered her. All she knew was she was no longer an immaculate. She wasn't what Dalia, or Crane, or any of the reborn wanted. She was immune.

She grinned, exposing all her teeth. "There is nothing in my blood for you at all."

Crane inhaled. "No!" he screamed, pressing back.

She drove the blade down, slipping it through his ribs and directly into his heart. His eyes went wide as she pressed him closer to her. "Yes," she whispered, her voice as soft as his fine silk shirt. "Don't you see? Women like *me* always get what they want."

CHAPTER 42

Nico buried Crane's head in the orchard and deposited his body in the cellar, Seraphina's knife still driven through his heart. He almost couldn't believe he'd decapitated the man he'd once viewed as his savior. Several months ago all of this would have been unthinkable.

Perhaps he should be used to having his world upended by now. He already knew that most things weren't as they seemed at first glance. A chimney sweep could be a gentleman. A princess could be a hero. Why couldn't a man be a monster, too?

By the time Crane was disposed of, the exhaustion had taken its toll on all of them. Colin and Greymont agreed to sleep in the barn with Rose, away from the reborn children. She was still an immaculate, after all.

"Are we sure the adult reborn never returned?" Nico asked Jocelyn and Seraphina as they headed for the main house.

Jocelyn nodded. "They must have realized they were outnumbered at the castle and fled," she said, wrapping her shawl tighter around herself.

Nico hoped she was right, and that they wouldn't be foolish enough to return—to Greymont's manor, or to the castle—tonight. On the porch steps a cluster of reborn children waited for them, silent with awe or fear. Maybe both. Dalia was among them, and she went with them to the kitchen to find whatever food was left behind by the former inhabitants.

Suddenly, Jocelyn let out a squeal, and Nico saw a rat go scurrying past them down the corridor.

"Apologies," Jocelyn said, one hand pressed to her chest. "I hate rats. Their tails are disgusting."

Seraphina patted Jocelyn's shoulder. "Crane would have done well to get himself a few cats. I haven't seen one rat at Eldridge Hall in all my four years."

"The master hates cats," Dalia said. "Well, hated, I suppose."

"Of course," Nico muttered. "Rats. They've been known to carry disease. I wondered how it was that no servants brought the plague with them into Eldridge, but I'm willing to bet it was because of all the cats!" He glanced at Seraphina to find her watching him with a bemused grin on her face.

He ducked into the pantry, emerging with some old potatoes and a sprouted onion. "They're ancient," he said, spreading the potatoes out on the countertop. "But I reckon they're edible."

Next to Seraphina, Dalia looked even more childlike than when Nico had first encountered her outside the castle with Colin. There was something about whatever the reborn were that seemed to stop them from aging, but he hadn't had time to puzzle that piece out yet. "There's a garden out back," Dalia said. "We could make soup."

Jocelyn nodded and rose. "I'll go with you, Dalia," she said, casting a meaningful glance at Seraphina and Nico. "You two can start the water boiling."

Seraphina had been silent since stabbing Crane. The front of her dress was spotted with his blood, though not as much as Nico would have expected.

"Are you all right?" he asked her when they were finally alone. Her hair hung loose around her face in waves, the hennaed strands faded to rose gold in the firelight. His heart was pounding, though he wasn't quite sure why.

"I don't know," she said, taking a step toward him.

"Seraphina." Nico closed the rest of the distance between them, the hammering of his heart almost unbearable now. "I'm so sorry for everything."

She lifted a hand and pressed a finger to his lips. "You need to stop apologizing, Nico."

"But—" Her sad eyes met his, and he felt for the first time in his life that he was looking into the eyes of his equal, someone whose soul understood his beyond custom and society and expectation.

"My people have a saying. 'He who saves a single life, saves the world entire.' I know your heart is heavy with the deaths of everyone you couldn't save. I know you wish you had done more for your family and Elisabeth. But you put your own life at risk to warn everyone at Eldridge Hall of the reborn, against all odds. You saved who you could. You saved *me*."

As she spoke, her finger slipped away from his lips. But before he could even miss her touch, she replaced it with her mouth.

For a moment Nico froze. He had imagined kissing her, but he couldn't have anticipated the lushness of her lips, the feel of her body pressed against his. And he wanted her closer. Just as he reached his hand up to cup her face, there was a clatter and they broke apart to see Jocelyn and Dalia watching them.

"Ahem," Jocelyn said primly as Dalia bent to retrieve the carrots she'd dropped.

Nico turned away, unable to meet anyone's eyes, a familiar heat creeping up his neck.

They talked for a bit while the vegetables boiled, though eventually Dalia seemed to grow tired and excused herself to sleep.

"We'll see you in the morning," Seraphina said, embracing her friend. When she was gone, she turned to Nico and Jocelyn, her eyes shiny with tears. "Will they be children forever?"

"I don't know," he admitted. "I've got a lot of thinking to do, now that we know how to kill the reborn. In the meantime, I believe the children can survive on animal blood."

Seraphina nodded and gathered their dishes, taking them to the sink. "We should all get some rest."

"I found two empty rooms on the third floor," Jocelyn said. "Princess…" She shook her head. "I'm sorry, *Seraphina* and I will take one and you can take the other."

"I'm happy to stand guard tonight," Nico offered, but Seraphina was already shaking her head.

"We'll lock our doors. It's important we all get some rest."

Nico stripped down to his breeches and washed himself with the basin of water in his room for the night. Its former occupant had been tidy; the bed was neatly made. But there was a blood-stained tunic hanging in the wardrobe, and Nico decided he'd rather wear his own filthy one tomorrow.

He pulled back the coverlet, thinking of what Seraphina

had said to him earlier. All this time, when he remembered his mother's final words, they'd felt like an accusation, proof of his failure. But what if "Nico, *help*" hadn't been his mother begging him to save her? What if, instead, she'd been imploring him to help others? And if that was the case, then perhaps Seraphina was right. Perhaps in this new world, a grave digger could be a physician, after all.

He startled at a knock on his door. "Who is it?" he called.

"It's Seraphina," came the soft reply. "Would you check my wound before I go to sleep?"

Nico unlocked the door, opening it just far enough to admit Seraphina before closing it behind her. When he turned to face her, she was staring not at his face but his chest. His bare chest.

"Good heavens," he blurted, rushing to put on his tunic. "My sincerest apologies."

She laughed gently. "Nico, I've seen a man without a shirt before. You don't need to sound so scandalized."

He was already halfway into his tunic, tangled in the sleeves, when he felt her tug on the hem, straightening it until his head found the hole and he was once again appropriately dressed.

When their eyes met, she was smiling. He hastily smoothed down his hair and smiled back. He almost apologized before remembering she didn't want him to.

"Can you check my dressing?" she prompted after a moment.

Good God, he'd been staring at her like a lovesick puppy. He cleared his throat. "Of course."

She removed her shoes and placed them neatly by the door, then sat down on the edge of the bed and lifted her leg.

Nico swallowed and knelt before her, resting her bare foot

on his knee. Gently, he unwound the dressing, sighing with relief when he saw that there was no fresh bleeding and no sign of infection.

As he rewound the dressing, his fingers pressed gently to her delicate ankle for leverage; he imagined taking her back to his old house to meet his family. Their home had been far less stately than Crane Manor, but it was clean and comfortable, and had always been inviting when his mother was alive. Lucinda had desperately hoped for a daughter, and neither of his brothers had married before the plague came. Nico doubted even his father could have resisted Seraphina's charms.

He wondered what *he* would have thought of Seraphina if he'd met her before the plague, but it was difficult to even imagine the circumstances. Their worlds were entirely separate. Strange to think that meeting her had come at the expense of losing everyone he'd ever loved.

He released her ankle when he'd finished and rose. To his astonishment, Seraphina was fully reclined on the mattress. And she was sound asleep.

He stepped closer to the head of the bed and coughed, but she only sighed dreamily, a soft exhale of contentment that he couldn't bring himself to disturb.

He slid down against the side of the bed, his back to the mattress. Soon enough, he felt his own eyelids growing heavy. Her breath was sweet against his neck, and the warmth from her body seeped out of the blankets and into his back. As tired as he was, he didn't think he'd ever been more at peace than he was in that moment.

His thoughts were beginning to turn strange and dreamy when he felt something brush his temple. He turned, still half-asleep, and opened his eyes to find her watching him, her face just inches from his. She held up a feather in her fingers.

"This was in your hair," she whispered.

He blinked, wondering if he was still asleep, but when he opened his eyes she was even closer. She dropped the feather and returned her fingers to his hair, her grip tightening suddenly and drawing him up.

He was on his knees next to the mattress now, facing her. She sat up, slowly releasing his hair and moving her hand to his cheek. He was conscious of all the blood pumping through his body, of how hot his skin must be against her hand. He kept his own hands clasped piously on the mattress in front of him. His scalp stung where she'd gripped his hair, and his throat was tight with longing. If he opened his mouth, his feelings would spill from his lips like nonsense, not the poetry he wished he could write for her. His thoughts were everywhere and nowhere. He couldn't even breathe from wanting her.

It was both a relief and an exquisite kind of torture when she pressed her lips to his. He released his held breath into her with a small sigh, still afraid to move his hands, of what they might do if he allowed them their freedom. As it was, his mouth was doing very ungentlemanly things, moving in a strange dance he'd never learned but that seemed to come as naturally as breathing: giving and taking and relishing the taste of her.

His eyes had closed on their own, but they opened when he felt her hands move to his tunic and tug rather insistently. Her eyes were still closed. Maybe she wasn't truly awake, didn't know what she was doing. Because it felt very much like she wanted him to climb onto the bed with her, and that was crossing every line of propriety that had ever been drummed into his head by his mother.

But for the life of him, he couldn't resist the pull of her hands, and she scooted over on the mattress as if she knew exactly what she was doing. He crawled up, still kissing her, afraid to break the contact, because what if it was the only thing holding them together?

"Nico," she breathed, plucking at his hands as if she wanted him to touch her. Her own hands were everywhere: in his hair, on his back, clutching his upper arms. He wanted to do all those things, too, but he was aware of how much bigger than her he was, and he never wanted her to feel like he was taking control from her. He knew she'd had enough of that for a lifetime. Touching her face seemed safe enough, so he allowed one hand to reach up and cup her cheek, his fingers tracing the curve of her jaw, where her scar ran, as fine as a seam.

Emboldened, Nico ran his hands through Seraphina's long hair, smoothing it away from her face. There was no sadness in her eyes now. He wondered if there ever had been, if perhaps he had mistaken her for a trapped creature, when all along she could have walked through the bars of the cage at any moment if she'd chosen to.

Her pulse raced beneath his fingertips, and he closed his eyes, inhaling her sweet scent. How could someone so vulnerable have survived so many horrors? How could she even allow herself to trust Nico this way? She ran her foot down his leg slowly, twining herself with him like a vine curling around a branch, and his eyes flew open only to find her staring at him, her lips curving in a seductive smile against his.

He realized his hands had traveled down to her shoulders, and he placed them with deliberate care on the mattress in front of him, like a boy caught with his hands in the cookie jar.

"You've never kissed a girl before, have you?" she asked, sitting up a little straighter and covering her legs with her skirt.

When he saw how red her cheeks were, he touched his own, hoping his stubble hadn't hurt her. "No," he admitted, embarrassed. His brothers had boasted to him about the girls they kissed behind the barn, but he'd been only sixteen when the plague came, and he hadn't known any girls other than the ones he went to school with. None of them had seemed particularly interested in him for anything other than help with their schoolwork.

"Good," she said, placing her thumb in the middle of his lower lip. "These belong to me."

He wondered if his lips were as raw and swollen as they felt. He kissed the pad of her thumb. "I imagine Jocelyn will be looking for you."

She dragged her thumb down his lip to the slight cleft in his chin. She shook her head, placing a small kiss where her thumb had just been. "She fell asleep the second she climbed onto the mattress."

"Oh." Her body was stretched out alongside his, and though he didn't dare look below her collarbone, he felt he could die happy if he never made it past this moment.

She tucked his long hair behind his ear. "You're a very good kisser," she said, her eyes fixed on his mouth as though she wanted to test it out again. Then she flicked her gaze up to his eyes. "It's your hands we need to do something about."

He laughed, a low rumbling sound he wasn't sure he'd

ever made before. "My hands are not the problem," he said, flexing them against the sheet. "They were only doing as instructed by my brain, which is trying very hard not to break every rule of decorum in the book."

She leaned closer, pressing her thigh against his. "Then I suppose I'll have to distract your brain well enough that your hands are left to their own devices."

He swallowed with an audible gulp, blushing so hard he wondered if he'd broken something.

Seraphina reached for Nico's tunic, pulling it up until he finally realized that she wanted him to remove it fully again. He did so with an almost boyish eagerness that made her laugh. When he emerged, hair mussed and cheeks flushed, she was resting against the pillows, and he gazed down at her with an expression that seemed to capture all her own feelings: wonder, pride, love, and desire all mingled into a silly grin. She began to reach up for him but he was already leaning down to kiss her.

"And these are mine," he said, brushing his lips against hers. The words that echoed hers were possessive, but she found she liked the idea of belonging to Nico, just so long as he belonged equally to her. "And this," he said, punctuating his words with a kiss on her neck that spread warmth through every inch of her body. He moved lower and she inhaled sharply, bringing the swell of her breasts even closer to his lips. "And this."

She caught his mouth with her own, and for a while they were far too busy kissing to speak, though they paused for a breathless moment every now and then to take in the sight of each other, smiled, and started again.

As lovely as the kissing was, she ached for more, and Nico was still keeping his hands selfishly to himself. She reached for them, placing them firmly on her waist, though she wanted them everywhere else, too. "You don't have to be afraid of me, Nico."

"I'm not afraid," he said, glancing down at his hands as if they belonged to someone else. "Well, maybe a little."

She grinned, leaning into his hesitant touch. "Of what?"

Now, she couldn't tell if his cheeks were flushed from embarrassment or lust or friction, but she liked him like this: open, vulnerable, a little undone. "That you'll burn me up, fiery one," he said.

She raised her chin and grinned. "And would that be such a bad thing?"

Finally, Nico ran his fingers up her back until he found the laces of her bodice and tugged gently. She released a breath that was part laugh, part sigh. It seemed that his hands did know the way, after all. He matched her grin and pressed his forehead to hers, their breath mingling in anticipation of all the things to come. "Truth be told," he said, nipping gently at her lower lip, "I can't imagine a more perfect way to go."

CHAPTER 43

Seraphina woke to find Nico watching her, his brown eyes hooded and dreamy, his hair mussed from her hands.

"Good morning," she said, stretching languorously. "Did you sleep well?"

He nodded. "You?"

"Never better." She smiled, but his brow was doing its furrowing thing again. "What's the matter?"

"It's... Well, it's just that I think I know why Crane no longer craved your blood last night. And I think I may know how to help the other immaculates."

Seraphina sat up, suddenly wide-awake. "That's wonderful news!"

He nodded. "It is..."

"And yet, you don't seem happy."

He shook his head. "It's just, what if I'm wrong? What if I hurt people instead of helping them?"

Seraphina settled into the crook of his arm and brushed his hair from his face. "I'm no scientist, but as far as I can tell, that's all science is—making educated guesses and hoping you're right. We already know what will happen if we do nothing."

He closed his eyes for a moment. "Yes."

"So whatever you think you've discovered, it's certainly worth trying."

He opened his eyes, and she was relieved to see that the worry was gone, replaced by something else.

"What?" she asked with a nervous laugh.

"You're a marvel, Seraphina. Did you know that?"

The warmth in her heart every time he said her real name radiated throughout her body, making her a bit dizzy. "I believe I did, once. Before everything I'd ever known or loved was taken from me."

He traced the curve of her jaw with one fingertip, then the bridge of her nose, as if he was memorizing the lines of her. "What would your life have looked like if the mori roja never came?"

She shrugged. "I've wondered that. Of course I have. But eventually I decided it was pointless. Even if we left this place to find the world unchanged, my parents still alive, Dalia still… Dalia, I wouldn't be able to go back to that tiny house in a walled quarter, waiting until a man decided he wanted me. I'm not sure I can ever stand to be told what I must do or where I must go again."

He smiled softly. "And you wonder if you still have that same fire."

She grinned, gazing up at him through her lashes. She loved that she could make him blush with just one glance. She kissed him breathless before climbing out of the bed. "So what's this plan of yours?"

"Which plan what now?"

She laughed at the dazed look on his face. "Your plan to save the world."

"Explain it to me one more time," Colin said as Nico made his preparations inside the barn.

"It's called inoculation," Nico replied, being remarkably patient with his students, who weren't familiar with medical terms. "A bit of the blood of an immune person gets into someone who doesn't have immunity, and it changes their blood. When I treated Seraphina's wounded leg, some of the blood from the cut on my hand must have gotten in."

Henry shook his head. "Makes no bloody sense."

"The hows and whys aren't as important as the *what*," Nico said. "Are you ready, Rose?"

Rose gripped Seraphina's hand as Nico used a sterile knife from the kitchen to make a small incision in her palm and another in Jocelyn's. Nico wanted to be sure it was the blood of any immune that could transfer immunity, not just his. They would wait a day before leaving the house, just to make sure the inoculation had worked. Once they were all immune, making their way back to Eldridge would be far safer.

Still, they'd already been gone two days, and Seraphina was worried about the people trapped in the library. But if Nico was right and this worked, they would eventually be able to inoculate everyone in Goslind. It wouldn't be long before the reborn ran out of prey.

Of course, that didn't answer the question of what would become of the remaining reborn. When Nico was finished, Seraphina found Dalia and asked her to join her for a walk.

"How are you?" Seraphina asked her as they made their way down the long gravel drive. "I know you must have been very frightened yesterday."

Dalia nodded, and Seraphina felt a pang of loss for her friend, for the nearly four years of development she'd missed. They were still the same age, but Dalia had been frozen in time, worried only about surviving. And while Seraphina had been trapped in her own way, she had also grown. She had read hundreds of books and met hundreds of people. She'd learned about politics, geography, science. She knew what lay across the ocean, even if she hadn't yet seen it for herself.

As if reading her thoughts, Dalia stopped and sat down on a bench in the shade of an elm tree. "You've changed so much," she said, her eyes huge in her pale face. Seraphina had asked her why her eyes weren't bloodshot like the other reborn, and she'd explained that she blindfolded herself at night so her lids would stay closed. Crane had taught her that, apparently. "I'm so grateful that you didn't leave Goslind without me," Dalia continued, "but even still, I can't help feeling as though I've been left behind."

Seraphina sighed, taking her friend's hand. "I'm so sorry it's been so difficult. I don't know why this had to happen to you, or me, or any of us. It isn't fair. But I'm not going to leave you behind, I promise." She squeezed Dalia's fingers. "Besides, I haven't changed that much."

Dalia arched a skeptical brow. "No?"

Seraphina rose, plucked a mushroom growing beneath the bench, and lobbed it at Dalia's face.

For a moment Dalia stared at her, openmouthed, a little smudge on her cheek from where the mushroom had hit her, and Seraphina worried she'd been wrong to joke around at a time like this. But then Dalia erupted in one of her signature giggles, grabbed a handful of earth from between her feet, and threw it back at Seraphina. By the time they returned to the manor, they were both filthy, and despite the long, difficult years that had separated them, suddenly things didn't feel quite so insurmountable anymore.

The next morning, after making sure there were several reborn children who knew how to hunt—*"Animals,"* Nico had reminded them sternly—they headed back down the drive to return to Eldridge Hall.

By midafternoon Seraphina found herself walking next to Rose. She and Nina were the last living descendants of King Stuart, and though they hadn't discussed it, they all knew she would be next in line for the throne, should anything have happened to Nina.

Rose had never been cruel to Seraphina. Vapid, ignorant, a little selfish, yes. But never cruel. So Seraphina was surprised when Rose said to her out of nowhere, "I'm really sorry, you know."

"For what?" Seraphina asked as they stepped over a fallen log.

"For everything. Taking you away from your family, treating you like you had somehow chosen to be Father's favorite."

"Did you resent Imogen when she was alive?" Seraphina asked, curious. She'd always assumed that Rose didn't care about being the favorite the way Giselle did.

"Me? No. Imogen was strange but sweet. She never said an unkind word against anyone. I think that was why she angered Giselle so much. She couldn't stand that Imogen was good without even trying."

Just then, Rose tripped on a stone, and Henry appeared as if by magic, taking her elbow and steadying her. "I've got you, Princess," he said, flashing his winning smile.

Seraphina snorted, and when Henry's eyes met hers, he smiled and shrugged as if he couldn't help himself. He was like a cat, always managing to land on his feet. Earlier, he had taken in the lovesick grins Nico and Seraphina were unable to keep from their faces, opened his mouth, and closed it again with a final nod. She supposed she couldn't fault him for looking out for himself. It was what he did best.

As for Branson, they hadn't encountered him again after coming to the manor, and Nico felt confident they wouldn't see him. Another man who always managed to cling to any advantage, although not nearly as clever as he thought he was. More like a fungus than a cat, really.

It was dusk when they arrived back at the castle. Colin remained outside to begin gathering the bodies. There were too many—and the ground was too frozen—for burial. They would burn them tomorrow. Seraphina wrapped her cloak tighter around herself as she took in all the destruction the reborn had wrought in such a short time.

The great hall was eerily silent without the ticking of the black clock, nothing more than a pile of dark rubble now. "We can use the wood for the pyre," Seraphina said, her voice echoing in the emptiness.

Nico took her hand. "We'll search for more reborn. Greymont, you and the other ladies should free the people in the library. Explain to them what's happened. We'll meet back here as soon as we've cleared the castle."

"Very well. Shout if you need help," Greymont said.

Seraphina and Nico walked the halls slowly, their weapons ready, but it was quiet here. They stepped over reborn and human bodies every now and then. When they reached the king's chambers, the door was open, the barricade shoved aside by the reborn who had come in through the king's window.

The king's body remained on the bed, undisturbed. Tomorrow they would take him to the royal crypt, along with Giselle.

Seraphina stepped up to his bedside, staring down at the withered body of the man who had become a father figure despite herself.

"Are you all right?" Nico asked from beside her.

"I don't know. I didn't love him. I couldn't. But I had affection for him. I'm sorry he died the way he did."

"Better than being eaten, I suppose."

Seraphina nodded, her eyes welling with hot tears. "And I hate him," she whispered. "I hate him so much and I'm glad he's dead. I'm glad he'll never kiss me again. I'm glad I'll never have to call him *Father.*" And still, she turned and buried her face in Nico's chest, crying for this man she despised.

When she was out of tears, they walked into the adjoining sitting room, where Seraphina promptly let out a startled screech.

The doctor sat on the green velvet sofa, his head in his hands.

"You're alive!" Seraphina said when she'd regained her composure. "We were sure you had died in the tunnel."

He rose shakily, clearly relieved to see them. "It appears I have the blood immunity you speak of," he said. "The monsters ran right past me in the tunnel. I turned back around, climbed out, and locked the trapdoor behind me. I could hear them banging for hours, but they never managed to get through the door."

"That means they're still in there," Nico said. "Trapped on both sides."

"I assume so," Dr. Lemin said. "I decided the best I could do was wait here for someone to find me. And I couldn't leave the king's body unattended."

At some point they would have to deal with the reborn. For now Nico piled some of the heavy furniture from the barricade on top of the trapdoor. "Let's check the remainder of the chambers. Doctor, you should get something to eat and drink. Come with us."

It took several hours to check all the rooms. They collected survivors who were still in hiding as they went. By the time they made it back to the great hall, a large crowd had gathered. Some of the lords were helping Colin and Greymont with the bodies.

Nina was clearly in charge by this point, despite being the most disheveled Seraphina had ever seen her. With her hair loose and her clothing in disarray, and with none of the affectation she normally displayed, Nina had never been more beautiful to Seraphina. She couldn't help thinking that without Giselle there trying to control everyone, things could have been very different. And as it turned out, Nina might make an excellent queen, after all.

"A few of the servants stayed," Lord Basilton explained to Seraphina and Nico as he helped them carry a body outside.

"They told us there are provisions in one of the storehouses, a secret stash they kept for themselves."

"We can hardly blame them," Nico said, wiping the sweat from his brow. "We should bring some food for the others. People need to eat or they'll weaken, and something tells me there will be a lot of work to do in the weeks to come."

Lord Basilton didn't seem to mind accepting orders. He nodded and disappeared to arrange the meal. Seraphina had to admit she'd been wrong about him, too. Perhaps he would make a very good king consort.

When all of the bodies had been removed to the courtyard, Nina commanded everyone to eat and rest at Lord Basilton's suggestion.

Tomorrow Seraphina and Nico would inoculate the immaculates in their midst. Then they would return to the country manor to take care of Dalia and the other children. Tonight they would get the rest they had not gotten last night. Without speaking, they made their way to the stairway leading up to Seraphina's tower. She removed her slippers at the bottom, took Nico's hand, and made her way back up to her little room. She knew it was the last time she would sleep in it and was surprised to find tears welling in her eyes again.

"What is it?" Nico asked, coming to stand next to her at the small window frame.

"I don't know, exactly," she said, placing her hand over his. "I was a scholar's daughter when I came here, and then I was a princess, and now..."

"Now you are whomever you choose to be, Seraphina." He smiled, but there was sadness at the edges. "I've seen so many terrible things these past few years. I felt completely alone at times, as if no one would ever understand me. The thought of losing you is like a knife in my heart, but if you ever feel like my presence would make you unhappy, I'll go. I'll let you face your battles alone, if that's what you need."

She rested her head on his shoulder. "I don't want to face the world alone, Nico. I want to face it with you, at my side. Together."

He sighed, tipping his head to rest on hers. "Thank God. I'm not sure what I would have done if you'd said you wanted me to go."

She laughed, then gasped as something brushed against her shins. She glanced down to see Fig there, purring contentedly, a dead rat lying at her feet. "Hello, Fig," she said, picking him up and cradling him in her arms, where he allowed Nico to scratch behind his ears.

"I thought you said you were a dog person." Seraphina grinned knowingly.

He glanced down at the rat and shuddered. "I might be coming around to cats."

After a few minutes Fig decided he'd had enough and leaped from Seraphina's arms, removing his gifted rat to make a meal of it. Seraphina led Nico to the bed wordlessly, and this time he found all sorts of creative uses for his hands.

Later that night, wrapped in Nico's strong grave-digger's arms, Seraphina heard him whisper her name—her beautiful, precious, *true* name—and she snuggled closer to him, relishing his warmth.

"Memento mori," he murmured, brushing her hair from her face.

"Hmm?"

He pointed to the only painting in her room, a small portrait of a skull amid drooping flowers, a tarnished pocket watch, an old book. "It means 'remember you must die.' Death comes for us all. Even kings."

She thought of her father's last words to her, his commandment to survive. The very fact that death was inevitable made life all the more precious. "Well, then," she said, pressing a kiss to his cheek. "I suppose we'll have to remember to live."

She could allow herself to worry about what would be tomorrow, but for once, she chose not to. The world outside Eldridge was wild and unknown, but for the first time it could be whatever they decided to make of it. There was something thrilling about endless possibility, and something terribly frightening. But unlike all the lies Seraphina had lived with for years, at least it was *real*.

And that was the most beautiful thing of all.

★ ★ ★ ★ ★

AUTHOR'S NOTE

A Multitude of Dreams is my fifth published novel, but it's a first for me in many ways. I was interested in playing with the idea of an unconventional retelling, but more importantly, I wanted to include Jewish representation—an integral part of my identity that I've always wanted to tie in to my fantasy writing.

I'm a fan of many of Poe's works, but "The Masque of the Red Death" has long been my favorite. I love the imagery of the colored rooms, the idea of nobles dancing at a masquerade ball while the world around them rots, and the final twist that reminds us that no one escapes death, not even princes. All of these things led me to write about a princess and a grave digger, neither of whom is who they appear to be, and the bizarre circumstances that bring them together.

Of course, I started drafting this book years before we'd all be living through a plague of sorts, before I'd come to understand the concept of social distancing or lockdowns. The Petrarch quote at the beginning of this book speaks to how I conceived of plagues before I experienced one for myself;

they really did seem like some kind of fable from the past to me, back then. Pretty naive, in retrospect.

But hey, at least *our* plague didn't include vampires.

While researching the history of plagues, antisemitism became a clear theme, though one I didn't necessarily set out to find. During the fourteenth century, Jews were accused of starting and spreading the Black Death. Fabrications such as well poisoning, and blood libel—an antisemitic trope falsely accusing Jews of consuming Christian blood—also emerged in the Middle Ages. With antisemitism on the rise even now, I began to see a place for some of its history within my story. And so, although *A Multitude of Dreams* is set in a fantasy world, it's one in which Judaism, and prejudice against those who practice it, exists. (I've also taken some liberties with the science and history of inoculation, so I hope I won't offend any scientists out there too badly!)

Seraphina, my reluctant Jewish princess, is misunderstood on so many levels, and her presence at Eldridge Hall forces the people around her to confront their differences, even as she confronts them herself. Most importantly, it provided me with the opportunity to explore the ways in which we are all, fundamentally, the same—and I hope *A Multitude of Dreams* will give readers that very same chance.

ACKNOWLEDGMENTS

As always, my thanks to Team Triada, especially my agent, Uwe Stender, who believed in this story from the beginning.

Thank you to some of my early readers: Jenn Link Leonhard, Lauren Bailey, Nikki Roberti Miller, Erin Sheley, and Ande Pliego. I'm so grateful for your insights!

Thank you to Connolly Bottum, for always being so kind and supportive. I miss you! And thank you to my editor, Meghan McCullough, who helped take this book to the next level.

Thanks to the rest of the team at Inkyard Press, including Brittany Mitchell, Laura Gianino, Bess Brasswell, and Kathleen Oudit. You are all brilliant! Special thanks to Elena Masci for creating a stunning cover illustration.

My unending gratitude to my Street Team, formed while I was promoting my last book but who were kind enough to stick with me. Special thanks to fearless leaders Niki Langlois and Lauren Kelsen. You are the absolute best.

Big thanks to my family: Mom, Dad, Aaron, Amy, Elizabeth, Jennifer, and Patti. And all the love to Sarah, my twinsie, who also read an earlier draft of *AMoD* (and everything else I write!). I jokingly call her my biggest critic, but she's also the one who pushes me to always be my best.

Thank you times infinity to my husband, John, and our boys, Jack and Will, for being my center.

And finally, to the readers: I've only been a published author for four years, but I've been writing for two decades, just hoping that one day someone would want to read my words. Thank you for coming on this journey with me. Your encouragement and enthusiasm mean more than you'll ever know.